Daughter of My People

ALSO BY JAMES KILGO

Deep Enough for Ivorybills

Inheritance of Horses

A Novel by James Kilgo

Daughter of My People

The University of Georgia Press   Athens and London

Published by the University of Georgia Press

Athens, Georgia 30602

© 1998 by James Kilgo

All rights reserved

Designed by Sandra Strother Hudson

Set in 12 on 15 Centaur by G & S Typesetters, Inc.

Printed and bound by Maple-Vail

The paper in this book meets the guidelines

for permanence and durability of the Committee

on Production Guidelines for Book Longevity

of the Council on Library Resources.

Printed in the United States of America

02   01   00   99   98   C   5   4   3   2   1

Library of Congress Cataloging in Publication Data

Kilgo, James, 1941–

Daughter of my people : a novel / by James Kilgo.

p.   cm.

ISBN 0-8203-2002-1 (alk. paper)

I. Title.

PS3561.I3668D38   1998

813'.54 — dc21   97-49962

British Library Cataloging in Publication Data available

This one is for

JOHN and SARAH JANE and ANN

who bless my life most richly

Behold the voice of the cry of the daughter of my people

because of them that dwell in a far country. The harvest is past,

the summer is ended, and we are not saved. For the hurt of

the daughter of my people am I hurt.

JEREMIAH 8:19−21

ACKNOWLEDGMENTS

Daughter of My People is based on events that occurred in South Carolina during 1918. While the major characters correspond in varying degrees to the people involved, all are fictitious, especially as to personality, and none should be taken as an attempt by the author to represent an actual person.

I want to thank the University of Georgia Center for the Humanities for supporting the work by a generous grant; my mother Caroline Kilgo for encouraging it with all her heart; my dear friend the late King Maner for giving it his blessing; Susan Aiken for helping me to understand the story; Lawton O'Cain and Paul Lawton for assisting with research; Stan Lindberg for reading the manuscript; Karen Orchard and Charles East for providing the kind of editorial help that all writers need and few receive; and Jane for everything.

The Creighton-Bonner Connection

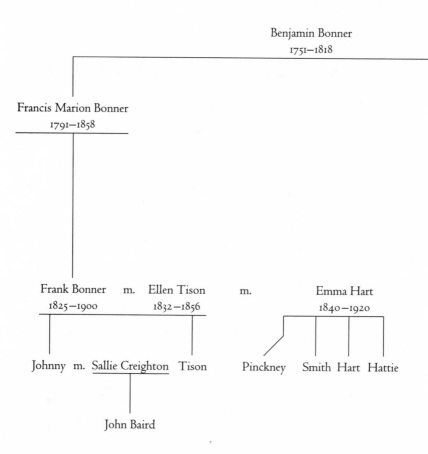

Benjamin Bonner
1751–1818

Francis Marion Bonner
1791–1858

Frank Bonner   m.   Ellen Tison   m.   Emma Hart
1825–1900   1832–1856   1840–1920

Johnny m. Sallie Creighton Tison   Pinckney   Smith Hart Hattie

John Baird

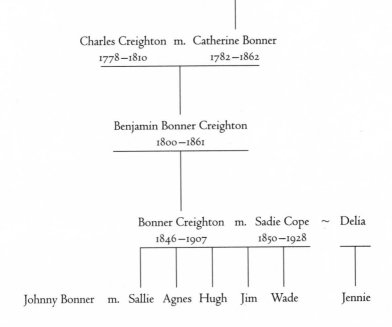

Charles Creighton m. Catherine Bonner
1778—1810   1782—1862

Benjamin Bonner Creighton
1800—1861

Bonner Creighton m. Sadie Cope   ~   Delia
1846—1907   1850—1928

Johnny Bonner   m. Sallie Agnes Hugh   Jim   Wade   Jennie

PROLOGUE

*J*im Creighton was lost. Hart Bonner's little setter bitch, the dog Jim called Darling, had run off into the piney woods and Jim had followed, trying to call her back. Now he had no idea where either of them was. He could see for a long way in all directions through widely spaced trunks, but nowhere in the dim reaches shone the light of a clearing. He had not brought his watch, and the sun was hidden by an overcast sky, but his stomach reminded him that the hour was well past noon. He sat down in thick pine straw and leaned against a tree, feeling its rough, scaly bark through the fabric of his coat.

He was annoyed but not panicked. He was not that lost. This, after all, was the country of his youth. He had to be within three or four miles of his sister's house. Sooner or later he would happen upon a lane that would lead him to a tenant shack, and the people who lived there would tell him where he was. Meanwhile, his wife Mattie would surely be outdone and he regretted that. They were to leave at first light tomorrow for Spartanburg and home, and he had promised to help with the packing. He could do nothing about that now. And it was not as though he had strayed heedlessly from the path. He had simply gone for a walk with Hart's setter, taking a lane that ran past Sister's barn and into the woods, but the setter, hardly more than a puppy, had scampered ahead and soon disappeared. When the lane forked, he had chosen the left, but another mile of whistling and calling had not brought her in. Attracted by a distant, muffled barking off to the left, he had struck out through the woods, but the barking had ceased and here he was. Not only lost and hungry but cold too. The thermometer was falling.

He had no option but to get up and start walking again, but he was tired, and the terrible events of the past three weeks—the Bonner tragedy, people were starting to call it—weighed upon him. At supper last night his brother Hugh had announced that the arrangements had been made. Jennie would go to Orangeburg tomorrow. They would leave first thing in the morning.

The family had received that news in silence, poking at their food, but they were all thinking the same thing. Jennie was practically one of the family.

"It's for her own good," Hugh had insisted, and still no one had spoken.

"Y'all know that as well as I do, and I don't like it either, any more than anybody else. But we might as well face it."

"We know all that," Jim had said. "I don't see any point in talking about it."

"That's what I'm trying to say, Jimmy. The sooner we forget her, the better off we'll be."

Forget Jennie? That was not what Jim had meant. The very idea was an outrage. Jennie would haunt him to his dying day—she and Hart and poor old Tison. Right now, shivering beneath the pine tree, he could not stop asking himself what he might have done, but each time he put the question he came up against the blank wall of impossibility. Maybe they were doomed from the start, those impassioned people, but he could not let it go at that. Out of their anguish something must be salvaged.

Part *One*

HART

*H*art Bonner had no use for an automobile. Even on cold, wet days he delivered mail in the buggy. But this morning he had grown impatient with the old red gelding. He slapped the lines smartly along the wide, dusty back. "Hum up, sir." But the horse paid no attention.

On any other morning he would have been content with Red's determined plod. The pace allowed him time to read in the damp sand of the shallow ditches the tracks of creatures that had passed that way the night before, or to discover by their songs which birds were just returned from their wintering grounds to the south. In fact, Hart fancied that the gait of an aged horse was closely attuned to the music of the spheres, the solemn spin of the earth on its axis as it swung through its orbit around the sun. But on this Saturday morning he was in a hurry. For the first time since he could remember, he had overslept, rising as the thin light of dawn seeped into his room.

He blamed the event on a restless night. Several times he had lain awake for long stretches, troubled by a dream that kept recurring. Even in the bright, early sun, it continued to haunt him. Though he could not connect its fragments into a coherent narrative, the dream had had deer in it, deer and dogs, but how and where he had entered the story he could not recall.

Just ahead on the left, in the shade of a live oak, stood his mother's mailbox. Through the branches of the trees of the avenue he could see the white of the big house where the old woman and his sister Hattie lived. He and his simpleminded brother Pinckney had long since been banished to a cottage out back. Most mornings Hart took a break here, stopping for a cup of coffee and giving the horse a rest. Red had been two hours between the shafts. But today they were pressing on, to make up the time he had lost.

He leaned from the buggy, canting it to the left, and deposited a letter addressed to Hattie. Before he had regained his seat, the old horse started forward, turning into the avenue. "Whoa up, sir," Hart said. "Not today."

Back in the big road again, the postman fished his watch, gold and wafer-thin, from a tight vest pocket. If he were not delayed by wagons wanting to stop and jaw all morning long, he might yet keep his rendezvous with Jennie. She would be there at ten, as she was every day, standing by Sallie Bonner's mailbox, waiting for the mail—at least as far as Sallie knew. Or anyone else for that matter. With the house a half mile back from the road, the box afforded the only daylight privacy they could count on. To anyone who might happen by on the long, straight stretch in front of Sallie's place, he was just the postman and she was Sallie Bonner's maid, out to see what the postman brought.

What he was bringing this morning was a pale blue cameo brooch, a birthday present for her, one day late. She had thought yesterday that he had forgotten. Not that she had said so. But a cloud had cast its shadow for a moment upon her face. It had taken all his strength to keep from telling her that the gift was on its way. And sure enough it had arrived last evening on the boat from Savannah. Jennie was going to love it. It was the kind of thing she might wear pinned at her throat, though for what occasion Hart could not imagine.

: : :

Hart had started the mail route seventeen years ago, the summer his brother Johnny married their cousin Sallie Creighton. His mother, Miss Emma, had hardly recovered from what she considered the humiliation of a fifty-year-old son marrying a girl young enough to be his daughter when news of Hart's job threatened her with relapse. She never thought she'd live to see the day, she huffed, that a child of hers would consent to work for Yankees. Hart reminded her that Smith had been working for Chatfield Sumner for going on five years, but Miss Emma said that was different, Mr. Sumner was a gentleman, which was a sight more than she could say for the United States government. Besides, Smith managed a plantation. Hart might have reminded her that that plantation had once been a major part of the old Bonner domain, ancestral land dating back to the Revolution, but he did not want to get her started again on the woeful tale of his father's misfortunes. What his mother thought hardly mattered anyway. He had never been able to please her. Nor did he give a damn for those who said behind his back that he was a ne'er-do-well. The mail route suited him. It hardly paid enough to keep him in shotgun shells, but it was better than working under another's supervision. He could not have managed that.

: : :

It had rained during the night, laid the dust in the sandy road, and the fresh, washed morning air was one of the pleasures of the job. The sun shafted through tall pines and a million wet leaves sparkled. The mail buggy creaked along behind the gelding's sleepy plod, past dark piney woods that crowded the road on both sides, past weathered tenant shacks, shaded by chinaberry, past wide fields of new cotton where, off in the distance, in small clusters, whole families chopped with relentless hoes at weeds in the furrows.

Hart passed the time by keeping a count, from the loud confusion of birdsong, of species he could identify. An indigo bunting zoomed across the road, a liquid streak of phosphorescent blue, and lit on the topmost branch of a flowering plum bush and sang.

: : :

On such a day as this, seventeen years ago, the sweet air rife with the smells of fresh-turned earth and the fragrance of new growth, he had just bought the blood bay Cassandra, paying not more than she was worth but every cent he owned. He had ridden her down the Black Gall to where that tea-colored creek entered the Savannah River Swamp and back up the Gall again past the old slave burying ground called Graveyard Corner. She was a filly still, a spirited animal, and all the way to the swamp and back, held by the bit, she had trembled between his thighs.

Coming upon a cotton field at sundown, he heard from across the way snatches of a voice singing. Field hands leaving for home, he supposed, but it was too late for that. Yet someone was surely singing, a plaintive soprano rising above the eternal chuck-will's-widows, as lonesome as the closing day.

From a plum thicket that grew between the field and a branch of the Gall stepped a tall, light-skinned girl, her hair tied up in a red kerchief, her long-sleeved dress the color of oatmeal. When she saw him riding toward her, she stopped and stood with her back to the thicket, looking down at her bare feet.

: : :

Hart tugged gently on the lines, said whoa, and brought Red to a stop. He needed to relieve his bladder and this was as good a place as any. With a long stretch of empty road in both directions, he wouldn't even have to step into the wet woods.

In the dream he had been running with a pack of dogs in headlong pursuit of a deer, though the deer they had not sighted. The dream was coming back, segments flickering like a moving picture show: he had begun to bay like a hound, startled by the rich depth and volume of his own voice, and he had scented through keen nostrils the hot, musky odor of a terrified buck. And then by one of those curious dream shifts, he had found himself in terror of the very dogs he was running with, had leapt ahead in desperation, but as hard as he had run the pack was ever at his heels, and then he'd felt the wide, hard rack of his antlers crashing through thick cane and the stalks of the cane hissing and snapping.

He climbed down from the buggy and peed in the ditch. He was buttoning his fly when he heard the automobile. It was coming in his direction, a black box of a machine growing louder by the second. Hart hated meeting the damn things, though hardly a day went by without his seeing three or four. Once this war was over and the soldiers got back home, he figured they'd be everywhere.

"Easy, Red," Hart crooned. The horse had never learned to tolerate the racket of a motorcar. As stiff as he was, he would shy at the noise and sometimes lash out with his hind feet when one was passing by. Hart wanted to climb back into the buggy, control Red from the seat, but this damn fool was driving too fast, holding by an effort to the middle of the road, trying to straddle the high ground between the ruts but drifting first to one side and then to the other. Hart stepped forward to the horse's head. Catching the cheek strap with one hand, he wove his fingers through the mane with the other and whispered soft words into the large twitchy ear. Red's eye was showing white.

And now the automobile was almost upon them—not a contraption bolted intact but a calamity of parts held in loose association by the fury of their vibration. If it slowed down at all, Hart thought, it would collapse upon itself in the road. But it came on, sidling right at them—postman, horse and buggy— and somewhere in the midst of that ramshackle machine hung a white, idiotic face, fixed in a rictus of either horror or delight. Hart froze, but the horse tossed his head and crow-hopped toward the ditch, almost knocking him to the ground. The automobile passed in a deafening clatter, all but sideswiping the buggy, and then backfired, a parting shot as loud as a pistol clap, and Red bolted. Hart grabbed a handful of harness and the animal jerked him off his feet. Stumbling alongside, he managed to lift a leg onto the buggy shaft and from there to the horse's back, and so he clung, right foot braced against the shaft, left hand clutching harness on the off side, and the weightless buggy rolled along behind.

If he could heave himself astride, he could get a hold of the lines, but as he tried the harness slipped, he felt a jolt and then the ground, his face against wet sand; the buggy was bouncing over his legs, and then it was past him, careening down the road. He pulled himself up and managed a shrill whistle, but the exhausted old horse was already slowing to a walk.

Hart limped toward the buggy, brushing sand from the seat of his trousers. They were torn where the wheel had struck his thigh, and the thigh was hurting. It might be bleeding. But he was more concerned about his watch, which was swinging free by its chain. As far he could tell, the watch had survived the fall; at least the crystal was not broken. He slid it back in place and patted the pocket of his jacket for the revolver he carried.

With hands and voice he calmed the trembling, lathered animal, but a black cloud of rage towered in his head. He looked down the road, maddened by the impossibility of running down the automobile. He had seen that face somewhere before. It was a remarkably narrow face, as colorless as a plate of hominy grits. Somewhere around Cypress Swamp he had seen it, probably on the gallery of Thompson's General Merchandise. Then it hit him. That was the same little son of a bitch who had bumped into him last week as he was coming out of Thompson's. Hart had never heard his name, or if he had he couldn't recall it, but Cou'n Bones Bonner, who made it his business to keep up with the business of the county, had told him that the fellow drove a jitney for the colored. Maybe he did, but the few times Hart had seen him he'd been hanging out at Thompson's, sucking on a grape soda. Hart would have paid no more attention to such a nondescript than to a stray dog in the street had the fellow not backed into him, knocking a cold drink from his hand. Hart had made an effort to conceal his disgust, but then the little no-account had said, "Well *scuse me*," as though the collision had been Hart's fault. Ignoring the bottle where it lay on the floor, gurgling out its contents, Hart had continued across the gallery. "You're not from around here, are you?" he'd said, and the no-account, grinning at his buddies, had said, "What's it to you, sport?"

Against such a pissant a gentleman had no recourse, and the pissants always knew it. Hart had paused on the steps long enough to light a cigarette, and flicking the match away had said, "Not a goddamn thing." That had not fazed the pissant, of course, and the last thing Hart had seen as he swung up into the saddle was that narrow grinning face, purple gums, and bad teeth.

And that was the fool who had just now come within a hair of knocking him into kingdom come. He was strongly tempted to turn around and drive back to Cypress Swamp. He was sure he would find the fellow on Thompson's gallery. But he had mail to deliver. And Jennie.

The mailbag had bounced from the buggy seat and spilled its contents into the road, white envelopes strewn for thirty yards in the wake of the runaway. Hart stooped for each one, sorting them between his fingers. Any chance that Jennie might still be waiting when he got there was gone now. To give her the cameo, he would have to take the mail up to the house and hope for the unlikely chance of catching her alone in the kitchen.

: : :

Two mailboxes stood at the end of Sallie's avenue. The other one belonged to Hart's older brother Tison, who lived directly across the road, though all you could see of his house was a grove of live oaks in the middle of a cotton field. As Hart approached the boxes, removing Tison's mail from the bag, a Model T emerged from the grove and came bouncing down the rutted lane toward the road.

Must be on his way to Carthage, Hart figured, business at the bank. Tison could not be persuaded to crank the machine for any other reason. For regular running around, he liked to say, it was too expensive to operate. Hart knew for a fact that the old miser siphoned the tank dry when the machine was sitting idle in the barn, to keep the gasoline from evaporating.

Hart turned Red into Sallie's avenue, away from the stink and noise of the approaching motorcar. He climbed down from the buggy and started toward the box with his brother's mail. The Model T turned into the road and stopped. Tison Bonner glared out from beneath the brim of his planter's hat, a heavy white mustache against a brick-red face. Hart handed him his mail.

"Leave it in the box. I ain't got time to look at it now."

"Why'd you stop, then?"

Tison leaned out the window and cupped a hand to his left ear. "Hanh?"

"I said, why did you stop?"

"Speak up. I can't hear you over this automobile."

"Then turn the damn thing off."

Tison turned it off.

"You don't look dressed for Carthage."

"Carthage? What the devil are you talking about? Have you seen Leonard Coe?"

"I don't know a Leonard Coe," Hart said.

"Oh yes, hell, you do. He's that sorry little trash that hauls niggers around. You'd know him."

"As a matter of fact, the son of a bitch just now ran me off the road."

"Where?"

"Between Wade's and home, right before you get to Willie Small's. What do you want with him?"

"That's my business."

With that, Tison stepped down from the auto and walked to the front to crank it. He was a big man, his belly bulging against his suspenders, but there was nothing soft about him. The engine caught, but Hart was already crossing the road. As he climbed into the buggy, he wondered what in the world the old man could be wanting with a washed-out little no-account like this Leonard Coe.

: : :

The sandy lane up to Sallie's house ran through tall longleaf pine for a half mile, as straight as a rifle shot to her front door. Halfway up the green tunnel, Hart could see that door, then the wide front porch, then as he emerged from the avenue into the yard, the gabled, boxy house with its tin roof and tall brick chimneys. It had not been repainted since Johnny finished it, just before he married Sallie Creighton. Now, scorched by the fierce low-country sun through eighteen long summers, it was blistered, flaked, and peeling.

Hart had spent the Sunday evenings of his young adulthood on that porch, playing guitar and singing, at Sallie's insistence, to a mostly female audience, for Sallie had been determined in those days to find a wife for Hart. The candidates were almost always cousins at one remove or another, for the Bonners and the Creightons and the Mayfields preferred to marry among themselves. What Sallie did not know was that Hart had already made his choice, and his chosen was usually present, standing a little apart from the gathered young ladies, her face in the soft blue shadow dark against the white post at her back.

: : :

She had stood backed up to the plum thicket. He had ridden right up to her, and still she had refused to lift her eyes.

"Good evening."

"Evening, sir."

"What do you have there?"

The girl lifted a sack. "Plums, sir." The sack swung with the weight of her gathering.

"Ain't it getting right dark to be out in the woods by yourself?"

"I was just now started home, sir."

Her bare feet beneath the hem of her dress were wide and dusty. She had gouged a half-circle in the sand with her toe.

"You ain't afraid of snakes? They're crawling now."

"I ain't got far to go."

"Where do you live? I don't believe I know you."

She looked up then and he almost tumbled into her large, dark, luminous eyes.

"I be's Delia's girl." There was amusement in her voice, the inflection that said, You knew that, *as though she was daring to tease him for having failed to recognize someone he had often seen as a child playing in Bonner Creighton's yard.*

Damned if she's not, he thought. Cou'n Bonner's outside child, half sister to Agnes and Sallie and the boys. Her resemblance to Agnes was unsettling. "You've done some growing," *he said.*

She looked again at her feet, but her cheeks broadened into a smile. He shifted his seat in the saddle, causing the filly to dance.

: : :

Red went straight to the watering trough, a mossy green box in the shade of a sycamore that was just now leafing out. While the horse drank, Hart walked up onto the kitchen stoop. "Postman," he called. From the pump he filled a tin cup that hung from a hook on the water shelf.

Surprised that no one had answered, he stuck his head inside the door. The kitchen smelled of biscuit dough, and pieces of a pullet had been laid out for frying, but the room itself was empty. Must be in the front of the house, he thought. Passing through the kitchen, Hart approached the dining room by a latticed passageway. As soon as he stepped inside, he knew the downstairs was empty. He heard footsteps from a room overhead, careful and unhurried— Sallie's mother Miss Sadie Creighton, who seldom came down these days except for meals and special occasions. He left the mail on the dining room table and returned to the stoop.

Except for a loud redbird—*cheer cheer cheer*—the yard was quiet. He filled and lit his pipe. Jennie's cabin stood fifty steps away—a neat little house with glazed windows, built tight and sturdy by Johnny himself—a familiar feature of that intimate yard but at night a lovers' secret rendezvous. For it was within those walls and nowhere else, unless you counted the mailbox, that he and Jennie had their life together. Settled into the routine imposed by their circumstances, she had not been willing for a long time to take the risk of slipping away to the woods on Sunday mornings, as they once had done. Too many eyes on this place, she had told him more than once.

The door of Jennie's cabin opened and Sallie appeared, a stout woman now, thickening with middle age. In the morning sun her hair, pinned up in a bun, showed more gray than Hart had ever noticed. By the way she walked, something was on her mind. She was halfway to the kitchen steps before she looked up and saw him.

"What on earth are you doing here?"

She asked the question as though his presence on her stoop was a breach of propriety.

"I brought the mail up. It's in there on the dining room table."

He offered his hand to assist her. She ignored it and took him by the elbow instead and steered him into the kitchen. "Come inside," she said. "I don't want Jennie to know you're here."

Hart went cold. He could not guess what his sister-in-law knew of his activities with her maid, but he had always felt sure that, no matter her suspicions, she was too much a lady to allow herself to imagine anything in particular or ever to mention the matter even to Jennie, much less to him. Now she had. He set his brown fedora on the kitchen table. He didn't know whether to sit down or to remain standing. He certainly did not know what to say.

"Can I pour you some buttermilk?"

"Yes, thank you."

Sallie opened the icebox and removed a stoneware pitcher. "We've had a little excitement this morning, Hart." She handed him the glass. "Do you know a man named Mr. Coe?"

"Better than I'd like to. He just now ran me off the road."

"Just now?"

"About an hour ago. Just this side of our place."

"Right after he left here then."

"Here? What on earth was he doing here?"

Hart licked at the thick buttermilk mustache on his upper lip. With the same frown she would have given her son John Baird, Sallie handed him a napkin.

"About Jennie. She's been owing him a dime for driving her to a wedding down at the landing a couple of weeks ago. She was a little short on the fare, and that's what he was here for."

That news rankled, as much for Jennie's having been in the same automobile with that little po buckra bastard as for her not having mentioned the matter to him, before or after.

"He came up here to collect a dime?"

"Marched right up to my front door, I'll have you know, and told Lois he was here to see the nigger girl that worked in the kitchen. Those were his very words. And didn't even have the decency to remove his hat."

Hart went as still as a bobcat when it spies a rabbit.

"I was upstairs when it happened, and while Lois was looking for me, Mr. Coe took it upon himself to go around back. I do wish you would sit down."

Hart chose the straight chair by the icebox, opposite Sallie, who stood with her back to the window above the sink.

"Now, listen to me, Hart. I'm going to tell you what Jennie said to that dreadful little man because it involves you, but I want you to understand that this is most distasteful. He must have asked for his dime, because just as I was walking through the door I heard her say, 'Mr. Hart Bonner pays my debts.' And to trash like that. I could hardly believe my ears."

Hart stared at the floor between his feet. This dear woman had treated him all his life with the kindness of a sister. He would gladly have given his left hand to have kept her from being confronted by the truth about him and Jennie, especially under such circumstances. "I'm sorry," he said. "She should have used better judgment."

"Don't you blame it all on Jennie. The time for better judgment was long before Leonard Coe."

So he was the one responsible, not only for Jennie's indiscretion but for Leonard Coe too—the whole catastrophe—and he had no defense against Sallie's righteous indignation. His part now was to tuck his tail and slink away, but there was more to the story than she had told him, and he meant to hear it all.

"Was that the end of it?"

"I'm afraid not," she said.

"Coe said something back?"

"About what you'd expect from somebody with the breeding of a spotted dog."

"But you won't tell me what?"

"It was not a thing a lady could repeat."

Hart stood up. He loathed himself for what he was about to do. "I'll just have to ask her then."

Sallie stepped quickly to the door and barred it with her outstretched arms. "Hart Bonner, I am astonished. That you would even conceive of such a thing. And in the broad daylight. With these children in the house. Just sit back down."

He sat, not knowing where to look.

"You should be ashamed of yourself." Sallie wrung her hands, looked out the window. In hardly more than a whisper she spoke. "What he said was, 'There ain't no need in us a-bothering a gentleman like Mr. Hart Bonner, not when me and you can swap it out in trade.' There. Are you happy?"

"I'm sorry, Sallie."

She turned, her blue eyes flashing. "No, you're not. If you were, you would not have forced a lady to repeat such a thing."

"I had to know," Hart said.

"Why? So you can go blazing up and down the big road, threatening to do who knows what to that pathetic little creature? I won't have it, Hart. Not a public display. This house has been humiliated enough already."

"I have other reasons."

"I don't know about that, but I must tell you, Hart, and it grieves me to say this, but if you say or do anything at all to make a spectacle of this family I will no longer be able to receive you here. Is that understood?"

"Yes ma'am," he said, rising to his feet. "Did you make it clear to Tison too?"

"I hope I did. But Tison is not encumbered by your circumstances. You are the last person on earth, Hart Bonner, who can even mention Jennie's name, to Leonard Coe or to anyone else for that matter. And you have no one but yourself to blame."

: : :

Hart walked out to the buggy, conscious of the sag of his left coat pocket, of the .38-caliber Smith and Wesson he had bought not long ago—too much firepower for the rattlesnakes and mad dogs that were always a possibility but a reassuring weight even so. Sallie might have known more than he had realized, but she could not know it all. For her to think of Jennie as a kept woman no different from any other colored girl was not fair to Jennie, but how could he tell her the truth? How could he tell anyone?

: : :

He saw her next a week later when the moon was full and redbreasts were bedding in the bends of the Black Gall. He had spent the afternoon fishing and was riding home at dusk by the same cotton field, only this time he was mounted on an old mule named Tough because the skittish filly would have grown restless while he fished.

"Picking plums again?" he asked.

"Yessir."

He lifted from the saddle horn a heavy string of redbreast. The fish gleamed like old pewter in the fading light. "Would you swap me your plums for these?"

That was a bargain for the girl, but he immediately regretted the offer. Whether she wanted to or not, she would not decline such a proposal from a white man. To cover his mistake, he hastened on. "I still don't think it's a good idea to be out walking around after dark. Climb up behind me, I'll give you a ride home."

"Oh no sir," the girl said, backing into the next furrow. "I better walk, sir."

"No reason to walk when you can ride." He removed his foot from the stirrup. "Come on now. The mule can carry us both."

The girl stepped forward, as reluctantly as a child obeying its parent. Without looking up, she handed him the sack. He looped the drawstring over the saddle horn so that it hung opposite the fish. When she put her foot into the stirrup, her dress rode up above her knee. He looked away, at the same time feeling for her hand. One bright star shone in the purple sky above the field. When he felt her slender hand in his, he swung her up behind him.

"Ready?"

"Yessir," she said, in a voice soft and small.

The mule was impatient to get to the barn, but Hart held her to a walk, down the long furrow into the darkening west. The girl was not touching him, even to hold on, and he sensed her discomfort. He was uncomfortable himself. His back tingled with awareness of the space between their bodies.

The cotton field was bordered by a shallow drainage ditch grown up in chinaberry. A path cut through the trees into a weedy field on the other side. Preoccupied by his indiscretion, he forgot to warn the girl of the crossing. The mule descended into the ditch. As it scrambled up the other side, he was seized around the waist by desperate arms, and he felt her cheek against his back. On level ground again she released him.

"That's all right," he said. "Hold on if you want to."

Carefully, she grabbed a handful of shirt on either side, and from there all the way across the weedy field, through the aroma of crushed dog fennel, toward the light that he could now see burning in her mother's cabin, he felt, in rhythm with the jogging of the mule, the brush of the girl's hard breasts against his back.

He continued to fish the hole on the Black Gall long after the bedding ceased and the days grew too hot for redbreasts to bite, but the girl came no more to gather plums in the thicket above the branch. He was not surprised. By forcing the peculiar intimacy of riding home together in the dark, he had violated a taboo they both acknowledged. So, while he hoped that he might stumble upon her again, he did not expect to.

As things turned out, she found him, on a Sunday morning three weeks later, while he was fishing near Graveyard Corner. For an hour he had reclined upon the roots of a pine, half dozing, smoking a pipe, entranced by the play of sunlight upon the sandy corrugations of the bottom. When he looked up she was standing there. Her apron, pinned up to form a pouch, was stained wine-red along the crease. "Blackberries," she said. She had smelled his pipe and come to see if he would like some.

He would.

She knelt on a bench of earth fortified by a thick root and opened her apron. He picked a plump berry from the glistening black heap. It tasted sweet, just tart enough. She invited him to scoop a handful. When he had eaten them, his palm and fingers were wine-red and sticky.

He could still feel the hard points of her breasts in his back. He looked into her dark, liquid eyes and almost leaned forward to kiss her, but the impulse shamed him. It was one thing to roll around in the dirt with a Negro girl, another to put your mouth on hers. He laid his red, sticky palm upon her cheek. She lowered her eyes. When he stood and offered his hand, she took it, her cheek stained where his palm had been.

His experience with women was limited to Columbia whores, twice, two years before. Now he stood and watched, trying to catch his breath, as she stepped out of her oatmeal dress and spread it on the sun-warmed pine needle carpet. When he beheld the freedom of her unrestrained pale breasts in the dappled shade, he wanted to kneel in adoration. He wanted to read her face, to find there a signal as to his next move, but he was too embarrassed to look her in the eye. So he stood addled as she lay down on the garment and turned onto her side, legs together, and rested her head on her arm. He allowed his trousers to fall around his ankles before he realized that he should have taken his boots off first. Trying to work his feet free, he tripped and fell to his knees, then crawled to where she lay. As carefully as a man gentling a skittish colt, he removed her undergarments, but when he saw her nakedness he lost all self-control.

If she cried out, in pain or pleasure, the banging of blood in his ears kept him from hearing. In a matter of seconds he was kneeling again on the pine needle floor, looking up through dark branches at a glaring sky. Getting to his feet, turning, and pulling up his trousers all at once, he stumbled off through the woods, more acutely aware than he had ever been of the smell of hot pine straw and the static repetitions of a summer redbird. He wanted to give her time to get her clothes on and leave, but when he turned again she was down at the sand-bar, kneeling among cypress knees, scrubbing her dress. He moved closer. The

*garment billowed pale in the tea-dark current, but the fabric she held bunched
in her hands was splotched blood-red.*

*She must have hurt herself, he thought, and for a moment, concerned, he
wondered how. Then it dawned on him. God almighty. Well, he was sorry—
damned if he wasn't—but how could he have known? She should have told him.
It had been her idea anyway. He sure as hell couldn't do anything about it now.*

*As she knelt by the water in her soiled pantaloons, he saw how thin she was,
how narrow her naked back, how frail her shoulders. And the way she scrubbed
and scrubbed, her determination to get that poor dress clean. He felt like crying.*

*She rose from the sandbar. Holding her wrung and wrinkled dress against
her bosom, she stepped onto the bench below the pine. He reached for her hand,
to bring her up onto the higher level of the bank, but she left it empty, poised in
the air. He wanted to see her face but she had turned her back to step into her
dress. He could not think of anything to say, but as she buttoned up her front
he took her by the shoulders and gently turned her. Her face was empty of reproach, empty of anything, but he put his arms around her. She let him. He almost spoke her name, but afraid of the risk he only stroked her hair.*

: : :

By the fall of that year Jennie, not yet nineteen, had surprised
everyone, and Hart most of all, by marrying a bright-skinned
boy named Joe Grant and moving to Florida, but after six years
she returned to Cypress Swamp without her husband. Sallie had
Johnny install glass windows in the cabin, and Jennie moved in.
By midsummer she and Hart renewed their acquaintance. On a
hot day in September Bonner Creighton, driving a wagon past a
cotton field, jerked the mules to a halt, stood up in the midday
sun, and died. After the funeral his middle son Jim, who taught
Greek and Latin at Wofford College in Spartanburg, suffered a
severe attack of malaria. His mother put him to bed in a tenant
house out back and sent for Jennie to nurse him.

: : :

*It was six weeks before Jim was well enough for her to return to her cabin. The
evening she did, Hart found her, fully dressed and sitting in the velvet-covered
chair that Sallie had given her, threading a needle. A pile of sewing lay upon
her lap. His attempts to engage her in conversation, clumsy and rushed by his*

impatience to get into bed with her, drew only token response. After a few minutes he got to his feet.

"If you're too tired to talk, you'd better go on to bed. I'll come back another time."

Jennie laid aside her sewing. "How are we kin to y'all?" she asked.

The question startled him.

"What?"

"I said, how close kin are y'all to us?"

"Let me think. Cou'n Bonner's father and my grandfather were first cousins, which means that your great-grandmother and my grandfather were sister and brother."

"Say it another way."

"Your father and my grandfather were cousins," he said.

"So what does that make us? You and me?"

"It makes us the same as Johnny and Sallie. Exactly the same, in fact, since Johnny and I are half brothers."

The light went out of Jennie's eyes, and Hart saw his mistake. Was ever a man so stupid? Unable to find the words he needed, he walked over to her chair and stood behind her. He put his hands on the back of her neck and rubbed her shoulders. Then he said, "Cousin Jennie."

She reached up and took his hands. "What does that mean? Cousin Hart?"

Hart had never said, "I love you," to any woman. Until these last few weeks of her absence his saying it to a colored woman had not occurred to him as a possibility. But now, as Jennie held his hands in a tight grip, that was what he wanted to say. "It means we are family."

She pulled his hands down to her bosom. "I imagine you love me then."

Hart leaned forward and buried his face in her neck. "I imagine I do."

: : :

The morning was well advanced by the time Hart headed out Sallie's avenue. The heavy pistol in his coat pocket rested on the leather seat at his side. Unreasonably, he was expecting to find Leonard Coe in the big road, maybe driving up and down the stretch that ran past Sallie's. Something had to be done about that man. The insult to Jennie could not be tolerated. But Sallie was right—it galled him to admit it—he was the last man on earth who could afford to right that wrong. The cost was just too high.

Like that time down at Thompson's a couple of years back. Jennie, entering the store, had overheard one of the riffraff on the gallery say that she was "the nigger girl Hart Bonner was fucking." She had not mentioned the incident to him, of course—in any case, she would not have repeated that word— but Cou'n Harry Bonner had. He had been there, just inside the door. According to him, there had been four or five of the no-accounts lounging on the steps, too trashy to get out of the way when Jennie came walking up. The mistake Hart had made was letting Jennie know what he aimed to do.

"And which one you planning to shoot, Hart?" she asked. "You don't know who said it. You gone shoot them all?"

"It would be a service to the community, but I am going to put a stop to that kind of filth."

"How? Tell them to keep their nasty mouth off your colored girl? Wouldn't that look good?"

That was the question to which he had never found an answer, and it threatened to stop him again. If only Coe would try one more time to run him off the road.

: : :

Throughout the winter after Bonner Creighton's death and on into the spring and summer, Jennie gave herself to Hart with an abandon he could never have dreamed. Three or four nights a week he came to her cabin. Often she would be in bed, dozing or merely drowsy, for he always waited until the lamps were out in the big house, but sometimes he opened the door to find her sitting by the fire in a cotton shift, wide awake and eager.

If he was trapped in a sober mood, as his temperament disposed him to be, she teased him out of it, teaching him to laugh at the clumsiness of bodies, the dumb insistence of the flesh, its sad little failures. She made him dance barefooted to the beat of her clapping hands; and by the merriment of her lovemaking, the delight in which she explored his shy white body and insisted that he learn hers, she outraged his stern Victorian scruples until they lay in a heap on the floor, as forgotten as their clothes. He grew to crave the vigorous leafy odor of her body, the mysteries of its lights and shadows, like honey and ribbon cane molasses, and he thrilled at the sound of his name in the dark timbre of her voice.

For the first time in his life he slept through the night in bed with a woman, setting his inner alarm to wake him an hour before daylight. One morning he didn't open his eyes until the room was filled with pearly light. Stumbling into his trousers, he paused to look at Jennie—the tangle of her unbound hair, the innocent abandon of her open legs beneath the cover. He could smell in the cold air the mingled odors of their bodies and their breathing; strangely, he thought of Johnny and Sallie, already awake and stirring about in the big house fifty yards away, and he muttered to himself as he stepped into his shoes, "This is as married as I will ever get."

: : :

A store stood at the junction of the Old Charleston and Union Church Roads, nothing so grand as Thompson's emporium but it boasted a gallery and in the heat of summer it enjoyed the shade of a splendid sycamore. Tison Bonner owned the building and the business it housed, but he had hired Wade Creighton, one of Sallie's younger brothers, to run it. The store was a losing proposition, but Tison said he had no choice. "If a man's reduced to working niggers," he said, "he's obliged to feed and clothe them, and I sho as hell ain't got the time to trifle with every field hand who finds a nickel in his pocket." Besides, Wade needed the job. The fellow was just a poor make-out at farming, always had been. "Don't talk to me about charity," Tison told the new Methodist preacher. "I'm Mr. Charity himself."

As a boy Wade, like his brother Jimmy, had followed Hart into the swamp, learning from him how to hunt the cane thickets, to fish the black water sloughs, but Wade's marriage to Clara Compton had put an end to that fellowship. Hart stopped at the store every day for a lunch of cheese and crackers.

An advertisement for Bull Durham tobacco had been painted upon the south wall of the store, but after many summers the rampant bull had faded to a ghost. Hart could not make it out until he was very close. He was glad to see that no one was about, but he was surprised that Wade was not sitting on the gallery.

Red stopped at the watering trough beneath the tree, and Hart left the horse unhitched. From the brightness of the April noon, he stepped into a cool, dark cavern, richly aromatic. It took a moment for his eyes to adjust to the shadows. Wade was not behind the counter either. Hart called out.

"Back here" came the reply, but the back of the store, as far as Hart could tell in the dim light, was empty.

He walked past the stove, down a long row of mostly empty shelves. "Where?"

"Right here."

Between a stack of fifty-pound sacks of rice and a pyramid of molasses cans, Wade Creighton in a white linen suit was squatting on his haunches, poking with a broom handle at the dark, dusty corner. "Treed me a dern possum, Bo."

Wade had called Hart Bo since boyhood, though no one else ever had.

"I kept thinking I was hearing something back here. Kind of a dry, scratchy sound. Finally got up and came back to set a rat trap and I wish you'd look at what that scutter's done to my rice."

Hart could see well enough now to discern the chewed hole and spilled grains and, backed into the corner, a bristly ball of dark fur, its pink mouth full of sharp little teeth. The possum growled, a sound exactly like that of a man's stomach grumbling.

"What are you trying to do with him?"

"I was trying to run him out. See if he might not go out through the same hole he came in at. So I could patch it up."

"Why don't you just go on and kill him?"

"I reckon I ought to. I just kind of hated to without giving him a chance."

"A possum? What kind of damn chance? Here, let me have that broom."

Wade handed the broom to Hart. "I kind of hated to with him cornered up like that."

Hart managed to get the handle behind the mean, pointed face, naked looking against the darker fur, and clamped the animal to the floor by its neck. The possum curled into a limp ball. All Hart had to do now was press down. Instead, he caught the intruder by its hairless tail and held it at arm's length. "This must be your lucky day, Br'er Possum. We're going to move you to a new neighborhood," he said.

Hart stepped out onto the gallery, followed by Wade. A man called Cholly Ross was coming up the steps. Unlike most black men around Cypress Swamp, Cholly Ross worked for himself, breaking horses to the saddle and mules to the plow and treating stock of any kind when they were sick or injured. Only way to stay out of the cotton field, he said. But those who had seen him handle an animal said he had a gift.

"You want a possum, Cholly Ross?"

"I ain't got no use for him, Mr. Hart. Thank you, suh."

"He's nice and fat."

Cholly Ross laughed. "Yessuh, Mr. Hart. You welcome to him. I don't know what all that possum been eating."

"He had rice for dinner, didn't he, Wade?"

"Yessuh, but we don't know what he et for supper last night. I was back een behind that Bethlehem church one evening, gathering me some red oak bark, and I seen a possum come up out of somebody grave, sho did. Said, 'Do Jesus, possum been eating the dead.' Had him a little hole wo' smooth. Been going een and out. Yessuh, Mr. Hart. You welcome to all the possum you wants."

Hart walked across the road and flung the animal by the tail as far as he could, out over a blackberry thicket. "Now stay gone, you hear."

They heard the small crash when it hit. "That ought to discourage him," Wade said.

"Possum ain't got enough sense to remember."

Back inside the store, Hart drew a ginger ale from the ice water of the drink box. "I been thinking about camping out tonight. See if I can't kill me a gobbler in the morning. You want to come?"

"I'd love to, Bo, but I can't close up till nine. That'd be too late, wouldn't it?"

Wade could close up any time he wanted to after six o'clock, but Hart allowed him the excuse.

"You going anyway?"

"I imagine I will," Hart said. "Do you know a man named Leonard Coe?"

"Sho I do. Comes in every day or so. And don't want a thing in the world but a dern grape cola. Seems to be a right pleasant fellow though. Talks all the time."

"About as pleasant as mange on a dog. What time does he generally stop?"

"Oh, you never know. Could be any time. You need to see him about something?"

"I have mail for him, but I don't know where he lives. He must not have a box."

"I can tell you where he lives, if that's what you want to know, though he don't strike me as the kind that somebody'd be writing a letter to."

Hart was carving a wedge from the orange wheel of cheese on the counter. With his pocketknife, he carefully pared away the rind. "Well, he's got one. How do I find his house?"

"Right after you pass Garrison Alexander's. You know those two roads off to the left, real close together? I understand he lives down the second one, but I couldn't tell you just how far."

"Can you find me a sheet of paper to write on?"

While Wade fished under the counter, Hart made a sandwich of a slice of cheese and two crackers. At the noise of an approaching automobile, both men stopped what they were doing. The automobile pulled in and shut off. "That might be him now," Hart said, but Wade said, no, it ought to be Cou'n Tison, this time of day. He tore a sheet of cheap, ruled paper from a tablet. "Is this enough?"

Hart folded the sheet into his pocket and stepped to the door. Wade was right. The old man, a cigar clenched in the corner of his mouth, was laboring through loose sand toward the steps, and the band of his panama was dark with sweat. Hart started down, touching the brim of his hat as they met. He had no inclination to pass the time of day with his ill-tempered brother. But Tison caught him by the upper arm as he passed. "You let me handle this Coe business, you hear?"

Hart had all but forgotten that Tison too was looking for Leonard Coe. Since Johnny's death he had been the guardian of the house, appointed by Johnny himself to see to the welfare of the women and children, and he took his responsibility with great seriousness. But he must not have found Coe yet, else why would he have just now warned Hart to leave Coe to him. Pleased by that, Hart half turned and looked up. The old man stood two steps above him, his thumbs hooked into his suspenders, blocking the sun. Hart felt the disadvantage of his position. Unable to plead Jennie as his rightful cause, he had no ground to stand on, but he'd be damned if he'd let Tison. "This cat's mine, Tison," he said, "and it's me that's going to skin it."

"And have the whole damn county talking about us? Miss Sallie won't stand for it. She's already told you that."

Tison's voice brought Wade to the door.

"I'd say you've done damage enough as it is . . . ." Tison broke off, but the unspoken words, from which neither man would have been able to retreat, hung between them.

"What're y'all talking about?" Wade asked.

"Nothing," Tison said. "Family business."

As though Wade were not Sallie's brother, Hart thought, not to mention Jennie's. But he didn't say it. He was already moving toward the buggy.

TISON

*T*ison Bonner was not accustomed to having men turn their backs on him and walk away before he'd had his say, but he didn't want to make a scene in front of Wade. He removed his wide-brimmed panama from his bald crown and with a red bandanna he mopped his sweating forehead. "Heating up early this year, ain't it?"

"Yessir," Wade said, "sho is."

Inside, Tison fished a cold soda from the drink box, snapped off the cap, and took a long greedy swallow. Finished, he wiped his mustache and belched. "You ain't seen a fellow name of Coe, I don't reckon?"

"No sir, not today, but he sho has gotten mighty popular all of a sudden."

"Hart looking for him, was he?"

"Well, he was just wondering where he lives."

"And you told him, I reckon?"

"Yessir. He had a letter for him, he said."

Wade Creighton's face, as guileless as a cow's, was alight with curiosity. He picked up a turkey-feather duster and went to work on a row of sardine cans, but he kept a hopeful eye on Tison.

Tison dropped a nickel for the drink in the till and stepped out onto the gallery. Wade followed but Tison saw nothing to be gained by discussing the incident with his clerk, Sallie's brother or not. He would see to Coe when the chance presented itself, as long as Hart didn't beat him to it. Which, come to think of it, might not be a bad thing after all. Tison came close to smiling at the thought.

Hart's carrying on with the girl in the kitchen was a thorn in Tison's side. A white man who engaged in relations with a nigger didn't deserve the skin God gave him. Hart might claim that what he did in his private hours was nobody's business but his own, but it made Tison sick. Worse than that, it defiled Miss Sallie's house and dishonored Johnny's memory, of which Tison considered himself custodian, as he was of Johnny's plantation and the welfare of his family. Designated as such by Johnny himself, on his deathbed. And Hart had been right there, heard it all from Johnny's own mouth. Tison named executor of the estate and not only that but guardian of the house. Sallie's brother Hugh Creighton, whose family lived upstairs, was gone all week selling ladies' shoes; Johnny said he'd rest easier knowing that there would be a man sleeping under his roof when Hugh was gone, and Tison was his choice.

And so Tison had—an arrangement from which he had seen enough to know that Hart was a regular visitor to the girl's cabin. He came at night, of course, after the lamps were out in the big house, but Tison kept an eye open, watching for one mistake, the opportunity he needed, for the sake of the woman and children, to banish Hart from the premises. Now this Coe business might turn out to be a blessing in disguise. If his hotheaded fool of a brother embarrassed the family by causing a scene on account of the girl, he would have given Tison all the rope he needed.

If Johnny had lived, the boy might have amounted to something. Johnny had had a way with him, had treated him special from the time Hart was a kid, taking him hunting and fishing, that kind of thing. Once, Tison remembered, Johnny had bought him a pony. And Hart would have come closer to working for Johnny than for anybody else. He sure as hell had refused more than once to work for Tison. Hadn't he offered the boy a place in the sawmill, even a turpentine crew, an opportunity to climb down out of that damn post office buggy and make something of himself? Nobody could accuse Tison Bonner of turning his back on his own blood, half blood or not. And Tison had yet to hear the first word of gratitude. For the sake of the family, such as it was anymore, he tried to get along with the fellow, but that business with the girl in the kitchen was an affront to them all. If Johnny had lived, things would have been different.

"Here comes Cou'n Bones," Wade said.

The light jersey wagon approaching from the north was drawn by a single white mule.

"Damn if it ain't. I've tarried about five minutes too long."

Some would say that Bones Bonner was the only friend Tison had. Of an age, and first cousins too, they had been boys together. For a year after the war, in fact, Bones had lived at the Frank Bonner place. But that didn't mean that Tison always had time to stop and jaw with the fellow. No point in trying to escape now, though. Bones was upon them.

With no apparent guidance from the man perched on the wagon board, the white mule turned in at the store and stopped beneath the sycamore. Tison and Wade watched closely as their kinsman unfolded his lanky, scarecrow frame and climbed over the side, his brogans, extending several inches from frayed cuffs, feeling blindly for a spoke. Safely on the ground, he removed his battered straw hat and wiped his forehead with the sleeve of his jacket, then looked up. "Y'all must not have nothing to do today, lounging about like the idle rich," Bones yelled.

Response was useless, for Bones was hard of hearing, or claimed to be, though Tison had often remarked that he managed to hear everything he needed to know and a lot that he didn't. For reasons that made no sense to Tison, Bones kept the temples of his head shaved clean and shiny but went for days without putting a razor to his face, and he never trimmed his heavy shingle of a mustache. A ragged cigarette, rolled from a pouch of Bull Durham, was pasted to his lower lip. Tison had been waiting for years to see him set himself afire.

Bones stopped on the bottom step, looked up. "You ain't seen no ball scores, have you, Bubba?"

Bones was the only man on earth, since Johnny's death, who called Tison Bubba.

"What kind of damn fool question is that? You know I've got no interest in ball."

"Why I can see that you're in a surly mood today," Bones yelled. "I didn't ask was you interested. I just thought you might have seen some. I was curious to hear if Chicago beat the Yankees. That Shoeless Joe, he's from right up here in Greenville, you know. I seen him play in Columbia one time, one of these exhibitions. Damn if he ain't a ballplayer now."

"You ain't seen that Coe fellow today, have you?"

Bones cupped his good ear. "Hanh?"

"Coe. That hauls niggers around. You seen him this morning?"

"I run into him a day or two back. What's today?" he asked.

"Saturday. Today's Saturday."

"I was hoping it was later in the week than that."

Tison rolled his eyes and looked away.

"I'm just ready for a little chess is all."

"We play on Tuesday. You know that."

"There ain't no law that says we can't play on Saturday too, is it?"

"I ain't got time for this," Tison said. "I'll look for you Tuesday evening."

HART

*J*ust beyond the store, Hart turned right onto the road that would take him back to Cypress Swamp and started up a long, easy grade. On higher ground piney woods opened onto wide cotton fields just turning green with young plants. Hart could see more sky from there than from anywhere else on his route. Off to the west, beyond the river swamp, a bank of cloud was building. Hart kept a slicker stowed beneath the seat. He hoped he wouldn't need it, but at this time of year anything could happen by late afternoon.

As the buggy creaked along, Hart wrote with a pencil on the sheet of paper Wade had given him. Then he folded the paper once, scribbled on the outside, and slipped it into his breast pocket.

: : :

When Hart heard that Jennie's husband was back in Cypress Swamp, he warned her to be on the lookout. Though she had refused steadfastly to talk with him about her Florida years, Hart believed that she had left Joe Grant because he had started beating her. Her response to his warning was not what he'd expected. "I ain't studying Joe Grant," she said, and her tone made him feel that he had trespassed onto someone else's property.

"Well, I bet he's studying you," he said. "You tell me now if he comes around here, you hear? I don't want him giving you any trouble."

"Looks like bossin' folks just comes natural to you, don't it? Why don't you tell him your own self if it matters to you that much. Just watch out he ain't drinking. Wine brings out the devil in that man."

That's what took his breath. "Do you actually expect me to go looking for Joe Grant? And what am I supposed to tell him when I find him? Not to do what he ought to be too scared to even think about in the first place?"

"Just do whatever you think," she said.

Going in search of Joe Grant was not something he wanted to do, but Jennie had issued a challenge and he had had no choice. She thought Joe was staying with his grandmother Lydie Baker back on Cou'n Harry Bonner's place, but Hart did not know exactly where Lydie lived, and he had no public business that would account for his riding up and down Cou'n Harry's roads until he stumbled onto the right cabin. What concerned him more than that was the uncertainty of his purpose. Jennie had said, "Do what you think." Did that mean Joe Grant had been causing trouble, maybe even threatening to hurt her? If Hart could be sure that was the case, he would gladly kick his skinny ass clear back to Florida. But if it was not, then Hart would have played the fool. To a colored boy ten years his junior. But why would she have set him up for something like that? He had not yet decided how he would handle the matter.

Hart remembered Lydie Baker from his childhood—a strong light-skinned woman, tall and spare—who lived for a few years on the Bonner place with a man named Pomp and worked for a while in the Bonner house. He remembered her vaguely as a silent yellow face moving about the rooms, high above the affairs of children, a woman not to be trifled with. From time to time through the years since, he would see her around Cypress Swamp and sometimes he would speak to her by name, but if she recognized him as the underfoot child from her years in the Bonner house she showed no sign of it. He had not seen her now for a long time. He thought she must be ancient.

He came out of the woods on a wide cotton field and stopped and sat the mare. The cabin stood across the way, pushed hard up against the dark green barricade of pines by the relentless pressure of expanding agriculture. Though it was not yet mid-May, a blue summer haze lay upon the knee-high plants, the rich black soil exhaling summer breath. The lane continued straight across the field.

A bottle tree stood in the cabin yard, its bare branches adorned with dispensary and patent-medicine bottles, glass of several colors, and an old woman was sweeping with a twig broom, making careful swirling patterns in the clean white sand. In spite of the mild temperature she had layered herself with skirts and petticoats. A lavender shawl cloaked her shoulders, and she had tied up her head in a faded purple rag. As Hart approached, she stopped sweeping and looked up. Her face was wide with the kind of features people called Indian, and her skin had faded to the color of old ivory.

As the mare entered the yard, a flock of guineas scuttled away toward the woods, going potrack, potrack. Hart was distracted by them when a small terrier-like dog burst from the darkness beneath the cabin with a salvo of infuriated yapping. The old woman raised her broom in halfhearted threat, but the little dog, stiffened and twisted by its frenzy, paid her no attention. When the old woman turned her face toward Hart again, he saw that her eyes were milky blue.

"Aunt Lydie?"

"Yassuh."

"How you this evening?"

"Ain't no good, suh."

Hart wished she would drive the dog back under the house. He was going to find it hard to make himself understood above its clamor, nor was he sure she could hear him.

"This is Mr. Hart. I'm looking for Joe."

"Suh?" She cupped her hand to her ear.

"Joe," he shouted. "I'm looking for Joe."

No response.

"Joe Grant. Don't he stay here?"

She mumbled something that sounded like, "'N' no Joe."

The little dog was inching closer to the mare, each outburst a paroxysm that propelled it one small jump forward, and the mare was starting to dance. Hart had just about decided he was wasting his time, when a man appeared from behind the corner of the cabin. Barefooted and shirtless, he wore loose, baggy trousers of a murky yellow check supported by suspenders. Dressed that way, he looked to Hart at first like a circus clown, but his naked chest, unblemished by any kink of hair, shone like cast bronze, and his shoulders were cabled with steel. If this was Joe Grant, he was more of a man than Hart had expected.

"Shut up, Boo," the man said to the dog, but it paid no more attention to him than it had to the woman.

"Are you Joe?"

"Depend on who asking."

The old woman, who had returned to her sweeping, stopped short and spoke sharply, "Cab." The mare continued to prance before the forays of the dog, and Hart almost fell from the saddle. No Negro had ever answered him with such impertinence. Yet, despite what the man had said, Hart had heard no hint of challenge in his voice, no belligerence. In fact he had spoken in the most friendly, bantering sort of way, his white teeth flashing as he smiled.

And that goddamn dog. Cassandra was agitated now, dancing like a barefoot child on hot beach sand. Hart took the crop from beneath his arm, tugged her head hard to the left, and sidled her toward the smiling black man. "I'm asking, boy." But somehow, shouted above the clamor of the dog, the words merely fluttered upon the damp air as weightless as butterflies.

"Yessuh, boss man. I goes by different names."

"Well if Joe Grant is one of them, I'm here about Jennie."

Joe put his hands in his pockets, stretching the suspenders. "Jennie now. She ain't got no last name?"

With that question the black man conjured up all that "Florida" implied, set before Hart's startled eyes the house in which he and Jennie had lived, opened wide the door and invited him to look in upon the intimacy of the lives they had shared.

"Jennie Grant," he shouted, trying to keep the horse under control. "You know who I mean."

"Yessuh, now, I sho does."

To this colored boy who had been Jennie's husband, Hart knew how he must look and he didn't like it. Jennie had invited him to her bed, by God, of her own free will, unthreatened by the color of his skin. He wanted Joe Grant to know that, he just didn't know how to tell him, how to say to a colored boy that he cherished the woman the colored boy had once abused. He felt caught in a game that other people were playing.

Easily and without warning, Joe Grant lifted the dog with his wide bare foot and launched it into the wall of the cabin. Cassandra shied, half rearing, the dog yelped, and Hart slid from the saddle, leaping clear of the horse and reaching for the reins at the same time. When he had caught her, he whispered soothing words and stroked her neck until she relaxed beneath his hand. Then he turned to Joe Grant, surprised to find that untroubled yellow face with its white, horsey teeth only inches away. Eye to eye, Hart felt the red in his own face, meaty jaw, and jowly neck.

"You remember how pretty she sings?" Hart said.

Joe Grant said, "Yessuh?" the response dying on a high note of expectation.

Hart did not know. This had not worked out the way he'd planned. He lifted his boot into the stirrup, feeling every pound as he swung aboard. He was looking down at Joe Grant now over his left shoulder. Cassandra stood, as though sensing that the man on her back had not completed his mission.

"I sing pretty fair myself," he said.

Joe Grant said, "Yessuh," again, but this time it ended with a period. Hart tugged at the rein, reluctant to look away from the man's toothy smile.

"You treat her right, now, boss man," Joe Grant said. And Hart thought, I'll be goddamned.

: : :

Over a little rise and there was blind Hezekiah, standing out at the end of his lane, as reliable as the sun coming up. God only knew how old he was. It would take God to make any sense out of the old man's babble, Hart sure couldn't. But Hart made it a point every day to save back something from his lunch—a slice of cheese, a stack of crackers—to put in the outstretched hand.

Hart had heard different versions of the story, but they all agreed that back when Hezekiah was in his prime, vigilantes had lynched his son for fooling with a white woman; Hezekiah found the body, still smoldering, and went blind on the spot. He took up preaching after that, called himself the prophet, but no church would have him, so the road became his parish. In recent years, unable to get about, he'd been setting up every day here in front of his granddaughter's house. Hart knew people who went out of their way to avoid the old darkie. Hezekiah's ability to tell the color of a man the second he heard him coming made them nervous, they said, but Hart paid no attention to such claptrap.

"Turn back, whitefolks, turn back now," the old man was chanting. "Jesus coming soon, better turn back now, wash all yo sins away."

"Whoa, Red." Hart pulled the buggy to a stop directly in front of the man. "Ain't it getting right warm out here, Hezekiah?"

"Nawsuh, whitefolks. Ain't too warm for Hezekiah, wash all yo sins away."

Hezekiah's hand was extended, palm up, a palm calloused into the shape of a cup, too stiff to close into a fist. Hart placed his offering in it.

"De Lamb o' God," sang Hezekiah, "dat taking away de sins o' de world."

: : :

Hart followed the tracks of automobile tires into the second lane according to Wade's instructions. The lane was narrow, choked by walls of blackberry that snarled the spokes as the buggy passed, and weeds stood tall in the ridge between the ruts. Rank undergrowth soon gave way to a stand of slash, a gloom in which no birds sang or flitted, but even as Hart entered it he saw a thinning up ahead and the light of an open place. It was a raw spot, so encroached upon already by the rife growth of spring as to leave little room for work or play. In the midst of the clearing sat a house—a tenant shack of weathered planks, listing to one side, without so much as a stoop to dignify its door. Hart stopped the buggy beside a dark, oily splotch in the sandy soil and knew it for the place where Coe parked his wreck of an automobile.

Trash, washed out from beneath the shack in the last hard rain, still lay where the storm had left it, and excrement both of dogs and people fouled the bare dirt yard. Three hens, their heads pecked raw, foraged among the filth. The place bore witness to the human enterprise defeated, and Hart felt the keen edge of his purpose dulled.

"Hello," he called. "Postman here."

In the silence he heard the muffled crying of a small child.

The door cracked. "What you want?"

Hart lifted his hat. "Afternoon, ma'am. Is your man about?"

"No he ain't."

"I'd like to leave you something for him if I may."

The door opened a little wider, admitting light on the woman who stood there. In her right arm she held a naked baby, and wet spots darkened the front of her flour-sack dress. "What?"

"Just a little piece of mail."

The woman's hair hung like wet string about her suspicious face. She was not going to budge from the doorway. Hart would have to go to her. He climbed down and picked his way through the yard. A child appeared from behind the woman, squirming between her skirts and the door, but the woman threw her hip and blocked its way. The child howled, and the woman with her free hand swatted it back into the darkness of the room.

Hart did not want to leave the note with her if she had learning enough to read it, but he didn't think she did. As close now as he dared approach, he held out the folded sheet of paper. "Is that your husband's name?"

The blank expression on her sallow face was all the answer he required.

"Leonard Coe? Is that his name?"

Her eyes widened; then slowly, as she realized what he had done, they filled with outrage. He had tricked her into embarrassing herself and for no reason she could understand. But she had dealt with his kind before, talking so polite and refined. She didn't owe nothing to this one, and damn if she'd be spit on, not in her own front door. "Why don't you kiss my ass?" the woman said.

Hart felt soiled. What he had done to her was no different from what her husband had done to the women at Sallie's house.

"I'm sorry, ma'am. I truly am. But I need you to give this to him. It's important."

He waved the note in her face, but she refused to reach for it. Hart leaned down and placed it on the split log that served as a step. The wind would blow it away, another piece of trash in that littered yard, but he no longer cared.

: : :

Shadows lay long upon the sandy road when Hart turned into the avenue that led to his mother's house. He had come full circle since leaving home this morning, yet nothing had been completed. Red had saved just enough for his final trot, and the buggy rolled smartly beneath the live oaks as the tired old horse headed for the barn.

Before the big white house, in the midst of an uncut, grassy yard, stood a set of steps, isolate and free of any building they might have served. With pillars on either side, they were twelve in number, fashioned of brick in Chippendale design, finished in mortar, and blackened for fifty years by the fire of Sherman's torch.

For a long time after the war, the family had camped in mean circumstances, slave cabins at first and then the hastily nailed together cottage now called the boys' house where Hart batched with his brother Pinckney. When at last the site of the former house was cleared of rubble for construction of the new one, Miss Emma decreed that the steps remain, and remain unscrubbed—a charred altar upon which she might lay anew each day her sacrifice of gall. Like any altar, the steps were sacrosanct, off-limits by her decree to the play of children. "No one has set foot on those steps since the last time your father . . ." she would say, trailing off.

Hart had heard the story from such an early age and so often through his childhood that it seemed to him even now that he must have witnessed the scene—the return of the family in April of '65 to the ruins of Live Oak Hall, the pile of picked-through rubble where the mansion had stood, the formal gardens rank with fennel, the scorched oak canopies. And Frank Bonner, still in the prime of manhood, had uttered not one word but ascended those steps in silence, with purpose in his stride, as though he meant to cross again his own threshold and resume the mastery of his domain. And then at the top had simply stood, addled by the empty air before him, until his wife came up to help him down.

: : :

Red stopped at his accustomed spot under the pecan tree and stood to be unharnessed. Robert Salley, the man who worked around the barn, came limping up to help.

"I'm going to camp by the swamp tonight," Hart said. "I'll need you to ride with me to bring Cassie back. Go on and give Red his oats and then saddle up. I won't be long."

The boys' house was a simple cottage, a living room with two bedrooms on the right and a kitchen at the back. Hart's ancient setter Dan lay on the porch, too stiff to stir himself when Hart walked up, though the tail went thump, thump, thump. Hart found Pinck snoring in his chair by the fireplace and tiptoed past him into his room. He had no time now for his brother's complaints. But he had no sooner taken blankets from the wardrobe when Pinck appeared in the door. His sparse, dry hair stood out in startled sprigs, and his trousers, hiked up to his armpits, were stained down the front. "I need you to see something."

Pinckney had never been quick, nor in recent years attentive to personal cleanliness. It was for that reason, in fact, that he had been banished years ago to the cottage. "You can tell where he's been by the odor," his mother used to say. "I'd as soon have a goat in the house." For a time their brother Smith had had him help look after bird dogs for Chatfield Sumner, but since Smith's final illness six years ago Pinck had kept more and more to the cottage, and the shadows that lay upon his mind had deepened steadily.

"What is it, Sport? I'm in a hurry."

Pinck settled on the bed and studied the knot of his right brogan. Directly, he began to tug at the lace. Hart put aside the bedroll he was making. "Here, let me do that."

When Hart had removed the shoe, Pinck held out his foot. "I hurt it," he said.

The heel of his dirty white stocking was frayed and stained, a place on the heel of his foot chewed to pulp.

"For God's sake," Hart said. He searched with his index finger for the nail in the boot and found it. "Why didn't you get James to see about this?"

James was Robert Salley's younger brother, the man hired to keep house and to take care of Pinck. He spent most of the day at the barn with Robert, but there was little Hart could do about that. James was the only man on the place willing to shave a dimwit.

"James ain't here."

"Then why didn't you take it off yourself? Don't you have better sense than to walk around on a nail?"

"I don't know."

Hart helped Pinck back to his chair by the fireplace, then put a pot of water on the stove. To his consternation the fire had been allowed to go out. When he had it going again, he packed his supper—a sack of coffee, three biscuits from the safe, three slabs of ham. He didn't have time to wait for the water to boil. It would be dark already when he got to the swamp. He took down from its hook a large canteen that Smith had brought back from the Spanish-American War and went out to the pump on the stoop and filled it. The water on the stove was getting warm. He put a cup and a coffee pot into the bag with the food, then went to his room for a tin of salve. Deciding that the water was warm enough, he took the pot into the living room and set it by Pinck's chair. Holding the wounded foot, lard-white and spider-veined, he bathed it and dried it and applied the ointment. "I want you to stay off of this tonight, you hear?"

: : :

Robert was waiting out by the pecan tree, holding the saddled mounts, the old mare Cassandra and a swayback riding mule they called Dolores. He was talking with James.

"Where the hell have you been?"

"Yessuh, Mr. Hart. Mr. Pinck done run me out."

"What did you do to upset him?"

"Ain't done nothing, suh. He just having one of his days, look like nothing go to suit him. Won't eat, won't let me change his clothes. Ax him do he want a shave, he say he gon cut me with that razor, sho did. I been waiting round for you, suh. See does you need me for some other little something."

James was probably telling the truth. Pinck could be a trial when the notion took him. "See if you can get him to go to bed. And try not to aggravate him."

: : :

There had been eight of them in all—Johnny and Tison by Frank Bonner's first wife Ellen, and Pinckney, Bess, Nell, Smith, Hattie, and Hart by Miss Emma. Consensus among the kinfolk divided the crop into wheat and tares: the four who were of a sweet and gentle nature, the four who were not. It was the wheat that had fallen—Johnny by cancer, the others by tuberculosis, which had become the family scourge.

With four of her children safely in the ground and the rest living within the sound of her voice, Miss Emma should be happy, Hart reckoned. It was what she'd always wanted, to keep her children right there around her, and unmarried at that. As a boy he had set his heart on Agnes Creighton. When his mother got wind of that, she went straight to Miss Sadie and told her to look to her daughter; the girl was behaving toward Hart in a manner unbecoming to a lady. What Miss Sadie had said in response, Hart never knew, but from that day on he found himself unwelcome at the Creighton house. Only Johnny, one of the tenderhearted, had had the grit to marry against Miss Emma's will, and he had waited until he was fifty years old to do it. Hart had taken a bitter pleasure in Johnny's choice of a bride; he often wished his mother could know that he now had a Creighton lady too.

: : :

As the sun went down behind the woods, Hart rode into the reddening west, down a narrow lane between a fence cloaked with yellow jessamine and a row of tenant houses, each one a two-room cabin with a stick-and-mud chimney from which smoke rose. Children played in the dooryards, and a mixed smell of collard greens and fatback filled the dusty street. Inside their cabins, framed by open windows, women were bending over hearths, their shining faces flickering as they prepared their family's meal.

Beyond the last cabin Cassie broke into a trot, and Robert's mule Dolores clopped along behind. They rode down cotton fields and along the edges of old fields rank with weeds, across shallow streams that ran as red as tea over pure white sand and into open groves of longleaf, fragrant with new growth. And as they rode, they cut a swath through the calls of chuck-will's-widows.

The way Hart took was the way they had taken in his youth when this had been Bonner land and they could drive deer every day for a week without ever crossing over onto another property. He no longer grieved the loss of that inheritance. Having grown up in the shadow of devastation, of burned mansions, ruined fortunes, crippled cousins, and one-armed uncles, he regarded the plantation as one more casualty of the war, deferred by thirty years, though August Belmont and Chatfield Sumner he did not blame. A stronger man than his father would have kept his patrimony, no matter how much money the Yankee bird hunters offered. "Your Pa was a good man, son," Cou'n Bonner had told him once, "but gracious a sorry man."

In the cool blue April twilight ghosts emerged from among the pines and brought their horses alongside and rode with Hart as they had when they were living—bluff Cou'n Bonner Creighton and Johnny, who had been more a father than a brother, and

Smith, the brother he'd grown up with, and Wade and Jimmy Creighton too, who though living still were dead now to the life of the woods. Their shades had greater substance than the black man on the mule, and the closer they got to the swamp the more substantial they became, until Hart recognized the very horses they were riding and heard the creak of their saddle leather. A damned select company they had been, the swamp the medium by which their bonds were forged. And of them all, Hart was left to camp alone.

: : :

Before him now in the deep spring dusk stood the dark wall of the swamp—the floodplain of the great Savannah River, which had enticed him as a child and embraced him as a youth. At the age of twelve Hart had thought that the joy of drinking black coffee with men who had slain deer and expected to again exceeded any pleasure his life might have to offer. Unlike most boys in their apprenticeship to hunting, he never in his excitement mistook a doe for a buck. By the time he was fifteen he had brought down four deer. At eighteen he knew the river swamp, its intricate winding sloughs, its barely perceptible ridges and landmark trees, as most men knew the fields around their houses, and Johnny and Cou'n Bonner, quietly and without a fuss, began to ask his opinion, given the season and the weather, on where to start the dogs. Long after the old-timers announced the demise of the last Savannah River bear, Hart continued to find occasional sign, and every year or so he reported seeing one. Once he was blessed by the appearance of a panther, the long, tawny cat crossing a dry slough not fifty yards ahead of him, harried by an irate thrasher into a solid wall of switch cane, as silent as smoke. But Hart kept the panther to himself because he did not want to be doubted when he knew what he had seen.

: : :

"Meet me here tomorrow morning," Hart told Robert. "Around ten o'clock." Dismounting, he took the L.C. Smith from its scabbard and leaned it against a tree. Then he removed his bedroll and the two bags that hung from the saddle, one with food, the other with gear he needed for turkey hunting. "Go on and get a fire started before you leave, Robert. These damn mosquitoes are eating me up."

Hart dropped his bedroll between the two young oaks that he had used for his last lean-to, back in the fall, and cut three sweetgum saplings for the frame. By the time he had the saplings lashed to the oaks, a fire was crackling. "Reckon it'll get cool enough tonight to chill these mosquitoes, Robert?"

"If it have a mind to, suh."

"You better get going. And be careful in the dark."

"This mule got better eyes than you and me both, suh. Got eyes in her foots, it look like."

: : :

Hart made his camp in an oak grove on the edge of the swamp, on the high ground they called the hill, though the difference in elevation was no more than a few feet. When he had set the coffee pot on a grill of green sticks, he sprinkled sulphur on the leaves beneath the lean-to to discourage redbugs, and then he spread the tarp for a roof across the frame and rolled out his blankets. His house in order, he sat in the doorway, facing the fire, and waited for the coffee to boil. The flare of the flames blinded him to the swamp beyond, but he did not need eyes to see it. At the base of the hill lay a wide lagoon and beyond the lagoon an expanse of oak flat, canebrake, and cypress slough. Hart inhaled the breath of the swamp, a sweetness of flowers—jessamine and bay—folded into the heavy musk of still water and rotting logs and leaf mold inches deep. He was where he wanted to be.

He took a biscuit and a slab of ham from the bag, and a bull gator roared, deep and resonant, from far out in the swamp. A barred owl, its peace disturbed, hooted back, a single hoot prolonged and quavering that ignited every owl in the woods. The chorus was like the clamor of incarcerated lunatics. Once begun, it went on and on, feeding upon itself as though the owls' lives depended on the noises they could make.

He chewed at the salty ham, aware of the ghosts. Summoned by the manic serenade, they came and sat around the fire, and though he could not see them now, their presence transformed the camp into every camp they had ever shared with him, and he was young again. He poured a cup of coffee, black and scalding, spilling a splash on the ground. He was glad of the owls. He hoped they would hoot at daylight. No other sound in the woods was as likely to provoke a turkey into gobbling. He was going to kill a turkey for Jennie in the morning.

When the fire had died down to a glowing bed, the moon came up. It rose through the trees of the swamp, yolk-red and hot, larger than any moon he had ever seen. Jab it with a pitchfork, it would break and bleed all down the sky.

From the time she returned from Florida and moved into the cabin in Sallie's yard, Jennie had become the reason for his hunting. For her he had killed wild meat and brought it from the swamp and laid it at her kitchen door, that she might convert it into good food for him and for Sallie's house—an innocent arrangement, yet the one unchanging ritual of their love for each other, the only outward and visible form it could take, and the world was welcome to watch.

A dog whimpered, close by in the shadows. Some mangy critter, it must be, strayed off from a shack out here on the edge of the swamp, or a famished waif looking for a handout. Hart didn't want it nosing around his camp, whining for something to eat. "Get," he yelled. "Get on off from here." The moon filtered down through the trees, casting shadows, dappling the ground with ghostly light. There was a stirring in the leaves, a shifting of light and shadow, and presently another whimper, from the right this time and closer. Hart stood. "Get on now. I ain't got nothing for you." He looked about for something to throw, but from the rustle in the leaves the dog was slinking away.

He would take a turkey to Jennie tomorrow morning, while Sallie and the others were off at church, and tomorrow night he would sit down to supper in her cabin, strips of fried turkey breast and rice and gravy, field peas and sweet potatoes.

A whimper again, and there it was, groveling on its belly, inching toward the fire. Long-eared, a bluetick, and by its head a handsome one, though its ribs in the moonlight stood out in bold relief. It reminded Hart of a hound he'd owned many years before, a dog named Brick that he'd lost to a hog. Not the best deer hound he'd ever seen but damn good. And a voice that could break your heart—a deep bass with something of a whine in it, eager for blood. But bad to run hogs if the scent was fresh and hot. He had finally run the wrong one, a big yellow boar with black spots, and bayed it in a switch cane thicket. The growls and snarls and squeals they'd made as Hart was coming up sounded like the end of the world, and for Brick it had been. Hart had found him lying on his side, his belly laid open from his balls to his gullet, everything spilling out, and those sad eyes pleading for forgiveness. Hart had buried him where he lay, in ground soaked with his own blood, and three days later he killed the boar.

Hart made a kissing noise with his lips. He knew better than to feed a stray, unless he meant to adopt it. Feed this one and it would follow him into the turkey woods tomorrow, ruining any chance for a gobbler, but he wanted a closer look at it.

It was not unusual for deer hunters to lose a dog. There was one in every pack that would follow a deer across the river or far downstream, beyond the reach of the hunters' horns. Often, these mavericks ended up at a Negro's cabin where their owners would find them a week or so later. But deer season had ended months ago. This hound must have been scavenging the river swamp since Christmas, wondering why its master hadn't picked it up. Hart reached into his bag. He wished he'd brought more than the three biscuits and three slabs of ham. He held out a piece of ham. The dog whined, inched closer. Hart spoke gently to it. He wanted the dog to take the meat from his hand. Finally it did, still on its belly, and when it had gulped the meat, Hart offered the biscuit. More trusting now, the dog approached, cringing but wagging its tail. "That's all now. Except for breakfast, and you ain't getting that. Not tonight you ain't." The dog seemed to understand. At least, it whined no more but stretched out by the fire, just beyond Hart's reach, and put its head between its feet.

Hart took a bottle of whiskey from his bag, unscrewed the cap, and turned it up. He chased it with a swig from the canteen. "Fire feels good, don't it, old noser? On a cool night like this. A dog without a hearth is a pitiful thing. About as bad as a man reduced to holding conversation with a dog."

Hart pulled again on the bottle. "I know how you feel. You might not think so, but I do. I spent a winter out here in the swamp one time myself."

Another drink, and Hart continued. "Cou'n Bonner Creighton used to say that a steady diet of wild meat would turn a man about half-wild himself. I think he was right about that. The longer I stayed out here, the longer I wanted to. People thought I'd lost my mind. Maybe I had, sleeping in the moonlight. Going straight from the swamp to Agnes Creighton's wedding was crazy as hell sho nuff. But I'd been in the woods so long by then until I wasn't thinking straight. It had been on account of Miss Agnes that I went to the swamp in the first place; it just made sense that she should be the reason I came back out. Anyway, my presence at the wedding was not appreciated, I can tell you that. I reckon it made people nervous to be sitting within reaching distance of a man with hair that hung halfway down his back."

Hart laughed. "Cou'n Alice Carpenter swore that she saw leaves in it, said I wasn't normal, and Cou'n Bonner said, 'Hell, you wouldn't be either, Sister, if all you'd had to eat for the last six months was coon fat and acorns. Hart just needs to clean out his system, the way you do a possum.' Cou'n Alice told him he wasn't fit for decent company. He probably wasn't, but I sho do miss him. Men are in short supply these days, wouldn't you say?

Used to, a man would defend the honor of his lady and not think twice."

While Hart had been talking, the hound inclined its head in his direction, ears cocked, but when he ceased, the dog closed its eyes, leaving him to preside over the dying of the embers.

: : :

Hart woke up cold. Pulling a blanket around his shoulders, he struck a match and looked at his watch. Four twenty-five. Outside the lean-to, the moon was so bright that the trees cast dark, defined shadows on the pale leaves. Hart crawled out, trailing blanket, and stirred the ashes of the fire. When he had the fire going again, he set the pot with last night's coffee by the flames and reached into his bag for the biscuit and the ham. Only then did he remember the hound. He was surprised that it had not appeared, but that was just as well. He had wondered how he was going to keep it from following him.

When he had washed down his breakfast with the bitter coffee, he blackened his face and the backs of his hands with a concoction of lard, sulphur, and soot, necessary camouflage in the turkey woods, and slinging his hunting bag over his shoulder he picked up his heavy shotgun and set out.

As moonlight grayed into dawn, Hart entered the swamp. He found the deer trail he expected and followed it north through a privet thicket. In the open woods beyond, dogwood blossoms shone brightly in the dimness, and high overhead rags of mist hung caught among branches—skeins of gauze or insubstantial Spanish moss. When an owl hooted, Hart stopped to listen for a turkey. Hearing none, he went on, bearing north. He skirted canebrakes and waded sloughs, flushing wood ducks that flew crying toward the light. The stink of hogs came to him on the damp morning air, and then soft gruntings. He walked right into them, a sow and half-grown shoats, and they squealed as they scattered.

As though the swamp air had worked a mysterious change in the chemistry of his system, Hart was pure hunter now, eyes focused, ears open, and he moved as an animal moves, with no sense of time or concern for location. His boots were wet, his trousers soaked to the crotch, but he was unaware of discomfort. Where he was was where he wanted to be—in the grove of swamp chestnuts that had been his destination, though he had no recollection of the bearings by which he had reached it or the time he had spent in getting there. The time now, he knew by the light, was the time for turkeys to gobble.

He stood as still as a tree, his whole body cocked in an attitude of listening. After a few minutes he hooted, resonant and ringing, but the only answer he got was the hoot of another owl. The time for turkeys to fly down came and went.

Several years before, Hart had constructed a crib of logs for a turkey blind. He had not used it since last spring, and it had been falling to pieces then, but it was a likely spot and not far away. When he found it, he had to cut away cane that obstructed his view of the oak flat beyond, and then he settled in. For the next thirty minutes he listened intently for soft clucks and distant gobbles. From time to time he yelped on a wingbone call, and constantly he scanned the far edges of the open, parklike grove before him.

The sun came up, filling the woods with pink-orange light. A hen was standing in the midst of the flat fifty yards away. Hart looked for a trailing gobbler, and sure enough, way off on the edge of the cane, what appeared to be no more than a black stump moved and the longing that had led him to the swamp found its specific object.

The gobbler took a long time to approach, veering first in one direction, then in another, opening its feathers into partial strut, then changing its mind. But for all its apparent indifference, every movement was controlled by the hen. Hart knew that and waited, his gun barrel resting easily on a log of the crib. Without warning his attention was shattered by the blast of a gobble. Another turkey, very close, and there it was, coming in from the east, out of the rising sun, looking for trouble. Hart watched breathless as the intruder displayed its shimmering plumage,

resumed its sleek, lean form, and then displayed again—an ir-
ridescent shape-shifting, expanding and contracting, both ludi-
crous and elegant.

Within seconds, the first bird had rushed to join battle. Separated by no more than eight or ten feet, the gobblers puffed
themselves into full strut, pulled in their pulsing, naked heads,
and began a slow minuet of blind pivots and tight circles, drawing ever nearer to each other. Ten-inch beards protruded rigidly
from their breasts, neither weapon nor phallus but suggesting
both, and Hart could not decide whether they were demonstrat-
ing their riches to the lady or trying to intimidate each other.
Their drumming—that mysterious pneumatic whine that gobblers produce when displaying to a hen—was at once a warning
threat and a vibrato of intense desire. The birds seemed paralyzed in the conflicting impulses of love and war. Hart wondered
if a cluck on the wingbone might break things loose.

The effect was instantaneous. Quicker than his eye could
catch the action, the gobblers were upon each other, breast
to breast, a flurry of hammering wings. They separated just as
quickly and resumed their showy promenade.

The hen, indifferent to their ardor, had pecked her way closer
to the blind, towing the fighting toms in her wake.

Without any cause that Hart could see, the gobblers were at
each other again, raking the air with thorn-sharp spurs, making
feathers fly. Locked in their determination to vanquish each
other, they swung like dancers through scattering leaves, and
when they separated this time they were almost in range of the
L.C. Smith.

Hart released a long-held breath.

The hen was standing only feet from the blind, head raised,
suspicious, looking all around with that round, black, shining
eye. Then she clucked—a querulous, inquisitive tone—and the
sound triggered a third round in the unresolved contest. Hart
saw two red wattled necks entwined like grapevines that have
grown around each other, and for one frozen instant the gob-

blers seemed suspended in the energy of their beating passion, inches above the ground. He brought the gun to his shoulder and fired.

The fury of the battle was nothing compared to the birds' dying frenzy. Flopping with antic abandon, they beat the ground with frantic wings, flinging up leaves and filling the air with feathers. Hart approached warily, gun up, prepared to shoot again if necessary. A pileated woodpecker, startled by the shot, was cackling furiously somewhere nearby.

The turkeys took a long time to die. Now and then one or the other, convulsed by a spasm, dug madly at the soft dirt with its claws or beat its wings in a violent shudder. The ground was churned up in a wide circle around them, and feathers lay everywhere.

When the birds at last were still, Hart knelt beside them, ran their coarse beards through his fingers, tested the prick of their spurs. Three-year-olds, siblings probably. He took a leather strap from his game bag and tied it from the neck of one of the gobblers to its feet and slung it over his right shoulder. Gripping the other bird by its legs, he threw it across his back. He was weighted down by forty pounds of turkey and he had a long walk back to the camp.

: : :

Hart was asleep on a blanket when Robert Salley came riding up, but the snuffling of the mare roused him. The turkeys had been gutted and covered by the tarp. Hart removed the tarp and tied it into a roll with the blankets.

"Two now," Robert said, looking down from the mule. "The Lord must a been with you this morning sho nuff."

"I wouldn't think the Lord would take much interest in turkey hunting," Hart said.

With the water left in the canteen he washed his face. Handing one of the turkeys to Robert, he instructed him to deliver it to Coretta, who cooked for Miss Emma. "I'm going to take the other one by Miss Sallie's."

: : :

As Hart rode into Sallie Bonner's yard, a calf bawled from the lot out back, unnaturally forlorn in the Sunday morning stillness, and a wren sang its exuberant song from the dogwood tree in front of Jennie's cabin.

Enticed by the smell of frying chicken, Hart rapped at the kitchen door, then opened it. Instead of Jennie, a large black woman named Wilma who sometimes helped with the cooking was standing at the counter. Disappointed, he asked where Jennie was.

"She ain't here."

Hart knew that the two women were not friends, but that answer bordered on impertinence.

"Where is she?"

"I don't know, suh. Gone to church, I reckon."

That seemed unlikely. When she went at all, it was usually on a Sunday evening.

"Where I needs to be. Easter Sunday too."

He had not realized that today was Easter.

"I reckon Nathaniel is too," he said.

"If it be Sunday."

"As soon as Nathaniel comes in, you tell him I said for him to pick this bird, and be sure you tell Miss Sallie." Hart could not instruct Wilma to let Jennie know, but eventually word would reach her, and he might get a good supper after all.

: : :

Hart slept through the middle of the day. Late in the afternoon he walked a mile to a branch behind his house and fished until dark. When he returned to the cottage, James was gone and Pinck was sitting at the kitchen table, stained napkin tucked into his uncollared shirt, staring at a plate of rice and butterbeans. He looked as though he were waiting for someone to tell him he had finished.

Hart cut a large square of cornbread from a pan on the counter and took a pitcher of buttermilk from the icebox. He didn't want to spoil his appetite for the meal he expected at Jennie's table, but it might be midnight before it was served.

"Why don't you get up and go to bed, Sport?"

"What are you going to do?" Pinck asked.

"I'm going to clean fish. You want to help me?"

"My back don't feel too good."

"You'd better give it some rest. Go on to bed."

Pinck winced getting up. "Night," he mumbled and shambled off.

"You forgot your napkin, Sport."

The older man stopped and looked back at the table, confused. Then his slack face flickered. "Oh," he said, and pulled the napkin from his neck.

Hart scaled and gutted his catch on the back stoop, working by lantern light, slapping mosquitoes with fish blood on his hands. When he had finished, he wrapped the fish in brown paper and placed them on the melting block in the icebox. Fry them for breakfast, he thought. On the stoop again, he poured hot water into a basin and stripped and washed, scrubbing fish slime from his hands, scraping shiny, translucent scales from his wrists and neck. But when he held his hands to his face they still smelled of bream.

Pinck's snoring filled the little cottage. Hart put on dark clothes. It made more sense to walk than to ride, but he had walked miles today and his legs felt dead. Time was when he could follow a bird dog from daylight to dark and get up and do it again the next day, but not anymore.

Without light Hart entered the barn, a crowded darkness warm with the heat of large animals, their bodies and their breathing. The bite of ammonia stung his eyes. Feeling for the lantern on its nail inside the door, he paused and listened to their stirring—the thud of a hoof, a low whinny of greeting. He struck a match and lit the lantern. By its glow eyes rolled in the dark, dusty corners. A horse blew softly, a flutter of lips.

In her day Cassandra had been the kind of animal men dream

about. When he entered her stall, she stepped toward him, pushing against his chest with her blazed forehead. He ran his cupped fingers along the underside of her jaw, laid his palm against her flat, hard cheek. Her muzzle was the softest thing he had ever touched. He pressed his face into the hollow place behind her ear and combed her mane with spread fingers.

When he had led her into the hall, he threw a blanket across her back and set the saddle in place. If a man was entitled to one great horse in his lifetime, he had had his. He cinched up the girth, then led the mare from the barn into the luminous April evening. Dan hobbled down from the porch to meet them. In earlier days Hart would have had to tie up the setter to keep it from trailing him to Jennie's cabin, lest it lie all night at her door, incriminating evidence. But Dan was too stiff now to go much farther than the end of the avenue.

"Damn if we ain't a broken-down old dog-and-pony show," Hart said.

He led the old mare down the avenue and crossed the road. Among the tall pines he mounted and turned onto the path his own feet had made. The darkness was all astir with chuck-will's-widows. Their loud, lashing whistles, breathlessly repeated, seemed to come from the pine straw at the mare's very feet or from the limbs of trees an arm's length away, and the air fluttered with the soft beating of their wings.

Hart leaned forward a little in the saddle, looking for the moon. By this time last night it had risen. He wished that the night were warm enough for a swim. He would like to take Jennie to a sandbar on the Black Gall—anything to escape that tiny, confining cabin. In the flickering darkness of those close quarters Hart sometimes found it hard to breathe, and lately he and Jennie had both been on edge, flaring up too easily at petty irritations. For the first time, they were discovering the difficulty of sustaining a secret passion. Without a community to turn to, a surrounding circle of family and friends who thought of them as a couple and believed in their future, they had no refuge from each other's recriminations. Jennie had been complaining more frequently of late that he spent too much time in the woods, ignoring her. He argued that it wasn't her but the lack of opportunity to do anything together but go to bed. She was surprised that he objected to that, she said; looked like bed was all he came for anymore. He asked what else she had in mind for the evening, supper in Savannah? She reminded him that they used to sing together.

He had eaten nothing since the ham biscuit before daylight, and he was hungry for fried turkey breast. Something brushed his cheek, a soft flutter, and just as the image of chuck-will's-widow flashed upon his mind he was struck hard in the face—a roar of light, quicksilver needles flashing through his skull. The next thing he knew, he was on his hands and knees, pine straw against his palms, trying to get to his feet. Unable to see, he reached out and felt the flaky bark of a pine trunk, steadied himself, and tried to think. The horse. The bird must have startled her, causing her to throw her head. The crest of her neck had caught him squarely in the face. He could feel his nose dripping. The mare blew softly off to the right. By holding to the trunk Hart pulled himself from the ground. He called to the mare by name. She came to him, pushed against his chest with her forehead. He rubbed her ear and told her it was not her fault; then, finding the path, he turned left, leading her by the reins, hoping he was headed in the right direction.

The side of the house shone through the trees. Hart tied the mare to a gallberry bush, stroked her neck, and promised to be back soon. Halfway along the hedgerow toward the box of Jennie's cabin, he realized that if she were cooking supper, there should have been light in the windows. By the time he reached the back door he knew that it would open upon an empty room.

He struck a match and found a candle. He wanted rags to clean his face, but finding none he took off his shirt and dipped its tail into a bucket of water that Jennie kept on the hearth. The fire had died down to gray ash, affording little warmth, and the room was chilly. Wherever she was, she had been gone for a long time. His nose was too sore to touch, but he wiped his lip and chin. Then he collapsed into the velvet chair and swore at her for not being there.

She'd gone to Annie Mae's, he'd bet anything. Lately that had become her second home. Annie Mae's George—Hart didn't know whether they were married or not—was half brother to Joe Grant, the man Jennie had married and moved to Florida with, and Annie Mae herself some kind of cousin to Jennie. "My aunt is Annie Mae's granny," she'd explained. He thought she meant her aunt on the side of the man she called her father, but who could keep their blood ties straight? He didn't even try. Kin or not, he could not understand why she would want to associate with a crowd of Saturday night no-accounts, drinking and dancing in a backyard frolic. She never had before. They weren't her kind of people, no matter who Annie Mae's granny was.

Hart's nose was throbbing badly. He thought it must be broken. The candle flame was a blur of light. He blew it out and felt his way to the bed.

The sounds of someone stirring woke him. Though he had been asleep, it seemed to him that he had never lost consciousness of the pain in his face. Without moving, he opened his eyes and saw the fuzzy glow of the candle, and beyond that Jennie moving and upon the wall behind her the huge, wavering darkness of her shadow. It seemed to him that she had shaken loose her long hair and was now leaning forward to massage her scalp, but he could not bring her into focus. She was fooling now with the front of her dress, descending the long row of buttons. The dress fell in a heap around her ankles, ticking against the floor. She stepped out, picked it up, and folded it across the back of the velvet chair.

"What time is it?" he asked.

"I thought you was sleep."

"I reckon I was. What time is it?"

"How I s'pose to know? I can't see the clock."

The defiance in her tone was a clear indication of where she had been, the lapse into heavy dialect a sign that she had been drinking.

"I was hoping you might have fixed supper for me tonight."

Jennie blew out the candle.

"Light that again. I'm going."

"Light it your own self. I'm wo out."

She lay back heavily on the groaning bed, her breath, the heat of her body, rich with wine. Careful not to touch her, Hart climbed out across her feet. To hell with her, he thought. I ain't getting into it tonight, not when she's like this, and my nose.

But then, pout swelling her voice, she said, "I ain't hired on to do your cooking." And that ignited Hart, though the words he spoke sounded thick and blunted. "Church in the morning, frolic in the evening. I don't think you even know who you are anymore. I know I don't."

He heard the bed complain. Jennie sitting up.

"Ain't that the truth."

Her feet hit the floor.

"Far as you concern'," she said, "I just a somebody waiting in the dark, do your pleasure, get up and go back to where you left off. And what I s'pose to do? Sit round here shelling butterbeans till you decide you ready for a next time? I'm tired of it."

Hart was feeling about for his shirt. His matches were in the pocket and he wanted light. "I'm getting the hell out of here," he said.

"And go where? Back een them dark old woods? You is a solitary man, Hart Bonner. Come and go to suit yourself. But you listen to me. Just cause you don't want nothing to do with folks don't mean I content to sit here by myself. If church where I feel like going, that's where I go, if Annie Mae', then that's where. And ain't nobody gon tell me different. Slavery time been over, Mister Boss Man."

Hart stumbled against the velvet chair, caught an arm, and found where to sit, Jennie's folded dress against the back of his neck. Her voice rose in volume, grew rounder and richer in dialect, until the little cabin echoed and resonated, Jennie from all directions. He had no idea where she was.

"And I'll tell you something else must not've cross your mind," she said. "Compny ain't all that easy to come by way out here in these old backside piney woods. Not for me it ain't. Peoples on this place act like I got some kind of disease. Meet me in the road, don't even speak, and the womens be worse than the mens. Quick as I pass by, they hide they mouth and go to talking. And it ain't the color of my skin neither. It's on account of you. They know what it mean to have to lay down for the marster. That's another thing freedom ain't change. And here come Miss Jennie, prancing down the road with her bright Creighton face, acting like that old misery ain't none of her concern. I goes to Annie Mae' cause I ain't welcome nowhere else."

Hart sat dazed, as blind with pain as when he was knocked from the horse, but this was a different pain. He wanted to run from it, to get the hell out of that clanging darkness without having to answer, but he could not rise against the battering of her words.

"Did you tell them about Leonard Coe?"

In the dark sudden silence, Hart could almost feel the sagging of her spirit, like a tent collapsing upon itself. When she spoke again, her voice was flat and crumpled, from off to his left.

"What I say at Annie Mae' is my business."

"It's mine too if it's about Leonard Coe. If this thing gets around, Sallie's going to blame me. She's already threatened to run me off. You need to mind who you talk to. You've already said too much."

"You just can't get it through your head, can you? What make you think I'm gon to tell them folks at Annie Mae' what I said to Leonard Coe? You know what they'd say? They'd say that Jennie Grant told a white man she was Hart Bonner's nigger whore."

For eleven years Hart had known that his relationship with Jennie came at a heavy price, but he had always thought he was the one who did the paying. He felt too stupid to open his mouth.

"I reckon I did," she said.

Hart touched his throbbing face, now hot to the touch. "I'm going, Jennie. If I can find my shirt."

"You been sitting on it."

Fumbling into the still damp garment, he felt his way across the familiar room, avoiding a table he couldn't see but knew the location of, and walked straight into the wall. "Goddamn," he swore, and hit the boards hard with his fist, skinning every knuckle.

"Just a minute," Jennie said. She struck a match and lit a candle.

As the flame quickened, Hart saw only light, dim and diffused.

"Lord Jesus," Jennie cried. "What happened to you? Come here and let me look."

Hart obeyed, squinting at the approaching yellow brightness.

"No wonder you blumping round like a blind man," she said. "Your eyes're all swole shut. And blood all down your shirt. What'd you do to yourself?"

He told her.

"You should've put cold rags on it. Lay down now. I'll be right back."

He heard the door open, heard the creak of the pump handle, the gargle and suck of the pump itself, the constant little frogs from a wet weather pond off in the pines, and then she was laying a cold wet cloth across his burning face. It felt like a blessing.

"Do it hurt bad?"

"It hurts."

"I bet it do."

She sat beside him, absently brushing back his hair with her long cool fingers. As from a great distance, he heard her ask, "Do it feel better now?" After a while she began to sing, a lullaby that he had heard her sing to the children in the big house, and he followed along in his mind.

: : :

On Monday afternoon, somewhere between Thompson's General Merchandise and his mother's avenue, the postman fell asleep in the buggy. His chin dropped to his chest, and his grip on the lines loosened, but the tired old horse knew where he was going and kept up his steady plod down the shadowed sandy road.

Hart had hardly slept at all the night before. Jennie had wanted him to stay at the cabin, but he had remembered Cassandra, tied to a gallberry bush at the edge of the woods, and said he couldn't leave her there all night. Jennie had seen him as far as the mare, fussing all the way through wet, moonlit grass that he had no business going anywhere in his condition. The ride home had been an ordeal, sure enough, and his face, hot and tight, had kept him from sound sleep until time came to get up and hitch Red to the buggy. Had he been able to get in touch with a substitute, he would have stayed in bed. Now, his route completed, he gave way to his weariness.

Then the horse balked and snorted, pitching back into the shafts, causing the buggy to lurch and jolting Hart awake. A snake lay in the road, a big one. Hart sawed the horse's head hard to the right, swinging the buggy broadside. The snake was a canebrake rattler. It was slithering backwards in smooth, tight loops, gathering into its coil, ten feet away. Hart took the pistol from his pocket.

Had the snake been crawling, he would have climbed down for a better shot, but, looped back upon itself, it presented an easy target. Red was a veteran of snake encounters and, though edgy, he would stand for the shot. Hart raised the .38, gripping it in both hands, and held it out at arm's length. The canebrake was about as big as any he had ever seen, maybe six feet—an old serpent, but its skin was bright and new, rich ochre marked by well-defined black bands. The black tail held the rattles aloft, stiff and poised to buzz, and the blunt, wedge-shaped head was drawn back, cocked and loaded.

Blam!

The whole snake jumped, a heavy knot, writhing and recoiling, its spine broken in at least two places. Hart was pleased to have killed it. He would have liked to see Red slice it up with his hooves and then to feel its thickness as the buggy wheels rolled over it, but he knew that the horse would continue to balk, for a dead snake smelled no better than a live one. He removed the spent shell from its chamber and dropped the pistol into the pocket of his jacket. Climbing down, he began casting about for a stick. "Let's get this evil-smelling son of a bitch out of the road, old man, and we'll head on home to supper."

He was approaching his mother's avenue when he heard the automobile—a tinny clatter and sputter-coughing engine—and here it came, swirling dust in its wake.

Hart had tried to forget Leonard Coe since his encounter with Mrs. Coe. Short of assaulting the fellow, there was no way to avenge Jennie's honor. But he had no desire to see him. He yielded the road, keeping a tight rein on the horse. To his surprise the auto began to slow and then suddenly it bucked to a halt just a few yards in front of him. The windshield had long since been broken out. Through the opening where glass had been Coe looked up and squinted, exposing bad teeth and purple gums. "Looks like you been messing with the wrong fellow, sport. I thought women was more your style."

"I'm going to give you an opportunity to explain that," Hart said, "and if I'm not happy with what you say I'm going to drag you out of that wreck and stomp your ass into a grease spot."

"As long as you gonna take the trouble to drive up to my house and insult my wife, looks like the least you could do is to leave me my dime and not no such shit as this." Coe held out the sheet of paper that bore Hart's message and let it drop in the road. "You hear?"

"Why don't I just let you have it now?" Hart said.

"Hit's high time."

Hart reached into the pocket of his jacket and produced the .38. An oily blue light played about its barrel.

Coe let out a yelp and tried to duck, but the automobile afforded no hiding place. "Please Jesus," Coe begged, his arm before his face. "I swear to God, Mr. Bonner."

Hart smiled. "Relax, Mr. Coe. I just carry this for snakes. Matter of fact, I just now killed a big one, back up the road a piece. You ought to see it when you go by. Now let me see if I can find that dime."

Coe gripped the steering wheel with both hands to stop the trembling of his arms and faced straight ahead through the empty front window.

Hart flipped a coin into the car. "Go buy yourself a grape drink, son, before you ruin your trousers."

But Coe didn't even try to catch it.

: : :

Two days later Hart met Cou'n Bones Bonner coming down the big road from Wade Creighton's store, driving his old white mule and even older jersey wagon. It was Bones's long-established habit to progress from one country store to the next, stopping wherever he found conversation, staying as long as it lasted. Wherever night caught him, he could usually find a cousin who would give him a bed, and so he covered Heyward County. Though he claimed to be deaf when it suited him not to hear, members of the family knew that if you wanted local gossip Bones was the one to ask. How a deaf man acquired such a wealth of information was a mystery, but Hart suspected that people didn't bother to lower their voices in the presence of a man who couldn't hear. Besides, many dismissed Bones as a fool, but Hart knew better than that too.

The two vehicles stood wheel to wheel, but that didn't keep Bones from shouting. "Lord, son, you look like you been a few rounds with John L. Sullivan. Who busted up your face so bad?"

"My horse, Cou'n Bones. She reared back and hit me."

"That little mare did? Well, think of that."

"It was an accident. She shied at one of these whippoorwills."

"Oh. Out riding at night, was you?"

If there had been any talk of the events of the day before yesterday, Bones would have heard it. Hart went straight to the point. "You heard anything about this Len Coe, Cou'n Bones?"

But that was too direct to suit the old man. "You ain't seen Bubba this morning?"

"No, I haven't."

"I need to see him on some business. Wonder where he'd be about now?"

"I wouldn't have any idea, Cou'n Bones. I don't try to keep up with him."

"Coe now. Is he the one that hauls niggers around?"

"That's him," Hart said.

"I understand y'all had you a little dispute the other day."

"Where'd you hear that?"

"Oh, it's all up and down the road, clear to Robertville by now, I'd imagine. But that ain't how I heard it. I got it hot, right out of the oven, you might say."

A horsefly landed on Hart's thigh. He slapped at it and missed. "It don't surprise me a-tall that the little son of a bitch is running his mouth, but I wouldn't rely on the truth of what's he's telling."

"Truth ain't something that fellow's closely acquainted with, son. I've done heard three different versions of it, but I know my own self what he was telling that evening down at Thompson's. The fellow's a dern fool, if you ask me. Come sailing up to Thompson's in that dangerous machine of his — right up to the front steps now — throwing dirt and scaring mules, making an awful racket. You'd a thought he had every intention of driving right on up them steps and straight on in to the drink box. I couldn't tell you how he got it stopped — I was too busy jumping out of the way — but what surprised people was when he come up on the gallery he didn't say a word, just went right on in like there weren't nobody around to tell whatever it was that had just now happened to him. Something had, sho as hell. That boy was just as white as new cotton and trembling like he'd caught the palsy. Well, he drawed him out a grape and drank it down in one draught, and then I be damn if he didn't go for another one." The old man shifted his quid of tobacco to his other cheek and directed a stream of juice at the hoof of his mule. "I believe that boy must live on them things. I ain't never seen him eat nothing, not that I recollect. Anyhow, it must have been that second one that restored his voice cause all it took to get him started was for Billy Coverdale to ask him whose henhouse was it he'd just got hisself run out of, and he said how that nigger girl of Hart Bonner's—that's him, son, not me—how she'd been owing him the fare for when he took her down to the landing and when he tried to collect it from her she told him that Mr. Hart Bonner paid her debts."

"He's got it right so far," Hart said.

"Hanh?"

"Nothing. Go ahead."

"So he'd been looking for you for the past several days and hadn't seen you, he said, till just then, back up the road a piece, driving that post office buggy, and when he did he said to hisself I'll just collect me my fare right now. And, son, he said you pulled a gun on him."

Hart laughed. "I just took it out of my pocket to find a dime."

"That ain't the way he told it, but you could tell by how white the fellow was that it had a gun in it somewhere."

"What did he say?"

"What he said was, 'I asked him for what I had coming to me and the son of a bitch drawed a gun on me, said if I was to ever trouble that girl again he was going to kill me with it. I told him if money meant that much to him, to where he'd wave a pistol in a white man's face, just to keep his goddamned dime.' Old Billy Coverdale snorted—you know the way he does—said, 'I bet you did.' And Coe said, 'You would of too, eye-to-eye with a blue-steel .38.'"

"He's got his dime," Hart said. "If he ever bothered to pick it up off the floor."

"You'll be fortunate, son, if that's all it ends up costing you. That fellow's doing you no good, talking all up and down the road about you and that girl. The public domain ain't the place for that kind of thing."

Hart laughed. "Well, if you can figure out a way to put a stop to it, Cou'n Bones, I'd be much obliged if you'd let me know."

TISON

*T*ison Bonner liked to say that the most dangerous animal in the woods is a turpentine nigger on Monday morning; he's strong enough to hurt you any time, but after a weekend of bad wine he won't be able to think of a good reason not to. For that reason Tison strapped a pistol to his hip when he went into the woods. On this Monday morning he was riding through a stand of cat-face longleaf with his woodsrider Raymond Crabtree. It was one of those low-country July days that dawns hot, warning all living, breathing creatures of the misery the next fourteen hours will bring. Against the possibility of trouble Tison kept the skirt of his linen duster pulled back on the right side to expose the gleam of his .38.

The hot smell of pine gum, as palpable as steam, permeated their clothes and clung to their mustaches while stinging deer-flies swarmed about their heads. As far as they could see in any direction through the silent open woods, wounded trees stood weeping and aggrieved. Tison Bonner was about as happy as he ever got. If the dry weather held, he should be able to ship three more freight cars before the first frost.

"How's that new crew doing, Mr. Crabtree?"

"They're green yet, but I put Peedro in with them. He'll by God show em how, if we can keep him sober."

"Seems like it would make more sense to mix the new ones in with the old, like you do young dogs," Tison said.

"A turpentine crew is more like a barn lot of mules, Mr. Bonner. You take a crew that's worked out their own little problems and throw in somebody green, why things can go to hell in a hurry. I had to do something about Peedro anyway. Much longer and I was scared he was going to kill that Jew."

"Jew? What the hell do you mean, Jew?"

"A nigger, Mr. Bonner. That's just what they call him, Jew, don't ask me why."

Tison sawed a chew of tobacco from the plug in his pocket. "Well, do as you see fit, Mr. Crabtree. You're the turpentine man."

"There they are," Crabtree said.

Up ahead four black men stopped what they were doing and turned to watch as the riders approached. Dressed in shapeless, resin-stained overalls, intent on the ground at their feet, they all looked alike to Tison Bonner. He didn't know any of them.

"Morning, boys," Crabtree said.

They responded in soft, indefinite gutterals.

"I don't see Peedro."

Nobody spoke.

"He started out with you this morning, didn't he, Tom?"

"Us must've lost him, Capn."

"Lost him?"

"Peedro say he need to answer nature," Tom offered.

At the same time another man said, "Say he sick, suh."

"How long ago was that?"

The black men studied each others' faces for the answer.

"Ain't been too long," Tom said.

"Which way did he go?"

Tom pointed east, the direction from which the white men had come, then waved vaguely through an arc toward the north and on around to the swamp until he had covered almost one hundred and eighty degrees. "Off yonder way, suh."

The white men knew that the crew had seen the last of Peedro for that day, but Crabtree said to them anyway, "When he gets back, y'all tell him I'm looking for him, you hear?"

"Yessuh, sho will," they said, all speaking at once as though eager to show their sympathy with the boss's righteous indignation.

Tison and Raymond Crabtree rode north through the pines toward the branch road, expecting to intercept the crew working the next crop. Sweating heavily in the wet, unbreathing air, they rode in silence, too hot to carry on a conversation. Crabtree suddenly reined in, said, "Hello. Looka yonder."

Twenty steps off to their left lay a black man, sprawled on the pine needles, face up.

"Reckon he's dead?" Tison Bonner asked.

"Who? Peedro? You couldn't kill that nigger with a chop axe, Mr. Bonner. He's drunk."

"Let me handle this, Mr. Crabtree."

"You watch yourself, Mr. Bonner. Peedro's a blue gum. You don't want to let him bite you."

"It hadn't occurred to me to, Mr. Crabtree."

Tison Bonner walked his horse right up to the unconscious man. Pine needles had worked their way into the tight kinks of his beard, and deerflies were feeding unmolested on the lumpy, welted face. Urging his horse one step farther, Tison stopped directly above the spraddled legs and looked down into the cavity of Peedro's open mouth.

"By God if he ain't."

Calmly, methodically, Tison worked the cud in his cheek. Then he leaned out from the saddle and spurted a heavy rope of juice. It struck the black man square in the forehead, splashing, but Peedro merely twitched his limbs and fluttered his eyelids. When at last he opened his eyes—red and smeary where they should have shown white—they seemed not to focus.

"Get up," Tison said.

Peedro did not budge, but knowing came into his eyes, like water seeping up into a hog wallow.

"Did you hear me? I said get up."

Peedro raised himself onto an elbow, causing Tison's horse to snort and sidestep, barely missing the black man's legs. As Tison fought the reins, Peedro sprang to his feet like a cat, crouched. To Tison's surprise, he held a chipping knife, a wicked sickle of a blade, and he was coming. What stopped him was the nose of Tison's nickel-plated .38, twelve inches from his face. Tison's hand was trembling. "Come on now. Just one more step, nigger."

Peedro dropped the chipping knife and backed off, hands held out to his side, but hate bleared his bloodshot eyes.

"I ought to go ahead and blow your goddamn brains against that pine tree. If you ever come at me again, I'm going to, you understand? I said, do you understand? Well, say so, goddammit. Now get the hell out of these woods and don't let me see your black ass again, you hear? I mean anywhere. Ever. Now march."

The black man turned and stumbled off to the west, in the general direction of the big road, weaving a little as he made his way through the trees. Tison, blowing hard, watched, his grip still strong on the pistol. When Peedro had at last disappeared among the hazy trunks, Raymond Crabtree said, "Peedro's about the fastest chipper we got, Mr. Bonner."

"Yeah. Well, we ain't got him no more," Tison said.

: : :

Shortly after noon that day Tison was leading a procession of three wagons down the dappled, sandy big road toward the depot at Cypress Swamp, still four miles away. As the wagons creaked and groaned behind him, threatening to break their springs beneath the weight of the turpentine barrels, Tison was counting profits. With two more cars after this one, and cotton looking like forty cents a pound, he was having his best year ever. He thought he might take a trip this winter, ride the train down to Florida maybe, drink orange juice and look at some of that real estate people were talking about. Might be a good investment.

Around a bend the store came into view—a white frame building on the right, squatting so close to the road that travelers could spit from their buggy seats right onto the gallery. Bones Bonner's jersey was tied up beneath the sycamore tree, his ancient white mule asleep on three legs in the oven-hot shade. Tison was not surprised, but he was in no mood for Bones today. Even so, he had to stop. Besides, he was hungry.

Now Tison could see them in the shade of the gallery, three men—Wade and Bones and somebody else—probably that underhanded bastard Richard Sanders. And now he could hear them, Bones and Wade yelling at the top of their voices, trying to communicate in normal conversation about something that didn't amount to a hill of beans, baseball more than likely. Tison told the driver of the lead wagon to go on, he'd catch up before they got to the depot. Then he swung the head of his horse toward the men on the gallery.

The third man was indeed Richard Sanders, a neighbor who had been after Tison for a year now about buying a piece of land that lay along the Gall between his place and Miss Sallie's. When Tison had said no, the land was not for sale, Sanders had made the mistake of going to Miss Sallie. Tison had let him know in terms not even Pinck could have misunderstood that he was not to bother the lady again, nor him for that matter; the land was not by God for sale.

"Gents."

"Hauling spirits, Bubba?" That was Bones, at the top of his voice, putting the question not as a casual observation intended to open friendly chatter but in the tone of earnest inquiry, as though he had not just seen and heard the loaded wagons rumble by. Tison ignored the question.

"Mighty hot, ain't it?" Bones said.

"Light and set, Cou'n Tison," said Wade. "Looks like you could stand a cool drink."

Tison grunted as he swung from the saddle. Tying his horse

to a banister, he climbed the three steps. "I ain't rich enough to idle through the middle of the day like you Vanderbilts," he said.

Without breaking stride he entered the hot, dusty, cheese-smelling dark, grabbed a box of crackers with one hand, a tin of potted meat with the other, and ended up at the drink box, from which he pulled a soda, more wet than cold. Before opening his wares, he walked behind the counter to record his purchase in the smudged ledger Wade kept beneath the cash box. Then, sawing open the tin with his pocketknife, he commenced spreading a cracker with the pinkish paste.

"Wade," he called.

Wade, who was young enough to have grown up regarding Tison Bonner as his father's contemporary, jumped to his feet and entered the store. "Sir?"

"How much does Peedro owe?"

Tison could have found the figure himself, for it was recorded in the ledger, but he wanted to see if Wade kept track in his head of accounts outstanding.

"A little over three dollars, I believe."

That was more than Tison wanted to write off, but the alternative was to let the Negro work it off through another week's labor and then fire him, and that was out of the question.

"No more credit to him or his woman."

"Peedro quit?"

"I quit him."

"I declare."

"He's lucky I didn't kill him."

"Great day." After a moment Wade said, "He and Alma sho do have a house full of younguns."

"You ever seen one that didn't?"

"I reckon not."

Tison finished his lunch on the gallery. Bones, his cigarette dead on his lip, appeared to be dozing, but he looked up at the racket of an oncoming automobile.

The buggy horses flinched and snorted, and Tison's gelding, hitched to the rail in front of the store, reared against the reins, kicking out behind him at the noise.

"Any of y'all know that fellow?" Tison asked.

Nobody did.

"You see a good many strangers passing through here lately, Cou'n Tison," Wade said. "If we had us a gasoline pump, I imagine a fair number of them might stop. Might buy them a little something from the store."

Tison didn't answer. Wade had mentioned gasoline before, but he couldn't see the percentage in it, not way back here, off the beaten path.

"Charleston Road's getting to be a regular thoroughfare. Next thing you know, Cou'n Bones will be driving one."

"Why?" Bones yelled.

"They go a sight faster than a mule and wagon for one thing."

"There ain't nowhere I'm in that big a hurry to get to," Bones said.

"I got too much to do to stand around jawing with you Rockefellers all afternoon."

"Where you going?" Bones asked. "You going to Cypress Swamp?"

"That's a good guess, Bones, since I'm headed in that direction."

Bones cupped his hand to his good ear, cocked his head, and squinted against the smoke of a fresh rolled cigarette. "Hanh?"

"I said yes. I ain't got time to repeat everything twice."

"Why you're an ill-tempered son of a bitch, ain't you?"

"No, just busy," Tison said.

"I think I'll ride with you anyway, whatever kind you are, long as you going that way. You ain't heard nothing on the war, I don't reckon?"

"Not today."

"I understand Horace Anderson's youngest boy's signed up to go."

"I wouldn't know," Tison said.

"I never saw anything like these automobiles," Wade said. "More all the time, it looks like."

"I don't reckon you've changed your mind about that sorry little old creek piece, Mr. Bonner?" asked Richard Sanders.

When Tison failed to answer, Sanders added, "Let me know if you do now."

The road stretched before them flat and mostly straight, loose white sand churned into powder by automobile traffic. Dusty ditch weeds drooped in the breathless heat. The two men rode in silence, one on horseback, the other by wagon, on either side of the sandy ridge that ran down the middle. Though Bones's mule kept pace with the horse, conversation in such weather, especially with Bones, required more energy than Tison owned. Out of nowhere an automobile came rattling up behind them, startling the animals with its imperious *ooga-ooga*, insisting on the road. The driver wore what looked like a bonnet, tied beneath her chin. When the machine had disappeared, dust drifting in its wake, a fine powder settled on Bones's dark clothes and turned Tison's damp white linen duster the color of dirt.

"Godalmighty," Tison said. "was that a woman driving that thing?"

"Appeared to be."

"I didn't know they let them."

"Must be from off somewhere."

"There ought to be a law against it, if there's not one already. Goddamn women. Wonder where the hell she thought she was going?"

Bones answered by saying, "I sho do miss old John."

Tison was not surprised by his cousin's abrupt change of subject—that was another of Bones's peculiarities—but he did not like to talk about his brother, even within the family.

"How long's he been gone now, Bubba?"

"Eight or nine years, I reckon."

"Has it been that long sho 'nuff? Don't seem like it, does it?

You remember the time me and John tried to get you to go out to Arkansas with us? You must a been busy with something. You sho missed a good trip though. They got these gambling palaces out there, see, and me and old John went in one one night—first night we got there, as I recall. Thought we'd try our luck, don't you know, but it didn't turn out too good. After a while John said, 'Bones, we done lost enough in this damn den of iniquity.' Well, no sooner had we stepped out on to the street when this pair of young ladies come up to us, said they'd been abandoned by their escorts and wondered could we see them back to their hotel. Well, John, you know, was ever one to rescue a dampsel in distress. I wish you could a seen the way he bowed to them little pullets. Tipped his hat, said we'd be honored, ladies. Course, we weren't nothing but country come to town, but I was somewhat more familiar with the wiles of the night than John was. I pulled him off to the side there and said, 'What we got here, John, is ladies of the evening.' Unfortunately, they heard me say it."

"I imagine the whole damn town did."

"Well, they commenced to laughing, and John said, 'Begging your pardon, ladies, but you'll have to overlook my friend, I'm afraid he left his manners in South Carolina.' Course, that was even better, far as they were concerned. One of them said, 'That's a good place for them, honey,' and the other one said, 'I hope he didn't leave his money too.' Lord, Bubba, I wish you could a seen old John when she said that."

What Tison saw was his brother's little yellow mustache, the way it curled beneath his upper lip, and the drawn beak his nose had become, and the bruised, glittery eyes.

"I'd just as soon not talk about it."

"Hanh?"

"I said shut up about it."

: : :

Tison was convinced that a darkened room was cooler than one in which sunlight was allowed to enter, if only by a degree or two. For that reason his house remained shuttered throughout the long summer, and the curtains and carpets and upholstered furniture became permeated with the odor of sweat-soaked clothes that were hung up each night to dry. Tison had long since grown accustomed to the smell. At sundown he was sitting in a blue enameled bathtub which his man Jonas had dragged from the back porch into the darkened bedroom, scrubbing his hard white body clean of the day's dust and dirt and turpentine. He scrubbed hard with a stiff brush, sparing his own no more than he would any living flesh, and as he scrubbed he entertained himself with figures, manhandling onto the flat car each barrel of spirits with the abacus of his brain.

When he rose dripping from the bath, his reflection shone like a haunt in the dark glass of a full-length mirror—a body as white as leaf lard, belly stout enough to bust its way through a crowd—but Tison, drying off his broad freckled shoulders, paid it no attention. He dressed himself in the white linen three-piece and plain black bow tie he wore each evening for supper at Miss Sallie's, changing only his collar from one day to the next. He regretted the time it took to return to his house each morning and change into work clothes, but he preferred that to keeping a wardrobe at Miss Sallie's. The day he moved his clothes across the road would be the day those women took the reins and that he would not abide.

The distance from his front door to his sister-in-law's was three quarters of a mile, a fifteen-minute walk. Driving the motorcar, had anyone proposed it, would have struck him as a senseless extravagance; when it was raining he put on a slicker and hitched up the buggy. But it was not raining this evening, hadn't in nearly two weeks, and that suited Tison just fine. With another crop to box he didn't care if the drought held on till Christmas. The cotton and corn were made.

He reached Miss Sallie's yard in a dying half-light, just dim enough for him to see the winking lightning bugs. As he opened the gate in the picket fence, a farmhand named Willie Tee, hardly more than a boy, came around the corner of the house.

"Yessuh, Mr. Tison, John Earl say come quick to the barn. Say us got a sick mule."

"Which one?"

"Little red mule, name Belle."

"What's the matter with her?"

"Got the staggers, what John Earl say."

Tison Bonner despised sickness. Having never been sick himself, he resented those who were, men or beasts, as though illness were a sign of weak character. That may have accounted for his affinity for machines. From the time he worked as engineer on the steamboat *Rosalee*, people with mechanical problems had called on him for help. Bonner Creighton had been especially bad about that. When Bonner was alive, Tison was forever repairing that little steam jenny of his. That machines could be repaired was what Tison liked about them. When people and animals broke down, a man had no way of knowing for sure what was wrong, and by the time the symptoms appeared it was usually too late for remedy. Tison had a particular aversion to treating sick mules and horses. He had little affection for them well; fevered and dull of coat, running at eyes and nose, they made him sick. Were it not for the value of an animal, he'd as soon let nature take its course.

"Tell John Earl I'll be down there when I finish supper."

"Yessuh. John Earl say best come quick, suh. That mule een bad shape."

Tison swore. Besides being hungry, he was not dressed for treating a sick animal. There was a man named Cholly Ross, lived on the Clifton place, who had a name for being a good horse doctor, but that was five miles away, and even if they could get him down here at this time of night he'd expect a dollar for his trouble. Supper would just have to wait.

The hallway of the barn was lighted by a lantern hanging at each end. Tison instructed Willie Tee to remove the one at the front and bring it to the stall of the suffering mule. In the pulsing yellow glow, the animal shone slick with sweat, its barrel and belly so distended that it looked like a carcass after a day in the sun. It smelled bad too.

John Earl led the mule into the hallway. It followed on unsteady legs, planting each narrow hoof with deliberation. Removing his coat, Tison examined the animal's glassy eyes, found the pulse and took it, and laid his hand upon her wet, bloated flank. "Tight as a damn tick, ain't she?"

"Sho is," said John Earl. "I believe that mule got the staggers."

"Staggers, hell. She's got the colic. Don't you boys know colic when you see it? Who's been working her?"

"She ain't been work. Not today she ain't. She been een this here lot all day."

Tison wiped his hands on a rag, took off his vest and tie and collar. "Where was she yesterday? That's when the damage was done."

"Same as today, suh."

"Then y'all must have let her get into the feed room."

"Nawsuh."

Those were the answers Tison expected, but he had his own way of making sure it didn't happen again. Sending Willie Tee to the big house for soap and hot water, he instructed the older man to throw a length of plowline over a hook in a rafter and then to hobble the mule. "We going to have us a little lesson in veterinary medicine," he said.

"Is?"

"If you ain't got no more sense than to let a mule eat itself sick, it's high time you learned how to fix it."

"Yessuh. That must have been somebody else left that feed room door unlock. Sho wan't me."

Tison left John Earl to his own devices and went into the room where medicines were kept. By the time he had mixed the ingredients for the drench, Willie Tee was back with two kettles of water. "They coming with the rest," he said.

When the purgative was ready, Tison poured a soda bottle full. Then, taking the end of the plowline that hung from the hook in the rafter, he pulled hand over hand, slowly winching high the reluctant hammer head until the mule's nose was pointed straight at the roof.

"Now climb up on that stool, John Earl, and see if you can get that bottle in her mouth. Just ease it in. That's right. Down in the corner more. Easy. Don't let it spill."

When the mule's throat began to convulse with involuntary swallowing, Tison released the tension on the rope, allowing the animal to lower her head.

John Earl, stepping down, said with great satisfaction, "That mule be ready to plow come morning."

"She might if you drench her every thirty minutes till midnight. Right now we're going to work on the other end."

"Oh Jesus."

"Take off your shirt now. What I want you to do is grease your arm real good with soap and water," Tison said.

"Naw suh. I ain't sticking no arm of mine up no mule' ass. Let Willie Tee. He ain't done nothing but bring water."

"It wasn't Willie Tee had responsibility for that mule. Now do like I said."

John Earl soaped his arm, muscles rippling the wet black skin like little minnows beneath the surface. With the despondency of a man resigned to the gallows, he leaned against the mule's left haunch and delicately fingered the black, puckered orifice.

"We can't hold her all night, John Earl. Go on and reach in. It ain't gonna bite," Tison said.

With a ripple of muscle and tendon, the hand disappeared. The mule hunched.

At that very instant tall Nathaniel appeared in the doorway swinging a kettle of hot water in each big hand. What he beheld was a congress of man and mule frozen into an astonishing statuary. It must have seemed to him for the briefest instant that not only the mule and the men but the barn itself and even the night outside had gathered themselves, sucked in their collective breath, and he had caught them trying to hold it for as long as they could. Then the mule brayed, a trumpet blast that released the tension by which the entire assembly held together, and the statue exploded. Willie Tee flew toward the door where Nathaniel was standing, still swinging the kettles; Tison disappeared amidst the flash of shod hooves and whipping rope, and John Earl landed fifteen feet down the hallway. The wretched mule had invested her last ounce of energy in that one mighty kick and now gave way to her misery, settling heavily onto the floor of the barn.

Tison looked at John Earl, still sprawled and badly injured for all he knew or cared. "You ain't worth the powder and shot it would take to kill you."

Disappearing into the medicine room, he returned immediately with a length of black rubber tubing attached at one end to a wide-mouthed funnel. His freckled shoulders glistened with sweat as he applied the soap.

"John Earl. All you got to do this time is stand here and hold this funnel and not drop it. Willie Tee, get ready to pour. Slow and easy now. When I say." Kneeling at the rear of the mule, Tison lifted the thick coarse tail and inserted the tubing. "Okay."

For a few moments all was still except for the quick, shallow pants of the mule and the glug glug of the gallon jug. Tison felt the hose grow warm between his fingers as he held it in place, and still the mule lay quiet. The jug was almost empty when the rumbling began, a remote, convoluted, subterranean rebellion. The mule struggled to get to her feet. As her hindquarters followed her front end, Tison jumped, snatching free the hose, but he was not as spry as he had once been and the arcing rooster tail, expelled with prodigious force, caught him full in the chest, appearing to knock him to the floor, though in fact in his haste to back out of harm's way he tripped over the stool that John Earl had left in the middle of the hallway.

John Earl and Willie Tee moved to lend a hand, but the sight of the boss man laid out and splashed brown with mule shit was more than they could bear. Nathaniel disappeared into the darkness while the young men turned their heads to keep from laughing in Tison Bonner's stricken face.

Fifteen minutes later Nathaniel reappeared, looming in the hallway door as rooted as a tree, holding out in huge, blocky hands a folded pair of faded overalls. Tison had stripped down to his drawers. Though that garment too was stained wet and brown, he would not expose his nakedness to black men. With fastidious step he picked his way through the fouled straw on the floor.

"Miss Sallie say your supper waiting."

Tison retired to the harness room to dress, peeling off the ruined drawers before stepping into the overalls. With nothing between him and the coarse denim, not even a shirt to clothe his lard-white shoulders, he felt as common as a sharecropper. So dressed, he would not allow himself to be seen by the household. Not that he was fit for company, reeking as he did of mule shit. He would eat a cold plate on the dark back steps. That suited him just as well anyway. Then he'd go back home to sleep.

He told John Earl to hitch up the buggy. Willie Tee was walking the sick mule in tight circles around the little lot. Apparently relieved, the animal was moving more easily now. Tison told the boy to keep it up till he got back.

He would have to let Miss Sallie know or she would worry. It was late, she was probably ready for bed, but maybe that girl was still in the kitchen. He was approaching the back of her cabin. No. There was a light in her window, the casement a softly glowing yellow square in the dark wall. The only nigger house in Christendom, he thought, with actual glass panes. One of Miss Sallie's notions. You'd think the girl was white, the way they coddled her. That business with Hart notwithstanding. He wondered if he should go around to the front and knock at her door, tell her to tell Miss Sallie. He knew who she'd think it was, this time of night. There was a good chance the son of a bitch was in there now. He eased up to the window. The rag of muslin barely filled the casement. He could see in.

What he saw was Jennie sitting on a footstool in the middle of a galvanized tub, bathing. Tison had never seen a completely naked woman in his life and the glory of her body all but struck him blind. Embarrassed, he jerked back his head. His ears grew hot. Directly he looked again. In the glow of the kerosene lamp her wet body shone all bold light and shadow—the column of her long neck beneath her loosely pinned-up hair, the glinting planes of her collarbones and chest, the shadowed cleavage between her breasts that still bounced when she moved like the breasts of a girl. Tison could hardly catch his breath. If she was to stand up now, he would faint sure as hell. He'd better get out of there. He turned to leave but stopped and looked again. And she was standing now, though turned from the window, so that what Tison saw was the curve of her waist and hips, the highlighted cleft of her buttocks. The hammering of blood in his ears alarmed him. Any second now she was bound to hear the pounding of his heart. Tison put his hands on his knees and lowered his head. He was as stiff as a poker.

⁘ ⁘ ⁘

In the breathless, overheated nights of that long August, as cotton made and split its bolls and cornstalks drooped and died for lack of rain and roadside weeds grew gray with dust, old Tison Bonner became a Peeping Tom, as addicted to spying on Jennie's nakedness as a wino to his bottle. Sleeping five nights of the week at Miss Sallie's, with authority to go and come as he pleased, he would retire to his bedroom after an evening cigar on the porch and stand at the window watching Jennie's cabin, hoping that the house would settle in for the night before her lamp went out. When stirring ceased in the rooms overhead, his heart began to pound in his ears. He fretted about bumping into Hart, arriving at her window as Hart approached her door, and that possibility forced him to contemplate what Jennie and his brother did inside—a cud of bitterweed that he could not help chewing. Yet he ventured out even so, for his eye was famished for Jennie's body, and the more he saw the more he craved.

Nothing grew beneath her window, neither grass nor weed to cushion the print of his boots, and Tison knew even as he eased his eye to the corner of the glass, lowered in spite of the heat to keep out mosquitoes, that he was scuffing the sand at his feet. Some nights he arrived to find her in a long white cotton gown, ready for bed, and some nights he came too soon, while she was still fully clothed, moving absently about the small cabin room, trifling with flowers in a vase or a hem she had just taken up. Terrified that Hart might step from the shadows at any second, he dared to risk one more minute, crouched against the wall, panting in the close hot night, looking not through the glass but out into the darkness, as though by turning away for a moment he might hasten her out of her clothes. One night, plagued by mosquitoes, he found her still dressed and sitting in a chair, a newspaper spread before her. That was the first time Tison Bonner had ever seen a Negro reading. Wondering just who the hell she thought she was, he abandoned his post and stole away into the trees, as aggrieved as the victim of a broken promise.

Often enough his daring was rewarded. Before his glazed and fevered eye she stepped out of her dress and pulled her undergarment over her head. The sight of her full cream-colored breasts rolling free would cause his heart to hammer so insistently against the wall of his chest that he actually feared he might fall stricken on the spot, to be found at daylight stiff beneath her window. One night as he watched she massaged her breasts, her head thrown back in bliss, and one night, fully naked, she turned from shadow toward his eye the secret roundness of her belly, the black triangle. Congested with desire, the old man crept away to the barn, and there amid the smells of animals and oats and new, oiled harness he spilled his seed in thick dust pocked by the conical pits of antlions. Returning to the house by way of the front lawn, he felt scalded by self-loathing, yet still refused to consider what he had done.

One night Jennie turned suddenly toward the window, looking as though she might have heard an unfamiliar noise, and her gaze met his, locked his eye to hers, and he could not pull away. He had always felt secure in knowing that she could not see through the reflecting glass, but this time he was certain he'd been caught. He waited three nights before going back, and when he did he found to his surprise the curtain open. Trembling, he dared to believe that she was inviting him to look, but the next night the curtain was back in place, a new piece of muslin stretched tight across the casement as though tacked at the corners. Then he knew for sure that she knew. But far from being dismayed by that knowledge he welcomed it, for it seemed to him they shared a secret now, a bond that shackled them soul to soul.

From that night he sought to engage her attention, but when opportunity occurred, the two of them meeting and passing in the dark hall or entering the parlor at the same time by different doors, his mouth went dry and he could not look her in the eye.

Then in a dream one night he saw her in a rope swing like the one old Nathaniel had hung from a live oak limb for the children. Back and forth, back and forth, higher and higher she went, legs outstretched, petticoats fluttering in her face. Her legs were bare for as far as he could see, and each time she went swinging by, arcing high above him, she smiled down at him and laughed. He awoke in darkness; the clanging of stove lids from the kitchen told him that she was already up and fixing breakfast, and it seemed to him that she had risen from his own bed just a short time before. If he went into the kitchen now, he felt, she would greet him with a sweet good-morning kiss.

As though the dream had opened a door into her guarded heart, Tison felt that they were friends now, and he began to court her. He did it with money, leaving coins beneath his napkin at supper. When a week had passed without her acknowledging the gifts, he left a shiny silver dollar—equivalent to four days' wages in the careful economy of that household. After breakfast the next morning he lingered in the kitchen, encouraging a thank you. When none came he prodded. "A gal that knows how to feed a man can do right well for herself, looks like."

Jennie turned from the dirty dishes. "That's kind of you, sir, but Miss Sallie looks after my little needs just fine."

Tison knew who looked after her little needs all right. Besides that, he was annoyed by her taking such care to be polite. When he spoke, his voice was harsher than he intended. "Of course she does. I know that. I just meant to show some gratitude, a little token of appreciation, you might say. And it ain't like you can't use it."

"No, sir. I thank you, sir."

Tison groomed his mustache with thumb and finger, giving the ends a quick twist. "If you want to know the truth, I got more damn money than I know what to do with. You let me decide how to spend it."

Jennie looked at her feet. "Yessir. I'm much obliged, sir."

One afternoon not long after that Tison arrived at Miss Sallie's much earlier than usual—a full two hours before supper—and contrived to overhear his sister-in-law tell Jennie to have Nathaniel saddle the pony for the children, they were about to drive her to distraction. Tison slipped away to a summerhouse smothered by a climbing yellow rose, and sat in the damp green shade. They should be along any time, but waiting was not easy for him. He was a man accustomed to getting what he wanted and getting it now. He was growing tired in fact of waiting for the girl to come around. If he could find a way to get her off by herself, away from the women and those wretched children, he could make her understand.

Nathaniel appeared from behind the house, seven shambling feet tall, leading a Shetland pony that hardly reached his thigh, and here came the rest of them, the children dancing circles around her, tugging at both hands, yelling, "Me first, Jennie, you promised."

Jennie was going in all directions keeping up with the youngest, an adventuresome three-year-old, while trying to settle the inevitable squabble between the older two as to which had had the longer turn on the pony.

"If y'all can't behave yourselves," Tison heard her say, "I'll tell Nathaniel to put that pony up and we'll see how long before you get to ride him again."

She lifted one whining child from the saddle and caught the other beneath his arms. He struggled free of her grasp, wanting to mount by himself, but unable to place his foot in the stirrup he submitted to her assistance. The three-year-old meanwhile was headed straight toward the summerhouse. Tison saw that the older girl, who was still pouting, had noticed her wandering little brother and decided that he was not her responsibility, and he thought how much he'd like to see her on the receiving end of a sound thrashing. Just as the child entered the door Jennie swooped down upon him like a chicken hawk, swept him up as high as her head, and, laughing, buried her face in his neck, making a wet racket of kissing.

"You stay out of this summerhouse, you hear me? Snakes and spiders be crawling round in here, waiting to eat you up."

Then she saw Tison. And jumped.

"Oooh, Mr. Tison. You scared me to death. What you doing lurking round so quiet?"

"Watching you, Jennie Mae."

"Me?"

"I have been for a long time," he said.

The three-year-old on Jennie's arm regarded Tison with wide blue eyes. Jennie gave a little sniff of wonderment. "What you mean a long time? We ain't been out here ten minutes."

Perhaps it was something she noticed in his face—Tison could not have said what his features were expressing—but suddenly her eyes quickened with understanding and she blushed. "And all this time I been thinking it was Willie Tee left them footprints."

"Don't you reckon Willie Tee knows better than to do a wicked thing like that?"

Confusion came into Jennie's face. "I hope he do," she mumbled.

"You're a fine looking woman, Jennie Mae."

She turned to leave, the child's head turning as she did so that he never took his eyes off Tison. Jennie stooped to get through the low door but then stopped and turned again and looked straight at Tison. Her large dark liquid eyes burned in the green light, but her voice was calm and sure. "I reckon you know. Mr. Peeping Tom."

Now it was Tison who was left in confusion. Jennie had boldly changed the footing of their relationship and he liked that, but she had done it by an impertinence unthinkable in a Negro. He hardly knew what to think.

∴ ∴ ∴

During the days following that encounter the air in Sallie Bonner's house became charged with Tison's awareness of the cook Jennie Mae, as he called her. Even a stranger might have felt its crackling current. Certainly the women of the house did. But Tison was like a man who had grabbed hold of a hot wire and couldn't let go. Jerked about so, he hardly noticed the presence of others, much less the frowns on their faces. By habit now he came for the hot midday meal and afterwards hung around the kitchen while Jennie, and often enough Sallie, washed and put away dishes, as though such behavior was perfectly normal for a sixty-two-year-old kinsman who for ten years had been too busy to spend five minutes passing the time of day with a soul in that house.

"Things must be going smoothly with the turpentining, Cou'n Tison," Sallie would say.

"Yes ma'am," he'd say, "long as the rain holds off."

"The cotton almost ready, is it?"

"Another week, I'd say."

But if Sallie left the kitchen, called away by any of a dozen little problems—for no one in that house, it seemed, could take a step without her help—Tison would try to talk. It was a painful thing to hear, like the catching and sputtering and dying of a cold auto engine. Accustomed to giving orders and answering questions, he had never acquired the grace of conversing with another person, especially a woman and a Negro at that.

"You ever been to Columbia, Jennie Mae?"

"No sir."

"Well you ought to go sometime. Columbia ain't at all like Charleston and Savannah. Columbia's an enterprising city. Sho is. They have this new hotel there. The Jefferson. Stayed there the last time I went. Indoor plumbing, electric lights, it's up to date now."

Then it occurred to Tison that even if Jennie Mae was able to afford train fare, she could no more get into the Jefferson Hotel than a sinner into heaven. Feeling foolish, he said, "I don't know why I never settled in Columbia. Back in those days, you know, it was still a pile of ashes, burnt to the ground. A man with gumption could have made himself a fortune if he'd gotten in on the ground floor. But I've not fared too poorly right here in Heyward County."

He took a swallow of water.

Jennie said, "No sir."

"But I didn't do it by working for the Yankee Post Office, the way Hart does. A man's got to be willing to take a risk if he expects to get ahead. I tried to tell him, Smith too, but they wouldn't listen. And look at Hart now. Forty years old and still sucking hind tit."

When Tison paused this time, Jennie made no response.

"Did I ever tell you about the time I saw the governor? Walking down Assembly Street. If he weren't so tall, you wouldn't have noticed him he had so many of his thugs around him. He damn sho needed them. People had rather see Cole Blease in his grave than the Kaiser."

Another day she told him that the children wanted to go for a ride in his automobile; he said he wouldn't do it unless she came along, he could show her what it felt like to go forty miles an hour.

She said she would like that, and she said it with a smile. Tison considered that progress. The girl had grown friendlier during the past week or so, no doubt about that. It had been longer than that since he had seen Hart around the place. He wondered what that meant. Over the years he had gathered that Jennie Mae and Hart waxed and waned. Not that he had paid attention. But he knew for a fact that two or three years back Hart had stopped coming to her cabin altogether. For almost a year, as he recalled. He had picked that up from talk around the barn. He wondered if something of the kind was happening now. He hoped so. The only reason he could see for her interest in a man like his brother was the color of his skin. Hart sure as hell wasn't much to look at, and the sorry son of a bitch had never had two dimes to rub together. It made no sense to Tison.

One day toward the end of the month Jennie served a peach cobbler for dessert. Tison thought it the best he'd ever eaten—the sweetest fruit, the lightest crust—and he told her so. He told her several times while the family was seated at the table and he mentioned it again as he rose from his chair. If there was a finer cook in Heyward County he'd like to know who. Didn't the ladies agree?

Of course they did, Miss Sallie said, but with a look in her eye that made it clear she had heard enough about that cobbler.

Tison's excuse for loitering about the kitchen that afternoon was a chair with a loose leg that needed fixing. Alone with Jennie, he said that if she insisted on tempting his palate with delicacies like that cobbler, she might have to suffer the consequences.

Jennie's large eyes flashed a smile. "What you talking 'consequences'?"

"If you get me to where I can't do without your desserts, I might have to hire you away from Miss Sallie, take you across the road."

"In that dark old empty house?" she said, but her tone danced with a playful challenge that left him mumbling to himself.

What he wanted most was to ask about Hart. He felt more comfortable with the girl than he ever had, but this Hart business was a delicate matter and Tison was not adept at innuendo. He was wondering if he could count on her friendship far enough to blurt out his curiosity when Miss Sallie entered the room.

Tison liked his brother's widow as well as anyone and better than most. She had more gumption than any woman he knew. But she was still a woman and women drove him crazy, busybodying around, forever straightening up, dusting off, disturbing sleeping dogs, improving on things. If he should ever be in danger of forgetting why he'd never considered marriage, he had only to spend an hour in that house. With three of them. It seemed to him that every time he tried to talk to Jennie Mae one of the ladies would come in and interrupt, often enough sending the girl off on some silly errand that one of the nigger women could have attended to as well. He waited to see what Miss Sallie wanted this time.

"Is it next week you have that jury duty, Cou'n Tison?"

She knew damn well it was. He had reminded her not two days past, explaining that he planned to spend as much of the week as it took at the new brick hotel in Carthage. Not to expect him back before Friday.

"And you think you'll be all week, do you?"

"That depends on the trial, Miss Sallie. That Parnell Truett case is on the docket, you know. If I get picked for it, I 'spect I will be."

"Oh Cou'n Tison. What a dreadful possibility. I pray you won't have to serve on that one."

"Somebody's going to. Twelve somebodys, as a matter of fact. Might as well be me as the next fellow."

"Well," she said, "it's no business for a lady, thank the Lord.

And I don't want to hear a word about it in my house, now or later."

Tison was forever astonished by a woman's ability to consume large amounts of time piddling, fussing with trifles that didn't amount to a row of pins. That was what Miss Sallie was doing now. Tison made up his mind to outlast her. He had thought of a way to ask Jennie Mae about Hart and he meant to do it before he left the house that afternoon. He requested another glass of lemonade. Before he finished it, Miss Sallie announced that she was going upstairs for her afternoon nap.

"You ought to stretch out a while yourself, Cou'n Tison," she said, "as hot as it is."

When his sister-in-law was gone, Tison cleared his throat. Jennie Mae was standing at the counter with her back to him, and he wanted to be looking at her face when he asked about Hart. Before he could speak, she opened the back door and set out a plate of scraps for the dogs. Back inside she spoke first. "You know that man, Mr. Tison?"

"What man?"

"That Mr. Truett."

"Not to speak of, Jennie Mae. He don't amount to much," Tison said.

"You think he did it?"

The question surprised him. "What have you heard about the case?"

"The woman they trying him for was raised up out here. I know some people used to know her."

Tison was not comfortable with this conversation. Back in June the body of a Negro woman had been found hung up on a log in the Coosawhatchie River. This Parnell Truett, an obnoxious little clerk at the feed and seed store, had been charged with manslaughter. Tison had heard that the local niggers were stirred up about the case, but he didn't like to think that Jennie Mae had been a party to their hushed and grumbling talk.

"Now you heard Miss Sallie, Jennie Mae. Not a word about it in this house. I reckon we'd better abide by that."

"They'll turn him loose," she said.

: : :

The judge had the look of a man who could be counted on for justice—a shy scholarly face in steel-rimmed specs, but the eyes behind them focused like drill bits. For this trial he barred women from the courtroom, and blacks were afraid that week even to appear on the public square. So Tison Bonner sat in a wilting crowd of white men—gentlemen, shopkeepers, gallused sharecroppers—democratically mixed and grateful for any seat.

Tison had been excused by the state, he could not figure out why, unless the solicitor had somehow sensed his sympathy for the defendant. But why make a pretense of procedure in a case as clear-cut as this one? The judge, he reckoned. But judge or no judge, the jury could not be seated—not in Heyward County— that would convict a white man under the circumstances about to be presented.

The earnest little solicitor tried, assuring the jury that the state would show beyond reasonable doubt that the defendant Parnell Truett in the heat of passion did strike the deceased, the Negro woman Almeda Dew, with a heavy object and did throw her unconscious body into the Coosawhatchie River, thereby causing her to drown.

The testimony of Sheriff Herliss Timmons: on Sunday afternoon, the 15th of June, 1918, he was summoned to a swimming hole on the Coosawhatchie River known as Little Egypt, where he found the naked body of the Negro woman Almeda Dew snagged on a log. Preliminary investigation of the site produced an empty whiskey bottle, a woman's undergarment, and a man's left shoe, all of which were entered as evidence.

The testimony of Dr. Banks Colham: examination of the corpse revealed a severe contusion on the back of the skull; further examination determined that the victim's lungs were filled with water, suggesting that death occurred by drowning, the victim having first been rendered unconcious by a blow to the head.

The testimony of Negro bootlegger Silas Finch: at about eleven o'clock on the night of June 14th the deceased appeared at his house in the company of a white man who was driving a black Ford automobile and purchased a pint of blended whiskey. Her manner at the time was high-spirited.

Asked if the white man was present in the courtroom, Finch indicated the defendant Parnell Truett.

Asked if Almeda Dew and the defendant had come to his house on other occasions for the purpose of purchasing whiskey, Finch said they had.

Recalled to the stand, Sheriff Timmons testified that the apparent mate to the left shoe found at the scene was discovered in the defendant's automobile, a black Ford.

Parnell Truett never denied that he was in the company of the deceased on the night of her death, but he didn't have nothing to do with her getting drownded, he said. As the sole witness in his own defense, he declared that he picked her up that night because she had access to "the nigger bootlegger," that after they bought the whiskey she enticed him against his better judgment to drive down to Little Egypt and drink it, that he got drunk and passed out and when he woke up the next morning she was gone. He never had relations with her and he never hit her and he "didn't have no idea how come her to be nekkid and hung up on that log." And that was the God's truth, he said.

Wasn't it known generally that he was keeping Almeda Dew? the solicitor asked.

Parnell said he wasn't in no position to say what was generally known, but he wanted the court to understand that he was a happily married white man with a steady job that went to church and his wife and daughter was just all to pieces over this whole mess, which was mainly his fault, he had to admit, but he hadn't drownded nobody.

In his closing argument counsel for the defense, a corpulent old shyster named Colham Burke, sweating freely, scoffed at the case presented by the state. They had shown no motive, no weapon, no incriminating evidence, he said. They had not even shown that his client was present at the scene; Mr. Truett had confessed that himself, to the defendant's considerable mortification.

"What we have here, gentlemen," Colham Burke said, "is a lively farce concocted out of an old shoe and a pair of drawers. That this case ever came to trial in the first place is an outrage against the taxpayers of Heyward County. That those people expect you to buy it and believe it is an insult to common sense, of which I am confident you will make full use in arriving at a verdict of not guilty."

The solicitor rose from his chair, shuffling papers. Calmly he approached the jury box. On the night in question, he told them, the defendant Parnell Truett had gone with his Negro concubine Almeda Dew to purchase whiskey from a bootlegger, and by his own testimony had then driven to the swimming hole known as Little Egypt. Those were the facts, established by sworn testimony.

"What Parnell Truett did not tell you, gentlemen, was that he took Almeda Dew to that notorious hideaway for lascivious and carnal purposes. No one this side of heaven, other than the defendant himself, knows exactly what happened in that midnight hour on the banks of the Coosawhatchie River, but God's good daylight, which discloses all dark and evil deeds, revealed the naked and battered body of this poor woman, who though colored is guaranteed the same rights by law as your own wives and daughters."

Colham Burke, dabbing at his streaming face, smiled at that miscue. "Counsel for the defense appealed to your common sense. The people of South Carolina, gentlemen, appeal to your sense of justice."

The judge gaveled the murmuring courtroom into silence, then turned his shy face to the jury. Tison Bonner would remember to his dying day the last words of the charge.

"Under the laws of South Carolina the purchase of bootleg whiskey is a misdemeanor and sexual intercourse with a Negro is a felony. But the defendant is not being tried today on those charges. While intercourse between the races is odious to all decent white people, you should not be swayed in your deliberations by your distaste for such behavior. The charge before you is manslaughter. You may allow the defendant's presence at the scene without concluding that he is guilty of acting in the heat of passion to deprive the deceased of her life."

So charged, the jury of Parnell Truett's peers took forty-five minutes to return a verdict of not guilty.

: : :

From his kitchen table Tison Bonner looked out upon a cotton field, chest-high and flocked with white, like clumps of wet snow melting in the sun. Tison broke the yolks of his eggs, stirred the flowing yellow into his hominy. Sundays ought to be canceled during cotton-picking time, he thought, hands kept busy in the field seven days a week, dawn to dark. If a hurricane hit the coast, and one might any day, its rainy wake would wash out the low country, bank accounts included. He'd seen it happen more than once. Unpicked cotton made him nervous.

Jonas was moving about in the front of the house, making the bed, emptying the chamber pot, sweeping. Tison cut a wedge of ham, sopped it in egg, wolfed it down. He ate like a man in a big hurry, though in fact he had nothing to do, not one thing that empty Sunday morning, until the folks across the road left for church. And left her alone in the house. The best chance he'd have for who knew how many days. He had been planning this since the week before the trial, had lain awake at night rehearsing a dozen different ways of telling her what he had in mind. The imminence of the opportunity unsettled his stomach, but with Hart out of the picture, as far as Tison could tell, the time had come. He called Jonas, told him to heat water for his bath.

With most of the morning to kill, Tison wandered through a house empty of anything to engage a man's idle hours—no collection of Indian artifacts to organize, no instrument to play, nor, except for ledgers, any books to read. For him a house was a place to eat and sleep, shelter from the weather. After his bath he blacked his shoes.

At the stroke of ten Tison set out for Miss Sallie's. It was already hot, steamy hot in the dusty lane that ran from his front door through a cotton field to the big road. The sun smote him, and far off in all directions dark walls of pines shimmered in the rising waves of heat. By late afternoon fat, puffy clouds would boil up in the west, towering hugely above the river swamp, but now the sky was a radiant cobalt dome. Sweat poured freely from beneath Tison's straw hat, stinging his eyes, wilting his collar, and the dust of that dry September powdered his shoes and trouser legs.

Across the big road he stepped gratefully into the deep shade of Miss Sallie's long avenue. Beneath the tall pines he removed his hat and swabbed at his bald crown, mopped the back of his neck, and wiped his stinging eyes. The woods reeked of heated pine straw and not one note of birdsong broke the Sunday morning stillness. He was already panting and he still had half a mile to go.

At the end of the shady tunnel up ahead shone the facade of the house that Johnny Bonner had built eighteen years ago. It was not as white as it looked, not when you got up close. Tison couldn't remember whether his brother had had it painted before his death, but he knew they had not done it since. Miss Sallie said she couldn't afford it. The brightness was the effect of the morning sun. As Tison emerged from the avenue into the open yard before the house, he could see its mottled face, paint flaking off. He headed around back toward the kitchen where he would find Jennie Mae making biscuits and frying chicken.

What stopped him was Hart's mare, tied to a dogwood branch. It stopped him cold. The truth was, Tison was afraid of his brother. He had not quite admitted that, even to himself; fear was not a thing he was much acquainted with, of Hart or of any man. But he had never been sixty-three years old before, standing cold in the broiling sun, fighting to catch his breath. He had to find a place to sit, out of the sun, and something cold to drink. He started toward the kitchen steps. If they saw him, what the hell. Didn't he have a right to be there? A damn sight more than Hart. He walked up onto the kitchen porch. He could hear them talking. He pumped a tin cup of water, wincing at the noise, but when he had drunk it, he pumped another. Then he eased down the steps and around to the front of the house, seeking the shade of the porch. Seated, he looked down the long dark avenue that would lead him straight back to his empty house. But he was too tired yet to get started. He'd rest a while first.

HART

*I*t was hotter in the kitchen than it was outside. A heat too thick to breathe. The door onto the back porch stood open, but no draft stirred the cooked air. Jennie stood at the high table by the sink, her back to Hart, slicing onions, a task repeatedly interrupted by her need to dry her eyes.

Sweat stains darkened the armpits of her wheat-colored dress, and her hair had tightened into kinks. She was not happy that Hart had stopped by. He could tell by the set of her shoulders.

He had spent the first two hours of the day sitting on the banks of the Gall, watching the float of his bobber—a forlorn hope in this weather, the water warm and low, the redbreasts lethargic—but Sunday morning fishing was his long-established excuse for stopping by Sallie's kitchen while the family was off at church. Today, with nothing to show for his effort, he felt unwelcome.

"I found a beehive this morning," he told her, "right on the Gall. A hollow tree had broken off about three feet from the ground, and they were in the trunk. You could see the comb. It looked like seashells except it was soft and pearly looking, like fungus. Ain't no telling how much honey's in there. I thought I'd get Uncle Silas to see if he can steal some. Do y'all—"

A noise outside, maybe the scrape of a shoe on the porch steps. Jennie started, looked toward the open door, then turned her apprehensive face to him.

"Settle down," he said, his tone betraying the irritation he felt. "They won't be home for at least another hour. What's got you so jumpy this morning?"

Wiping her eyes on her sleeve, Jennie returned to her onions. "I ain't jumpy. I just got dinner to fix and you ain't making it any easier."

"Well, let me do the onions then." Hart stepped toward the table.

"I don't need no help. I just ain't got time to carry on a conversation, hot as it is."

Hart was troubled. Her mood might be explained by any number of ordinary circumstances—maybe her time of the month was coming on—but ever since that night back in the spring when he had broken his nose, she had grown more distant. He was sure of it. He should go now, come back when she was feeling better, but he wanted one sweet word before he left.

The squeak of the pump handle startled them both. Hart stepped to the screen door. There at the water shelf, three steps away, stood Tison, working the handle, looking straight at him. Hart eased back into the kitchen, anger boiling up. Tison was forever on the prowl, but lately he had gotten worse, hanging around the house and yard at any hour, day as well as night. Hart thought of his mare Cassandra, tied to the hitching post at the trough. Realizing that he had already been discovered, he stepped again toward the door as the pump sucked and gurgled. He was looking for a fight, but Jennie caught him by the arm, a finger pressed to her lips, a frown on her glistening face. Arrested, they stood. Tison's feet descended the steps.

Hart pulled free of Jennie's grip. "What the hell is he doing over here this time of day? On Sunday at that?"

"Shh," Jennie warned. Then in a lowered voice: "I reckon he's got as much right as anybody else."

Hart knew who she meant by "anybody else," and it made his stomach heave. Then it struck him: if Hart's mare had not been tied at the trough, Tison would have come on in, would be standing in the kitchen right now, talking to Jennie. "I hope you don't mean he's got more right."

Hart could not really believe that Tison would be welcome in that kitchen, that Jennie or any other woman for that matter could take pleasure in the old man's company, but he was hot and edgy.

"You too hard on Mr. Tison. He's been real nice to me."

Hart could hardly believe his ears. How often through the years had he and Jennie made sport of the old curmudgeon, laughing at his proprietary attitude? Hart felt betrayed. "Tison ain't got it in him to be nice," he said.

Jennie turned, brushed a plastered curl from her forehead, and her large, dark eyes were wet with onion tears. "Listen to me, Hart. I been trying to tell you, I ain't got time for this. Look like all you want to do anymore is hang around your own self, interrupting people's work. You run on now and let me do my biscuits. We'll talk another time."

Hart had always been able to locate bream beds by their faint but distinctive odor, even when others said they couldn't smell a thing. What he was smelling now betrayed an underwater presence. He just didn't know what it was. He grabbed his hat. "Don't wait up," he said.

TISON

*I*n the heat of the afternoon, when plants as well as beasts and men kept still, and even breathing was an effort, Tison hollered old Jonas out of the dark little den of his cabin and had him hitch the horse to the buggy. He was going back now, while the folks in the big house were stretched out in their under-clothes, on their beds in the rooms upstairs, as hot as ovens be-neath the tin roof. He was accustomed to the walk, in almost any weather, but he had walked it once today already and his bad toe was acting up again.

Jennie Mae would be lying down too, fanning herself. Tison could see the bed, could see her on it, barely clothed, her limbs slick with sweat.

The old gelding plodded, sleepwalking through a swarm of deerflies and horseflies that danced and zoomed in the long green avenue. Except for the creaking of harness and buggy, the gritty whisper of tires in the sandy lane, Tison heard nothing. He had not changed clothes all day. When he shifted position in the buggy seat, he caught a whiff of himself.

Heat rose in waves from the tin roof of Jennie Mae's cabin, sound asleep in the open sun. Tison pulled up in the shade of an oak not far from her front door. If anyone from the big house happened to be looking out a window at that moment, so what? He was Tison Bonner, master of the place. If he needed to call on the colored girl that worked in the kitchen, that was nobody's business but his own.

He knocked. Waited. Knocked again.

The door opened a crack—Jennie Mae's face, sleepy, hair falling down around her ears. Blinking in the glare, she looked more baffled than surprised. "Mr. Tison," she said. "Just a minute."

When she opened the door again, she had wrapped a garment around her, something old and striped. A man's dressing gown, it looked like. Tison wondered whose. It revealed the shapeless swell of her bosom. He had to ask if he might step inside.

Though he had never entered that cabin, it felt as familiar to him as Miss Sallie's kitchen. By habit he removed his hat, realized that this was a colored girl whose house he'd entered, started to return it to his head, thought better of that, and ended up holding it before him, turning it by its stiff brim as though it were a plate. He stole a look at Jennie Mae's bosom. She folded her arms across it. Tison didn't want to think that she was resorting to modesty with him.

Jennie did not sit nor ask him to but stood like a person prepared for business, arms crossed, guarded but interested.

"I'm a plain man," he began, "a plainspoken man. No taste for frills."

He studied the hat in his fingertips as though he were seeing it for the first time, turning and turning it.

"I don't know but one way to say a thing and that's just to come right out and say it."

Jennie tightened her arms.

"Now I have a proposition for you, Jennie Mae. I'm prepared to be generous."

Jennie's dark eyes shone in the dim light.

"You just tell me what Mr. Hart's been paying you and I'll double it."

Jennie reeled, her face wrung in disbelief.

Tison attempted an engaging smile. "I might do better than that."

Wild panic broke out in Jennie's eyes, the terror of a squirrel unable to decide which way to evade the swooping hawk. Then she drew herself up, pulling the wrapper more tightly about her bosom, and her face shone clear. In a measured tone that required greater effort than Tison had any idea of, she said, "You ought to be ashamed of yourself, Mr. Tison, a fine gentleman like yourself talking such trash. You must not be feeling good."

With that, a mottled flush commenced to blemish her throat and her eyes brimmed, betraying her composure. Tison put on his hat. The enormity of what he had done threw him off balance, as though the floor had heaved beneath his feet, causing him to stagger. This was exactly the reaction he had been expecting but he had not known it till now. He could see that she was about to lose control.

"Now, Jennie Mae."

Tears ran down her cheeks like quicksilver, but still her voice held steady. "I want you out of my door, old man. And if you value my goodwill, you better stay out, you hear?"

: : :

During the week following the fiasco in Jennie's cabin, Tison lay low, coming in after dark, going straight to his room, leaving the next day at first light. When Sallie caught him slipping out one morning before eating breakfast, he explained that it was a busy week, cotton picking begun, this and that to tend to. She told him he ought to slow down. "None of us are getting any younger, Cou'n Tison," she said. "And in this heat."

On Sunday evening he came in from surveying the progress of the picking in Sallie's fields, his coattail sagging with the weight of an almost empty pint of whiskey. A blue haze had settled on the yard, blurring even the near trees and shrubs, and the dry racket of insects prevailed upon the twilight. Tison advanced through twinkling lightning bugs toward the citronella candles on the porch. The ladies of the house had assembled there—an old woman, her daughter and daughter-in-law—hoping to catch a breeze. They had laid aside their handwork and now sat talking quietly, rocking very gently.

They greeted him. He tipped his hat, made a bow, a bit extravagantly. "Ladies."

Miss Sallie mentioned the weather, the grainy heat, the drought, and that got Miss Lois started. Tison could not abide that woman, forever whining in her nasal Yankee twang. She came from up North somewhere, Tison wasn't sure just where, maybe Baltimore, and nothing about South Carolina had ever suited her. And she took it out on her husband. He had heard her say things to Hugh Creighton that no man should tolerate. Tison could understand why the poor fellow stayed on the road all week. If it was him now, she'd be the one in the road. He wouldn't put up with it one damn minute. But what could you expect from a pantywaist like Hugh Creighton, a squeamish man, mincing and contentious. As a boy he had refused to go barefoot. Well, it was his bed, let him lie in it.

Miss Sallie knew better than to let her sister-in-law get up a head of steam. "You just missed the new preacher, Cou'n Tison."

"That right?"

"He stopped by a little while ago. I wish you'd been here. I think he's going to be just the thing for our little church."

Miss Sadie said, "He's a nice little fellow."

Talk of church made Tison uncomfortable and he knew Miss Sallie knew it. He'd better watch himself. The pint in his pocket was almost gone, and that on an empty stomach.

"I do wish you'd come hear him, Cou'n Tison. You might be surprised."

"I reckon the church'll have to get along without me, Miss Sallie."

"It has so far," Miss Lois said, not looking up.

Tison started toward the door. If he responded at all to that bitch, he would blast her off the porch.

"Have you had your supper, Cou'n Tison?" Miss Sallie asked.

"No ma'am. I was just on my way to the kitchen."

"I'm afraid Jennie's out with the children. Let me see what I can find you."

"Keep your seat, Miss Sallie. I really ain't all that hungry. Thank you just the same."

The kitchen was almost dark, its tall windows luminous with the last light of day. Tison felt in his pockets for matches, stepped over to a window to see where to strike.

Jennie was standing in the midst of the darkling lawn, in her long white dress a column of light as children swirled about her, tugging at her gown, holding out to her their jars. Tison pulled at his mustache, sniffed. "Lightning bugs," he muttered. He wanted a cigar, decided to smoke it in the summerhouse, maybe finish off the bottle.

Coming down the kitchen steps, he heard the children squealing. "Count mine, Jennie, count mine. I caught a heap."

Like an outcast dog, Tison slunk along the shadowed fringes of the yard, gained at last the summerhouse. Beneath its heavy bonnet of climbing rose, the little bower never dried out completely. At this time of day it was as dark as night inside. Tison felt beneath his soles the squishy mat of leaf litter, beneath the seat of his trousers the damp, punky bench.

Smells like a goddamn tomb in here, he thought.

The summerhouse offered no surface dry enough for striking a match. Tison flicked one into flame against his horny thumbnail. Thought, I'll fumigate this place.

"Time to go in," Jennie called to the children, and the sweet soprano pitch of her voice caused Tison's heart to ache. "Mosquitoes starting to eat me up," she said.

"You said dark, Jennie. It ain't dark yet."

"Jennie Mae," Tison called.

She must not have heard him.

"Jennie Mae." A bellow, like that of a bull gator silencing the pond and the woods all around.

The children stopped their play, drew closer to Jennie.

Tison took a pull on the bottle, drained it, set it on the bench. Then he stepped to the low door and stooped through. "Over here," he said. He sucked on his cigar, saw the coal glow cherry-red.

Without looking his way Jennie picked up the three-year-old. "Time to go in, y'all." She meant business.

"Didn't you hear me, girl? When I call, by God, I mean for you to come, you hear?"

The children were scurrying toward the front steps, a litter of little pigs racing to cover, Jennie herding them along. Tison followed them with his eyes all the way to the foot of the steps where Miss Sallie waited, anxious to receive them, and Miss Lois from the porch stood looking straight at him.

They must have heard me, he thought.

He retreated to the darkness of the lair, an old snapping turtle drawing in its head, and felt for the bottle. Maybe there was enough left to wet his tongue.

: : :

Tison found Jennie's letter in his mailbox on Wednesday. A problem at the turpentine still had kept him in the woods until past noon, causing him to miss dinner, and he was vexed almost beyond endurance by the team of young mules he was driving. Unaccustomed to working together, the animals had been out of sync all morning, and for the last two miles they'd grown edgy, alternately balking and lurching in the traces. Tison pulled them in at the mailbox, and there found the letter, a plain white envelope lying atop the stamped mail. *Mr. J. T. Bonner*, it said, in soft pencil, childish and loopy.

Having never seen her writing, having never even considered the possibility that she could write, he had no reason to guess that it had come from her. Curiosity caused him to open it, right there at the end of his avenue, unprotected from the midday sun, while the restless mules, eager for water, stamped and started.

"Whoa mules," Tison kept saying, attention focused on the

letter. It was neither long nor hard to read, but his vision blurred as he raced through the lines:

I told you the next time I caught you watching me I would forfeit our friendship. He stumbled on, scanning, halting. *I could not be anything to a man I don't have respect for and you have killed it in me.* Large shelves of self, like an undercut river bank, sloughed off and slid into a roiling stream. His eyes stung with sweat. *I cannot go back to being what I was to you. I will not be treated like a dog even if I am colored. Everybody saw you Sunday evening. I am sick and disgusted with the whole affair.*

Tison wiped his eyes with his damp bandanna, reread, and the swirling current ate deeper. Just then one of the mules started forward. Its mate, not to be left behind, bolted to overtake it, jerking the lines from Tison's loose grip. "Whoa now goddammit," he yelled, trying to keep his balance. The off mule stepped on a slack line, pulling it free of the wagon, and the other tossed its head and lunged away from the tongue. Tison fell forward, catching the dash with his knees. The mules broke into a trot.

Tison's face turned a darker beet-red and every vein in his neck and forehead bulged like stiffened cord. He stuffed the letter into his coat pocket and reached for the whip. Just then an old black man stepped from the chest-high cotton, reached for the headstall of the near mule. "Whoa up here, missy."

The mule tossed its head, trying to avoid the hand, but the man caught it by the cheek strap.

"Yessuh, Mr. Tison. Don't want to let these here young mules get all het up. Sho don't."

"Hand me the lines, Ezra."

Ezra patted the mule's dark, lathered neck, soothed the animal with hand and voice. "Y'all just a little young yet to know what's what. You'll learn."

"Goddamn right they'll learn," Tison said. "Hand me the lines, old man."

"Let me walk 'em on up to the barn for you, Mr. Tison. Ain't but a little piece. Calm 'em down."

"You want me to climb down out of this wagon?"

The old man gathered up the lines. "You ghy ruin them mules sho nuff, you don't watch out. Hot as it be."

"Stand back."

"'Fore God, Mr. Tison," Ezra said, but he stepped back into the protection of the cotton.

Tison Bonner stood, sore knees braced against the dash, whip raised. "All right, you iron-headed sons of bitches. You want to run"—he laid the whip across the back of the near mule, a sharp lash—"then run."

The leap of the team jerked the wagon out from under Tison, landing him on the seat, but in a second he sprang to his feet again, the mules in full gallop. Leaning forward, he laid into them both, first one and then the other, methodically, rhythmically, drawing upon the deep well of his frustrated lust, spending it in rage.

The whip was a buggy whip, too slight to do much damage, but Tison stung the mules with his fury, blistered them with his relentless obscenity. The wagon bounced and clattered up the washboard avenue. Hot air blasted his face, whistled in his ears. His hat went flying. He'd not stand for disobedience in anything of his—not in a man, not in a mule. These two would think twice before they tried to run away with him again.

Up ahead loomed the trunks of the live oaks that stood like massive gateposts to the bare front yard of his house. Tison dropped the whip, looped the lines twice quickly around his wrists, and leaned back against the team's headlong flight. He might as well have tried to hold a freight train. He would have to turn them. To the right, into the grassy lane that ran along the upper end of the field. Else they would all pile up in a heap on his porch—man, mules, and wagon. Gripping the right line in both hands, he hauled back against the rigid head and neck, leaning all his considerable bulk into the pull. The mule's head began to yield, and into the cotton they went, the wagon jouncing so high when it struck the edge of the field that Tison lost his balance and all but toppled forward into the team. With shins scraped, he tried to shift his weight with the swing of the wagon's career, cotton stalks thrashing, flailing, bolls popping, trash boiling. The wagon broadsided a swath across that corner of the field and skidded on two wheels into the grassy lane, remaining upright only because the mules were slowed by the woven stalks.

With an open path before them again, they renewed their determination, but Tison could tell that something in them had broken. Both animals were laboring, their breath coming in ragged gasps, and the lane was deep with sand. It was not as hard to haul them through the next turn, back toward the big road, and fewer plants were trampled. The mules were wanting to walk, but Tison would not let them. Swearing, he tried to reach their heads with the whip, driving them down the narrow path between the ends of the cotton rows and a drainage ditch. When he turned them into the big road they were toiling, eyes rolling white. Thick ropes of slobber swung from their mouths and suds of dirty foam flecked their necks and flanks.

Seated now, Tison trotted them past the mailbox and into the avenue again. And then stopped. Lined up on both sides, as far as he could see, stood the field hands, two rows of black faces drawn from their picking to witness the boss man's wrath.

Tison climbed over the dashboard, stepped down onto the tongue, and from there clambered onto the sodden back of the off mule. As the sweat soaked his seat and thighs, he cried, "All right then, you trifling niggers, stand clear." With that he struck the other mule between the ears with the swinging butt of the whip and kicked the one he straddled hard in its heaving sides. The mules lurched forward, plunging and stumbling, heads low, breathing in agonized cracked wheezes, between the rows of field hands who stood as mute as statues, their faces glistening and blank. Tison cursed each one as he passed, yet never ceased hammering at the head of the near mule. He saw blood on his hand, and the mule fell, front end first, pulling its mate onto it. Tison landed in a maelstrom of wet, struggling mule flesh, the wagon sailed in a wide arc and toppled onto its side, twisting singletrees and traces, and Tison Bonner was tumbled by hooves and hames and trace chains, a tormented, broken-winded braying in his ears, bristly mane in his face, the stink of terrified mule all over him.

After a while the wreckage began to quieten down—now and then an exhausted bray, a twitch and heave of haunch, but that was all. Tison was bleeding from his head, but beyond that he could not tell how badly he was hurt. He lay still, afraid that any movement might ignite the pyre of hurt flesh—the mules' as well as his own. Negro faces floated in the dusty, burning air. Dozens of them. Somebody was saying, "Easy now, just lay easy," and there was Ezra, knife in hand, cutting, pulling, untangling. One of the mules struggled to extricate itself; out of the madness of snarled limbs and lines it got to its feet, an animal intact, recognizable. Ezra was leading it away.

"Y'all see to Mr. Tison," he said.

Part *Two*

JIM CREIGHTON

*T*he color of the sky above the Savannah River Swamp was a thin winter orange when Jim and Mattie Creighton entered Heyward County. The air smelled of wood smoke and a blue layer of haze lay upon the blackened cotton fields. It would be dark by the time they reached their destination and Jim was tense. He turned on his headlamps, slowed down to twenty-five miles per hour, and leaned forward toward the windshield, peering into the feebly lit patch of road immediately before him. He didn't like to drive after dark. Mattie drew the blanket she was wrapped in more snugly about her shoulders. "I do wish you'd drive a little faster, Jim. They'll be waiting supper for us, and I can just hear Brother Hugh."

"Brother can hold his horses. A little exercise in patience won't kill him."

"Now don't be cross, Jim. You'll just spoil the holiday spirit."

"I'm not cross, but it's been a trying day," he said.

The young couple had been on the road since first light, motoring down out of the red clay hills of the Piedmont, across the low sand ridges of the fall line and into the flat Savannah River valley, bringing with them on the fenders of the Buick the various soils of South Carolina. Since leaving Spartanburg they had suffered three punctured tires, an overheated radiator, and long waits at two river ferries, and now it was dark.

But it wasn't the frustrations of the trip or the anxiety of driving at night that affected Jim's spirits. It was the prospect of home, of having to try once again to find a comfortable place within the family circle. Though he was the one who had chosen to leave, to devote himself to books, to the life of the mind, he had never expected to be treated like a sideshow freak by his own people. Only Sallie understood, the sister who had taught him everything he knew before he left home for college. Hugh openly scoffed: why a grown man would choose to piddle away his life in a schoolroom instead of rolling up his sleeves and taking on the real world was beyond him. And Hugh's wife Lois never missed a chance to parrot his opinions. When Sallie had raved last summer about the new preacher at Cypress Swamp Methodist, Lois had chimed in, "I doubt Mister Atkinson is smart enough for the professor, but he suits our little church just fine."

Jim turned from the highway onto the narrow washboard road that would take them to the house, and it seemed to him that he was entering upon a backwater of the last century.

"I just hope Brother don't get started on politics tonight," Jim said. "He can ruin a good meal quicker than anyone I know."

"Try to relax, dear. By expecting the worse, you only encourage it. Don't you see that?"

What Jim saw but could not explain to her was that she was the chief cause of his anxiety. The family had from the beginning found his wife a bit too modern to suit their tastes. The first Christmas after they were married, she had insisted that Jim take her on the annual Creighton-Bonner deer drive—a thing no lady had ever even considered—and then, as if to rub their faces in it, she had stepped into an old pair of trousers and ridden to the swamp on horseback. But it was her friendship with the maid Jennie Grant that caused real consternation. To laugh and carry on with Jennie in the kitchen was one thing—they all loved Jennie—but to spend Sunday afternoons in her cabin was unseemly to say the least.

In a conversation reported later to Jim by his younger brother Wade, Lois Creighton had vowed that Mattie and Jennie were out there smoking cigarettes, but Wade's wife Clara had disagreed. Mattie might be smoking—Clara wouldn't put it past her—but with the help?

"Well now, Clara," Wade had said, "Jennie ain't exactly what you'd call 'the help.'"

And Clara had fired back, "Well, what would you call her then, for goodness' sake?"

Sallie had told them all to hush. Mattie was a dear, sweet girl, more sophisticated than they were used to perhaps, but that came from living on a college campus.

Well, Lois had sniffed, Cypress Swamp was not Spartanburg, and socializing with a colored girl was not acceptable behavior down here. Sallie ought to put a stop to it before Miss Sadie noticed.

Wade had reported the conversation to Jim, not in malice but in sincere concern for Mattie, and Jim had accepted the warning in the spirit in which it was offered. He had been concerned too. He loved Jennie as much as any of them did, probably more. It had been Jennie who nursed him so attentively when he was stricken with malaria right after his father's death, and he had believed ever since that by the special intimacy that often develops between a nurse and her patient they had forged a bond, a mutual understanding that each of them knew who her real father was, but he had never quite named the relationship, even to himself.

So Mattie's affection for Jennie was not surprising, but for her to flaunt it served only to antagonize the household, especially his sisters-in-law. He had been wanting to bring up the matter for the last fifty miles, but fearing her reaction he had put it off, and now they were passing the churchyard where his people slept and approaching Cypress Swamp, the crossroads that served the lower end of the county as a village—post office, general store, cotton gin, and depot—and now the house was just four miles up the road. A lamp was burning in Thompson's General Merchandise as they rattled across the railroad tracks, but the dusty street was deserted.

Jim said, "I know you enjoy Jennie's company, my dear, but I want you to be careful how you spend time with her."

Mattie turned to face him. "Why shouldn't I spend time with her? Jennie is a delightful person, which is more than I can say for Lois and Clara Creighton, and there's more substance to her too."

"I know there is," he said, "but this is their home, Matt. Try to understand how it looks to them."

Jim could not see his wife in the darkness, but by the heat of her indignation he could imagine the look on her face.

"Who are they that I should have to tiptoe around them? If the truth were told, Jennie is more my sister-in-law than they are."

If Jim had just hit an unseen pothole in the road, he could not have been more stunned. He swallowed hard. "Not exactly. And don't you dare say such a thing to anyone else but me, do you hear?"

: : :

Jim stopped at the front yard gate. Mattie turned to the pile of presents on the back seat, but he told her to leave them for the servants, they had kept the family waiting long enough. And here they came, pouring through the door out onto the porch, women and children, waving handkerchiefs and calling "Merry Christmas."

Torches illumined the walkway up to the steps, and the porch was hung with swags of smilax. Amidst the flurry of hugs and kisses, Jim managed to evade everyone but Sallie. "We were growing so anxious," she said as she held him by the elbows and smiled up at him. "Were the roads very bad?" Eager hands took their coats, gloves, and hats. "Come on in by the fire now,"

Sallie said. "I know you're just half-frozen. Supper will be on in a jiffy."

"Where's Jennie?" Mattie asked.

"Why, I don't know. She was right here a minute ago. She must have gone back out to the kitchen. Go on back and see. She's just been beside herself all day."

Jim followed his wife and sister down the hall and through the dining room. The table, dressed in white linen, shone with silver in the lamplight. "My," Mattie said, "don't it all look pretty?" Without pausing, the little group continued out onto the cold, latticed passageway that connected the house to the kitchen.

They found her taking biscuits from the oven, a tall woman in a dark, floor-length dress, a white apron, and a perky little servant's cap. "Oh," she cried, looking up, and joy suffused her pretty, light brown face.

Jim hung back—an awkward pause. One might hug an old mammy, a family retainer who had changed one's diapers, made one eat his peas, and grumbled about one's bringing in too many quail for her to clean, but Jennie was no old mammy. She was younger than Jim, just as tall, and with a bosom that he had always had trouble not staring at. In the instant of his hesitation Mattie rushed to Jennie's arms, squealing like a schoolgirl. The mulatto woman was a full head taller than Jim Creighton's wife, and Mattie was like a child in her embrace. When they had broken from each other, Jennie took a step toward Jim, extended her hand, and smiled. "Merry Christmas, Mr. Jimmy. And welcome home."

: : :

There were four men in the sitting room drinking sherry by the fire as they waited for supper. When Jim entered, three rose to greet him. The one who remained seated was an older man, his left leg extended and resting on a stool. "Merry Christmas, Cou'n Tison," Jim said. "I hope you're feeling well."

Tison Bonner's hand was as hard and abrasive as a brick. "Except for this damn leg," he said. "How are you?"

Tison had broken it back in September. Only in the last few days had the cast been removed.

Jim shook hands with his brothers—Wade, the only blond Creighton in three generations, and Hugh, the eldest, as dapper as a man in the Sears and Roebuck catalogue, his dark hair carefully parted down the middle and plastered to his skull with a scented pomade.

"I hope you don't keep your classes waiting like this, professor."

Hugh's attempts at teasing never quite came off. Jim ignored him and turned to the dark man in the shadows, his friend Hart Bonner. Though six years Hart's junior, Jim had grown up following him into the woods, recipient of Hart's considerable knowledge of woodcraft. Like the others, Hart was dressed in a dark three-piece suit, but his looked like it been slept in, and one dark lock kept tumbling down upon his broad forehead. He had the look of a man who had been kept awake too many nights by a great anxiety. But he managed a smile for Jim. "And how's Miss Mattie, professor? Pert as ever, I hope."

A framed photograph of the Creightons' late brother-in-law Johnny Bonner stood at one end of the mantel, balanced at the other by a picture of their father—an appropriate pairing, for the men had been good friends. Jim picked up the ornate frame that held the photograph of his father, the old man dead now ten years or more, and gazed upon the innocent, bearded face. In three sons Bonner Creighton had failed to reproduce his high spirits, his bulk, or his appetite for pleasure.

"Looks just like him, don't it?" Wade said.

"A glass of sherry, Jimmy?" Hugh asked.

"Cou'n Tison's got something a little stouter, Jimmy, if you'd care for it. Just don't let Sister catch you."

"You boys ever hear about the time Johnny and your pa went to the game supper over at the Grenville Club?" Tison asked.

They all had, dozens of times, but the story, never mentioned in the presence of the women, remained a favorite among the men.

Jim lit his infrequently smoked pipe. "You were there, weren't you, Cou'n Tison?"

"I was. But I had more sense than to see how much liquor I could drink. The last I saw of your pa that night he was sprawled out across the billiard table, drunk as a lord, and John was passed out in a corner somewhere. They didn't get home until the next day, way on up in the day. You know they must have reeked to high heaven, but Bonner said Grenville had locked their coats in a closet and it was too cold to ride home without em, that's why they had had to spend the night. Miss Sallie was still too new at being a wife to know just what to say, but not Miss Sadie. 'A man who will drink whiskey with his own son-in-law is no better than white trash,' she said. And Bonner said, 'Hell, Mother, me and John have been drinking together too long now to let this in-law business interrupt us.'"

The Creighton brothers laughed at their father's rough wit, as they had a hundred times before, and a smile even flickered across Hart's somber features. Except for Tison, a contemporary of their father's, they were all of an age. Through the years of their childhood and youth, they had accumulated a mutual fund of rich experience. The tension Jim had anticipated must have been relaxed by tobacco smoke and the rich, old stories, repeated in front of the fire. Already he was settling into the fraternity.

"You ready for the deer drive tomorrow, professor?" Hart asked.

"With all that education," Hugh said, "I hope Jimmy's learned how to tell a buck from a doe."

Oh Lord. They would never let him live that down.

"You were hunting with Cou'n Johnny that day, weren't you?"

"Yes," Jim groaned.

Hugh's attempt to embarrass his brother betrayed his resentment of Jim's various successes, but Jim knew that it was better to endure it than to try to defend himself.

"Exactly what happened, Jimmy?" Hugh continued. "I never can get it straight."

"Then I wouldn't have brought it up if I were you," Jim countered. To change the subject he turned to Tison. "That's a mighty handsome suit you're wearing, Cou'n Tison. Is that a Christmas present?"

Of dark serge, the suit was conspicuously new, still sharply pressed and more stylish than anything Jim had ever seen the old man wear. Even the wine-colored tie looked new.

Tison hooked his thumbs in the pockets of his vest and reared back, as though to show off the outfit. "I bought it in Savannah. Just last week. At a good price too. You can't beat Savannah for a bargain."

Tison leaned forward to spit tobacco juice in the fire, and Hart from across the room spoke up. "I can see why you got it cheap, Tison. I'd be looking for another tailor if I were you."

Hart's unnecessary comment might have been as easily deflected as Hugh's lame gibes, but Tison seemed edgy tonight, more so than usual, and Hart should have known better.

"What the hell are you talking about?"

"He left the lining of your coat hanging out. You've been walking around all evening with a tail," Hart said.

The laughter of the Creightons did not improve Tison's spirits. Sputtering, and with some difficulty, he removed the jacket and, sure enough, the pale blue satin lining had pulled loose from the hem. "Well, ain't that a hell of a thing," he said.

The tinkling of the supper bell stifled Tison's bile, but he took his seat at the table in an evil mood, his face an apoplectic red against which his heavy mustache seemed whiter than ever. Hart sat down directly across from him, and Hugh at the head. He and Lois had moved into an upstairs room twelve years ago— "just until we can find a place of our own"—and since Johnny Bonner's death he had presided at family meals as he was tonight, in a manner natural to an eldest son, carving a pork roast with a long ivory-handled blade. Lois on his left, her mouse-brown hair pinned up in an old-fashioned bun, assisted her husband in serving plates. With Wade and Clara and Hart and Tison too, the table had been extended by three leaves, and Hugh was slicing the roast mighty thin.

"Just a small piece for me, son," Miss Sadie requested from down at the other end, "and trim off the fat, if you would, please."

Since sitting down, Hart and Tison had acted as though the other weren't there. The tension was palpable. Something of greater weight than Hart's ill-considered remark had come between them. Half brothers actually, they were now the oldest and the youngest of old Cou'n Frank Bonner's children, separated by twenty years, and while they had never appeared particularly close—had never hunted together, for example—they had always been governed by good manners. Until now.

Hart looked tired. His usually lean face seemed fleshier than Jim had ever noticed, his jaw fuller, and there was a weariness about his blue-gray eyes.

The clinking of silver and the passing of dishes—sweet potatoes, field peas, spoon bread, and collard greens—kept conversation down, and when all the plates were served Jennie came in with a basket of hot biscuits.

"Why, Jennie," Sallie said, "you've just outdone yourself tonight."

The table voiced its agreement, and Jennie responded with a smile that brightened the room.

When she had come around to Jim's side, standing between him and Tison as the older man helped himself to a biscuit, Jim saw that Hart's pale eyes were fixed on her. They shone in his dark face with naked adoration.

Jim had no idea who knew what or how much. The keeping of Negro women by white men had been going on in Heyward County for so long as to have become almost a custom, and if not universal it was widespread enough to have involved every family he knew. Yet no one acknowledged the practice, certainly not women and rarely even men. It was as though the community had tacitly agreed with the offending members to participate in a great charade: we will gladly pretend that you are not engaged in this abomination if you will have the decency not to confront us with it. As long as both sides played by the rules, life limped along. If undeniable evidence occasionally appeared on the scene—Jennie herself, for example, with her bold Creighton face—no one had to notice. Even now she was serving Jim's mother, who was taking a biscuit from her hand as though she were any Negro servant and not her late husband's daughter.

"Well," Sallie said, "tomorrow's the big day." She was referring to the Christmas hunt, the annual deer drive for the men of the Creighton-Bonner connection. It would begin at dawn and after a midday picnic, brought to the edge of the swamp and prepared by servants, continue until dark. Even Hugh Creighton was expected to participate.

"Have you heard who all's coming, Hart?"

In that uninflected drawl that was already beginning to sound quaint to Jim's academic ear, Hart said, "Ralph Carpenter's supposed to be here, and I heard the Brodies."

"Oh good. I do hope they brought Emily with them."

Jim asked Hart if he had been seeing many bucks.

Hart laughed. "How many do you need, professor? If you fail to put meat on the ground tomorrow, I don't want to hear you blaming it on a dearth of game now, you hear?"

"I'm not sure the professor remembers what a buck looks like, Hart," Hugh said. "With all that education."

Hugh just would not let it drop. His crack gave Lois the opportunity she'd been waiting for. "I wish you mighty hunters would save your men-talk for later. The rest of us really aren't that interested."

Jim could hardly believe his ears. His own wife might be outspoken but she was never rude. Across the table Hart had colored deeply but, too much the gentleman to respond, he applied himself to his plate. Hugh cleared his throat and announced that

Birth of a Nation was returning to Savannah, he was looking forward to seeing it again.

"Once was enough for me," Jim said. He had never seen a picture so well made, but he deplored its depiction of Negroes and its incitement to mob violence. Brother should have known better than to mention it in Jennie's presence.

"I don't see how you can say that, Jimmy," Hugh said. "There's never been a moving picture like it. Lois and I are planning to see it again. I'm hoping Wade and Clara will go with us. What about you, Hart? You haven't seen it, have you?"

Hart gave Hugh a look, chewing his food. "I don't care much for that form of entertainment."

"They tell me it costs three dollars," Tison said. "I can't imagine a man wasting his money on such a thing."

"Y'all are just impossible," Hugh said. "*Birth of a Nation* is the most advanced picture ever made, and besides that, it's about South Carolina."

"It's not about me," Jim said.

That remark might have inspired Hugh to new heights of indignation had not Tison brought the discussion to an end. For the last minute or two he had been struggling with a pickled beet. Twice he had tried to cut it with the edge of his fork and twice it had slipped away. Impatient, he tried again and this time the beet skidded from his plate and landed on the tablecloth with a dark red plop. In his haste to scoop it up he knocked over his glass of tea.

Tison's embarrassment was painful to watch. He was a man who took himself with great seriousness, and he had never found it easy to apologize. As he pushed back from the table, dabbing furiously at his lap with his napkin, he mumbled amidst the sudden flurry of activity, "Clumsy old fool."

Across the table Hart was enjoying his brother's distress. "Contrary little devil, ain't it, Tison?"

The remark itself was not funny, but the consternation on

Tison's face, the wreckage he had made of his end of the table, and Hart's droll tone combined to produce in the Creightons a fit of mirth. Except for Miss Sadie, who behind her flashing spectacles continued with earnest composure to attack her meal, people were giggling up and down both sides. Even Jennie found the laughter contagious. As the family struggled to bring itself under control, she burst out afresh and rushed from the room.

Tison looked like a man one breath away from a stroke. Beads of sweat had popped out on his bald crown, which was flushed pink, and his cheek was twitching. "If that girl knew her place," he said, "she'd be in here cleaning up this table instead of ridiculing a white man."

Every face looked up, shocked into silence, but Hart's heavy features had darkened like an oncoming storm. Rising from his chair, he placed both hands palms down on the soaked linen and leaned forward, his dark hair falling onto his forehead. "You leave her out of this, old man," he said.

He might as well have fired off a pistol in the room; the family could not have been more stunned. For an instant, each person at the table was frozen in an attitude of utter disbelief. Then Hugh rapped furiously with the handle of his knife. "Hear, hear. For God's sake, gentlemen, remember where you are."

Tison pushed back from the table and heaved himself from the chair. Nodding at his hostess, he said, "Ladies, my apologies. I'll ask to be excused." With that he went limping toward the door, his walking stick striking the boards with anger and the lining of his coat flapping behind him like a flag in retreat. Hart settled back in his chair, sank into himself, and they all sat mute as the sound of Tison's stick went stalking up the hall. At the sound of the front door closing, Hart's chair scraped from the table and without a word to anyone he followed his brother.

When he was clearly out of the house, Sallie raised her eyebrows and with an expression of disbelief said, "I just can't imagine what possessed them."

Is that all you have to say? Jim thought. Hart has just proclaimed before us all that he is the lover, defender, and champion of the colored girl who lives in the yard and works in the kitchen, and all you can say is, "I can't imagine." But then he remembered his nephew John Baird, Sallie's sixteen-year-old son who was sitting on his mother's right. Though recently allowed to join the adults at the table, John Baird was still a child in his mother's eyes, too young to participate in a family discussion of scandal.

But Hugh's wife Lois must have forgotten that he was present. Seething with indignation, she said to Sallie, "Well, I can."

"Be quiet, Lois," her husband commanded. "Nobody needs a postmortem from you."

Lois left the table in a huff, and Miss Sadie, in her deliberate fashion, soon followed. At the sound of her feet climbing the stairs, Wade and Clara left the room to gather up their children, Mattie went along to help, and Sallie headed out to the kitchen.

"Run along, son," Hugh said to John Baird. "Uncle Jimmy and I have things to talk about."

"Aw, Uncle Hugh."

"I mean it now. Don't trifle with me."

"Well," Hugh said when the boy was gone, "what are we going to do?"

There was something about Hugh's tone that Jim didn't like, a smugness, as though the incident had just proved him right in all their disagreements, and the smugness had an edge, as though that incident were somehow Jim's responsibility.

"We can start by getting this tablecloth off, before it stains the table."

"Don't dodge me, Jimmy."

Jim handed his brother a napkin. "Wipe that dry while I get this."

As he gathered up the sopping linen, the weight of Hugh's expectation that he be the one to handle the situation settled on his tired shoulders, and he resented it. "What makes you think it's my place to do anything, even if I could?"

"You're his friend, aren't you?" Hugh said. "You know Sister can't say anything. She's already tried to once and you see how much good that did."

Jim tossed the wadded linen into a corner and walked over to the fire. At this moment he wished that he and Mattie could turn right around and drive back to Spartanburg. Just because he had once encouraged Hart's confidence, had listened ten years ago with the prurient curiosity of a boy to his cousin's confessions, did not mean now that Hart and Jennie were his responsibility. He and Mattie had made a life for themselves clear across the state. What happened down here was no longer any of his business. If Hart still regarded him as an ally and confidante, that was just too bad. Jim lacked the moral energy to get involved.

"And now we got Cou'n Tison to deal with too," Hugh said. "You saw what happened. Tison's mixed up in it too."

Jim looked hard at his brother. "What? Mixed up in what?"

"With Jennie somehow," Hugh said.

For at least the third time in the last two hours Jim was all but knocked off his feet. If there was a man in this world more indifferent to a woman than Tison Bonner was, he would like to know who. Living his parsimonious bachelor life in that cold house across the road, he refused even to have a woman cook his meals but used old Jonas instead. That the old man might in any way be involved with Jennie, or she with him, was simply more than Jim could comprehend. But before he could ask for details, Lois called from the top of the stairs, "Hugh! I need you. Right now, please."

: : :

The shot fired by Hart at the table the night before still rang in Jim Creighton's ears, but with John Baird in the back seat of the Buick, neither Jim nor Hugh spoke of the incident, though Jim knew that all three of them were thinking of nothing else. Instead, they talked about how cold it was. Hugh said Jim must have brought it with him from Spartanburg.

Jim had had trouble cranking the automobile, but once the

engine was running the uncomfortable ride took only a few minutes, for the Bonner place was no farther than two miles down the road. Though the big house was occupied now only by Hart's mother Miss Emma and his spinster sister Hattie, the deer drive had always started in the Bonner dining room: a sleepy crowd of men in stocking feet because Miss Emma forbade boots on her polished pine floors.

Though never an ardent deer hunter himself, Jim had once looked forward to this event with great excitement, but in recent years he had found himself haunted by the dead: his father, bigger than any of his sons, assuring each of the young men that they would kill a buck today; Cou'n Johnny, who, though titular huntmaster, had always deferred to Hart; and Hart's brother Smith, dead of tuberculosis five years ago in Tucson, Arizona. There were others as well—Sam Carpenter and Creighton Mayfield in particular, who had drowned drunk in the flooded river swamp, herding cattle.

These had been the tall men of Jim's youth by whose stature he and his brothers had measured themselves. Jim stood by the fire sipping coffee from one of Miss Emma's china cups. He could almost believe that those old stalwarts were milling among the crowd this morning, and sometimes he could swear that he'd just heard among the random conversations the hearty laughter of his father. But that was not surprising. The faces and the voices of the dead were repeated in the living. Jim did not know the names of several of the young men there that morning, but they were clearly members of the tribe, their faces blends of Carpenter and Creighton, Brodie, Bonner, and Mayfield. They were indeed one people.

And so many this year—seventeen—that they had to eat in shifts. As Jim waited for his turn at the candlelit mahogany table, deaf old Cou'n Bones Bonner came sidling up. "Reckon where Bubba's at this morning, son?" he yelled. "He ought to have been here by now."

"I don't know, Cou'n Bones. He must not be feeling well."

Bones cupped his large, knuckley hand to his right ear and leaned toward Jim. "Hanh?"

Raising his voice, Jim repeated what he'd said, but the answer was not satisfactory to the old man. Bones turned and spit tobacco into the fire. "It could be his leg, I reckon, but this ain't like him."

: : :

By the time Jim was seated, the smell of frying sausage had made him ravenous. Every black man on the place, except the dog handlers, was employed in cooking and serving, and he and his fellow hunters were met with steaming bowls of hominy, platters of sausage and bacon and ham, and more fried eggs than they could eat. Hart, seated at the head of the table, showed no sign of being troubled by the episode last night but wolfed down his breakfast with the appetite of a field hand. Jim was still eating when Hart rang the bell to assemble the group. "Y'all go right on," he said to the table, "but it's time to get this show on the road." From outside came the whines and snarls and barks of the deer hounds, rearranging the pecking order.

"The men of our family have been gathering in this room on the Saturday before Christmas every year since the war," Hart began, "and this morning we continue that tradition. Welcome to the Creighton-Bonner Christmas deer drive, gentlemen."

Hart called next for introductions of the boys who were present for their first hunt, gave the schedule for the day, and announced the draw for stands.

Head of the hunt, the professor thought. Hart of the hunt. Or better yet, heart of the hunt. Now that was more like it. With him the heart had always taken precedence over the head, in hunting as in everything else. Not a bad legend actually—better heart than head. How would that go in Latin? *Cor melius capitas?* Something like that. But what did it mean? Better to hunt with the heart than the head? Or better to hunt the heart? It applied either way, he reckoned. Jim envisioned a coat of arms for his kinsman—a gloved fist lifting a hunting horn, the shield crested by a running stag. A hart. In one word the hunted and the hunter. *Cervus. Cor.* Not quite the homonym that it was in English, but close.

The professor's musings were interrupted by the announcement they were all waiting for. "Now, gentlemen, put on your boots and let's go hunting." As men pushed back from the table, gulping a last swallow of coffee, Wade asked Jim what stand he'd drawn, but Jim didn't know; he hadn't been paying attention.

HART

*L*unch on the hill was a steaming, savory stew ladled from a black washpot into enamelware bowls. Hunters leaned their guns, unloaded, against the trunks of trees and squatted on their haunches in small groups, while the mules and horses, gathered in rope corrals, munched hay, and the only deer slain that morning, a spike buck, hung cleft and cooling from a limb on the edge of the camp.

Hart sat apart from the others, beneath a young oak, holding his bowl in a large, dirty hand. From time to time one or another of the cousins came over to ask a question, mostly about the hunt, but he offered no encouragement to anyone to sit down and stay. He was preoccupied by the events at last night's supper, and he wanted to discuss them with Jimmy Creighton. Hart glanced across the way at the Creighton brothers, squatting with the boy John Baird, the nephew they had in common. He was sick with remorse for John Baird's sake. Hugh would be indignant, he suspected, Wade sad and baffled, but Jimmy would be inquisitive—the detached professor seeking to understand. Willing to listen, he already understood more than the others.

Hart wished that he'd come over. Instead, here came Cou'n Bones, stew sloshing from his bowl.

"Howdy, young Hart." Like the others, the old man was attired in coat, tie, and vest, though his hunting outfit was a relic from the last century, rent and mended many times, the cuffs frayed to fuzz. For a deaf man he was a stout talker, loud and high-pitched in a way that could set your teeth on edge, and there was no way to guess what he might come out with next. People still told of the time, at Johnny Bonner's on a Sunday afternoon, when Bones observed that that girl Jennie "sho did favor the Creightons." You could tell it by "them fine bosoms" if nothing else. It was just good luck that Bonner Creighton had not been standing within reach of his voice, for Bones never paused to consider his audience. "We was just debating the contents of this stew. Some said venison, some pork. I maintained possum, a touch of squirrel maybe."

Hart said, "You'll have to ask the men who made it, Bones. I just eat it."

"Me too. I sort of thought Bubba might have shown up by now."

"I wouldn't look for him."

"I reckon the deer drive's got to where it's too much fun for Bubba, setting out here in the cold, dining on possum stew. Bubba enjoys pleasure less than any man I know."

Bones stopped long enough to light the cigarette he'd been working on, the flame of the match disappearing beneath the ragged shingle of his handlebar. During that pause, Jim Creighton came walking over, a man of slight build wearing gold-rimmed glasses. Hart got to his feet, brushing leaves from the seat of his pants. The professor looks pale, he thought. Probably hasn't been outdoors since last summer.

"It's been a pleasure," Jim said, "but I'm not feeling well. I think I'd better call it a day."

"What's the trouble? I was hoping we'd get to spend some time together."

"I know, me too, but I'm afraid I might be coming down with something. I think I'm running a fever. With this flu going around I don't want to take a chance."

Hart took Jim by the lapel of his coat and playfully tugged at it. "Listen now, professor. Here's what we're going to do," he said. "You and I are going to find us a pretty place out on the river and sit and smoke until we've caught up on the news or a buck runs over us, one. Seriously now, you'll feel better out here in the fresh air anyway than cooped up at Sallie's with all those chirren."

Jim wavered, Hart could see it in his face. He had always been one to please others. Someone called out his name. It was Hugh, who was pulling John Baird by the hand into the back of a crowded wagon—the social hunters headed for the hill. He was beckoning Jim to come on. Jim waved back, shook his head. Hart smiled. "Old Hugh don't look real natural in those hunting clothes, does he?"

"Brother is a fastidious man."

"I know he is. You remember when he was a child he'd never go barefooted? Didn't want to get his feet dirty."

: : :

Hart and Jim left their mounts with the handler Robert Salley and walked for twenty minutes down the river, the wide expanse of the Savannah the color of gunmetal in the wintry light. From a thin stand of switch cane they emerged into an oak flat, park-like in its generous spacing of big trees and extensive in its reach. As late in the season as it was, the foliage was still autumnal, the canopy intact, and bleak light filtered down through the leaves. The two men found a log and sat. The ground was flat and free of underbrush in all directions. Though Hart had brought them to a major river crossing, there were too many standers along the trails between them and the hill for any buck to make it that far, but Hart seemed not to mind. He filled his pipe and lit it.

"I hadn't figured on this illness," Jim said. He looked peaked. "I'm just scared I'm not going to be feeling well enough to take

Matt to church tomorrow, and she's been looking forward to it so."

"Looking forward to church?"

"I don't mean Cypress Swamp. I'm talking about Bethlehem. She wants to hear the singing, and I promised I would take her."

"Oh. That's no problem," Hart said. "I was half thinking about going myself. If you can't make it, she can go with me." Most people in Cypress Swamp considered Hart's love of Negro spirituals peculiar, but they dismissed that interest as one of his more harmless eccentricities. "In fact, that might not be a bad plan," he continued. "I ain't sure I'm quite as welcome there as I used to be."

"Has something happened?"

"Jennie's been attending. For a right good while now. I don't know how much those people know, but I don't feel as comfortable as I used to." Hart raised his hand. "Shh. Listen. You hear the dogs?"

They were a long way off but in full cry. "Sounds like they've made game," Jim said. "Can you tell where they are?"

"Still on the other side of Clearwater, but if that's a buck they're running there's no telling where he'll lead them."

Hart put a match to his battered old brier. As he sucked at it, blue smoke wreathed around his head. "I don't understand it. Jennie going to church. Don't care much for it either."

Jim slid to the ground, rested his head against the log he'd been sitting on, and pulled his hat down over his eyes. "Well, it can't hurt her, can it?"

It can hurt us, Hart thought, already has. But before he could frame an acceptable answer, he heard the muffled boom of a gun.

"Was that a shot?" Jim asked.

"Yes. I don't reckon you saw her after I left last night?"

"No, I didn't."

"Look, Jimmy," Hart said. "I'm sorry about last night, I truly am, especially for Sallie and John Baird. There's no excuse for it,

I know, but how could I just sit there? Could you have? I know my brother was just trying to provoke me, but there're some things a man can't tolerate, and call himself a man."

Jim pulled himself up onto the log. "I'm afraid I'm really sick, Hart. I hate to trouble you, but I'm going to have to go on in."

A shot—not close but close enough to pay attention to.

"Hello," Hart said. "Let's just wait a minute, see what the news is going to be."

The baying of the dogs was growing louder by the moment. Hart's face lit up, losing instantly all traces of concern about Jennie. "They're off a ways yet, but they're coming this way."

Boom! went another gun.

"Who was that? Doug Mayfield maybe."

Whoever it was had missed, for the baying of the pack did not cease but swelled in volume. Hart got to his feet and picked up his shotgun. "Get ready, Jimmy. We might see something any second now. Come on now. Get your gun. I want you to kill this buck."

It took an effort for Jim to stand, but this would be his best chance at a buck until next year, and Hart urged him to it. As the race came steadily toward them, Hart envisioned the dogs as clearly as he heard their desperate bawling, the strung-out pack in headlong pursuit, muzzles to ground, and just as clearly, the galloping, ghost-pale buck, bearing down on them, to burst any second now from the pale green wall of switch cane on the far side of the flat. And there he was—God almighty, what a stag—but he was running too far out for a shot. The buck thundered across the open park with his head held back, his rack against his shoulders, and his feet seemed not to touch the ground. And here came the dogs, driving the buck straight toward the river, on a line well out of shotgun range. And then the buck turned, for what cause Hart could not tell, unless it was in compliance with a pattern long ago ordained.

Hart turned, oblivious now of Jim. This one was his. He rose, bringing the L.C. Smith to his shoulder, and the buck saw him and leapt, right into the charge of his right barrel. The shot seemed for an instant to stagger the animal in midair, but it hit the ground without breaking stride, lunging toward the safety of the wide Savannah River. Hart stood, the gun at his shoulder as the dogs streamed past, and black smoke clouded around his head.

The buck was down and the dogs were upon him. Hart hurried toward the flailing animal, wading into the snarling, moiling hounds, kicking as he went. "Get back now. Get back, goddammit."

With the dogs at bay, he nudged the buck with the toe of his boot, and then he took the horn that was looped around his shoulder and, tilting his head back, sent one long, sweet, mellow note quavering through the river bottom forest.

The tines on one side had been driven by the fall into the sandy soil, twisting the muscled neck. Still kicking at whining dogs, Hart reached down and freed the antler. The stout beams, walnut dark and knurled at the bases, swept outward in a wide arc of paling horn, curved forward dramatically, and concluded in symmetrical ivory points. Hart lifted his hat in tribute.

Jim had come up behind him. "I don't think I've ever seen a rack like that. Have you?"

"Maybe once. But it's been a long time."

"Well, congratulations, Hart. That was a beautiful shot."

Now that the deed was done, Hart's joy was edged with regret, for having snatched the buck from Jimmy, for the death itself.

Robert came riding up, leading Hart's mare and Jim's mule, and soon other hunters began to appear. When they saw the animal on the ground, they marveled, climbed down from their mounts, and admired it, hefting its head by the antlers, but no one wanted to come right out and ask who had killed it.

"Gentlemen," Jim said, "shake the hand of the huntmaster."

While the hunters smoked and talked, the drivers caught up the hounds and leashed them and bled and gutted the buck. A bluetick, still roaming free, nosed among the steaming entrails.

"I imagine he whipped some ass in his day," Tom Brodie said, examining the scars on the animal's neck.

"Enjoyed a world of it too," Tom's brother added.

"Full of piss and vinegar, a buck like that. Tough as hell too."

"Well, anybody who wants a share will have to pick it up at Miss Sallie's house this evening," Hart said. "The professor's not feeling well, and I'm going to take him on in. Might as well take this gentleman as long as I'm going."

Hart surprised himself as much as the others by that announcement. By custom, they divided venison at the end of the day, back at the Bonner house. But he had never slain such a trophy, and though the impulse was childish, he wanted to show it to Jennie.

"I think I'll let you keep mine, Hart," Charlie Carpenter said.

"Fine with me. I got plenty of folks at home that'll be glad to get it. Ain't that right, Eli?"

The driver named Eli grinned. "Yassuh, Mr. Hart. Sho will."

"What'll he go, Eli?" Wade asked.

"That buck, Mr. Wade? That buck gon make two hundred pound."

"More'n that," another driver said.

Exaggeration was the black men's tribute, and everybody knew it.

"I was about to get y'all to swing him up on the back of my mare, " Hart said, "but if he weighs that damn much, I'm afraid you'll hurt your backs."

The drivers laughed, and gray-haired Eli said, "I tell you what, Mr. Hart. You catch hold of his horns and I'll catch his back feets and let's us see who get his end up first."

With Hart holding the reins, the mare stood for the loading. Hart snugged the carcass against the cantle, tied the legs to the stirrups, and mounted. "I believe she'll carry us both. You ready, professor?"

Between the hunters and the hill lay a mile and a half of floodplain forest, a patchwork of canebrake and hardwood grove veined by a dozen winding waterways, the stillwater sloughs called guts in that part of the country. The going was slow and deliberate, Hart gripping the antlers in his left hand to protect the mare as she skidded down embankments or crashed through thickets, Jim struggling to keep up. It took them an hour to reach the place of their nooning. Hart's thigh had suffered considerable abuse from the tines, and Jim was too feverish to remain any longer on the mule. Fortunately for them both, two wagons were parked beneath the pines.

"Why don't you stretch out in back," Hart suggested as they approached the vehicles, "if you don't mind a bedfellow?"

"I'll sit up front."

Hart unfastened the stiffening carcass and dumped it directly from the back of the mare into the wagon bed; he tied the mare and the mule to the tailgate and gave Jim a hand up.

Seated haunch to haunch, the two men took a narrow, hard-packed sandy lane through an endless gloom of tall loblolly pine, the team of mules plodding along with no sense of destination. At some point in that creaking, interminable ride, Hart spoke: "I wonder if Jennie's around today."

Jim was seized by a chill. Shivering uncontrollably, he wrapped his arms about himself and tucked his chin into his chest as though a cold wind were blowing. Hart took off his coat and draped it over Jim's shoulders. "Does that help?"

Jim nodded, or seemed to. It was hard to tell because of the violence of his chill.

Beyond a row of bare trees, the tall brick chimneys of Tison's house rose against a lead-gray sky. The road would take them through the old man's yard. Before they got there, though, Hart turned the heads of the team at an intersection, toward Wade Creighton's house, adding by that decision a full thirty minutes to Jim's ordeal.

"Sorry, professor, but it wouldn't do for me to encounter that son of a bitch right now, not after last night. I lack the self-restraint," he said.

: : :

As the laden wagon approached Sallie's house, Hart considered his chances of seeing Jennie. With so many people about he could not expect a private moment, but by long practice they had learned to communicate by code. He wanted to see her face when she saw the buck.

Hart pulled up at the gate in the picket fence. "Go fetch Sister," Jim said. "I can't go inside not knowing—" and then he swooned. Hart caught him before he fell. Jim was right. If this was flu, he would endanger the household. The epidemic had spread across the country, killing more soldiers than the Germans, and now it had come to South Carolina. Men and women, often in the prime of their lives, were dying right and left. People were terrified.

Hart maneuvered the unconscious man into the back of the wagon and laid him alongside the buck. He would have to see what Sallie wanted done with the patient. Before he reached the steps, she came out onto the porch, followed by Mattie.

With the women hovering at his elbows, Mattie wringing her hands, Hart lifted Jim from the wagon. He was not heavy. "Where shall I put him, Sallie?"

"Upstairs, Hart. In John Baird's room," she said, leading the way.

As Hart climbed the front porch steps, Jim awoke. "Put me down, please," he said, embarrassed by his weakness. "I can walk."

"Right at the end of the hall," Sallie said, "but, Hart, can you carry him up those steps?"

: : :

Forgotten by the household, Hart led the team of mules around to the back. With Nathaniel's help he unloaded the buck, punched a gambrel through its hocks, and hung it from a cross-bar used for butchering hogs. Then he told Nathaniel to unsaddle the mare and clean the blood from her matted flanks.

The butchering rack stood in view of the kitchen window. Hart glanced in that direction, then removed his coat and tie and collar and rolled up his sleeves. Testing the edge of his blade, he cut circles around the hind legs just below the hams; then, splitting the skin, he worked it away from the flesh and peeled it back, first one leg and then the other, exposing the meat of the hindquarters, dark red beneath the silver fascia. It felt good to be doing something that required care and deliberation. Gripping the buckled hide with both hands, one on either side, he used his weight to strip the back and ribs. When the skin had cleared the shoulders, he made precise cuts along the backs of the front legs and worked the skin away from the chest and neck until it hung like a wet and heavy cape over the deer's antlered head. The right shoulder was bruised purple-black where the buckshot hit it.

Kneeling at the muffled head, Hart cut through the thick muscle of the neck, just behind the skull. Fetching a saw, he completed the decapitation, then stepped back, wiping his hands on his soft corduroy trousers. In the deepening twilight the carcass shone like a ghost. Hart loved its clean muscularity, grace apparent in the lean efficiency of the shoulders, the vigor of the loin, the power of the haunches.

Damn near the ideal animal, he thought.

A table for butchering extended from the side of the smokehouse. Hart removed his vest and unbuttoned his shirt, looking back toward the kitchen as he shed it, but the window reflected the failing light. Taking hold of the carcass by grips he had cut between ribs on either side, he hoisted it so that the gambrel lifted free of the hook, and waltzed it over to the table. With the carcass on its belly, he removed the shoulders with his skinning knife. Connected to the trunk by only tendon and muscle, they separated easily beneath the blade. Next, he sawed through the spine at the small of the back, and then he split the hindquarters right down the middle of the pelvis.

Jimmy might like a cutlet of loin for his breakfast, Hart thought, though he doubted the tenderness of this old buck.

With the point of his knife he traced a line from just back of where the right shoulder had been, along the top of the rib cage, to the end of the trunk. Then he made a parallel cut along the spine, slicing deep. Working his fingers gently beneath the delicate meat, he slowly tugged it free of its attachment to ribs, lifting it in both hands, conscious of its weight. A skein of smooth fascia sheathed the outer face but underneath the meat was a deep maroon. Hart held the wet plank of muscle in both hands and looked about for a clean surface. Finding none, he peeled off his undershirt, dipped it into a bucket of water, wiped the backstrap clean, and wrapped it. When that was done, he hung the quarters and the rib cage in the smokehouse. If any of the hunters showed up for a share, they could help themselves.

Hart turned now to the only part of this business he found distasteful—the removal of the antlers. The skinning and butchering had been a kind of sacrament whereby the animal was reduced to meat that in turn would be converted into living flesh again, causing those who ate it to run a little wilder than they had before, as Cou'n Bonner Creighton used to say. But the sawing off of the rack required a mutilation that Hart found offensive. Nevertheless, he knelt to the task, first bringing forth the head from the blanket of hide that had concealed the shame of its protruding tongue. The antlers were for Jennie, a hatrack if she wanted. He placed the saw directly behind the bases of the beams, chewing through thick hair, and angled his cut down toward the eyes. Gripping an antler with his left hand to steady the head, he made a cut high on the bridge of the nose, just below the eyes. The skull plate made a sucking sound when he pulled it away, exposing to the air of the world the packed gray brain.

Hart looked up to see Nathaniel standing there, his huge hands hanging like blocks of wood at his side.

"Don't you tan hides, Nathaniel?"

"Sometimes I does."

"Well how 'bout tanning this one for me. It has some buckshot in it, but I got it off in one piece."

"Yessuh."

"And take this head off somewhere and bury it." Hart could not bear to think that the head might be flung into the woods for a possum to drag around in the leaves, worrying it to pieces.

"Bury it?"

"Yes. Deep enough to where something won't come along and dig it up."

Nathaniel wrapped the emasculated head in the blanket of its hide and shambled off into the deepening shadows while Hart stood alone gripping the bloodstained antlers. The buck was now unmade, as his father used to say, and Jennie had not appeared. Hart tossed the antlers toward the smokehouse. They bounced when they hit the ground and tumbled toward the wall. His thigh was sore where the antlers had gouged him during the ride across the swamp, and he wanted to see what the place looked like. He sat down on an old cypress stump that someone had dragged up to the smokehouse and loosened his trousers. If anyone from the kitchen should see and be shocked by his naked legs, well let them.

: : :

Hart stood uncertain at Sallie's front door. Because of Friday night he could not simply turn the knob and walk in, as he always had, but neither could he bring himself to knock. Mattie Creighton solved his dilemma by opening the door herself. Though bundled up for the long ride to church, she had an anxious look. "Oh Hart. I just don't know."

She had caught him just before he left the house last night and asked about the service; Jim had insisted. Hart had told her to be ready by nine, and here she was.

"How is he this morning?" he asked.

"He seems to be much better, thank you. He says he is, and his fever broke in the night. But I do hate to leave him."

Hart liked Mattie Creighton. He had from the first. She reminded him of a wren, pert, and while she looked like a girl with that pinch of a freckled nose, she had gumption. Jennie liked her too. "He'll be fine, Miss Mattie. Sallie can see to him."

"I know, but I just hate . . . with all she has to do."

Hart assisted her into the buggy, climbed up beside her, and arranged a plaid robe across their laps. The thermometer had dropped below freezing for the first time that winter—cold enough for them to take the automobile, but Hart was not confident of the machine; the church was a mile back in the woods, he explained, at the end of a little piece of road that had washed out in places in the recent heavy rains.

Hart was anxious for a report of Jennie, no matter how scant, but he dared not ask. He had no idea how much Mattie knew. Most men considered such information too sordid for their wives, but Jimmy and Mattie were a modern couple, and after Friday night who could guess what all they might have discussed? Mattie seemed preoccupied anyway.

The buggy creaked along behind Hart's old red gelding, louder than usual because of the cold, and bumpier too. Hart focused his attention on the polished harness, the way it lay upon the horse's well-groomed coat, shining in the sun. The steady plod and the rhythmic creaking of the springs produced in him a sense not of progressing toward a destination but of merely moving in place, the unchanging stretch of road no more than occasion for the exercise.

"Will any of the people I know be there this morning, Hart?"

"I imagine so, Miss Mattie. I'm sure Nathaniel will. And Jennie, I suspect. She didn't say anything to you about going?"

"No. No, she didn't."

Hart turned Red from the Old Charleston Road into the guttered lane that led to the church. The horse arched his tail and emptied his bowels. Hart directed Mattie's attention to the open woods on the left, site of an old slave burying ground long since grown up in scrubby hardwoods. "Used to always be a covey of birds in there," he said.

They heard the singing before the church came into view, a chorus wordless and indistinct yet vibrant despite the distance, swelling resonant and full-throated, falling away and rising again, as they came around the last bend in the road. Mattie's gloved hand clutched Hart's forearm. "Oh listen," she said. The little church could not contain that music. Set amid pines tall and pencil thin, the small frame box listed to one side, its weathered boards warped, sprung loose from studs. Hart fancied he could see fervor like steam escaping from crack and seam. Otherwise, he thought, the power of the singing might lift the roof right off its moorings.

"They've already started, Hart. I do hate to come in late," Mattie said.

"Late ain't something you can very well be to a Negro church, Miss Mattie. They'll keep at it off and on all afternoon."

The spaces among the trees were filled with the dilapidated, jury-rigged modes of conveyance available to plantation blacks—crippled buggies cast off from the big house, ingeniously repaired, battered wagons with straight chairs set upright in their beds for the aged and arthritic, even an oxcart or two, meanest of vehicles; and the beasts that drew them, mules of every size and color, every one with a droopy lip, used up, too damaged by age or abuse for field work. Standing among them were a few lethargic oxen, long-horned and harlequin—all asleep on planted hooves, hitched to pine trunks in the cold, bright sandy yard, suffering servants impervious to the singing. Hart drove the buggy to the far side of the clearing, up against the woods, climbed down, and tied the reins to a bare gum branch.

BethLeHIM A. M. e. cheRch

The board was hand-lettered, black on white except for the HIM, which had recently been painted over, bright red as was the door beneath it, in celebration of the season.

"We'll just slip in and find a place in the back," Hart said.

The red door opened upon the back of a congregation sway-
ing in unison, shoulder to shoulder, like treetops rocked by a
mighty wind. The heat and the smell of close-packed bodies,
sweating in exultation, nearly took their breath away, but it
was the singing that caught them up and held them, a pulsating
chorale ascending in pitch and swelling in volume until Hart
thought he might actually rise upon its buoyant energy. Again,
Mattie took him by the arm, too enthralled to remove her gloves
and heavy coat.

The song ended like smoke rising, drawn out and fading, but
before the last note died a clear baritone rang out,

> If you want to get to heaven . . .

and the congregation in one voice answered,

> Got to re-born again
> Yeah, got to re-born again.

Hart helped Mattie with her coat, removed his own, and
worked his way over to the side of the room to hang them from
already burdened pegs. He looked for Jennie, but all he could see
were the backs of hats, a wide variety brim to brim, moving in
rhythm to the music.

It's mostly women here, he thought.

Again a solo voice came in upon the trailing garment of the
song they'd been singing, but this time it was a soprano, as sweet
and clear and lonesome as the sun coming up over young green
fields in May. Hart grew tense. "That's Jennie," he whispered.

> I know I been change', I know I been change',

and the congregation:

> Angel in the heaven done change' my name.

When the congregation was seated at last, some of the women
still rocking and softly moaning, a man of short stature, elderly
but obviously strong, emerged from the confusion down front,

stepped up onto a platform, and took his place at a pulpit hammered together out of stray boards. He was barely able to see over the top. The man was Ezra Jeffords, Hart whispered, who worked on Tison's place and led the Sunday service here at Bethlehem. In a shy, gravelly voice, Ezra announced the Reverend Doctor Brewster Simmons, guest preacher from the Mount Zion African Methodist Episcopal Church in Charleston.

Amid the applause of the congregation, the Reverend Doctor Simmons took the pulpit. He took it in both hands, with authority, reducing it by his stature to something a child might play with. The sun, angling steeply through the tall glazed window to the right, glinted on the lenses and the fine gold frames of the preacher's spectacles.

"Much obliged, Brother Jeffords," said the preacher. Just that, but the voice rumbled from deep inside like news from an approaching storm. Without greeting or preamble, the Reverend Doctor Simmons produced a Bible, smaller than the hand that held it, and waved it about on high, as a man brandishes a torch against the darkness. "The Word of God," he pronounced. Opening it, he presented it to the congregation like a bite of something to eat.

His chosen text was from the second chapter of Luke. Without so much as a glance downward, he recited the familiar story of the poor carpenter who brought his espoused wife, great with child, into the crowded streets of Bethlehem.

"Lost in the dark street, beloveds, cold and hungry and no place to lay they head."

The congregation had begun to move, not with a motion one could see but with an impulse Hart could feel, a sort of spiritual harmonizing with the growing rhythms of the preacher. And the preacher responded.

"The whole creation groaning, groaning and moaning up and down the world, awaiting its release—liberation, children, from the cold dark night of sin."

The preacher paused, gripped the pulpit with his bear-paw

hands, and his glasses glinted so that no one could see his eyes. The people held their breath, waiting for the thunder. Instead, the preacher whispered:

> But look who coming here,
> Yeah just look who coming now—
> Virgin Mary great with child
> Toiling down that rocky road
> Into the town of Bethlehem
> Heavy laden with the Bread of Life,
> Press down, shake together, and overflowing, children.
> Oh look who coming here.

A scatter of moans, a wailing "Yes Jesus," and the Reverend Doctor Simmons was pacing about the pulpit stage, confined by its narrow space like an animal behind bars. Hart was surprised to see that he had removed his coat—he had not noticed when that happened—but there the preacher was, white sleeves billowing from a bulging vest and the hands at the ends of those sleeves cleaving the air like hatchets.

> Po folks been lost that night, peoples,
> Strayed off from home and disperse' in the wilderness,
> And no light to find they way.

"Take your time now."

The preacher stamped the hollow floor with a foot the size of an anvil and proclaimed again, "No light," and it seemed to Hart that the midday sun streaming through the tall windows lost a noticeable measure of brightness.

> But shining, peoples.

"Don't hold back now."

> Bright with the light of the world.

"Preach it now."

The preacher paused, mopped the sweat from his glistening

brow with a red bandanna, dabbed at his eyes, and Hart saw that the glasses were gone.

And Joseph knock at the door of the inn.

The Reverend Doctor Simmons struck the pine of the pulpit with a massive fist. Rap, rap, rap.

> But the boss man say no room
> And he slam shet the door.

The preacher clapped his hands, a *pow* like a gunshot.

> Slam it shet in the face of the sweet Baby Jesus.
> The Light of the World
> But the boss man can't comprehend it,
> Flood them street with glory,
> But darkness brood in the boss man' heart,
> Yeah,
> And the Bread of Life
> All spread out on the welcome table
> Feed the multitude
> And the boss man starve to death
> Go hongry een his heart.

Hart shifted his seat on the hard bench, plucked his watch from a tight vest pocket, impatient for more singing.

> Behold I stand at the door and knock, peoples.
> Yeah my Jesus knock
> Knock at the door to my heart
> Knock at the door to yours.
> Rich man, poor man, white man, black—
> Light of the World
> And Bread of Life—
> And what you gon do?

From the congregation a single voice cried, "Amen, brother,

open it," but the preacher asked again, hand cupped to his ear. "Do what?"

"Open it."

Hart leaned toward Mattie. "Are you about ready?"

"Oh no, Cou'n Hart," she said, placing a firm hand on his arm. "I just couldn't leave now."

> And watch how fas' the Lord come in.
> Fill yo' heart with light.
> And spread yo' board with bread.

"Amen. Amen."

The preacher waited for the clamor to die down—a long cessation—until he was sure he had the full attention of the congregation, and then, his voice rising in pitch, quivering along the edge of hysteria, he shouted,

> But keep it shut, peoples—
> Yeah, you jes' keep that front do' shet—

Another pause.

> And Gawd have mercy.

The four words fell like individual stones, boulders from a great height, each word upon the open hearts of the people, and a sound like grief, low and turbulent, began to rock the assembled body, that brown body of Christ, and with one voice it mourned for the hard-hearted bosses who chose to dwell in a hungry night.

Hart was ready to go. He said so to Mattie.

"Oh Hart, look."

A thin, dark man in a tight-fitting gaberdine suit had leapt from the congegation and stood in the narrow space between the pulpit and the mourners' bench. Then he began to move, a slow and stately rubber-limbed strut, and as he strutted he began to sing, and the song and the dance were a single act of praise.

> I gwine to sit at the welcome table,
> I gwine to sit at the welcome table
> Some of these days, hallelujah.

Then the congregation joined in:

> I gwine to eat and never get hongry
> Some of these days, hallelujah.

Hart had heard that old favorite more times than he could remember, but this time he envisioned an outdoor table of warped and weathered boards, stretching away beneath the pines as far as eye could see, laden with fried chicken and country ham and dumplings, baskets of biscuits, and every kind of vegetable grown in Heyward County and cakes and pies without end, and, lined on both sides, laughing black faces, converging in the distance like the rails of a train track. The welcome table. Well, they were welcome to it. He was too hungry to stay any longer, Mattie or not.

A woman rose from the seated congregation, tall, light-skinned. It was Jennie. She raised her arms, and the singing broke off.

"For God's sake," Hart muttered.

With the back of her wrist pressed to her forehead, the tall mulatto woman shivered from head to foot, like a tree sawn almost clean through and poised to fall. Then she swooned, sank lightly like a rag doll into the billowing of long skirts and petticoats, and disappeared among the people around her.

Hart caught Mattie by the arm, gripped it firmly to communicate the seriousness of his intent. "Let's go."

"Wait, Hart. I fear for Jennie. Something's wrong."

The congregation had closed in around her, a swarm active with solicitude. Above the babble came a man's voice, high-pitched and hoarse: "Make way. Make way. Let this lady breathe." And the swarm parted before the authority of the preacher, who was standing now with Jennie's unconscious body, skirts trailing, in his arms.

"Stand back now. This lady's burning up."

The word clanged like a fire bell in Hart's head. He bolted forward, but Mattie had grabbed his coattail, stopping him in his tracks. "No, Hart," she said. "You mustn't. Let me see to this."

The agitated crowd parted like the Red Sea before the rod of Moses, and the big preacher from Charleston, spectacles back in place, emerged, Jennie's limp body draped across his arms. Her face was hot and dry, her lips parched, but it was her dangling feet, her laced black shoes and ruffled pantaloons, exposed to these people, that made Hart's heart tumble like a downhill stone. To hell with Mattie's scruples. He started forward again, but Mattie had never released her grip.

"This lady needs attention," the preacher said.

Mattie moved in front of Hart, placing herself between him and the Reverend Doctor Simmons. "We will take her home," she said, "but we'll need a wagon. We came in a buggy."

Through the confusion of milling bodies, Mattie led the preacher to the door. To Hart's surprise a light jersey wagon was already there, parked and waiting. A young man sat on the seat, lines in hand, and people were bringing quilts from all parts of the yard. The wagon looked mighty frail, but no worse than any other vehicle parked amid the pines. Mattie turned to Jennie, still in the preacher's arms but somehow already bundled up, cocoon-tight. Hart might almost have believed that angels had been at work had it not been for Jennie's mother, poor old Delia, hovering, smoothing back her daughter's hair, tucking in a trailing edge of quilt.

Outside, in the cold and now bleak afternoon, Hart stood at the back of the wagon, the plaid lap robe draped across his hands, as women prepared a pallet for Jennie. Mattie took charge, directed the lifting in of the patient, the laying on of cover. As quick as a darting wren, she was in the wagon herself, kneeling by Jennie, tucking, tugging, arranging for comfort. Then, turning, she assisted heavy Delia, who had climbed up onto the spokes but could not hoist her bulk over the side. Taking her hand, Mattie pulled, and in one motion Delia came aboard. Together, the two women settled at Jennie's head, and Delia made a pillow of her lap.

And still Hart stood expectant, the now unnecessary lap robe still hanging from his hands. He felt stupid, unnoticed, and unnecessary.

"You'll need that more than we will, Hart. Come on behind us now," Mattie said.

A cloud cover had thickened in the west, filtering a sorry light. The pines that stood close on either side of the sandy track cast no shadows, and the dim woods, carpeted with pine straw, were drained of color, vacant of all flitting, chirping creatures. Except for the clink of traces and the creak of axles, the groan of old wood, and the gritty whisper of tires in sand, the little caravan made a silent progress.

A slow one too. In spite of his years Red had more spunk than the plodding, decrepit mule up ahead. Impatient, he would gain on the wagon until his broad chest was all but touching the open gate. Then Hart would tug on the lines. They could have made better time on foot. Jennie needed a doctor as soon as possible, but locating Sam Pettigru would not be easy. Half the houses in the county had somebody sick. Sam could be anywhere between Cypress Swamp and Carthage. Wherever he was, he'd be worn to a frazzle. You could bet on that. There wasn't much the doctor could do anyway, to be honest. Rest and chicken broth, the universal prescription. If the patient was strong enough, she would pull through.

The thought of losing Jennie to Jesus, so upsetting just a short while ago, was taking on a different meaning, as bleak and threatening as the clouded western sky. Fear closed upon Hart's chest and gripped his throat. He fought it back, concentrated upon his hands. They lay against the plaid blanket as white as candle wax, useless, keeping a little tension on the lines.

Up ahead, the wagon's off rear wheel was wobbling, causing the wagon to ride with a pitching motion. In the last few minutes it seemed to have gotten worse. The wagon had held together thus far by a miracle of coherence. Any sudden bump could shock it into pieces. Hart winced and held his breath each time it lurched through a gutted place in the road.

Hart imagined himself standing against a heavenly host, fighting for the right to carry Jennie home, to her cabin, their home. He wanted to be the one who put her to bed, built up the fire. He wanted to crawl in beside her, snuggle up. That's what he'd been missing—not so much the pleasure of her body as her bed and the comfort of lying together, touching along their length. Those nights he had found her already asleep, he had curled up against her back, warmed his chilled thighs and feet, breathed in her smell. Often it had seemed to him that he was absorbing, inhaling the essence of her, and the more deeply it permeated, the more complete the peace he felt.

Who was driving that damned catastrophe of a wagon? Couldn't he touch up the mule? Hart tapped a little dance to warm his feet. The wheel was wobbling worse than ever. Just then, as though his concern had caused it, the rut on the left side of the road fell away. The wagon yawed, throwing Delia into Mattie, and the weight of the loaded vehicle came to bear on the wobbly wheel. The wheel screamed. Goddamn, Hart thought, holding his breath. But the wagon creaked on, canted now, Mattie braced against the angle, and with each slow turn wood screeched against worn wood.

If Jennie was set on giving herself to Jesus, then Jesus had better make her well, Hart breathed, as close to praying as he ever came.

The wagon lurched, shivered, stopped dead. The bad wheel was jammed in a narrow but deep washout, what Hart called a churn hole. He should have remembered to warn the driver about this place. Coming in, they had had to climb down from the buggy and lead the horse around it. The wagon was tilted so dangerously that Mattie had wedged herself against the side board to cushion Jennie, and it was all poor Delia could do to keep from sliding into them both. The driver was already on the ground, scrutinizing the stuck wheel as though he had just come walking up and had no idea how this accident had occurred. He was a dark-skinned boy, younger than Hart had realized.

"What's your name?"

"Tucker, suh. Stays over to Mr. Gus Mayfield place. Sho is a bad hole, ain't it?"

"How on earth did you miss it?"

"I ain't did miss it. Not with that back wheel, I ain't."

Hart turned to the women. "We're going to have to unload, Mattie. Y'all come off the high side if you can. That wheel won't stand much more."

Mattie backed over the side board, as agile as a schoolgirl, felt for a spoke with her foot and found one. Hart caught her by the waist and eased her to the ground. Delia was another matter. But before he could devise a strategy, the big woman was on her way, backing over the side as Mattie had. Mattie and Hart both jumped to assist her, but Hart hesitated as though he wasn't sure where to grab hold.

"Wait now, Delia," Mattie was saying. "Just hold still a second."

Mattie grasped the older woman's shoe, which was searching blindly, and set it on a spoke. "Come on, now. We won't let you fall."

Hart caught Delia by the arm as Mattie steadied her with a hand at her elbow. As soon as her feet touched ground, Delia moved to the other side of the wagon, to where her daughter lay, and resumed the stroking of her hair, singing to her in a soft, low guttural croon.

"Tucker," Hart ordered, "take the lines and say gee when I tell you."

Hart examined the stuck wheel.

"Delia, stand back a minute. We'll be out of here in no time."

As Hart prepared to step down into the washout, he paused and looked at Jennie. So pale was her cheek that it showed a red spot, like paint on the cheek of a doll. Her eyelids fluttered, then opened, and there could be no doubt of the fever. No longer luminous and liquid, her eyes had a glazed, heated look. Hart's hand hovered, as though to touch, but beneath that mound of quilts she lay as wrapped as an Egyptian mummy, only her face exposed. And now her eyes were shut again. He laid his hand on her hair, felt against his palm the familiar coarse waviness, unbound and loosened by her mother's desperate stroking. He leaned close. "Rest easy now," he said. "I'll get you home." Then, without looking at either Mattie or Jennie's mother, he leaned forward and kissed her on the forehead.

The wagon was light, it was true—old, dried wood wired together—but if it had weighed a ton, that would not have mattered to Hart. Instead of taking a spoke and dislodging the wheel, as he might have, he slid down into the hole, set his shoulder beneath the bed, and stood up with it, shouting, "Now!"

: : :

The little caravan came at last to the rise that would take them up into the big road. The wagon groaned as the poor mule leaned into the pull. Out of the woods and into the thoroughfare, Hart pulled the buggy alongside the wagon, hub to hub. Jennie seemed to be asleep. Mattie turned toward him, her freckled child's face almost annoyed by the distraction. You've done what you could, she seemed to be saying, we can handle it now.

"I'm going to get the automobile," he said, though he knew that by the time he returned they would be close enough to Sallie's not to need it.

His horse broke into a stiff trot, little streams of sand flowed from the spinning tires, and Hart slowly pulled away from the crippled wagon.

: : :

The entire household, except for Miss Sadie and Jim, kept vigil that night, sitting around the dining room table, drinking coffee, anxiously awaiting reports on Jennie. They came almost hourly, either from Sallie or Mattie. Delia would not be dislodged from the chair at her daughter's bed, but the two white women took turns sitting with her. Jim had been forbidden to leave his room. His temperature had climbed a bit through the late afternoon, and Sallie wanted him to remain upstairs, both for his sake and the family's.

Hart had gathered that much from his position on the porch. In spite of the cold, he refused to go inside but settled into a rocker that squeaked when he rocked. After a while Sallie brought him a cup of coffee. "We'll keep you posted, Hart," she said. She did not invite him in, but neither did she suggest that he go on home. For that he was grateful. He was having trouble keeping his pipe going. He got up and walked around the yard, edging toward Jennie's cabin, drawn like a moth to the lamplight in her windows. He felt like that old stray that had crept up to his fire that night last spring, too fearful to approach but too hungry to leave.

: : :

A lamp wick fluttered low on the table by Jim's bed, a feeble blue flame, as Hart eased through the door. Jimmy was asleep, he thought, but immediately from the bed the sick man spoke. "Who's there?"

"Hart."

Jim leaned toward the lamp.

"Leave it. We don't need light."

Jim sat up, adjusted his pillow for support. "How are you doing?"

"Not worth a damn."

Hart moved toward the window. From there he could look down upon Jennie's cabin.

"Why don't you try to get some rest, Hart? You could stretch out on the sofa in the sitting room."

"While the rest of the family sits up all night? What a hell of a thing to say. I wish to God Sam Pettigru would get here."

Jim said, "I wouldn't look for him before morning."

"She could be dead by then. And I have so much to tell her, Jimmy. So much to explain. She don't know." Hart's voice broke. Kneeling at the window, his arms about his head, he gave in to the exhaustion of having borne on his shoulders for twelve lonely hours the weight of his anxiety. The spell was brief. Gaining control of his voice, he got to his feet. "It just don't seem fair, Jimmy. The whole damn house can go out there, and the one who really has the right is not allowed to."

"No one's out there but Sallie and Mattie, Hart."

Hart settled on the cot where Mattie had slept.

"I don't think she knows who's with her, from what they tell me," Jim continued. "She's in God's hands now."

"Don't talk God to me. God is one thing I've just about had enough of."

"I know you're under stress, Hart—we all are—but that's a terrible thing to say."

"Let me tell you something, professor. She claims she's found Christ or something, but it ain't a thing in the world but nigger religion, and she's too good for that. I've tried to tell her, but she won't listen. She won't even talk. I haven't spent a night with her since way back in September, and even then we didn't—"

"Hart. Listen to me," Jim said. "A person's spiritual life is her own business. Even if you were married, you'd have to respect that."

"You know, Jimmy, for a professor you can be pretty goddamn stupid. What do you mean, 'if you were married'? Do you think that if that was Mattie out there, you'd be one bit more distraught than I am right now?"

: : :

Sometime in the night Hart woke. He was on the cot in Jimmy's room. He could hear the regular, heaving breathing of a sleeping man. He sat up. Jennie was dying, might be dead already, and not even Jimmy Creighton was prepared to accord him the rights of the aggrieved. They had all decided that Jennie was Cou'n Hart's nigger wench. Not that they would have used those words, but that's what they thought.

Listen, he wanted to tell them, you think you know what color she is? She is many colors. It depends on the light and on her temperature and mood and what part of her body. She is the color of pears and ribbon cane molasses and rye whiskey in a glass. The skin of her back in the late afternoon sun is the color of honey poured down the valley of her backbone, and the small of her back gathers to the richness of scuppernongs. But her belly when she stood waist-deep in the Black Gall one morning shone like ivory. The tendrils of hair upon her neck are as black as the hair below her navel. And there is a particular rose that we found in Sallie's garden that is exactly the color of the inside of her mouth. Listen: Once when she was a child a playmate pushed her down and she fell upon an old plow point and I am the only man on the face of the earth who knows where the scar is. I would like for y'all to know these things so you could understand my right to be at her bedside. I have nursed her. Listen: When the family was gone to Glenn Springs one summer—the summer of 1914, I think—I found her in a fever, vomiting in her bed, and I changed her linens and held her on the chamber pot and emptied her slops and then I bathed her and brushed her teeth. I could tell you all her smells. We made love one afternoon in the greasy-smelling darkness of the smokehouse, standing with our feet wide apart, our heads among the swinging hams, and I thought that my knees would buckle, but she held me to her and not with her arms but by the urgency of her desire. And once, in the spring of 1912, I put her on my mare and took her out to the river and showed her a fawn in a canebrake and the look on her face when she saw it was the true Jennie revealed. I know her better than God. She has gnawed my earlobes and trimmed my toenails and inspected every inch of me for ticks when I've come out of the woods. By virtue of that degree of knowledge do I claim the right, yet here I sit, like any distant cousin, waiting for word of her death. But it is only for her sake that I suffer this condition, not for mine or for your comfort, for if, by walking into her room right now and lifting her in my arms and sucking the germs from her fevered mouth, I could save her life, don't think for a moment that I would hesitate. One Sunday morning before Johnny died we came upon a pair of fox, in a pine grove back of the Joint Stock field, and the vixen was crouched head down, her blond tail lifted to the side, and the dog fox, springing on stiffened legs and yipping with delight, leapt into a shaft of sun and his tail caught fire, and we yipped too and it was as one person laughing. And two nights after that I lay asleep in her bed, alone in her cabin, and I dreamed that I was burning off the woods, dragging a burning rope through pine straw, and the rope became a fox with his tail on fire and he set the room ablaze and I awoke to Jennie tugging at my buckle and we laughed again just as we had yipped with the fox and I believed then, and I still do, that she had been inside my dream and somehow dreamed it with me.

JIM CREIGHTON

*T*he boredom of Christmas afternoon, like a fine dust suspended, spread throughout the rooms of the house. The candles on the tree were extinguished, the men stretched out for naps, and the children, their presents cast aside, whined that there was nothing left to do. The weather had warmed up and rain was expected.

It was Sallie who saved the day. "I have a good idea," she said, and the children perked up. "Let's spend the rest of the afternoon making presents for Jennie, and then, just after dark, we'll all light candles and take our presents out to her house and sing Christmas carols."

The suggestion was met with enthusiasm. The rest of the cloudy day was devoted to clipping and pasting, collecting pecans and walnuts from forgotten Christmas stockings, baking cookies, and, in the case of Wade and Clara's Julia, composing a poem. Lois helped with the wrapping and Mattie with the carols, making sure that the children knew the words of first stanzas at least, and as the windows grew dark the children gathered in the hall, crowded against the door, stamping their feet.

"Now listen," Sallie said to the impatient little throng. "Does everyone have a candle? And be sure you have your mittens on or the melting wax will burn your hands. We'll light our candles on the porch."

Sallie opened the door and the crowd surged out, overwhelming Hart Bonner, who was just coming in. He was bringing a fruitcake from his sister Hattie.

As though we need anything else to eat, Jim Creighton thought.

"Oh Hart," Sallie said, "you're just in time. We need your voice for the caroling."

Hart glanced desperately about him, like a cornered animal seeking a way of escape. He had not shaved in three days at least.

"No ma'am, Miss Sallie, I'd better run. I didn't mean to crash your party."

"Nonsense, Hart. We're all going over to Jennie's to sing Christmas carols. Just set Hattie's cake in the hall."

This won't suit him, Jim thought, not being one for group activity, especially having to do with Jennie.

"No running now," Sallie said. "We're all going to walk to Jennie's like ladies and gentlemen. But no one is to go inside. Is that understood? Jennie is still very sick. So here's what we're going to do. We'll put our presents on a tray and give the tray to Delia to take in to Jennie. Then we'll sing three Christmas carols and yell with all our might, 'Merry Christmas, Jennie!' And when I say it's time to leave, I don't want to hear any argument."

It was fully dark by the time the last candle was lighted and the little troop, attended by as many grown-ups, arrived with their carefully protected flames at Jennie's door. Sallie knocked, Delia opened the door, and Lois presented the tray of gifts. Delia, all smiles and nods, said she'd be right back and closed the door with her foot. When it opened again a minute or two later, it opened wide and Jennie was sitting up in bed. Framed by the rectangle of the doorway, she was leaning back against a hill of pillows, her hair tied up in a ribboned cap, her dark eyes bigger and rounder than ever. Too big, Jim thought, and then realized that her face and throat were wasted. What concerned him even more was the stillness of her features. She lay as unresponsive as a wax dummy. He wondered if Hart could see her too. He was tall enough to look over the heads in front of him, but he was standing too far to the right to see through the door.

With Mattie leading, the little choir trudged through the first stanza of "O Little Town of Bethlehem," all faces fixed on her ardently swinging hand, and then plunged into "Joy to the World." They were halfway through when it occurred to Jim that Hart was not singing. In fact, he had backed out of the wedge of light that fell through Jennie's door and was standing in the darkness.

The last carol was "Silent Night."

> Round yon Virgin Mother and Child
> Holy Infant so tender and mild,
> Sleep in heavenly peace.

With Mattie's help they made it through the second stanza and then attempted the last. Suddenly, from out of the darkness, rose Hart's clear tenor:

> Silent night, holy night,
> Son of God, love's pure light,

By its pure and resonant tone, it hushed the sweet, uncertain babble and overwhelmed the off-key adults. One by one, voices faltered, ceased, until Hart was singing alone:

> Radiant beams from thy holy face,
> With the dawn of redeeming grace;
> Jesus, Lord at thy birth,
> Jesus, Lord at thy birth.

Jim was amazed that he knew the words.

When the last note had faded, the children screamed, "Merry Christmas, Jennie!" Delia thanked them and said goodnight, and the crowd started back to the house, but Hart lingered in the darkness outside Jennie's door. When he failed to appear later for coffee, his absence went unmentioned.

: : :

Late that night, as Mattie and Jim were getting undressed, Mattie said, "Don't Hart have a beautiful voice? I'm so glad he finally let us hear it. I hope he believes what he was singing."

"He was singing to Jennie," Jim said. "To let her know that he was out there. About like a dog howling at the moon."

Mattie laughed. "Mind what you say, dear. You know that old saying."

"About a dog that howls on Christmas day?"

"Don't that mean that he'll go mad in the coming year?"

Part *Three*

HART

The fields were too muddy for bird hunting, but Jim and Hart, frustrated after four days of rain, went anyway. Hart's dog, a rangy pointer of mediocre talent, overran three coveys and no telling how many singles. Still, when they had opportunity, he and Jim shot well. By midafternoon they had bagged nine birds, but now a cold wind was kicking up, and they decided to call it a day. Back at the buggy, Hart handed his gun up to Jim and lifted the wet, panting dog into the back. With trousers wet to the crotch and boots clumped with mud, he pulled himself up onto the cold leather seat. "How about it, professor? Will that do you?"

Jim reckoned it would have to. The holiday had been a disappointment as far as quail hunting was concerned. His illness had kept him in the house until Christmas day, and the day after that the rain had begun—a slow, cold drizzle just above the freezing point that continued into the weekend. By Sunday he and Mattie had been ready to return to Spartanburg, but the roads were not yet passable. Today, with skies clearing, he and Hart had been able at last to get out and follow a dog.

"Y'all still planning to leave tomorrow?" Hart asked.

"At first light if the roads look good. Now that Jennie's on the mend, there's no need to stay, and I have a good deal of preparation for my classes."

Hart had heard nothing of Jennie's progress since Christmas night. Afraid that he had worn out his welcome, he kept his distance from Sallie's house, declining even to take the mail to her door. Until now Jim had not mentioned Jennie all day, and Hart, assuming that to mean good news, had not asked. "She's up and about, is she?"

"She hasn't come up to the house yet," Jim said. "Mattie says she's still mighty weak. You always worry about a relapse, but I think she's taking it slowly. She had a close call."

"Damn close."

For the better part of an hour the men rode in silence. From time to time the raised top of the buggy caught a strong gust that rattled the frame and knocked the vehicle back on its heels. "We're in for a bitter night," Hart said.

They heard the regular blows of an ax before they reached the yard, the soft clonks of Nathaniel splitting firewood. Hart fished a handful of ruffled, blood-matted quail from the generous pocket of his jacket—three, four, five—the ones he had killed. "Put these with yours, Jimmy, and suggest to Sallie, if you will, that Jennie might like some for supper. Jennie's mighty fond of birds and gravy."

Jim consented to Hart's request. "But won't you come in for a minute, long enough for a cup of coffee?"

The men left their muddy boots on the back porch and entered the kitchen in stocking feet. Wilma was standing at the cast-iron stove. Jim asked if there was coffee in the pot, would she please heat it up. He was placing the birds on the table under the window when Sallie came bustling in, followed by John Baird.

"Why Wade Creighton won't get a telephone is beyond me. Go crank the automobile, son. I'm going to have to get you to run me over there. And tell Delia we're ready. We'll drop her off on the way." Sallie turned to Jim Creighton. "Jimmy, what on earth are you doing with those birds?"

"Jennie's supper, Sister. I was just getting ready to ask Nathaniel to pick them. There's enough here for y'all too."

"Not tonight," Sallie said. "Wilma's just put spoon bread in the oven. Birds would be too rich for Jennie anyway. And get them off that table, please. Wilma, we should be back by the time that's ready, but be sure you keep an eye on it now."

Hart stood, his coffee steaming but untouched. If Sallie was taking Delia home, Jennie would be alone until her supper was ready. Unless Mattie went out to keep her company. Hart would take that risk. He had not seen her, except from a distance Christmas night, since Sunday a week ago. But he would have to leave now. He took a sip of coffee, scalding the roof of his mouth, then extended his hand to Jim. "I'm afraid I have to run, professor. I'm glad you're feeling better. Tell Miss Mattie goodbye for me."

"I wouldn't even consider such a thing. She would skin me alive. Just hold on a minute and I'll run get her."

The southwestern sky glowed a soft yellow through the live oak branches, and dead leaves went skittering across the yard between the back porch and Jennie's cabin. John Baird was cranking the Model T when Hart stepped into his muddy boots. Jim and Mattie came out onto the porch. Mattie was shivering. "Hart Bonner," she said, "you ought to be ashamed of yourself, leaving without kissing me goodbye."

Hart lowered his unshaved cheek to Mattie's soft peck. "Just didn't want to disturb you, Miss Mattie. Y'all have a safe trip home now, you hear. And happy New Year."

Delia had emerged from Jennie's cabin and stood waiting by the automobile. Sallie came out onto the porch, pulling on her gloves. Hart had wanted to start before they did, but it was too late now. Then Mattie said, "I think I'll go too if y'all have room. I just need to get my coat."

"Well, do hurry, Mattie," Sallie said. "I want to get back in time to take Jennie her supper."

That was all the lead Hart needed. Mattie had not yet returned when he headed into the avenue. They would pass him before they reached Wade's house, but all that mattered was that they see him headed home.

He was almost to the big road when he heard the automobile coming up behind. He looked back through the isinglass window at the approaching headlamps. When he turned back, a horse and buggy had entered the avenue up ahead. It was Tison. Now what was that old fool up to at this time of day?

Hart had not seen his brother since that fiasco at the table, though he'd heard that Tison had stopped briefly at their mother's house on Christmas day, after he himself had finished dinner and returned to the cottage. Just yesterday the old woman had grumbled about Tison's not coming by more often; she had business to discuss with him. Now here he was, blocking the avenue. His horse whinnied and stepped forward until he was neck and neck with Red. Hart could not see Tison's face in the shadow of the buggy, and he doubted that he could make himself heard above the automobile, but he yelled anyway. To no avail. He could not believe such pigheadedness in a grown man.

John Baird came walking up. "What's wrong?"

"His majesty yonder is too high and mighty to yield the road. Run tell him, son, that your mother's in a hurry."

TISON

*T*ison's leg was extended straight out in front, lying along a one-by-six that rested on the dash. He had thrown a blanket over it, but even so it hurt, and he was cold. He was in a hurry to catch John Earl before he finished feeding up the stock and left for home, and here was that damned mail buggy filling the avenue. And Hugh Creighton behind it. Well, they could both back up. The horse he was driving had not come with a reverse gear, never willingly retreated.

Hart yelled. Tison could not understand what he said, but he could guess. Tison gestured, back up. It would be a tight squeeze but they had room. He shook his fist.

Was that John Baird speaking with Hart? Where had he come from? Now he was headed toward Tison, running his hand along the flank of the horse.

Five sons old Frank Bonner had sired, and this boy the only male of his generation to carry on the name. Johnny's boy, but he favored the Creightons. After Johnny died, Tison had tried to be a father to the kid, but the kid had never taken to him, not like he had to Hart. Hart had always spent time with him, of course, something Tison had never gotten the hang of. Children made him nervous. "Uncle Tison," the boy was saying, "Mama's in a hurry to get to Aunt Clara's. She wondered if you could back out and let us by?"

That put a different face on the situation. The boy must be driving the automobile. Maybe backing up in close quarters was too much to expect. And since it was Miss Sallie. Tison hauled back on the lines. "Back up, sir," he said. The horse danced in its harness, crowhopped, balked, took a step backward. With each lurch, Tison felt his leg.

Hart rolled by without a word of gratitude, followed by the automobile.

Tison had not shown his face at Sallie's house since that embarrassing episode at the table, when Hart scandalized the household. Yet here the fellow was, as shameless as a roadside dog. Hanging around the kitchen, Tison would wager, hoping to see that girl. From talk around the barn, Tison had gathered she was getting better.

The avenue stretched before him, a dark tunnel in the twilight. He flicked the horse's rump with the whip, and the horse picked up his pace.

The window of Jennie's cabin glowed a warm yellow as Tison rolled into Sallie's yard and turned the horse's head toward the barn. He could hear an ax chopping wood. Nathaniel, he reckoned, laying in a supply for the night. People were going to need it.

The door of the cabin opened. Someone stepped out into the dooryard, an old man, it looked like, long coat and hat, leaning on a cane. Who in the hell could that be? Tison wondered. He stopped the buggy. The person turned to face him. A red scarf was wrapped around the face, so that only the eyes were showing. They burned in the dusk. Tison recognized them. He had not seen her except in public situations since the accident, and then only a time or two. Confronted by her now, he found it hard to breathe. Heat rose from his neck, blurring his vision. He was sorry he had stopped, but he couldn't ride on now. That would look like shame. But if he remained, he would have to speak, and he could think of nothing to say.

The girl turned and started toward the big house, one hand on the cane, the other holding her hat in place, and the wind whipped at her coattails.

"Look here, girl." Tison's voice rasped high against the wind.

She stopped. Looking over her shoulder, still holding her hat in place, she said, "You talking to me?"

It was her tone as much as anything that flew in his face. By an effort he suppressed his irritation. Nothing to be gained by getting her riled up now, as sick as she had been. Managing a friendly voice, he said, "Now what kind of way is that? Here I drag my poor old leg all the way over here just to see how you coming along, and you speak rude words to me. I thought you were raised better than that."

Jennie made a little curtsey, as gracefully as she could with the cane, and let the scarf slip from her face. "I'm sorry, sir. I'm doing fine, thank you."

"Now that's better, ain't it?"

Tison could not think of a way to keep the conversation going, but he was not ready yet to let her go. She wouldn't leave until he dismissed her. He liked that, enjoyed holding her there, dependent on his pleasure. He smiled down at her. He had never understood why she rejected him. He might be getting a little long in the tooth, but he was still worth twenty Hart Bonners, hadn't he told her that? He would have let her name her price. The memory of her letter took the smile from his face. That a nigger girl would have said such things to him caused him to gasp. He was breathing hard.

"I'd better be getting back in, sir, cold as it is."

She was still clapping that idiotic hat to her head, leaning on her cane, and the red scarf fluttered in the wind like a pennant. Chilled to the bone, she was. Served her right.

She turned toward the cabin.

"Don't you walk off while I'm talking to you," Tison said. His voice was shrill, a rasp cutting through the wind. "Who do you think you are?"

She paid no attention but continued toward her door.

"Answer me something, girl. If it ain't money, then what is it? Hanh? Tell me that."

That stopped her. "I don't know what you talking about," she said.

"Sho you do. I'm talking about Mr. Hart, talking about your beau. Figure he must be a real bo' hog to satisfy a wench like you."

Jennie came toward the buggy, three steps, her cane jabbing the sandy ground. She was close enough now for him to touch her with the buggy whip and still she took another step. She looked up at him from under the brim of the crumpled fedora, and her face was all ablaze. "You wretched old goddamn stiff-leg," she said, and then she spat. She spat at the ground beneath the buggy, turned, and walked with purpose toward the cabin. Entering, she slammed the door behind her and slid home the bar.

Tison sat, cold and stunned. The wind moaned in the tall pines. It was dark now. He sawed the head of the horse to the right and lashed its rump with the whip.

HART

 art parked the buggy in a grove of pines less than a quarter of a mile from Jennie's cabin. He whistled the dog Flint from his bed in the back and sent him off in the dark to find his way home. Then from a fifth of whiskey he had stowed beneath the seat he took a long drink.

The path was familiar, the path his feet had made and memorized through countless pitch-black nights. There was just enough light in the woods for him to avoid wet pine boughs, but even so he brushed against them time and again, soaking his trousers.

When he came to the edge of Sallie's barnyard, he stopped and took the bottle from his coat pocket, unscrewed the cap, and took another swallow. Jennie's windows were dark, but that did not surprise him. She was probably napping. He slipped like the shadow of a deer across the open space between the woods and the barn and then along the hedgerow to her cabin, but the back door stopped him. He was actually about to knock, such a stranger he felt, but, thinking her asleep, he let himself in quietly.

The odor of illness in that unaired room did not surprise him either, but he was unprepared for the chill. Jennie lay asleep, on her stomach as far as he could tell, and the fire had died down to an ashy bed of coals. He stuck his head out the door he'd just entered. A stack of new split wood, clean and pale, stood against the wall. He loaded four or five sticks into the cradle of his right arm, re-entered, and laid them in a rick. Kneeling, he blew upon the coals, spraying feathery ash, and the coals came to life, igniting the dry, resinous pine, and firelight was soon dancing upon the chairs and the lacquered table by the window and the little tinselled pine at the foot of the bed where Jennie lay. Hart stood with his hands to the flames. He thought he might touch her on the shoulder, to see how deeply she was sleeping.

And then she sobbed—one racking, involuntary gasp, like the last convulsive sob of a heartbroken child.

Hart was at her bedside, on his knees, his hands gripping her shoulders. "Jennie. It's me."

She started, rose and turned. Like a person terrified, she folded herself into his large embrace, hiding. Her frailty alarmed him. Fabric bunched in his hands. He had no idea what she was doing with a dress on. And why had she been lying on the bed instead of in it, beneath the covers?

Hart took Jennie's face in his hands. Firelight pooled in her swimming eyes and glared on her raw cheekbones. He wiped her tears with his thumbs, dried his thumbs in her hair, placed his lips on her forehead.

"Now what is this? What's wrong?"

She freed her face from his hands, hid it against his shoulder, and shook her head.

He insisted that she tell him.

"I said a terrible thing," she confessed, her voice muffled by the folds of his coat.

"To who?"

"Who don't matter. The book say thou shalt not take the name of the Lord thy God in vain."

She spoke in a haunted whisper, almost catatonic.

Hart took her face in his hands again, held it at arm's length.

"Now listen, Jennie," he said. "Look at me. Tell me what happened."

"Why? You got the power to forgive? Don't nobody need to know but Jesus."

"Has somebody been here? Who's been here?"

Jennie looked away, her eyes downcast. Her neck rose like a thin stalk from the loose, high collar of her dress.

Then Hart remembered the encounter in the avenue. By God, he thought. "Has Tison been here? Is that who it was?"

Jennie did not answer.

Hart was growing impatient with her remorse. If she had cussed Tison, Hart was sure he had done something to deserve it, and he wanted to know what. He removed his hunting jacket and laid it across the foot of the bed. "What was he doing here?"

"I don't know."

"He came here to the cabin?"

"He just come driving up. While I was out front," she said.

"What were you doing out?"

"Cause I wanted to. All cooped up in this nasty old room, can't even get out of bed without my mama got to say her little something. I went to tell Nathaniel to chop me some wood."

"What did he want?"

"He just being Mr. Tison."

"That's bad enough by itself. What did he say?"

"He say he just come to see how I was doing."

"Was that all?"

The question seemed to awaken Jennie from the trance that had held her. She looked around the cabin as though to make sure that no one was hiding in the dark, flickering shadows, and for the first time since Hart entered, she seemed to recognize him, to relax in the warmth of the man who had shared her bed for eleven years. The air between them stirred with old intimacies, mutually acknowledged. She touched his cheek. Her fingertips were warm.

"You got to promise, Hart. Trouble the last thing I be needing now."

"I promise," he said.

"I hope you mean it."

"Go ahead."

Jennie related the account in broken, halting phrases, up to the point at which she, half frozen, had turned away. "And that's when he said what he did," she told Hart. "That made me cuss him." She said that last with a tone of finality, as though relieved to come at last to the end of a tale that she had never wanted to get started on in the first place.

Hart waited, but Jennie was finished.

"Well, what was it? What did he say?"

"Just something nasty, like Mr. Coe that time."

"About you and me?"

Jennie looked pale. In the dark, flickering room her eyes shone as wide and frightened as those of a rabbit caught in a rabbit box.

"I want you to tell me, Jennie. No matter how bad it is. I need to know," Hart said.

"Let me have a taste of what you got in your pocket."

Hart reached for the coat, patted it to find the bottle. She drank from it straight and returned the bottle to him.

"You promised now. No trouble."

"All right."

"He said you must be a bo' hog to keep me satisfied."

Hart felt as though he had just stumbled onto something dead in the woods, like a deer or a pig, very close, and the odor gagged him. "That rotten son of a bitch," he said.

This time she didn't ask for the bottle but simply reached and found it in his hand.

"You go easy with that now."

"That's what he said. And that's when I shamed myself. I been standing out in that cold wind, freezing to death, and just as quick as Mr. Tison say what he did, I taste the devil in my mouth, and it felt like my face caught all on fire with hate."

"So that's when you cussed him?"

"I spit on the ground, right next to the wheel of his buggy, and I cussed him for a wretched old goddamn stiff-leg."

As though the tale had consumed the last of her resolve, Jennie crumpled. Hart caught what was left of her, held her as she softly wept, spent. He could feel her bones, her shoulder blades and rib cage as she shuddered.

"There now," he said. "Stop crying now. Tison's been called worse things than that."

Jennie did stop. She pulled away from Hart's embrace and turned her face toward the wall. "That ain't what I mean."

It was the way she said it that alarmed him—neither cold nor angry but weary with resignation, as though she had just given up. Given up on him, on them.

"You're weak, baby. You shouldn't have gotten out of bed. You've been a very sick lady."

"I'm sick of men," she said.

Like a shotgun blast, that declaration blew him across the room. Without knowing exactly how he got there, he found himself standing before the fire, his back to her, seeking warmth, seeking words. But nothing came to him in that silent room but the pop and crackle of the dry pine and the loud ticktock of the clock that was staring back at him from the mantel. The whistle of the wind outside made him shiver. A gust down the chimney flattened the flames and blew smoke into the room. The clock ticktocked on. Sallie had given that clock to Jennie on her birthday, he couldn't remember how many years ago. He thought of the old Dutch clock that watched the suicidal duel between the gingham dog and the calico cat, and he smiled bitterly to think of the tumblings this one had witnessed. He fancied that the hours of their life together, lived mostly in this room, were somehow registered and stored in a secret compartment deep inside the timepiece.

A blast of wind struck the cabin, causing it to shudder on its piers. Twenty past six.

The clock was ordinary, except for Roman numerals on its face, plain and inexpensive, but its chime had a sweet tone. When Jennie had first opened it you would have thought from her reaction that it was carved from ivory and set with precious stones. When they were alone that night, she had shown Hart the little door in back that opened upon the compartment where the key was kept. That was the cleverest thing she'd ever seen. And she had turned the hands to make the hour chime.

Just a girl she had been.

At first the loud ticktock had bothered him. Even in bed, he had been unable to hear anything else. One night he had risen from her embrace and said, "That damned thing is timing me."

Jennie had laughed. "Maybe timing just what you need."

If he could only talk to her—not now, not here in this abominable sickroom where you could not think for fear of some busybody coming through that door any second—but outside, in warmer weather, with nothing to do for an entire afternoon but talk things right again. He would talk her back to who she used to be, before Tison and Leonard Coe and Joe Grant, before church and all that Jesus business, back to the girl who had asked him one night, many years ago, "How are y'all kin to us?"

Hart discovered that he was still gripping the bottle. He removed the cap and took a drink.

He loved her. He would make her understand, by God— make her remember that she loved him too.

He turned. The room was darker now, the flames subdued to fiery orange. The little house creaked and groaned from the bitter cold outside. She was lying on the bed, face down, as he had found her when he came in. He spoke her name: "Jennie."

She made no response.

He moved across the room, to the foot of the bed, and sat down. He reached out to place his hand on the curve of her hip— that flesh as familiar as his own—but stopped. It seemed to him that familiarity was no longer his right, at least not now.

"Jennie, I want you to listen to me. I'm confused about some things, I'll admit, but you're acting like a stranger, like someone I don't know, and that scares me. It really does. But, listen now, no matter what, we're still us. We have to remember that. Still Hart and Jennie. And we're right here where we've always been. Can't you sit up and look at me?"

She lifted herself onto her elbows, turned and with one easy motion swung her legs off the bed. She was sitting now, beside him but with a space between. He noticed that she had accomplished that shift without touching him.

"We need to talk, Jennie. I don't know how long it's been since we really had a chance to talk things out."

"Talking's just your way of seeing what you think," she said. "I'm too wore out, Hart."

"Then you talk. Tell me what you're thinking. I don't know what you're thinking any more."

"I ain't got it worked out in my mind yet. Let me get my strength back. We'll talk another time. You need to be getting on now."

"I can't leave like this, Jennie. Not without something to take with me."

Even in the dark he could see the change that came over her, or maybe he just felt it, the way she suddenly grew more present, focused, and he dug in his heels.

"All right," she said, her voice at last composed and confident. "But it ain't going to suit you."

"I'm listening."

"The last thing I recollect from before I got sick was when I went to church to hear Brother Simmons."

"You don't remember that I was there, that I brought you home?" he said.

"That's what they tell me, but I'm talking about me now. Ain't that what you ask me? Well, I went through the fire, Hart, out of my head and burning up, lost track of day and night, I don't know how long. Then the fever broke, and it felt like I had come back from a long trip. Everything looked different. It ain't you,

Hart. It's me. Who I used to be was wrong. Maybe it took Mr. Tison to show me that. But that old self is dead. I think it must have burned up in the fever. It's like that old spiritual, Angel in the heaven done change' my name. I'm still getting acquainted with who I am now, but all I know for sure is Jesus."

Hart groaned. "And so that's all you know?"

"He came to me when I was sick," she said.

"Oh really. And how did he get in? Did he knock on the door or come down the chimney?"

"I don't know but he stood right there at the foot of my bed and he filled this room with light."

Hart got to his feet. He wanted to smash through something, to swing out, as he had when he was a boy on a rope swing over the swimming hole on the Black Gall, and slam his body into and through the walls that hemmed him in, banging from wall to wall like a wrecking ball until he demolished all barriers or obliterated himself.

The door rattled but he paid it no attention. The cabin was creaking and groaning like a ship in a storm. But then it rattled with purpose. He looked at the door. Jennie had slid home the bar. Of course she had, against Tison's outraged face. Then above the wind he heard Sallie's voice: "Jennie. For goodness' sake, open this door."

Jennie leapt from the bed, frantic, and pointed Hart toward the back door.

"Just a minute," she yelled. Then to Hart she mouthed the word "go."

"I'll come back later," he said.

She put her finger to her lips, frowned, and shook her head. "My mama," she whispered.

"When then?"

By way of answer, she pointed emphatically, her arm straight, like that of a sibyl or an angel, and it seemed to Hart that he was being banished, against his will, from the only place that felt like home. For one mad instant, he considered staying, presenting himself to Sallie when she came in, let her think what she wanted.

As Jennie slid back the bar, he jammed his hat down on his head and slipped out the back, into the windy freezing dark, and plunged into the woods, heedless of his way, his wet feet too numb to feel the ground. Needled pine boughs lashed his face, and twice he stumbled, sprawling headlong. He had left behind his liquor bottle and his hunting jacket—soft corduroy with feathers of bobwhite quail stuck to it—but he was not suffering from the cold. He had left behind the only life he knew, the life contained in Jennie's cabin, and he was walking away from it as hard as he could go, with no assurance that he would ever enter her door again. Yet he had no clear idea of where he was headed. He had to get Red home—he knew that—out of harness and put up for the night. The poor animal must be miserable. But beyond taking care of the horse, he had no certain purpose. Wherever his footsteps led, to whatever brink of fire or flood, there he would go, there and beyond.

He stumbled upon the buggy before he expected to. The horse was standing with head lowered, an index of his misery. Hart had never felt much affection for the old gelding, not as he did for Cassandra; Red had kicked him more than once, and his shoulder bore a discolored scar that he would take to his grave. But seeing the animal in such a wretched state, Hart wrapped his arms around the neck and buried his face.

: : :

Flint came out of the dark to meet the buggy when Hart pulled up in front of the cottage. "I bet you're hungry too," he said.

He took care of the animals, feeding Flint and the old setter Dan and the puppy in her pen. Though Red's eye showed resentment at having been left so long in the windy dark, Hart gave him a pan of oats and a good rubdown. Then he went inside. Without a word to Pinck, who was sitting in his chair by the fire, Hart entered his bedroom. From the wardrobe he took a wool jacket and from the drawer of his bedside table his Smith and

Wesson .38. He loaded the revolver and dropped it into his coat pocket.

The automobile, a 1913 Model T inherited from Smith, sat parked for long periods in an old carriage house. Chickens walked about on the torn fabric top. It was used only on those infrequent days when the weather was too wet for Hart to deliver mail in the buggy. It was never easy to start. He switched on the ignition, opened the throttle, and turned the crank. It took several tries, but at last the engine coughed, caught, and sputtered into action.

Hart turned left out of his mother's avenue, north toward Tison's house, and left behind all need to understand, any need to explain. His way was clear, a highway that would lead him to his moment, his ultimate opportunity to protect and reclaim.

TISON

*T*he dark, empty house creaked with cold, and gusts of
wind rattled the windowpanes. Tison put a pot of water on the
stove and went to fetch the chess set from the parlor. He and
Bones would have to play in the kitchen this week. He couldn't
heat the whole damn house. Last week's game — Christmas
Eve — had been suspended because of the hour, with Tison in
trouble. He studied the board, the chessmen fine pieces of onyx
and ivory that had belonged to his father. The old man had
taken the set with him when the family fled from the Yankees —
one of the few artifacts of that opulent world that survived the
war. Everything else had been burned up or, in the case of the
silver, dug up and stolen. Nine pieces remained on the board,
Tison's the four white, and he had lost his queen. Bones could
checkmate in four moves or less. Tison picked up the board,
careful to keep the pieces from sliding. He wondered if Bones
would notice. Probably so. An unworthy notion anyway.

Tison placed the board on the kitchen table. The water on the
stove was boiling. He added four tablespoons of oatmeal to it
and slid the pot to the edge of the burner. They would not play
until tomorrow night — their weekly date — but he wanted to

consider the possibilities. There may be a way out yet. If he could just slide his castle to the right. The prescribed movements of the various pieces always afforded him a measure of comfort. He wished people were so constrained.

Tison prepared for himself a bowl of the hot cereal, poured a cup of coffee, and sat down to his supper. He had wanted to tell John Earl to be ready to leave for Carthage at daylight—he was taking the wagon to get a load of guano and he would need the Negro's help—but in the heat of his rage he had forgotten his purpose. He was halfway down the avenue—too late to turn back— before he remembered. That mistake was liable to cost him two hours in getting away tomorrow.

If Jennie Mae had agreed to work for him, he would have built her a nice house out back.

Hart was a sorry man, always had been, a whiner as a child, a piddler ever since. For the life of him, Tison couldn't understand it. A girl as apt as Jennie Mae, and she didn't have the sense to see how much better off she would have been with him. He would have bought her things.

If she had treated him more kindly, he would not have had to speak so harshly to her. He hated for her to think of him as that kind of man.

Tison washed out his bowl and put it away, turned down the lamp, and stepped out onto the back porch to pee. God, it was freezing. A gibbous moon was rising in the west, out over the river swamp, and its thin light made him feel even colder. It shone on the brass headlamps of his automobile. Though the machine was backed into the barn, the water in the radiator was likely to freeze. He reckoned he'd better drain it. He wished he had thought of that earlier. He hated having to drag his leg out into that cold.

: : :

Tison spread two extra blankets across his bed and turned back the covers. He undressed and removed his glasses and put on a flannel nightshirt. His left leg from the knee down was hairless and discolored. He rubbed it vigorously to keep up his circulation. Then he blew out the candle. The sheets were icy, but it felt good to lie down and stretch out. But his head was cold. He ought to get up and find a nightcap or his old bald scalp might ice over before morning. Stockings too, he reckoned, as long as he was up.

He struck a match and lit the candle, set it on the dresser, and opened a drawer. Was that somebody knocking on his door? He paused and listened. Yes, no doubt about it. Now who in the hell at this hour? Not Bones. Bones would have come around back.

He stepped into his trousers, stuffing in his nightshirt, and looped a suspender over his left shoulder. He couldn't think of any business too urgent to wait for morning. His vest lay on the trunk at the foot of the bed. He withdrew his watch from its pocket. Quarter past eight. Maybe something had happened at the big house. You never could tell. "Just a minute," he shouted, though he knew that his visitor could not hear him above the wind. He pulled on his stockings, stepped into his shoes, and took the candlestick. "Coming," he shouted.

He had reached the door to the hall before he remembered his pistol. Limping across the room, he took it from the drawer of his bedside table and stuck it in the pocket of his trousers. The rapping on the door continued. Lifting the candlestick before him, he lighted his halting way up the hall. "Hold your damn horses," he grumbled. It couldn't be niggers. There wasn't one in Heyward County who would come to his front door, night or day. When he reached the door, he yelled, "Who is it?"

He did not understand the reply.

"Who?"

Again the response was muffled, but something made him think of Hart. He peered through one of the small panes to the right of the door, but the reflection of candlelight prevented him from seeing. Transferring the candle to his left hand, he unlocked the door and turned the knob. He lifted the candle but the screen caught the light. "Who is it?"

"Bad news, old man."

Tison recognized the voice, saw the striking tongue of orange, and felt that a mule had kicked him in the chest. The blow spun him all the way around, but he kept his feet, falling into the door and slamming it shut. Hardly able to breathe, he reached into his pocket, but the pistol snagged on fabric, would not pull free. Glass shattered, a windowpane. He reeled down the hall. *Blam!* The sound of the shot rang in the closed space, knocking him to his knees. He struggled to get to his feet. *Blam!* The noise was deafening. *Blam!* The hall reverberated. He reached for the pistol in his pocket. *Blam!* A blow to his lower back knocked the breath from his chest. They were shooting him to pieces. If he could just get his pistol. He rose to his knees, got one heavy foot underneath him. If he could just stand up. *Blam!* His leg was knocked out from under him. He fell across the threshold of his bedroom. He thought it was his bedroom. He reached for his pistol but his hand refused to move. Maybe he'd just rest a while, but God it was cold. If he could slide that castle, he might protect his king.

JIM CREIGHTON

A large brown bowl of hominy sat on the kitchen table steaming up the windowpanes. Sausage was frying on the stove, and Sallie Bonner—floury arms and apron—was putting a pan of biscuits in the oven. Outside, the sun was just touching the frosty tops of the pines. Jim Creighton was pouring his first cup of coffee. The weather had frustrated his plans again. He and Mattie had meant to leave on Friday, but the rain had started Christmas night and not let up till Saturday. In addition to ruining the roads, it had kept him out of the field. So when Hart had urged him to stay over and hunt on Monday, he had not put up much of an argument. He didn't like to travel on Sunday anyway. Now here it was Tuesday morning and colder than he had ever seen it in Heyward County. He and Hugh had drained the radiators of the automobiles last night, and a good thing they had. The glass of water on his bedside table was frozen solid when he woke up, and the thermometer on the back porch was holding at twelve degrees.

"People are being lazy this morning," Sallie said.

"If they could get a whiff of that sausage, they'd be out here in a hurry."

"Well, they'd better get to stirring pretty soon because I'm ready to crack these eggs."

Jim was still in his nightshirt and dressing gown, not inclined to go back up to his freezing room and put on his clothes. It was going to be a lazy morning for them all.

"I wish you'd get Buddy up, Jimmy," Sallie said. "He needs to get started on his chores."

A sharp rap on the outside door startled them both.

"Who on earth?" Sallie said, wiping her hands on her apron.

She opened the door to find a dwarf shrouded in a patchwork quilt, the edges trailing the ground. A murky green scarf was wound around his face, showing only his eyes, and a scarf of red paisley was tied about his head, holding his hat in place. It was old Jonas Stubbs, who lived in Tison Bonner's yard. What they could see of his face was ash-gray.

"Why, Jonas," Sallie said, "what on earth? You come into this kitchen this minute. You must be perished."

But Jonas stood his ground. "Yessum. Somebody need to come right quick and see to Mr. Tison."

"You come on in now and warm by the stove and then you can tell us about Mr. Tison."

Once inside, Jonas kept reaching for his hat only to be reminded each time that it was tied in place by the scarf. "He sick and laying een the floor."

"Oh no. Did he say anything, Jonas?"

"Naw'm, he ain't say nothing. Just laying een the floor."

Jim started from the kitchen but met John Baird in the door. The boy was dressed but hardly awake. "Good morning, son," Jim said. "Jonas here says that your Uncle Tison's sick."

"And Jimmy: knock on Brother's door. Son, you run get Nathaniel to hitch up the surrey. The surrey now, not the buggy. Here, Jonas, drink this coffee."

Jim took the steps two at a time, suddenly invigorated. If Tison was sick why had the old black man not helped him into bed? That "laying een the floor" sounded bad. Like a stroke or a heart attack. The promise of catastrophe had charged the day with meaning. He felt renewed. He rapped at Hugh's door with the authority conferred by the circumstance, then opened it a crack. "Brother, get up. Something's happened to Cou'n Tison. We need to hurry."

Mattie was buried beneath a burden of quilts and comforts, whether awake or asleep Jim couldn't tell. He pulled on whatever garments came to hand—flannel shirt, blue-striped sweater, overcoat. When he returned to the kitchen, Jonas was hugging the stove and Sallie was beside herself. "If I get my hands on that boy, I'm going to skin him alive. Oh Jimmy, do something. I send him out to get Nathaniel and the next thing you know he's tearing across the yard on a mule. Bareback, I'll have you know. And no more dressed for this weather than a grasshopper. Is Brother coming?"

While Jim waited, Jonas warmed up enough to tell how he had sat by the fire listening for Mr. Tison's whoop. It came every morning at six o'clock—or every morning that Tison woke up in his house—and every morning Jonas waited till he heard it to stick his head out the door. And Tison would say, every morning, "Why I have to stand out here and whoop you up after all these years is beyond me. Looks like you could get up here and start my fire without me having to come stand out here and whoop you up." And Jonas, every morning, would say, "Yessuh. I was jes befo' stepping out the door." It was the ritual that started their day.

But this morning, Jonas said, "I wait and wait, huddle up by the fire, and no whoop come. 'Mr. Tison must be refuse to got out of bed,' I say, 'cold as it be this morning.' I hope that the case. But by and by day commence to shine through the cracks, and it come in my head, must be something the matter. 'I better get up and see,' I say, so I wrop up een the quilt and step out the door and do Jedus it feel like I can't catch my breaf, it that cold, and no smoke coming out of Mr. Tison' chimbley. I calls him from the stoop and ain't hear nothing so I goes een the kitchen. Then

I calls from the kitchen and ain't hear nothing. Then I steps into the hall and there he lay, his foots sticking out the door to his room. I call his name. 'Mr. Tison,' I say. But he don't say nothing. That's when I start over here, suh."

: : :

By the time Hugh came down—his hair neatly combed, his tie carefully knotted— the surrey was waiting at the kitchen steps, the sorrel mare Molly standing stiff in her misery. Jim helped the old black man up.

"At least he had the presence of mind to leave the mare for us," Hugh said. "Get up, Molly."

The leather seats were as cold and hard as iron, but Molly moved at a lively clip, warm breath feathering from her nostrils, and the surrey creaked and groaned down the long, shade-latticed avenue. Hugh turned to Jonas on the rear seat. "You say you think he's sick, Jonas?"

Jonas was hunched into a knot. His full gray lips barely moved. "Nawsuh," he said, his voice low and husky. "He ain't sick, suh. Mr. Tison been shot with a gun. All een his back."

Jim was numb with cold, not just his body but his brain and heart also. He turned his head to the breeze and pulled his lapels up in front of his face. Would he have been stunned were he not so cold? The mare clopped along, her hooves ringing on the hard-packed sandy lane. All he could muster was, who? He would react when he got warm. They crossed the big road and entered the freezing sunlight of Tison's avenue. The house among the live oaks up ahead, shuttered and silent, was devoid of holiday decoration.

"Looks like you would have gone over to Mr. Wade's, Jonas, it's so much closer," Jim said.

"Yessuh, but Mr. Wade so tenderhearted. Now go on round back, suh."

John Baird's mule was standing loose in the sun, naked except for a halter and the rope dangling from it. The boy was at the foot of the back steps, on hands and knees in the dirt, retching and drooling.

Hugh caught him by the arm and pulled him to his feet—too roughly, Jim thought. "Have you taken leave of your senses, son? Your poor mother's frantic. Now go on with Jonas and get warmed up. We'll be back out in a minute."

John Baird wiped his face with the sleeve of his thin jacket. He was sobbing or shivering too hard to speak. "Uncle Tison. Dead," he managed to say.

"I know he is, son. Now run on with Jonas."

: : :

Jim had visited Tison's house only a few times through the years, and on those occasions he had entered at the front door and never ventured beyond what Tison called the parlor. He let Hugh lead the way through the kitchen, a room bare and spacious, into the back hall. At the far end panes on either side of the front door—small squares of brightness—admitted light, but it spent itself before it reached their end.

"Open wide that door," Hugh said.

Light from the kitchen revealed a white-stockinged foot. Then they saw the other, shod in a black high-top. As Jonas had reported, the feet extended from the bedroom into the hall. The corpse filled the doorway. Jim and Hugh, braced against the doorjambs, leaned in. Tison Bonner lay face down in a pool of blood that gleamed in the dim light like congealed motor oil. It looked as though he had pulled his trousers on over his nightshirt, for the nightshirt was only partly tucked in. The back was splotched with dark, oily looking stains. Jim knelt beside the legs. The threshold had dammed the pooling blood, held it in the bedroom. The side of the old man's face lay in it, his bristly white mustache, and the eye that Jim could see was wide open.

There was an odor. Not just that of unwashed man flesh but something unexpected, vague but rich and fecal. Jim's empty stomach heaved. He retreated to the kitchen, but a minute later

Hugh called from the front of the house. Jim found him at the door.

"Look at this."

The lowest windowpane on the right was broken out; shards of glass lay on the floor. "Looks like somebody tried to break in."

"But how did they manage to shoot him in the back?" Jim asked.

"He was going back to get his gun," Hugh said.

"You think they shot through this little window light?"

"Look around for shells, but don't touch anything."

Hugh unlocked and opened the door, and light flooded the hall. "Here they are. Out here."

Jim followed his brother through the screen door. Five brass casings lay scattered on the porch.

"And look," Jim said. He put his finger through a hole in the screen, chest-high. "Was this already here?"

"Somebody was trying to break in," Hugh said. "Probably thought that Tison was sleeping over at our place, and when he tried to stop them they shot him. That's exactly what happened. We'd better get back and call Herliss Timmons."

Good, Jim thought. As long as he had something that needed doing he would be all right.

: : :

Like most servant's houses, Jonas's cabin had neither porch nor stoop. Hugh rapped on the rough pine boards of the door, then opened it upon a dark, smoky den, flickering with firelight, for the windows were shuttered tight. John Baird was sitting at the hearth, Jonas on the bed. Jonas stood when the Creighton brothers entered, firelight playing upon his face.

"Are you thawed out yet, son?" Hugh asked. "If you are, go on and tie that mule to the surrey. Jonas, there'll be a crowd of people in and out over the next few days. It would be best for you to lay low. If anybody gives you trouble, you just let me know, you hear? Now as soon as you get warmed up, I want you to light the stove in the kitchen and then go over and tell Mr. Wade. Tell him we'll be back in a little while."

"Yessuh."

Back in the surrey, they headed out Tison's avenue.

"Uncle Hugh, Jonas said they heard an automobile."

"Who did?"

"Jonas and Liza, last night. They said it sounded like it was coming up to Uncle Tison's house and then it turned around and went away."

"You can't put any stock in what a darkie tells you," Hugh said. "Don't you know that? Whoever it was that shot Cou'n Tison can't drive an automobile. I'll warrant you that."

"When did they hear it, son?" Jim asked.

"Right after they went to bed."

"Hello," Hugh said. "Who is this?"

A buggy was turning into the avenue and coming toward them. The horse pulling it looked like Hart's red gelding. Now what can he be up to? Hugh wondered. Hugh pulled over.

Hart drew alongside, his horse blowing plumes of smoky breath. "Mighty airish for a morning ride, gentlemen. Is something wrong?"

Hugh gave Jim a look. After what seemed a long moment, he said, "It's Tison, Hart. He's dead."

Hart's coat collar was turned up, guarding his neck and cheeks, and the brim of his brown fedora was snapped down low. Jim could read little in that hidden face, but he thought he saw a shadow pass across his friend's blue eyes, like the shadow of a moving cloud upon still water. Hart shook his head twice, hard shakes as though he were flinching. "You don't mean it," he said, but his voice betrayed no more than his face.

"He was murdered, Hart."

That jolted Hart out of the cover of his collar. "Murdered? Tison? How could he have been?"

"Somebody shot him, must have been last night," Hugh said.

"Jonas found him first thing this morning and came up our avenue. We're on our way right now to call Herliss Timmons."

Jim wanted to tell Hart that he was sorry, but it didn't seem quite the thing to say. On the other hand, it felt worse to say nothing at all.

"Could you tell anything about who did it?"

"Whoever it was must have come up to the front door. One of the window lights is busted out. Looks to me like they were trying to break in, and Tison must have heard them and gotten up to see, and that's when they shot him. He must have turned and run because they shot him in the back. Several times."

"It ain't like Tison to turn and run."

"Well, he's got three bullet holes in his back, that we could see," Hugh said. "He's lying in the door to his bedroom. Jonas told John Baird that his wife heard an automobile not long after dark, but you can't put stock in that."

"Did they steal anything?"

"Not that we could see. But we didn't really take the time to look."

"If I were you," Hart said, "I'd call the coroner first. His name is Bert Akers. You might know him. He'll have to assemble a jury. Let him get in touch with Herliss. Does Wade know?"

"I sent Jonas to get him. He ought to be over here directly."

"Oh Lord. And I'm the one who'll have to tell Mama."

When the vehicles had parted, Hugh turned to Jim. "Did he ever say what he was doing over here?"

"No, why?"

"He ought to be delivering his mail, this time of day."

"He could have had any number of reasons, I reckon. Tison is his brother, after all."

"Was," Hugh said.

They were almost home when John Baird piped up from the back. "It don't seem right, Uncle Jimmy. Does it to you? I mean, just to leave him lying there. All by himself, I mean."

"He can't be moved, son, until the coroner's jury examines the scene," Hugh said.

"But shouldn't somebody be staying with him?"

The boy's lip was trembling.

"Uncle Wade's on his way over there right now," Jim said. He reached back and put his hand on the boy's skinny knee. "It's going to be all right."

: : :

Hugh called the ladies into the sitting room, away from the ears of the children. The room was dark, its heavy drapes still drawn, but in spite of that and a new fire crackling on the hearth, the chill of night lingered.

Hugh stood with his back to the fire and spoke in a lowered voice, in the manner of a government official who can't suppress completely his pleasure in the opportunity to be important. "It's bad news, I'm afraid."

The response was predictable—shock, dismay, the ladies holding each other.

"But that's not all," Hugh said. "It looks as though Cou'n Tison was shot. Somebody apparently tried to break in and Cou'n Tison was killed trying to stop them."

Expressions of sympathy turned to fear. They wanted to know more. Miss Sadie asked if Wade and Clara were all right.

When Hugh told her that he had sent Jonas to tell Wade, Miss Sadie was outdone. "You mean y'all didn't stop by Wade's yourself? Oh, son. For all we know, they may have tried to break in over there as well."

"I'm sure we would have heard by now, Mama."

"And to think we depended so on Cou'n Tison to keep us from harm," Lois said. "And just look what's happened to him now."

"We've never had any trouble, though, have we?" Sallie asked.

"We've never had a maniac running loose in the neighborhood either."

"Well, we mustn't panic," Sallie said. "Brother will be here for the rest of the week, and you'll stay too, won't you, Jimmy? Surely by then the authorities will have apprehended the person responsible."

"Humph," said Lois. "Hugh don't even own a gun, do you, Hugh?"

"Poor Miss Emma," Sallie said. "I don't see how that old soul can endure another blow."

∴ ∴ ∴

When Hugh Creighton tried to ring Central, he discovered that the line was dead. It had been dead since early morning, Sallie said; she was so undone by this terrible thing that she had forgotten to mention it. So he and Jim had to put water in the radiator of the Model T and try to crank it. When at last they had it running, they drove down to the depot at Cypress Swamp to wire the coroner at Carthage. While they were at it, they sent telegrams to Sheriff Herliss Timmons, to Dr. Sam Pettigru, and to the undertaker, Mr. Newsome. In all that coming and going, John Baird, heavily bundled up, rode with his uncles. Jim had seen to that.

They found Wade sitting on the back steps of Tison's house, blinking in the sun. A motley flock of chickens, fluffed up against the cold, had assembled at his feet, clucking and whining, but he paid them no attention.

Hugh asked his brother what he was doing outside when it was warm in the kitchen.

"I just can't stay in there, Brother."

"You could've closed the door."

"I know it."

"How long's Hart been gone?" Hugh asked.

"Hart? I haven't seen Hart."

"He wasn't here when you got here? That's peculiar. What time was that?"

Wade fumbled through the layers of his clothes until he came upon his watch. He snapped it open, then squinted into the sun. "An hour ago?"

"He was driving up when we were leaving. I told him you'd

be here directly. I assumed he'd hang around. He's an odd bird, that fellow. Well, I'm going on in," Hugh said. "Are y'all coming?"

"Now that y'all are here, I reckon."

"I wonder if anybody's fed those chickens," Jim said.

"Not since I been here," Wade said.

"I bet there's a sack of feed on the porch, John Baird."

The boy got up and looked, found the feed, scooped a pan of it, and the chickens renewed their clucking. He led them away from the steps, kicking them out of his way as he went, and scattered the feed along the outer edge of the sandy yard while his uncles went inside.

Wade went straight to the stove. "Y'all close that door to the hall," he said, holding his reddened hands over the heat. Hugh sat at the kitchen table and stared out at the brightness—a field of frozen broom sedge.

"I just saw him yesterday," Wade said.

"Sister and Jimmy did too."

"He came through the yard in his buggy. Didn't say where he'd been. Didn't say much a-tall, come to think of it. I was out chopping wood. Cou'n Tison said I'd better lay in a good supply, it was going to be a cold night. That's what he said. 'It's going to be a cold night.'"

"What time was that?" Hugh asked.

"Late in the afternoon."

"Jimmy saw him after that. What time was it?"

"When I was taking Sister over to your house, Wade. We met him coming up the avenue. He said he had to go by the barn."

"I'll be back in a minute," Hugh said, and he went into the hall, closing the door behind him. John Baird came in shivering and went to the stove.

"You came over here this morning by yourself, son?"

"Uncle Hugh and Uncle Jimmy were right behind me."

"Jonas said it was you that found him."

"Well, it was Jonas that found him first. But I was the first one of us."

"And you went right on in by yourself?"

"Yessir."

"Great day."

"I couldn't understand why he had just one shoe on."

Hugh returned. "Wade, did you take a look at Cou'n Tison's desk?"

"I didn't go in there, Brother. Why?"

"It's all cleaned out. Ledgers, bills, letters, everything. Just as bare as a widow's cupboard."

: : :

You could judge the rate at which word traveled by the order in which they came—kinsmen first, the ones from around Cypress Swamp, and then neighbors, both landowners and sharecroppers, whether they knew Tison Bonner or not; then, as the day wore on, cousins from Carthage; and late that afternoon a carload from Savannah. Without a designated host to receive them or a grieving family to whom to pay respects, the guests shifted for themselves, separating into small clumps according to their station or the degree of their kinship to the dead man. Only closer members of the Creighton-Bonner clan were admitted to the backyard, domain of Hugh Creighton; distant kin settled on the front porch steps, smoking cigars, while curious neighbors kept a respectful distance beneath the live oaks, and the wool-hat crowd congregated among the ramshackle wagons they had come in, out by the cotton field. Whatever the differences among them, all were male and all were white, and the topic of discussion from one group to the next was who killed Tison Bonner.

By noon the front yard was jammed with automobiles and buggies. It reminded Jim of the town square on court day. Restless, he moved among the crowd, speaking to men he knew, but there were many he had never seen before. The farther he moved from the house, the wilder the rumors he heard, until it seemed to him that they were originating, like sparks from a brush fire, out at the edge of the dead cotton field, among the ill-favored, meanly clad crowd that was squatting on its heels in the harsh winter glare.

They looked underfed, those sharecroppers, washed out and faded. To a man they agreed that it was niggers that killed Tison Bonner. Stealing money for liquor. One, with a sunken eye socket, said Tison Bonner had a name for being hard on niggers; maybe this was one time he had been too damn hard. But an older fellow with grizzled whiskers said no, he'd heard that it was the husband of a nigger girl the old man was messing with. A young man with buckteeth said, "These Bonners is bad to fuck niggers. Always has been." The one-eye shook his head and spat. "I'll just tell you now, it'd take a sorry white man to fuck a nigger, I don't care if his name is Bonner." The bucktoothed boy said it didn't make no nevermind to him why they done it, he just wanted to be there when they caught them.

Jim was sickened by such talk. This was the same crowd you'd find at a freak show. Not one of them would have counted Tison Bonner a friend, yet here they were, gathered about the house of death like buzzards perched above a carcass, not even feigning grief.

But what about Hugh and Wade and the other cousins? Every member of the family he had talked to was concerned only to know who had done it. And what about himself? How was one to mourn the passing of a hard-nosed, tight-fisted old miser like Cou'n Tison? The truth was, Jim had never liked him, had often cringed at Tison's harsh treatment of Negroes, his rough hand with animals. And what he had heard of Tison's infatuation with Jennie had disgusted him. So why was he disturbed by the general indifference to Tison's death? If he couldn't grieve, how could he expect others to?

He entered Tison's barn, shafts of dusty sunlight, a burning of ammonia in his nose. Jonas had turned the stock into the lot. Except for one, a poor looking mule in its stall. Perhaps one of the mules Tison had ruined last summer. Jim stepped over to it.

Something beneath his heel cracked. He bent down. A pair of eyeglasses. They must have slipped from the owner's pocket. Could they have belonged to Tison? The left lens was shattered, one temple twisted. He tried them on. Reading glasses. He had never seen Tison wearing glasses. At the image, an unaccountable sadness descended upon him. That such a man should sit down alone at his desk, fit glasses to his face and study his accounts, then, recalling some little thing undone at the barn, slip them into his pocket and come out here, only to lose them from his pocket and wonder later, when he found that pocket empty, what on earth had become of his glasses. Tison Bonner was dead.

: : :

They had built a fire in the backyard. Jim joined the men gathered around it.

"Has anyone seen Cou'n Bones?" Wade asked.

Harry Bonner thought that Bones had gone to Carthage. "I doubt he's even heard yet."

Here came Sam Pettigru, taking care to watch where he put his feet. A pair of glasses sat perched on the end of his nose. He greeted each man by name and touched his hat brim to John Baird. Dispensing with pleasantries, he told Hugh he was ready to get on with it, if Hugh would show him where to go.

"Just go on in through the kitchen, Sam. He's right in there in the hall."

Doctor Sam had not been inside five minutes when Hart came riding up. He came on horseback, along the lane that ran from Wade Creighton's avenue to Tison Bonner's backyard, sitting the horse tall and easy—a dark three-piece suit and a brown fedora smartly blocked. The men looked up, some spoke, but Hart rode past, the reins held high, intent on his well-groomed, dancing mare.

"Mighty independent, ain't he?" Harry Bonner said.

At Jonas Stubbs's cabin Hart swung his leg heavily over the saddle and dropped to the ground. Afoot, he moved like a man carrying too much weight. He tied the reins to a chinaberry branch and came walking over. He touched his hat. "Gentlemen."

"Where'd you get to?" Hugh asked.

"Akers here yet?"

"We haven't seen him. Sam Pettigru's in there now. Where have you been?"

"Looks like half the county's gathered over here."

"I figured you'd have stayed around until Wade got here at least. Somebody should have."

Hart reached inside his pocket for his pipe, filled it, and struck a match. During the time it took to get it going no one spoke. When the blue smoke was curling from the bowl, he looked through the smoke at Hugh, eyes squinted. "Maybe you'd better run on back home, Hugh, and see if you can locate your manners."

Hart had just made it clear to Hugh that he was in charge now, that Hugh had no more authority in that yard than any other cousin, and Hart was damned if he would be interrogated. Everyone who heard him understood the message, including Hugh, who opened his mouth to say something but then thought better of it.

"How's Miss Emma, Hart?" Jim asked.

"She's all to pieces, Jimmy. The whole house is."

: : :

Sam Pettigru wasn't sure it was a good idea for John Baird to hear what he had to say, but Hart told him to go ahead. The doctor reared back, exposing a gap of white shirt between his vest and trousers, and tugged at his white goatee. "It is my observation, gentlemen, that Tison Bonner was shot four times by a .38-caliber pistol, the first ball taking effect in the sternum, the second in the upper back, passing inward and lodging near the left nipple, the third entering the lumbar region and passing inward, and the fourth entering the left hip, breaking the femur a few inches below the joint. Any of the shots was sufficient to cause death, the one to the breast instantly."

"Could you tell when it happened, Sam?" Hart asked.

"That's impossible to ascertain, but judging from the state of coagulation, I'd say sometime before midnight."

John Baird touched Hart's elbow and asked in a lowered voice, "When are they going to move Uncle Tison? I mean, the body?"

"We're still waiting on the coroner, son. And the sheriff will need to take a look too."

"I don't know what good you think that will do," the doctor said. "Herliss Timmons couldn't track a bleeding elephant through the snow." Turning to Hugh, the doctor asked, "How's the girl?"

"Mending, I understand. I haven't seen her."

"She had a damn close call. I'm losing people from here to Carthage. Charles Dargan last night."

"You don't mean it. Charlie ain't as old as I am. And all those children."

: : :

Hugh was ready to leave. He had not had a bite to eat all day. John Baird hadn't either, but he said he wasn't hungry. Hugh insisted that he go anyway. "You need a rest, son. We'll come back later."

Sallie met them at the door, her sweet face hardened into a look of anxiety. Where had they been, for goodness' sake? Didn't somebody have a watch? She had expected them back an hour ago. What was going on that they couldn't have come home for dinner? If the rest of the men had no more sense than her brothers, she had figured she'd have to send something over. Mattie was helping Delia put up lunches. Would ten be enough? She couldn't feed the entire county, but she did want to send sandwiches to Wade and Ben and Cou'n Harry and Cou'n Bones. And to Hart. Had they talked with Hart? How was he taking it? Had the sheriff uncovered anything? What were people saying about who did it?

Jim had never seen his sister in such a state. Usually the calm at the eye of the hurricane, she was wringing her hands now.

Hugh retreated to his room upstairs, but Jim and John Baird followed Sallie out to the kitchen, and there to his surprise sat Jennie, warming in the sun that streamed through the window. An old housedress hung loose around her shoulders, but it was not her gauntness that shocked him so much as her ravaged face. She looked like a woman cut loose from the rack. Yet she managed a smile, a weak, "How you doing, Buddy? Mr. Jimmy?" She moved to rise, but Sallie ordered her to keep her seat.

She's uncomfortable sitting in our presence, Jim thought.

"Tell us now," Sallie said, "what they've found."

"Sam Pettigru just got there a little while ago, Sister. We haven't seen the sheriff yet."

"What in heaven's name could be keeping him? The people who did it are probably all the way to Georgia by now."

Jennie was dabbing at her eyes with a napkin.

: : :

When the Creightons returned an hour later, the crowd had thinned out and the coroner's jury had met and rendered a verdict: the deceased had come to his death at his residence at Cypress Swamp, South Carolina, on December 30, 1918, by pistol shot in the hand of party unknown to the jury.

"That's what we stood out here freezing all day to hear?" Ben Carpenter said.

Sheriff Timmons had arrived with two deputies and two detectives from Savannah.

"Herliss and his boys have been real busy keeping folks away from the house," Ben said. "The detectives are still inside."

So was the undertaker. Hart had conferred with him and then left without a word to anyone, Wade explained to his brothers.

"Well, he missed his dinner," Hugh said, as though he were personally offended.

The detectives from Savannah were a matter of much curiosity. They were the reason, it turned out, that Herliss Timmons had taken so long to get there. He had waited for them at Thompson's since eleven o'clock that morning.

"Was it Herliss who sent for them?" Hugh asked.

"I think so," Ben Carpenter said.

"I wonder who told him to."

"I don't know, but if he thought it up by himself, it's the smartest thing he's ever done."

The sheriff had posted the deputies on the front steps to keep the curious away from the porch; he himself was stationed at the back. Jim followed Hugh over to him.

"I'll have to ask you not to go in, Mr. Creighton," Herliss Timmons said.

"Oh, for God's sake, Herliss."

Herliss Timmons was short and fat, but hard fat, nobody to mess with. His coat was pulled back on the right side to reveal the revolver that rode high on his hip. He wore his authority with great seriousness.

"I was just wondering about these fellows from Savannah," Hugh said.

"Two of the finest homicide detectives in the country, Mr. Creighton."

"I'm glad to hear it. You send for them yourself, did you?"

"Yessir, I did."

"Have they turned up anything yet?"

"You'll have to ask them about that, Mr. Creighton."

: : :

The detective who seemed to be in charge was a foreign looking fellow with a blue five-o'clock shadow. He wore a gray hat, the brim snapped up, and when Jim shook his hand his fingers felt blunt and moist. He introduced himself as Martinetti. His partner, a stocky man with crinkly blond hair, hung back. Jim failed to catch his name.

"There's blood under the broken window on the porch," Martinetti said, his accent crisp and northern. "As soon as the sheriff finds us a nigger with a fresh cut on his hand, we'll have this case wrapped up. Now I understand that the body was discovered by the yard nigger. Who was it said his wife heard an automobile last night?"

"That was my nephew here," Hugh explained.

Martinetti ignored the boy. "We'll be speaking with them in a minute."

While the detectives were busy with Jonas and his wife, the undertaker came out of Tison Bonner's house. Jim had never seen the man before. Short and dumpy with apple-red cheeks, he wore a black duster and a homburg. A cigarette stuck at a jaunty angle from a corner of his mouth, and he was trying to strike a kitchen match. He lifted his hat to greet the Creightons, a perfunctory gesture that revealed a bald dome.

"Did Mr. Hart Bonner speak to you about the arrangements?" Hugh asked.

The question caught the undertaker off guard. Buying time with the lighting of his smoke, he glanced furtively, quickly, about the yard, as though trying to decide on the appropriate tone of voice.

"I don't believe I've had the pleasure, sir," the undertaker said. "Do you belong to the immediate family?" His voice was alarmingly high-pitched.

"He didn't have an immediate family. I'm the one who wired you," Jim said.

"Oh yes, Mr. Creighton, of course. Then I'll tell you, sir. This is highly irregular, highly irregular."

"I don't understand you."

"I explained to Mr. Bonner—to the brother, I mean—that it is customary in such cases to remove the remains to my place of business, but he insisted, sir, that Mr. Bonner—the deceased, I mean—be left right here in the house. I tried to explain to him that there would be problems with that—professional problems, sir—I'm just not equipped—but he was in no mood to listen. No mood a-tall. The shock of it, I'm sure. Said his mother would want to view the remains before the service tomorrow, and he was afraid that we wouldn't be able to get them back out here in time. I told him that he wouldn't want her to view them if I were not allowed to take them in to town, and you won't believe what the fellow said to that."

Mr. Newsome paused to suck on his cigarette. "He said she couldn't see well enough to know the difference, just do the best I could. Now what do you think of that? You hear all sorts of things at a time like this, Mr. Creighton."

"I imagine you do."

"Now I don't want to be crude, gentlemen, but we can all be thankful for the weather. Under the circumstances, I mean. I didn't say that to Mr. Bonner, of course, him being the brother and all, but I sho am glad it ain't July, ain't you?"

The undertaker's laugh was hideous. When the Creightons failed to laugh with him, he resumed his doleful manner. "Yes. Well. I've done the best I could under abnormal conditions. He's in there on the bed, stiffened up considerable what with the weather like it is, but I've cleaned him up as best I could. If y'all want to lay out a suit of clothes for him, we'll get him dressed first thing in the morning. But he ain't going to look natural, I'm just warning you."

"You want to go in, Jimmy?" Hugh asked.

The prospect of looking upon the old man naked, stiff and contorted, his blue flesh penetrated with bullet holes, was more than Jim could stomach. "No," he said.

: : :

Through the bare branches of a pecan tree, the sky glowed bleak orange, and against that desperate color an endless string of blackbirds sought their evening roost. Jim and his nephew were sitting in the Model T, hoping to hurry Hugh, but Hugh was still finding people to talk to. Jim was exhausted by the problems of Tison's death, of having to decide what face to wear, what words to say, what to think and feel. Hugh, on the other hand, had sailed through the day without any trouble, except for that little confrontation with Hart. He wasn't exactly glad that the old man was gone, he had told Jim after lunch, but it sure did solve a lot of problems, and he didn't see anything wrong with saying so. Within the bosom of the family, of course. And then he'd gone in to look at the body.

Jim was worn out too by having struggled all day to get warm. John Baird must surely be. He wished Hugh would come on.

"Uncle Jimmy? Is anybody going to sit up with Uncle Tison?"

"I don't know who, son."

"I don't reckon Uncle Hart."

"No, I don't reckon."

"I wish somebody would."

Here came Hugh. He bent over and cranked the Ford. It coughed, sputtered and caught. The vibrations of the running engine felt like a blessing to Jim.

Hugh seated himself at the wheel, opened the throttle, and turned on the headlamps. Except where they shone, the yard went dark. As they turned into the avenue that led to the big road, a mule and wagon appeared up ahead, a white mule glowing faintly in the dusk, beyond the reach of the headlamps. Hugh jerked the wheel to the right and stepped on the brakes. "Here comes Bones."

Hugh got out. The old man loomed above him on the buggy seat, a tattered silhouette against the low glow in the southern sky. The coal of a cigarette burned against his darkened face.

"Evening, Cou'n Bones."

"Who's that? Is that Hugh Creighton?"

"Yessir," Hugh yelled. "And Jimmy and John Baird."

"I'm here about Bubba."

"Yessir."

"I been in Carthage since yesterday."

"That's what I heard."

"They said it was niggers shot him."

"They don't know for sure, Cou'n Bones."

"Hanh?"

"I said, they don't know for sure. That's what they think."

"I imagine they took him on in to town."

"Nosir. He's right back there at the house."

"Well. I want to see what they done to him. I didn't hear about it till just this afternoon."

Hugh stepped one step closer to the buggy, placed his hand against the rump of the mule. "He's in no condition for viewing, Cou'n Bones."

The old man leaned forward on the wagon seat, the coal of his cigarette aglow. "I'll be the one to decide that, son. Me and Bubba don't need no permission."

"Yessir. Let me turn around. We'll go with you."

: : :

The kitchen was still warm. A lamp was burning on the table.

"He's right in there in the bedroom, Cou'n Bones. We'll wait out here," Hugh said.

The Creightons and their nephew sat in silence at Tison's kitchen table. As eager as Jim had been to get back home, to turn his back upon the harrowing day—the prurient crowds, Sheriff Timmons and the detectives, the stiffened, naked corpse one room away—he was glad Bones Bonner had come. A burden had been lifted from his shoulders, a responsibility he had assumed because no one else—not even Hart—had been willing to. But he had not been able to carry it. Now Bones could. Let him grieve for Tison Bonner. Jim could hear the old man's feet moving from one room to another. Aimless and random, they sounded, and the cold house creaked with his rambling. When he returned to the kitchen, he was holding his battered hat in his hands, close to his chest, and his old eyes were red-rimmed and rheumy.

"They shot him all to pieces, boys," the old man said. Then he walked over to the window and stood for a long minute staring out into the dark backyard. When he turned again to the room, his face had clouded up like an autumn afternoon, dark and working. "They took our chess board too. What you reckon they wanted to do that for? The son of a bitches."

When no one answered, the silence grew awkward, as though Bones expected an answer.

"I don't know," Jim said.

"Well, y'all go on. I imagine Hart will be on over directly."

Jim and Hugh looked at each other. "I don't think so, Cou'n Bones. He didn't talk like he was."

"He'll have to do as he sees fit, I reckon. Y'all go on now. We're much obliged."

HART

*I*t was a small and threadbare family that was left to grieve for Tison Bonner. Miss Emma claimed a mother's right. "He was one of mine," she whimpered to Hart and Hattie, "every bit as much as any one of y'all."

"Yes ma'am," Hart said.

His mother's face, like sun-baked clay, had long since hardened into a sour expression, but who could blame her? She had come to Heyward County before the war, bride to a widower twice her age and mother to his two little boys; she had wept over the ashes of Live Oak, suffered her husband's long twilight, buried four of her children, and here she was this morning prepared to say goodbye to another.

She would never forget, she said, the afternoon Mr. Bonner brought her to Live Oak, the shadows on the lawn and those two little men, Johnny and Tison, dressed up in their sailor suits, standing on the verandah to welcome their new mama. She had reared them, schooled them, put her stamp upon them.

You also did your best to keep them from marrying, Hart thought, just as you did with us. But it didn't work with Johnny, did it? Tison never tested your resolve, but Johnny did, though it took him thirty years to get around to it.

"Tison was a sweet child." she said.

She had insisted on viewing the body.

Hart had tried to discourage her. "He ain't going to look very pretty, Ma."

But the old lady was adamant. "Suppose it was you," she said. "How would you feel?"

She was playing the part assigned her, but in spite of her vast experience in that role, she had never learned to get it right.

I just hope you're as blind as you say you are, Hart thought.

"Is Pinck going?" Hattie asked.

Hart's sister, so close to him in age that as children they were often taken for twins, had withered into a creaky middle age, her sole purpose in life to care for her mother.

"I don't think it's a good idea," Hart said. "He sounds like he's scared to go over there, acts like he thinks Tison's still alive. James is with him."

"I do so dread having to see people," Miss Emma said. "Daughter, fetch my lavender shawl."

Hattie arranged the shawl around her mother's shoulders.

"Tison gave me this shawl for Christmas. Was it this year or last year? I don't remember."

Hattie had knitted the shawl herself. She and Hart exchanged a look, as if to say, let her think what she wants.

: : :

With difficulty Hart installed his mother in the front seat of the Model T. Hattie, veiled in black, climbed into the back, and off they went in the strong, cold sun, rattling along the washboard road toward the house of the deceased.

A small crowd had gathered in Tison's yard. They were standing not in the shade of the live oaks but around the edges, their backs turned to what little heat the sun afforded, men in small clumps, dressed for Sunday, smoking, spitting tobacco, speaking of weather or bird dogs or the influenza epidemic or who killed Tison Bonner. Their wives remained seated in the automobiles or surreys they had come in, as though intimidated by this bastion of male prerogative. There were not many—men or women—and none who were not related to the Bonner family. They had been waiting for Miss Emma to arrive and go in first. Now that she was here they began to stir, arranging themselves in positions of respect. Once she had had her private minute with the dead, they could express their sympathies and get back home to things they'd rather be doing until the funeral at three o'clock.

Hart brought the automobile bucking to a stop between the live oaks. Climbing down, he tipped his hat to the guests as he walked around to the other side and opened the door for his mother. Hattie emerged from the back seat. Taking an elbow each, the brother and sister helped the old lady toward the porch. She made a slow and painful progress, her old black taffeta arustle. As she labored up the steps a solitary blue jay squawked.

Hart suspected that this was the first time she had ever been to Tison's house. She was not the kind of woman who went visiting, and Tison had never been one to entertain.

The undertaker—Hart could not remember his name—was standing on the porch, smoking a cigarette, the grimace on his face offered as sympathy. As the party approached, he bowed and held the door open. A small pane on the left-hand side had been broken out.

It was dark inside, the drapes drawn in respect for the dead, but not dark enough, and there was no greenery in the room to ease the harsh fact before them—on a velvet-draped bier an open pine coffin and inside the remains of Tison Bonner, his formerly florid complexion drained to a blue pallor, his mustache faded to the color of dead grass, his features somehow sunken in upon themselves. Hart thought how fragile his bald dome looked. Miss Emma gasped and collapsed, her eyelids aflutter. Hart caught her and with an effort held her up while Hattie pulled over a chair. When his mother was seated, Hart stepped out onto the porch and asked if anyone had smelling salts, but by the time he returned his mother had allowed Hattie to guide her to the parlor across the hall.

With its claw-footed chairs, velvet-skirted stools, and horsehair sofa, the room struck Hart as something of an extravagance for Tison. On the wall opposite the sofa hung a picture of three dingy cherubs, sweetly dimpled and suspended weightless in celestial ether—the last thing Hart would have expected in Tison's house. A gift from one of the sisters, he'd bet, nailed up and never looked at again.

Miss Emma, restored by the smelling salts, sat in lamplight, propped by a pillow at the end of the horsehair sofa, Hattie at her side patting her hand, while Hart stood by to remind her, as each guest approached, who this was.

"Cou'n Sallie, Mama."

Miss Emma looked up blinking, her mouth pursed. Powder was caked in the creases of her dewlaps.

"We're so sorry, Miss Emma. Cou'n Tison was very good to us."

"I know he was," the aged lady said, her voice a startling croak.

John Baird followed his mother, as awkward as any sixteen-year-old in this unfamiliar situation. "Grandmother," he said, and leaned forward to peck her powdered cheek.

"This is John Baird, Mama, Johnny's boy."

Miss Emma turned and looked up at Hart, her face a mask of exasperation. "I know who it is." But she offered her hand instead, arthritic fingers protected by the lace that extended from her sleeve.

Jim Creighton made a bow. "We're all so sorry, Miss Emma. It's just a terrible thing."

The old woman fingered the edge of the shawl draped across her shoulders. "Tison gave me this for Christmas," she said.

Hart caught Jim's eye and shook his head. He wanted to get out of that room, light his pipe, and talk with Jim. When Jim had paid his respects, Hart drew him aside. "Let's go outside," he whispered. "I need a break."

Hart stood at the stall of one of the ruined mules, his black suit dusty in the rays of morning sun, his polished shoes fouled by the offal of the barn, and sucked fire into his pipe. "Look at that poor mule," he said when his pipe was lit. "Tison was hard on animals. Hard on people too. Just a contentious sort of man. I heard my pa say one time that if Tison was to drown in the river, they'd have to look for his body upstream, it was too contrary to flow with the current. I know you're not supposed to speak ill of the dead, professor, but I never knew a man so ill-tempered. I can't think of a single soul that he really cared about, unless it was Johnny. He took Johnny's death real hard. And Bones, of course. He was fond of Bones. They had been boys together, you know. Bones lived with us for a year or two after the war."

Hart paused, beguiled by a recollection. "Did I ever tell you the story of Tison's shoes? I must have been eight or nine years old. Looking for relics, or arrowheads maybe, in that Joe Pye field behind the house. And Tison came riding up. You probably don't remember how he looked in those days. He was thin and to me he seemed very tall. He had hair back then and a beard too—red hair and a bushy red beard. Tison was a handsome young man, especially when he rode that tall bay gelding. He called that horse Caesar, I remember. He didn't keep him long. Anyway, he rode right up to me that morning in the Joe Pye field. 'Son,' he said, 'come with me. I want to show you something.' And he lifted me up—caught me under the armpits and lifted me up and set me in the saddle in front of him, and he wrapped his arm around my waist to keep me from falling off. I remember that. His hands were freckled and the hair on them looked like copper."

Hart patted the mule on the rump. "When the family got word that Sherman was crossing the river and marching on Robertville, he told me—though I had heard that part of the story a hundred times, I reckon—the whole household went into a frenzy—what to bury, what to take, frantic to leave. Tison said he was just about my age and all in the world he cared about was a pair of shoes Papa had brought him from Savannah. In those days, you know, a cobbler on the place made shoes for everybody, black and white, but these were store-bought, fancy lace-ups for church and such. While the family was busy burying silver, Tison wrapped those shoes in an old flannel shirt and hid them in the hollow of a live oak tree, in that grove between our place and yours—where you grew up, I mean. And that's where he took me. The tree was still standing after all those years, and he rode us right up to it.

"When they got back from Darlington—on up in the spring—the house was gone, the slaves were gone, the stock was gone. Even the silver was gone. One of the people had shown the Yankees where it was buried. But those shoes were all Tison could think about. He went straight to the tree, and damned if the shoes weren't gone too. He held me around the waist and told me to lean forward and look real good. He had always figured they must have slipped on down into the hollow, beyond reach, and he wanted me to see if I could see them.

"For a minute I had the strangest feeling—that the war had just ended and I was the one who had hidden the shoes. I don't know. It's hard to explain. Anyway, that's the only time I remember Tison ever touching me, other than to shake hands. The only time I ever had his full attention. As a rule, Tison didn't take up time with children. In those days any more than recently."

A barn cat rubbed itself against Hart's leg. He reached to pick it up, but the cat eluded his grasp. "I don't know what made me think of that," he said.

"Well, I'm glad you did," Jim said. "I appreciate your telling me. What do you think went wrong?"

"With Tison?"

"Between the two of you."

Hart gave Jim a searching look. "Has anybody told you about Tison and Jennie?"

"Brother did. A little."

"What did he say?"

"Just that Cou'n Tison developed a romantic interest in her. I could hardly believe it, especially of him, after all these years."

"Well, it's true," Hart said. "But I never have learned just how it started. She won't talk about it. Did Hugh say anything else?"

"Just that Cou'n Tison made a fool of himself. He told me about that episode at the summerhouse."

"There's more to it than that, but I don't know what. I know she told him to leave her alone, but I have reason to believe that for a while there she was not altogether displeased with his attention. I mean, goddamn. Can you imagine? It nearly drove me crazy. Old Tison of all people. Never been looked at twice by a woman, and Jennie sits around the kitchen laughing and cutting up with him. I know that for a fact. But then something happened, I don't know what. Tison must have done something to offend her, and then he turned that wagon over and broke his leg, which he richly deserved after what he'd done to those young mules, and he's been out of commission ever since."

Hart realized what he had just said and gave Jim a look. "But not like he is now."

"Good Lord, Hart. I hope you've got sense enough not to say such a thing to anybody else."

Hart leaned back against the mule's stall. "Professor, most of what I've told you over the last fifteen years I've said to you alone. I've confided a great deal in you, but if you're standing there waiting for me to look you in the eye and tell you that I did not kill my brother, then it's time we went back in."

: : :

The little church was full. The pallbearers—the Creighton brothers, their nephew John Baird, and two Bonner cousins—were seated in the tiny choir loft, and the pine coffin reposed upon a bier before the altar. A murmur of hushed conversation ceased as people noticed that the Bonners were coming down the aisle, Miss Emma a squat Queen Victoria, with Hattie at her elbow and behind them Hart and Pinckney.

Hart guided his brother into the front pew and took his seat on the aisle. "Just sit still," he whispered. Pinck did not like church and had long since stopped attending. "This won't take long." He wasn't sure how much Pinck understood. The man was not an idiot, but in recent years, as he increasingly kept to the house, he had grown more childlike. More difficult too. Hart had told him only that Tison had died, not that he'd been murdered, and Pinck had gotten angry, blaming the messenger for the message. By this morning, though, he had decided that Tison had not died after all. When Hart had insisted on his coming to the funeral, Pinck pitched a fit. Hart wanted to leave him at home, but Miss Emma wouldn't hear of it. "What will people think?" she said.

"Well, you see what you can do with him then."

His mother had her ways, he had to admit. He had remained at the big house to greet an old friend of Tison's, a lawyer named Edmund DeSaussure, just arrived from Savannah. When he returned to the cottage, there sat Pinck, shaved, dressed, and ready to go, as docile as a lamb. James Salley had wet his hair and plastered it to his skull, but now it stood about his head in dry sprigs.

Bones Bonner came down the side aisle and eased into the pew alongside Miss Emma.

Just what she needs, Hart thought. His mother despised the old man, said he was forever in need of a bath. Hart would have bet a dollar bill that Bones was rolling a quid of tobacco in his toothless gums.

It was a shame that neither Bones nor Miss Emma could hear the preacher. Mr. Atkinson made Tison Bonner sound like the leading citizen of the state. Most of what he said was standard funeral fare, but when he started on Tison's devotion to the church—"Mr. Bonner may not have been as regular in attendance as some of our little flock, but he loved his church and supported it with his gifts and his prayers"—he went so far beyond the bounds of propriety that the congregation began to squirm, people exchanging glances.

Pinck hiccupped loudly, a torn sob. Hart placed his hand on his brother's knee. "Shh now," he whispered. Pinck's shoulders were trembling. He could not control himself. Wet, blubbery sobs attracted the attention of the congregation. Hart offered him a handkerchief, his nose was running. Pinck took it but wailed aloud. Hart had had enough. Taking his brother by his meaty upper arm, he lifted him from his seat and pulled him gently into the aisle. Pinck covered his large face with his hands. Hart put his arm around his brother's trembling shoulders and guided him toward the back of the church.

James Salley was standing there, beneath a framed picture of Jesus kneeling in Gethsemane, as though he'd been waiting for just such a development. "Take him outside," Hart whispered. "See if you can get him to sit in the auto."

: : :

The service at the graveside was brief—a shivering crowd in the January glare, the preacher's prayer blown away by the wind, a creaking of ropes as the coffin was lowered into its hole. And then, as people departed, the scrape of shovels and the thud of dirt on the box.

Hart guided his mother among the tombstones of her children—Betsy dead at twenty-eight, Nell at thirty-seven, Smith at forty-four—all of tuberculosis—and Johnny of cancer in the gut. The old woman had wanted to keep them in a tight orbit around her, unmarried and within reach of her voice. Now Tison was safely laid away with the four who had gone before. Miss Emma could rest in the assurance that he was taken care of. Hart directed her away from Betsy's grave. "Watch that coping, Ma."

: : :

Sheriff Herliss Timmons was waiting beneath the tall pines at the wrought-iron gate, his hat in his hands. Hart wondered why. He appeared uncomfortable having to greet each of the mourners as they filed through. Hart nodded as he passed, and the sheriff made a deferential little bow. When Hart had seated his mother and started around to the driver's side, the sheriff came over to the automobile. "My sympathies to the family, Mr. Bonner. We've had a development, something come to light, and Detective Martinetti thinks it'd be a good idea if you and the Creighton boys was to meet with us at Mr. Tison's place. Just as soon as you can."

Something come to light? Hart could not imagine what.

: : :

Edmund DeSaussure was a handsome man, tall and slender and impeccably dressed. A silver mane of hair fell upon his collar, and he moved with an air of authority. Hart was glad he had come. Walking away from Tison's grave, he had invited the lawyer to stop by the house after the funeral, but when he came driving up in his shiny maroon Franklin, Hart had to excuse himself. "A little meeting with the sheriff," he explained. "Something's come to light, they say."

"Mind if I come along?"

The request took Hart by surprise. "Well, no, Edmund, I don't mind a-tall, but I don't know what those lawmen will think."

"We'll just say that I'm an out-of-town guest of the family. Which is simply the truth. Why don't you let me drive?"

During the short ride the lawyer asked if it was generally believed that Tison was killed by Negroes trying to break in. That's what he had heard.

"It sho looks that way."

"Was anything taken?"

"I wouldn't know about that."

It was past five when they arrived at Tison's house. Shadows in the sandy yard were growing long, and the parlor was almost dark. The Creightons were sitting in a group on one side of the room, the sheriff and the detectives on the other. The two groups seemed not to be conversing with each other. Edmund DeSaussure was already acquainted with Wade and Hugh, had spoken to them at the funeral. Hart introduced him to Jim and then more formally to the lawmen.

"I'll have to ask you what you're doing here, sir," the sheriff said, "not meaning to be rude, you understand."

"Mr. DeSaussure is a guest of the family, Sheriff, here from Savannah for my brother's funeral," Hart said.

Wade struck a match to the wick of a nickel-plated lamp, and all but the sheriff took seats.

"Gentlemen," the sheriff began, "a new piece of evidence has just come to our attention, and Mr. Martinetti thought y'all ought to be advised of it as soon as possible. So that's how come we're here. Seems that Mr. Alston Bonner, that sat up last night with the remains, took it upon hissef to make a search of the premises, said he didn't have nothing else to do, and he found this letter here"—the sheriff produced a smudged envelope—"in a coat pocket that was hanging in the chifforobe. He give it to me first thing this morning, but I didn't want to bother y'all with it till after the services was over. Now that they are, I'd like to ask one of you gentlemen if you'd read it out loud and see can you tell us who might have wrote it since Mr. Martinetti here suspects it might have a bearing on the case."

Hugh Creighton said he would read it, but when he opened the envelope he found it too dark in the room to see. He moved over to the table where the globed lamp was burning and held the letter at arm's length down by the light.

> I told you the next time I caught you watching me I would for-feit our friendship. I could not be anything to a man I don't have respect for and you have killed it in me. I cannot go back to be-ing what I was to you. I will not be treated like a dog even if I am colored. Everybody saw you Sunday evening. I am sick and disgusted with the whole affair.

Hugh's voice ceased. No one spoke a word. Hart forced himself to remain calm. Jennie had surely written it, but in response to what offense, he did not know. He wanted to hear it again.

"Well, I'll be," Wade said. "It ain't signed, Brother?"

"Well, what do you think, Wade? They wouldn't have asked me to read it if they knew who wrote it."

"Could you read it again, please, Brother?" Jim said.

Hugh did so.

Jennie's words in Hugh Creighton's mouth sounded soiled to Hart. He could hardly bear it.

"I hate to say this, gentlemen, but it sounds to me like the woman who lives in our yard. Jennie Grant's her name."

The woman who lives in our yard, Hart thought: he had no right to speak of Jennie that way.

"What makes you think so, Mr. Creighton?" Martinetti asked.

Hart was seated in a straight chair at the end of the sofa, leaning forward, his body tensed. He was breathing heavily.

"I think we are all aware of the fact—my family, I mean— that Tison Bonner developed a romantic interest in Jennie some time last summer," Hugh said. "This letter was apparently written in response to that."

"Back last summer, you think?"

"That would be my guess."

"Who would have wrote it for her?" the sheriff wanted to know.

"Oh she can write," Hugh said. "This is her hand. As I said, Cou'n Tison was interested in Jennie. We all knew that. But, frankly, I'm surprised that Jennie would have consented to a relationship, as this indicates"—he waved the letter before them—"but it just goes to show, you never know."

Hart rose from his chair, his face congested with rage. "You smirking little pissant. You don't know what you're talking about," he said. "Who the hell do you think you are to say what's going on with Jennie Grant? I ought to break your neck."

"Hear now, Hart," Wade said. "For goodness' sake. There's no call for that."

Edmund DeSaussure took Hart by the arm and urged him back into his chair. Hugh, badly ruffled, drew himself up and ran his finger around the inside of his collar, as though the celluloid was plastered to his neck. "There certainly isn't," he huffed.

Composed now but still with labored breath, Hart said, "Jennie Grant did not consent to a relationship with my brother, as that mincing little pantywaist put it. Tison was tormenting her. I'm sure that's why she wrote the letter."

"And you knew about this, did you?" Detective Martinetti asked.

"I knew nothing of the letter until five minutes ago. I have known of the harassment for some time."

"And how did you learn of that? Did your brother tell you?"

Edmund DeSaussure stood up. "This is not a court of law, gentlemen. No one in this room is on trial. Neither Mr. Hart Bonner nor anyone else here will be coerced into answering questions that might damage their reputations as decent men."

"And what business is this of yours, sir?" the sheriff asked.

"I'm an attorney, Mr. Timmons. I represent the family."

The sheriff turned to consult in whispers with the detectives.

"Hand me that letter," Hart said.

Hugh, though refusing to meet Hart's eye, handed the letter to him.

I told you the next time I caught you watching me I would forfeit our friendship. Something had happened between the old man and Jennie—whatever she meant by "watching me." Could that have been the episode at the summerhouse? It was the word "friendship" that most puzzled Hart. Jennie was speaking out of an extraordinary familiarity, alluding to a private moment in which she had made it clear to that intimidating white man that she would not tolerate his treatment of her. The letter by its tone bore witness to an intimacy between them that Hart could not bear to contemplate. Could Hugh Creighton have possibly been right? She had once respected Tison, the letter implied, but could not "go back to being what I was to you." What in the name of God could that have been? That was the thorn in Hart's

side—he did not know. The ambiguity of her final phrase—
"even if I am colored"—almost broke his heart.

"Ain't this Jennie Grant some kind of kin to the Stubbs
woman?" Martinetti asked.

"I believe Jennie is Liza Stubbs's niece," Wade said.

"Well, gentlemen, there's something hereabouts that stinks to
high heaven. I am going to ask Sheriff Timmons here to lock
those women up. Just for questioning at this point."

"Now you hold on just a goddamn minute." Before he realized what he was doing, Hart had leapt from his chair, as com-
mitted as a rattlesnake and just as dangerous. "The first man that
lays a hand on Jennie Grant—" He was headed for the sheriff,
but Edmund DeSaussure, surprisingly agile, tackled him around
the waist and swung him about. Hart looked over his shoulder,
struggling to wrest himself free of the lawyer's hold, refusing to
take his eyes from the sheriff, and the veins in his neck and forehead stood out thick. "You touch Jennie Grant, Herliss Timmons, and I'll break your goddamned neck."

"Shut up, you fool," whispered DeSaussure. Suddenly the
room went still, everyone frozen by the lawyer's command. Hugh
and Wade were on their feet, the deputies and detectives closing
in, and Sheriff Timmons, red-faced and trembling, held his
snub-nosed pistol in both hands, aimed at Hart. "Don't be coming in my face like that, Mr. Bonner," he warned, and for a stout
man his voice was surprisingly shrill.

"Put that gun away, Mr. Timmons. There's no need for it."

The lawyer was in charge.

"Edmund," Hart said, breathing hard, "I can't let them take
her. She's in no condition. She didn't have anything to do with
it. I swear to God she didn't." Then he caved in, just crumpled
upon himself like a tent, hiding his head in his uplifted arms and
sobbing like a man who has let go of all that matters to him.

Edmund DeSaussure said, "Gentlemen, if you'll excuse us,"
and led Hart from the room, out into the hall and past the

bedroom door where two days ago Tison Bonner had fallen dead, and on into the dark kitchen. "Now sit down here and get control of yourself. And from now on, you let me handle things. I don't want you to open your mouth to a soul about this case. Is that understood?"

Hart wiped his face on the back of his sleeve and nodded. "But, Edmund, you can't let them take her. She is completely innocent, I swear to God."

"I'll take care of it. You just sit right here."

When the lawyer had disappeared up the hall, Hart got up and followed, easing along as quietly as he could.

"Sheriff," Hart heard the lawyer say, "I'm going to ask that you not arrest the woman Jennie Grant. Out of consideration for the feelings of the family. I can't see that justice will be served by making this scandal any more public than it already is. Go ahead and take Liza Stubbs if you must, but leave Jennie Grant."

"No sir, I'll not take one without the other," Sheriff Timmons said.

"Then leave them both. I'll talk to Jennie Grant tomorrow. In fact, I can probably get more information from her than you can."

With an ugly grin the sheriff said, "Oh I can get a nigger to talk when I need to now."

"That's just what I'm afraid of, Mr. Timmons. But Jennie Grant is a Creighton servant. I 'spect you'll want to keep that in mind."

: : :

When the sheriff and the detectives had left, Hugh Creighton suggested that they all repair to Sallie's house for a bite of supper. Wade said thanks but he needed to get on home, Clara was anxious enough as it was. And DeSaussure declined on Hart's behalf. The poor fellow was distraught; the lawyer feared a nervous breakdown.

Hart smoothed back his hair. Supper at Sallie's meant a chance of seeing Jennie. He straightened his tie and entered the parlor. Smiling at the Creightons, he said, "Thanks, we'll be happy to."

JIM CREIGHTON

*J*im cranked the Buick, anxious to get back over to Sallie's, eager to think through all he'd seen and heard, but as soon as he climbed in, Hugh erupted. "Well, Jimmy, are you satisfied? I knew he was guilty from the minute we met him in the avenue, but I'm surprised that he was stupid enough to incriminate himself that way. He really nailed himself to the cross just now."

"I can't see that he incriminated himself. What did you learn that you didn't know before?"

"You astonish me. He just made it clear enough for a blind man that he's keeping Jennie."

"Well, that's big news, ain't it?" Jim said.

"It is to those detectives, Jimmy. It provides the motive they're looking for."

"But it don't explain why he would have waited so long. If Cou'n Tison was harassing Jennie last summer, or if Hart had any idea that Jennie had encouraged him, why would he have waited until now, four or five months later, to do something about it? That's what a lawyer's going to want to know. Hart is an ardent man, Brother. You saw him just now. I can't put my finger on it exactly, but he reminds me of what men must have been like in the old days. You've read *The Iliad*, haven't you?"

"You and your damn books. This is Heyward County, South Carolina, Jimmy. If driving a mail buggy and screwing a colored girl and threatening decent folks is your idea of a hero, you've got too much education for me," Hugh said.

: : :

If Hart had accepted the invitation for the purpose of seeing Jennie, he was surely disappointed, for Jennie was nowhere around. Except for Sallie, no one was. In awkward silence the men sat down to a supper of cold fried chicken, rice and gravy, collard greens, and sweet potatoes. Jim asked Edmund DeSaussure if he liked his new Franklin, but before the lawyer could answer, the front door bell rang. Hugh jumped to his feet and announced that he would get it, but every man at the table followed him out into the hall, linen napkins tucked into their waists. It was the sheriff.

He stood at the foot of the steps, his hands on his hips. His automobile, parked out by the gate, continued to run, its putt putt putt punctuating the prepared speech. "I hate to trouble you again, Mr. Creighton, but after discussing the matter with the detectives, we have decided that it's best to arrest Jennie Grant after all. We don't want no trouble now so I'd be obliged if you could show us to her house."

Jim glanced at Hart. Edmund DeSaussure had a firm grip on his upper arm.

"Herliss," Hugh said, descending the steps, "let me have a word with you in private, if I may."

The two men walked out toward the gate. In just a minute or two they parted; the sheriff returned to the auto and Hugh came back up onto the porch. As the vehicle turned into the long avenue, Hugh said, "I explained to him that Jennie has been sick, that she's just now gotten up from flu, and that we were afraid she couldn't stand the drive to Carthage in this cold night air."

"And he accepted that?" Jim asked.

"Not at first. But I assured him that if she had a relapse and died in his jail, we would hold him responsible. I think that got his attention. Just to show that we wanted to cooperate, I invited them in to supper, but he declined."

The men returned to the table praising Hugh for what he had done, but no one seemed interested in eating. After a few minutes Edmund DeSuassure got to his feet. "If you'll excuse us, gentlemen. It's been a long day, and I have a feeling that tomorrow may be even longer."

Hart stood obediently, took his napkin from his waist, but instead of leaving remained at his place. He started to speak but ran his fingers through his thick dark hair instead. "Before we go, Edmund, just a minute. Hugh, I insulted you before these men this afternoon. It's only right that I offer my apologies in their presence. And thank you for what you just now did. I'm much obliged to you all. For everything."

Hugh looked up from his place at the head of the table, his small white hands palm down on the linen tablecloth. "Jennie is our servant. What I did, I did for her. And for our house."

"That's uncalled for, Brother," Jim said. "Hart, we accept your thanks. I hope you'll be able to get some rest now."

Hugh rose to his feet. The corners of his mouth were white with anger. "Since you're so hell-bent on defending him, Jimmy, why don't you ask him what he was doing over at Cou'n Tison's first thing yesterday morning. Before anybody had heard. Let him answer that."

In the stunned silence that followed, Hugh looked like a man suddenly appalled by what he had said, but he tried to put a face on his regret.

"This is highly inappropriate, gentlemen," Edmund DeSaussure said, and his tone was such as to brook no objection. "We are grateful for your hospitality."

"No," Hart said, pulling free from the lawyer's grasp. "Hell no. If Hugh Creighton wants an answer, fine. I have nothing to hide. I was going over to Tison's Tuesday morning to deliver a message from my mother. He had not been by the house since Christmas afternoon. I think she wanted to see him about some financial arrangements. I don't know, she didn't say. When y'all told me what had happened, I decided to take the papers and bills from his desk. As his only competent male relative, I regarded that as my responsibility. I took the chessmen too, in case you're wondering. That set is a valuable family heirloom, and I had no idea who all might be wandering through his house in the next day or two. I'm telling you this, Hugh Creighton, so you won't go revving your engine on nothing but idle speculation. Do you understand me?"

Hugh nodded and excused himself.

: : :

Hart and Edmund DeSaussure had left. John Baird had gone up to bed, and Jim and Hugh were standing in the dark hall at the foot of the stairs, Hugh holding a candlestick. "That was a fine thing you did tonight, Brother," Jim said. "I was proud of you."

The door at the top of the stairs opened and Sallie appeared, a candlestick extended before her. Jim and Hugh looked up as she came down in a long white flannel gown and nightcap. With the candle flickering upon her features from below, she looked shockingly old. The holiday had been hard on them all but harder, Jim thought, on his sister. Nursing Jennie alone had taken a toll.

"Who was that at the door?"

"We've taken care of it, Sister," Hugh said. "It's nothing you need to fret about."

Fire flashed in Sallie Bonner's blue eyes. "Now you listen to me, Hugh Creighton. This is still my house. I'm thankful to have you men here, but I mean to know what's going on. Is that clear?"

Hugh gave Jim a look. Raised eyebrows. "Yes ma'am. It was Herliss Timmons, Sister. Those Savannah people wanted to arrest Jennie."

"Arrest Jennie? Over my dead body. What on earth for?"

"Because of her connection with Liza Stubbs, they said. They just wanted to take her in for questioning, but we talked them out of it. For the moment at least."

"Brother did," Jim said. "You should have seen him."

"What else?" Sallie asked.

"That's all, as far as I know."

"What about that meeting? What are y'all not telling me?"

"It's complicated," Hugh said. "Can we discuss it in the morning?"

"I want Jennie in this house tonight."

"Why, for goodness' sake?"

"I just do. With everything."

"Where do you plan to put her?" Hugh said. "Mama will have a fit if she sleeps upstairs. You know that."

"Jimmy and Mattie will just have to move back up to John Baird's room."

"And where's he going to sleep?"

"He can find a corner," Sallie said. "Jimmy, I hate to disturb Mattie at this hour, but go ahead and get her up. Brother, you come with me. And let's try not to wake the whole house."

By the time Mattie was up and stirring, Sallie was leading a frightened Jennie into the hall, her large eyes rolling in the candle light. Mattie rushed to help, and the two women led the mulatto woman into the downstairs bedroom, to the bed still warm from where Mattie had been sleeping.

"Lois ain't going to be very happy about this," Hugh said. "Mama either."

"Well, Brother Hugh, it's like Sister said. This ain't their house."

HART

*H*art was sitting on the cottage porch when the hawk struck. The morning was still a little chilly, but he was on the lookout for Edmund DeSaussure, anxious for news of Jennie. The lawyer had left early that morning, hoping to advise her before the detectives got to Sallie's. It was time he was back. Hart had just decided to walk out to the big road to see if the Franklin was on its way when a chicken cackled in distress and he looked up to see, out by the smokehouse, a flurry and a flash of great wings swooping. The hawk swung through its stoop, pulled up in the backyard right above the washpot, banked over the kitchen, talons empty, and headed for the fields.

Hart hurried out to the smokehouse. One of Hattie's bantam hens, a little red pullet, was flopping in the dust, feathers everywhere. The hawk would be back. Hart rushed into the cottage for his .22. That old bandit had terrorized the chicken yard all winter. Hart was glad that he was at home this morning to put an end to its marauding. By the time he got back out, the hawk was beating heavily toward the pines beyond the yard, the pullet dangling from its talons. Hampered by that burden, it lit on the branch of a tall pine less than a hundred yards away. Hart could make that shot. Using the carriage shed for cover, he slipped inside, past the Model T, and stationed himself at the rear window. The hawk's white breast shone in the sun. Hart sighted along the barrel. The hawk was bending over its prey, going to work. Hart squeezed the trigger and the big bird dropped from the limb like a sack of rice.

It was still dying when he walked up, its yellow talons contracting, but its convulsions grew feebler as he watched. When it was dead he picked it up by its feet. The large wings fell open and the copper-colored tail flopped over backwards. Hart lifted the hawk and felt with the ball of his thumb the sharpness of its polished hooked beak. What a splendid bird, he thought. He was sorry that he had had to kill it.

He was on his way back to the porch when the Franklin pulled into the yard. Edmund DeSaussure got out, an unruffled man, smiling with self-assurance. "Good work," he said when he recognized what Hart was carrying. "You saved a world of partridge with that shot."

"I don't begrudge a few partridge. They can take care of themselves. It's these poor defenseless chickens that need protection. This old pirate picked the wrong backyard."

Edmund DeSaussure gave Hart a long look, an expression that stopped him in midstep. Then quietly he spoke. "Did you do it, Hart?"

Hart walked on past the lawyer. When he reached the steps of the cottage, he turned. "Now that I've shot the damn thing, I don't know what to do with it." He headed for the barn. "Robert," he called.

The black man came out to meet him. When he saw the hawk, he clapped his hands and cut a little caper. "Lord God, Mr. Hart. You the one that killed that chicken hawk?"

"Yes. Go throw it off in the woods for me, will you?"

: : :

"I want to hear every word," Hart said to Edmund DeSaussure. "Everything she said." They sat in front of the fire facing each other. "How did she seem to you?"

DeSaussure clipped the end from a long panatella, put it in his mouth, and rolled it around on his tongue. "She was right undone about the letter, but I assured her that she is not a suspect—not of the murder, at least. She was far too weak to have accomplished that." DeSaussure raised his eyebrows at Hart as he lit the cigar. "But they will be interested in how much she knew ahead of time. Prior knowledge would make her guilty of conspiracy."

"She didn't know anything."

"Maybe you had better tell me what you know before we go any further. If you expect my help, you're going to have to cooperate."

Hart got to his feet, backed up to the small fire. "What makes you think I'm going to need any help?"

"That little outburst yesterday, to begin with. Not very smart, my friend."

"Okay. So Jennie is my woman. That's no secret. Any man would have done the same, given the provocation."

"Such as Tison's run-in with her Monday evening?"

"You know about that, do you?"

"I do, and so do the detectives. The yard man says he witnessed the encounter. He gave a statement. What I find of considerable interest is that you know about it too."

Hart groaned. "I hope to God Herliss Timmons keeps his mouth shut about that. If it gets out, Jennie could be in danger."

"I wouldn't rely on the sheriff's good judgment, but she has been moved into the big house. Miss Sallie saw to that last night. But Jennie's not the one that I'm worried about."

"She's the only one I am," Hart said. He put his hands behind his head and stretched. "I don't reckon there's any way for me to talk to her, but if she's in the house I could at least catch a glimpse of her."

Edmund DeSaussure rose and stepped right up to Hart. With

the fire at the end of his cigar he punctuated the sentence he delivered: "If you are fool enough to set one foot on that place, my
friend, there is nothing I can do for you, and take my word for
it, you are going to need my help. Now. I made it clear to her
that she is not required to answer anything she doesn't want to.
But that cuts both ways. Refusal to cooperate never looks good.
They'll be over here this afternoon, I expect. If I were you, I'd
make myself scarce, go to the woods maybe. I'll tell them you've
gone hunting. That at least ought to buy us a little time."

: : :

Hart saddled Cassandra in the barn and slid his L.C. Smith into
the scabbard. He was not going out for the purpose of hunting,
but it paid to go prepared. He might well flush a covey of birds
on the way, or a young buck might cross his path, even a turkey.
He wished he had his old corduroy jacket. He felt unequipped
without it.

Restless, he galloped the mare down the street of cabins and
into the fields beyond. Through tall dead grass and open pines,
he made his way, scattering dingy sparrows before him, until he
came to the sandy lane that would lead him to the swamp. The
lane was crosshatched with shadows of bare limbs, oak and hick-
ory. A black-faced fox squirrel fled at his approach, racing up the
road, its silver plume afloat.

Around a bend and way up ahead, he spied an oxcart, and
perched on its side an old black man that Hart knew to be Uncle
Simon, on his way to his shack at the edge of the river swamp.
Hart had no idea how old Simon was. Born in slavery, he had
seemed ancient when Hart was a child. Through the years Hart
had made a practice of taking the old man game—a couple of
quail, a string of fish, a cut of venison—and though you could
see the sky through Simon's roof Hart had often taken shelter in
the shack from a sudden storm.

He overtook the cart, the mare swinging wide of the long-
horned ox, and reined in. "Afternoon, Uncle Simon."

The old man's face was the color of yellowed ivory and just as smooth. Hart had often wondered who his pa could have been. For all he knew, Simon might be a real uncle of his. Simon nodded in response, touched the brim of his hat.

"You staying warm, Uncle Simon?"

"Yessuh."

"Got enough to eat?"

"Yessuh."

Hart sensed the absurdity of his questions. This old man had outlived need, any need that Hart could supply. It was he whose need was dire. "Reckon it's going to rain tonight?"

"Not tonight, suh. Rain tomorrow. Big rain tomorrow."

Hart wondered, as always, at the confidence of the old man's weather forecasts. "I'm going to leave my horse in your shed, hear?"

"Yessuh."

: : :

Hart rode west, into an increasingly cloudy sky, and the river swamp beckoned, a powerful call that his spirit responded to. He urged the mare on. No one knew the swamp as he did, for ten miles upstream and ten miles down. Among its winding sloughs he could lose himself so completely not even dogs could find him. He knew he could, as he had that winter Miss Sadie Creighton forbade him to call on Agnes. On more than one occasion he had been startled by human voices, timber cruisers, or black folks going fishing, and stood invisible in thin cane like a buck, watching as they passed, understanding what people sound like to a deer. He could live that way again or he could make his way along the river, downstream to Savannah and there jump a freighter bound for Suez. If not for Jennie, he could. She needed his protection, now more than ever, and more than ever he felt helpless to defend her. He could not even identify the enemy.

Three hours later he was sitting by a slough, leaning against a sycamore. He had awakened from a nap to find, right before his eyes, a pair of summer ducks swimming. His hand had crept toward his gun but never reached it, so entranced was he by their beauty—the heavy-crested, war-painted drake, his demure but lovely wife, their images in perfect color reflected perfectly upon black water. Hart's legs had gone to sleep. He needed to stand and stretch. But he was reluctant to startle the ducks. Maybe they would drift on down the slough.

A loud nasal honk, like a blast on a woodwind, distracted him from the ducks. It was a strangely familiar call. And there was the bird, a big woodpecker swinging in to alight at the top of a naked snag just across the water. Hart caught his breath. It had been years since he had seen an ivorybill. He had feared that it, like panthers and parrots, was gone from the Savannah River forever. In the subdued light the scarlet crest glowed. Without taking his eyes from the bird Hart reached for his shotgun. He was hungry for a closer look, eager to hold the bird in his hand. He had always wanted to. Indians had made necklaces of their strong white beaks. There probably weren't enough left to keep a population going anyway. As his fingers closed on the grip of the stock, the woodpecker flew, flapping slowly, majestically in the fading light, calling as it went. Hart stood, sending the summer ducks splashing and squealing. He was glad of the lost opportunity, though he knew he would never see an ivorybill again. He wondered if he really would have shot it. He reckoned he'd never know.

: : :

The sheriff had assured Edmund DeSaussure that Hart was not a suspect, but the lawyer didn't believe him. That had been yesterday when Hart was in the swamp. They would be back today, just to ask a few questions, the sheriff had said, but DeSaussure suspected that arrest was imminent. It was past nine now. Hart had not slept well, had never fully waked up this morning.

He sat slumped in his chair by the cold fireplace. He needed to get up and shave. He had not even brushed his hair. But he could not take his eyes from the painting that hung on the opposite wall, a smoke-darkened oil done by some old aunt, long since dead. Hart's mother had acquired it somehow and passed it on to him because it depicted a deer. But the scene resembled nothing he had ever seen or would ever be likely to——a stag at bay, marooned on a rocky little island in the midst of a stormy sea with dogs or wolves swimming through the waves to attack. Not a sporting scene but something out of ancient myth or legend.

Somehow, one way or another, he was going to see Jennie today.

"The first thing they're going to want to know is where you were Monday evening," DeSaussure said. He was pacing back and forth in the small room. "And I'm afraid that you had better have an ironclad answer."

"I've already told you that," Hart mumbled, his voice dispirited. "I was up at the big house. Sister knows that."

"Yes, but what time did you get there. They'll want proof."

At the sound of an automobile, both men jumped. Someone was out there. Hart stood. "Don't let them take me, Edmund. Not yet. Think of something."

DeSaussure answered the knock. It was John Baird and Jim Creighton, dressed in hunting clothes. Relieved, Hart walked over to greet them, extending his hand to Jim. "Good morning, professor. What an unexpected pleasure. Please come in. You've met Edmund, I believe."

The lawyer stepped forward. "How's the professor this morning?"

"Uncle Jimmy and I wanted to use your dogs if we could, Uncle Hart."

"We just thought we'd see if we could kick up a covey or two," Jim added. "We'd like to have y'all join us if you'd care to."

"Much obliged," said Hart, "but I 'spect we'd better not this morning. But if you'll step outside with me a minute, Jimmy, I'll show you to the dog pen."

When John Baird moved to join them, Hart said, "Keep Mr. DeSaussure company for me, Buddy, would you please? We'll be right back."

The second they came within view of the pen, the dogs set up a racket, yelping and whining and springing into the air, straight up, as high as the top of the fence.

"They must think they're going hunting," Hart said. "They don't do that when I come to feed them. What I can't understand is how that little setter knows. She ain't been shot over since I've had her. She must have learned it from old Hardhead there."

Hart opened the door to Flint's pen. The big, rawboned pointer took off as though shot from a cannon and careened through the vast backyard, scattering hens and startling the washwoman who was taking clothes off the line before it rained.

"Let's give him a minute, work off some of that piss and vinegar."

The setter yelped and whined, cringed and begged. "No, darling," Hart told her. "You ain't going today. We'll take you another time, by yourself. I don't want you learning bad habits."

Flint came thundering past, skidded to a halt, raised his leg, and squirted the corner of his pen. Then he was off again, rocketing down the lane toward the street of servants' houses. Hart placed his tongue against the back of his teeth and gave a piercing whistle. It did not faze the dog. "I don't know why I don't go ahead and shoot that son of a bitch. How's Jennie?"

"I haven't seen much of her, Hart. But Sister says she's doing pretty well, under the circumstances. You know we moved her into the house."

"Edmund told me. I was much relieved. I wonder where she's sleeping?"

"In the downstairs bedroom, on a cot. She didn't want to sleep in the big bed."

Hart found that information pleasing. He allowed himself a smile of satisfaction. "Are they treating her well?"

Jim looked taken aback. "What do you think?"

"I'm sorry," Hart said. "Forget I asked. I should have known better, with Sallie there." After a pause he added, "It's just that

I—" He took a coil of rope from a nail on the side of a shed. "Let's walk back here and find that dog."

With the setter whining piteously behind them, the two men entered the street of servants' houses, unnaturally empty at this hour.

Hart whistled again for the dog, that piercing blast, then walking through the alley between two houses, headed toward a field recently plowed. Cloven tracks, cut perfectly in the thin gray crust, showed where a deer had walked. "They're coming clear up to the house these days. Where they have no business. When are y'all planning to go back?"

"I don't know, Hart. It sort of depends."

"I need to ask a favor of you."

When Jim did not respond immediately, Hart gave him a look. Jim was anxious. He could see that and it saddened him. Of the three Creighton brothers, Jim had always been most loyal, most ready to understand, but today he was keeping his distance. At last he said, "If I can."

Hart reached down and picked up a clod and crumbled it in his hand. "I don't know what's going to happen to me, Jimmy. Edmund thinks they'll be coming for me by tomorrow afternoon. I want you to take Jennie back to Spartanburg, and the sooner the better. Can you do that for me?"

Jim knelt, picked up a fragment of glass, and wiped sand from it. "Do you think they plan to arrest her too?"

"No, I don't. I could stop that anyway if I had to. But she might be in danger from some of these white trash bastards. I wouldn't put it past them."

"Me either, I'm afraid. I just now had a run-in with that Leonard Coe down at Thompson's."

"I'd like to kill that son of a bitch. What did he say?"

Jim looked distressed. "Hart, I'm going to tell you again: you must be careful what you say. I know you don't really mean that, but under the circumstances—" He hesitated. "I had gone in to buy a box of shells. As I was walking out, Coe piped up; asked me if I was a Creighton, wanted to know if I was related to you. I told him yes and he said something vile."

"What?"

Jim offered a perfect imitation of Coe's hard-bitten, piney-woods accent: "'I wouldn't feel too bad about it if I was you, sport. I got some cousins ain't worth a shit my own self.' Something to that effect."

Hart laughed in spite of himself.

"Mr. Thompson told him that he was not going to stand for that kind of language, not in his store, and Coe got all huffy and indignant, said that you had insulted his wife and 'drawed a gun' on him, 'all on account of a nigger girl,' and if that didn't give him the right to say nothing, then this must not be America. And then he said he reckoned Herliss Timmons would be glad enough to hear it. Which is the reason I'm telling you now, Hart. I hadn't wanted to trouble you with it."

"I can't do anything about that now. But that's the very reason I want Jennie away from here."

"If we do take her, Hart—and that's assuming she'd be willing to go—she'd just have to turn right around and come back down. You know she would have to testify."

"There's not going to be a trial."

"You sound mighty sure of that."

Hart stooped and picked up something from the ground. "Well what do you know?" he said. "A birdpoint. A pretty one too." Taking it between his thumb and index finger, he held the delicate artifact to the light—a long, narrow triangle, translucent white, with serrated edges. "The only time I feel close to God is when I find one of these." He slipped the point into his pocket. "There's one other thing, Jimmy."

Jim waited, concern in his face.

"I need to see Jennie."

"Hart. I don't know that that's such a good idea. Under the circumstances, I mean. The house is full of people."

"I didn't mean up there. I can meet her in her cabin."

"Have you thought about the risk to her? Suppose y'all were to be seen? Those detectives have been questioning people all over the place."

"Just give her this." He handed Jim the arrowhead. "And tell her I'll be waiting for her at half-past four this afternoon. At least, let her be the one to decide." Hart hated having to beg, resented Jim for forcing him to. "For God's sake, man. This may be my last chance."

"Okay. I'll do it."

Hart extended his hand. "You're a good man, professor. God bless you."

Jim's grip was weak, involuntary.

"There's that hardheaded son of a bitch." Hart whistled again and the dog came running, bounding across the plowed field, kicking up dust, as though they were the ones who'd been lost and now he had found them. Hart squatted on his heels to receive him, and the dog bowled him over, licking at his face. In seconds Hart had the rope through the collar. "Once y'all have your guns," he said, "he'll go to hunting. But I can't promise he won't bust a covey. You remember how he was the other day?"

"That don't matter," Jim said. "I just wanted to get John Baird out of the house this morning."

"How's he doing?"

"He's holding up."

"How much do you think he knows?"

"How much is there to know, Hart?"

Hart had counted on Jim. Right now he would have welcomed a word of encouragement, even the touch of Jim's hand on his shoulder. "Look. I know this has been hard on y'all," he said. "If I could change it I would. I wouldn't hurt Sallie for anything in the world."

"I know that, Hart. I'm sure she does too, but I 'spect we'd better get moving. I promised the ladies a bird supper tonight, and it looks like it's about to rain."

Hart looked at the sky. The afternoon was growing dark though the hour was not yet four. He had had to take a longer route to Jennie's because of the vigilance of Edmund DeSaussure. "Going for a walk," Hart had said and set out in the direction of the swamp, west when his heart was tending northward. It was as warm as a spring afternoon. Thunder was rumbling in Georgia, rolling his way. He doubted he would beat the rain, but getting wet did not concern him. What did was the likelihood of the rain stopping her. He hoped that she would see it coming and leave for the cabin in time. If Sallie was around, she would never hear of Jennie's going out in the storm, for even so short a distance. A good thing too. He did not want her soaked to the skin any more than Sallie did, certainly not on his account.

He crossed the Charleston Road not far below Wade's place. Among the tall pines on the other side it was almost as dark as night. He wanted Jennie out of Heyward County before he was arrested, but that looked doubtful. She might not yet be well enough to travel such a distance, and even if she were he could not be sure that she would consent to going. That was one of the things he had to tell her. She must go, for her own safety. He was not aware of any organized Klan activity in this neck of the woods, but those boys down at Thompson's were capable of mischief. If they got the notion that she had put him up to killing Tison, they would need no better excuse, and he would not be there to stop them.

Hart had not allowed himself to think about a jail cell. He did not see how he was going to survive confinement, any more than an Indian could.

He would insist that she go with Jim and Mattie, and he would assure her that there would be no trial. In spite of Edmund DeSaussure. Edmund seemed convinced that with Hattie's support of his alibi they had a good chance of acquittal, but entering a plea of not guilty would expose the woman he loved to the drooling grins of every wool-hat yahoo in Heyward County. Hart Bonner's nigger whore, they would call her; the prosecution would treat her as such, and newspapers would parade her through their headlines like a defeated Cleopatra through the streets of Rome. The possibility was too painful to contemplate, but that was one thing he could still prevent. He wanted her to know that. If she went to Spartanburg with Jimmy and Mattie, she would not have to live in fear of coming back for a trial.

It was starting to rain, a pattering of drops. Suddenly the woods went white with lightning, and on its heels a crash of thunder that all but deafened him. As though that were the awaited signal, the skies opened. Before he had gone ten steps he was drenched. By the time he reached the barn his boots were full. Rain fell in sweeping sheets, obliterating all prospects. Even from the barn, he could not make out the cabin. By the same token, though, he could not be seen from the big house. He made a dash for the back door, splashing through puddles. It was dark inside but he knew instantly that she was not there. The room smelled empty. He removed his soaked hat and placed it at the end of the mantel. His hair was plastered to his forehead; he wanted something to dry it with. Too wet to sit down, he stood in front of the cold fireplace, placed his arms on the mantel, and put his head down. He was cold.

She had waited too long to leave. He could not expect her now until the rain let up. Even then it would take a good excuse for her to gain Sallie's consent.

Lightning illumined the room, a startling flicker, revealing the little tinseled Christmas tree, its needles all but shed, and there across the foot of her bed, where he had left it, his corduroy jacket. Hart took off his soaked coat and dropped the heavy garment on the bricks. Then his shirt and undershirt. Somewhere he might find a rag to dry off with, but first he wrung out his garments over the bucket she kept on the hearth.

The clock on the mantel had stopped. Shivering, he removed

his watch and snapped it open: 4:20, it said, but it too had stopped, drowned out.

He found a towel on one of the shelves in the curtained recess. When he had dried himself from the waist up, he put the jacket on over his naked skin and felt a weight in the left-hand pocket. His fingers closed on glass. Jennie had put the bottle back where it had come from. Bless her heart. It was still half-full. Hart turned it up, and the whiskey burned its way to his belly.

The rain was beating so loudly on the tin roof that even if she were here they would not be able to talk. He unlaced his boots, stepped out of them, and emptied them into the bucket. Then he wrung out his stockings. She was probably standing at the kitchen door right now waiting for the rain to slacken. He wished he could build a fire.

He had not thought beyond his refusal to plead not guilty. He needed to see her first, to know that she knew that he loved her, no matter what lay ahead. They would not have time to talk, not as he wished they could, but what he needed to hear would not take long.

: : :

Hart wondered what time it was. Jennie's windows had grown almost as dark as night. The rain seemed to have eased up, though it was still coming down in a steady drizzle. He took another drink. Sallie must be in the kitchen. He sat down on the hearth, folded his arms around his knees, and put his head down. His head was hurting, right behind his eyes, and he was chilled to the bone. She was probably hoping that the storm had kept him from coming, but she knew him too well for that.

A noise startled him from sleep. For a moment he dared to hope. "Jennie?" he said, and though he had known that she was not there, the sound of her name in the chill, damp darkness of that cabin was almost more than he could bear. He stood and reached for the bottle on the mantel. Edmund may have warned her that he would try to see her; Jimmy may have advised her not to go. He opened the back door. Trees were dripping but the rain had stopped. He walked outside, still barefooted. A lamp was burning in the room where she was staying. She was not coming.

Nothing Hart had ever done was harder than putting on his wet clothes again—his undershirt and shirt, his stockings, and his heavy, waterlogged boots. What happened to him now did not matter. He took another drink, seeking oblivion, but the whiskey merely lay like a cold stone in his gut, absorbing the last of his vitality. He felt as though he was moving underwater. She had not come because she thought he was going to tell her that he had killed Tison, that he had done it for her sake, and that knowledge she could not bear. That was why she had remained in the big house.

He thought about writing her a note but what could he say? That he had waited long past the time the rain had stopped, hope dying with the failing of the bleak light outside? That would only cause her to feel bad. The wet spot by the hearth was calling card enough.

: : :

Hart was not drunk but his cold feet never found the path in the flooded, pitch-black woods. For a while he splashed through darkness, blundering into wet brush. At last he stumbled into the big road, surprised to see that he had not gotten beyond Willie Small's. A dim candle glowed in the window of the cabin, and Willie's dogs were barking, dogs that came running out to greet him every day when he passed in the mail buggy. They were coming now, but one—a big dog of no recognizable breed—was growling. They were after him. He walked on, faster, but the pack was closing in. One, snarling, nipped at the back of his leg. Hart spun, wishing for a stout cudgel. The big dog rushed in. Hart swung his bottle at it and cursed them all, goddamn mangy curs, hell dogs, and walking backwards he brandished the bottle, daring them to try. But they fell back, having driven him beyond their territory. He stopped, drained the bottle, and flung it at the sound of their barking.

: : :

The whiskey hit him before he reached the cottage. He stumbled in, too intoxicated to respond to Edmund DeSaussure's tirade. Settled in the chair by the fire, he struggled to unknot his boots. "Been for a walk," he said, noticing that his speech was slurred.

The sheriff and detectives had come by again that afternoon, DeSaussure said, just before it rained, and they were not very happy to find him gone. Timmons expected to be back out here tomorrow afternoon with a warrant for Hart's arrest. They had to settle some matters tonight.

Hart knew that DeSaussure would not urge going to trial if he did not think they had a good chance of winning. But it seemed to him that the lawyer was too insistent. The trial would be a sensation, covered by every newspaper from Columbia to Savannah, and Edmund DeSaussure would be at center stage.

"The jury cannot convict unless the state removes the last shadow of doubt," DeSaussure said, "and they cannot do that. Four people can testify that you were in your mother's house Monday night."

"My family and an old Negro cook. Who is going to take their word for it?"

"Just a shadow of a doubt, Hart. That's all it takes. And I can create that, I assure you. I'm good."

Hart stood. "I'm sure you are, but I will not enter a plea of not guilty, Edmund. There will be no trial. I cannot subject my mother. At her age it would kill her. And poor Sister, who knows so little of the world. I will not."

"Then you are a fool," the lawyer said.

"If I didn't think you were trying to help, Edmund, I would demand an apology for that."

"You are the one who should apologize. If you refuse to plead not guilty, you know the alternative. Is that what you want?

Don't think that a guilty plea is going to save your neck. It might, since the evidence is circumstantial, but I wouldn't bet my life on it."

"No, I'll not do that either," Hart said.

DeSaussure threw up his hands. "Then what in God's name do you propose? Running like a coward? That would amount to the same thing but with worse consequences. If you aren't willing to heed my advice, Hart, you might as well take the honorable way out. You leave yourself no choice."

: : :

Hart lay awake in bed, chased from sleep by the hounds of Willie Small. Sunlight framed the drawn window shade. It seemed to him that he had not slept at all. His head was pounding. He got up, put on a bathrobe, and stepped into the living room. Edmund DeSaussure was sitting by the fire, shaved and dressed, writing in a tablet. He looked up and smiled. Hart nodded and went on into the kitchen. He put a pot of water on the stove, poured a cup of coffee, and walked out onto the back stoop to pee. The sun was coming up through the bare branches of trees, shining in his face. The air was brisk—a good day for a deer drive. That's what he would be doing if not for this.

He gave the water time to heat, making his coffee last, lifting his face to the sun. He fancied he could feel it on his forehead.

When the pot was steaming, he carried it to his room and poured the water into a flowered basin on the washstand. He took his razor from the drawer, his brush and mug of soap, honed the razor on a leather strap and tested its edge. He leaned toward his reflection in the mottled mirror and massaged his cheeks and jowls.

Sagging with mortality, he mused. Out loud he said, "My name is Joseph Hart Bonner. I was born in Cypress Swamp, South Carolina, on the twelfth day of June in 1875. I am forty-three years old."

He lathered his chin and jaws, and the skin of his face went dark in contrast to the thick white soap. When he had shaved and put away his brush and razor, he made up the bed and put on the same dark suit he had worn to Tison's funeral. The spicy scent of the bay rum with which he had splashed his cheeks was strong in the room.

Edmund DeSaussure looked up from his tablet when Hart walked in. "Feeling better this morning?"

"Much better, thank you. I hope you slept well."

The lawyer said he had.

"I think we'll have dinner at the house today, Edmund. I wonder if you'd run over and let Sister know."

"Right now?"

"If you don't mind. I just don't feel like facing them yet."

"It's not too early?"

"For those folks? They've been up for hours."

As soon as Edmund DeSaussure had closed the door, Hart returned to his room. His brother Johnny was on his mind, Johnny's last buck. A sorry little deer it had been, a small cowhorn spike, but Johnny had known that it was the last one he would ever kill and he wanted to show it to John Baird. The boy had almost died of scarlet fever, and though he was mending he was still confined to bed.

Hart drove Johnny home in a borrowed step-down buggy, designed for the sick and elderly, and the mule that carried the buck came along behind. As they rolled into the yard, Johnny said, "Stop right here. I'll be right back." By the time he returned from the house the boy was at the upstairs window, his white face pasted to the glass. Johnny caught an antler of the buck, but the neck had stiffened so that he could not lift the head. "Give me a hand with this," he said.

His freckles stood out like blotches on his face, and pain was etched in every line. Hart took the other antler, and slowly the stiff neck yielded. In the upstairs window small hands waved like fluttering moths. Though Hart could not see her behind the reflecting panes, he knew that John Baird's nurse was holding him up to the window, her face so close to the child's that her hair tickled his cheek. She had spent the last two weeks sleeping on a pallet in the sickroom, taking turns with Sallie at the bedside. Who could imagine what those two women talked about through the long, dangerous watches of the night? One evening a few days back Hart had ridden by to check on his nephew, and in the upstairs window the shadow of a woman had loomed upon the wall, but he had not been able to tell which of the women it was.

When Nathaniel had led the burdened mule around to the back and Johnny had gone in to lie down, Hart stopped in the kitchen for a cup of coffee. She poured it. He asked how the boy was doing. She said he was almost well, she thought at last that she might be able to sleep in her house tonight. Her own bed sure would feel good after all those nights on the floor.

The cabin had not been warmed by a fire since John Baird got sick. The bedclothes smelled of old ashes. Hart lay stretched on the lumpy mattress, fully dressed in the damp chilly dark, praying that she would come. If she could get away she would, but Sallie might decide she needed her again tonight, especially with Johnny sick.

A fire was out of the question. Someone would notice the glow in the window or smell the smoke, someone who knew that Jennie was sleeping at the big house. But maybe he would get up in a minute and lay in some wood and kindling, be ready. It was ten now and he was weary. He'd better get up and lay the fire before he fell asleep.

The woodshed stood out back where he was not likely to be seen from the house. Hart made two trips, loading his arms with fat wood and as many sticks of dry split pine as he could manage. Inside, he dumped the wood onto the brick hearth, knelt in the ashes, and carefully built the sticks into a loose crib, slipping the greasy kindling underneath. When it was ready for the match, he returned to Jennie's bed.

Almost immediately he eased into a haze in which he was burning off woods, as he had done the winter before, working for Johnny, preparing a crop of longleaf for turpentining in the spring. He was walking through the pines, dragging a burning rope across pine straw, watching the spreading V of little flames, al-

most invisible in the pale winter sunlight. Then the rope became a fox with its tail on fire. It ran between his legs and raced ahead through open trees, a living torch streaking through the woods like fireworks, laying a path of flame as it fled, yet unconsumed itself. Then somehow Hart found himself in Jennie's cabin, watching from the bed as the firebrand pinwheeled through the room, setting it ablaze. Surprisingly unalarmed, he was idly wondering where he might find water to quench such a conflagration when he felt himself being lifted from the middle by his belt, and opening his eyes he saw Jennie, kneeling beside him on the bed, trying to solve his buckle.

"I was starting to think you were too hard asleep to be woke up," she said.

Illumined only by the flicker of firelight, she went about the task of skinning his trousers down over his hips as efficiently as a nurse preparing a patient for a bath. She seemed amused by something, he did not know what. He thought he must have died and was waking up in heaven.

Sitting astride his hips, she pulled her chemise over her head. Hart placed his big hands on her rib cage, felt its ridges as it rose and fell with her deep inhalations. In that light his hands seemed darker than her skin. Hart imagined that her Creighton blood was running high, blushing her breasts pink. As an infant he had nursed at a chocolate bosom, dear ample Alma, because his mother had no milk. That's what he wanted to do now. As he took her nipple in his mouth, it seemed to him that he and Jennie were more than cousins, closer than man and wife.

By a mere shift of her hips they became one. He closed his eyes upon a red darkness in which embers floated, glowing. When he opened them again, she was looking down at him, her large eyes hot and dark, her face suffused with joy. An ache to merge completely, to blend mind and soul as well as body, overwhelmed him. With his arms around her back he gathered her to his chest, rolled over, almost falling from the bed, and willed himself into herself. If only he might cease thinking and lose himself in her, past finding. But he could not. Even then he was conscious of her hair against his cheek, an itch in the corner of his eye, the need to adjust his rhythm to hers, and then, dear God, too soon, all need was met forever and forever and forever amen.

Yet it had remained, that need, through all these years, a cavity somewhere behind his heart. He sat down at the table by the

window, a plain pine table with a single drawer, hammered together by Johnny before he was born. He held out his hand in
the sunlight, closed it and opened it again. What a marvelous
machine, he thought. And the hair on the back of his hand, bur-
nished by the sun. And his strong clean nails. He opened the
drawer and removed a fountain pen and a bottle of ink and a
small stack of yellowed stationery. Any man unwilling to lay
down his life for the woman he loved lived a life not worth the
effort. Thank God he had the opportunity, at last. He wished
that he could explain that, but he had no way of knowing into
what hands his words might fall. For her sake, he could not risk
so much as the mention of her name.

He dipped the pen into the ink.

> In full realization of the fact that this terrible, shocking decision
> I will shortly make will tend to prove conclusively that I am
> guilty of the murder of my brother Tison, I am leaving this last
> statement with the earnest hope that it will some day, and that
> in the very near future, clear my good name of the suspicion now
> resting upon it. I can only feel that God will not permit it to re-
> main always with my memory to be a stain on the honored name
> of the Bonner family.

Hart paused, lifted his eyes to the bright backyard. Then wrote
again, the scratchings of the pen loud in the room.

> He above all knows I am innocent of any connection whatso-
> ever. My dear sister Hattie and my poor dear brother Pinckney
> know that I am innocent as I was with or near them both con-
> tinually from the time I reached home in the late afternoon of
> December 30, 1918 to the time I retired for the night which was
> about eleven o'clock. My last wish is that other relatives and
> friends of mine will share their belief.

Hart read over what he had written. Edmund would be back
any minute. It would have to do. He signed his name, "Hart

Bonner," and waved the sheet in the air. Then quickly he took another sheet and hastily he scrawled.

To the Administrators of my estate. It is my desire that all saleable property and belongings of mine be sold and converted into cash, and after all my debts are paid, every penny that I own, including moneys, Georgia State Certificates, Liberty Bonds, and everything that would have come to me be used in employing competent detectives or offering rewards for the apprehension and conviction of the guilty murderer of my brother.

He lowered the window shade. Against the light it shone bright orange. He returned the pen and ink to the drawer and removed the owlhead .32. It felt so light and rickety in his palm.

JIM CREIGHTON

*J*im had lain awake much of the night pondering what he would say to Hart. The poor man had been crying out for understanding yesterday afternoon, and Jim had turned his back. But what does one say to a friend who has killed his brother? Jim still didn't have an answer to that question, but he was determined to see Hart as soon as possible this morning. At daybreak he was dressed and ready to go, but Mattie persuaded him to wait. If Hart were still asleep, she said, it wouldn't do to wake him; the poor fellow needed his rest. Jim idled his way through two more cups of coffee, and then, as he was walking out the door, Hugh came into the kitchen. As usual, he was in a hurry, a man with important things to do and no time to waste. He wanted Jim to take him by Wade's house; he'd be ready in a minute.

"How do you plan to get back? I'm going on to Hart's."

"I'll get Wade to drop me off on his way to the store."

A blustery wind out of Georgia was scattering clouds, and the morning sun was slanting through. As Jim and Hugh drove south down the Charleston Road, the wet pines sparkled and the water in the ditches reflected light.

It was half-past eight when Jim turned into Wade's avenue—

a rambling, one-story frame structure their father had built the year he was married and spent the rest of his life expanding, adding rooms as children were born, in whatever direction his fancy took him. Now it was showing signs of neglect, a shutter hanging askew, its walls in need of paint. And the plants his mother had tended all her life—the azalea borders, the camellias and japonicas—had grown leggy or scabrous or they had given up and died, and the yard was littered with the playthings of children, broken and forgotten. Wade had more than he could handle.

They found him in the pecan grove on the left side of the house, dressed for work. The wind must have prevented him from hearing the approach of the auto, but when he saw it he came over to greet them.

"Y'all are out mighty early. Anything going on?"

Before Jim could speak, Hugh said, "Yeah. We need to talk about Jennie."

Jim was astonished. "Now look here, Brother," he said. "I agreed to drop you off, not to sit here at Wade's discussing Jennie. Why involve Wade anyway? It's none of his concern."

"Hart ain't going anywhere. Not yet anyway."

Hugh got out of the car and a gust of wind took his hat, tumbling it across the yard beneath the pecan trees, and he went chasing after it. Wade came around to the driver's side, one hand on his hat, and his kind face was troubled. "What's going on with Jennie?"

"Nothing. Brother wants to move her back out to her cabin. Or Lois does. But I don't see what that has to do with you. If you want to discuss it with him, you go right ahead. I'm on my way to Hart's."

Jim put the automobile in gear and eased forward, but Hugh stepped into his path. "Just hold your horses, Jimmy." Wade followed Hugh to the window. Jim looked up at his brothers. "Now I'm as fond of Jennie as y'all are," Hugh said, "but something has to be done. With all the talk that's going round, it's just too dangerous for her to stay here."

"In the house, you mean?"

"I mean in Cypress Swamp."

Jim switched off the ignition and got out. He had had about enough of Hugh's proprietary manner.

"Where would she go?" Wade asked. "We can't just put her in the road. You know Sister wouldn't hear of that, doing her that way."

"For God's sake, Wade. What do you think I am? I'm not talking about putting her in the road. I know some people in Orangeburg. A doctor and his wife. They're kin somehow to the Gilberts in Camden, good people," Hugh said.

"How do you know they'd take her?"

"I've already spoken to them. They need help and they have a servant's house in the backyard. They'll treat her well."

"And what makes you think that Jennie would agree to go?" asked Jim.

"Jennie might not have the luxury of a vote. If Hart's arrested, and I don't think there's any question he will be, I'm worried about the wool-hat crowd. They're stirred up as it is, and she's the one they're blaming. As long as Jennie's on the place, she endangers us all. It's just that simple."

"Not to mention the danger to her," Jim added.

"Well, of course, Jimmy. That goes without saying."

"I think I have a solution," Jim said. "I spoke to Mattie about Jennie's going back to Spartanburg with us. She's in favor of it."

"Jennie will be subpoenaed. Don't you realize that?"

"What's this?" Wade said.

A black man had burst from the oak grove that stood between Wade's house and Miss Emma Bonner's place and was running toward them through Wade's cornfield, knocking down dead stalks. It was James Salley, who looked after Pinckney and kept house for Hart. He was coming fast, like a herald out of an Old Testament tale, and his yellow face was congested with unannounced catastrophe.

Jim placed his hands on the top of the Buick and leaned forward, scared to death that James's long strides were measuring out for him the last moments of ordinary peace, of hearty appetite and untroubled sleep, that he would ever know.

James reached them out of breath. He stood for a moment bent over, his hands on his knees, trying to catch his breath. When he looked up, his face in spite of the cold glistened with sweat. "Y'all better come quick, sir. It's Mr. Hart."

: : :

Black people stood out by the smokehouse, yardmen and field hands, huddled together, keeping their distance from the cottage. When the Creighton brothers piled out of the Buick, Jim could hear them moaning, low and restrained but threatening to swell. Edmund DeSaussure came down from the porch to meet them, shaking his handsome silver head. Guarded and deliberate, he shook hands with each of them, greeting them by name. The lawyer's hand was cold and moist.

"I saw it coming, gentlemen, but I didn't think this soon."

There was something in DeSaussure's manner that rubbed Jim the wrong way, something close to relief and an assumption that the Creightons felt the same.

"When did it happen, Edmund?" Hugh asked.

"Just now, Hugh. Not twenty minutes ago. He asked me to go up to the big house and tell Miss Hattie that we'd be having dinner with them today. I stayed for a cup of coffee. Not more than twenty minutes. And when I got back—"

Wade was having a hard time, his face working to hold back tears. Jim could not allow himself to look at him. He needed a place to sit down, to be alone, away from these others. That damned smooth lawyer. And Brother, who might have been discussing a business matter, for all the feeling he was showing.

"You didn't hear the shot?" Hugh asked.

"No. As I said, he waited until I'd left for the big house. But I just had no idea."

Jim walked over to the steps of the cottage. The front porch and door were the same as he had seen them dozens of times before, no different from the way they had looked yesterday afternoon. If that were really the house of a man who had turned his hand against himself, twenty minutes dead and still bleeding on the floor, there should be a sign of it somehow, a sympathetic scaling off of paint, at least a shattering of windowpanes. Jim sat down, his head in his hands, and the discussion plodded on against the background murmurs of the black men.

"How was he, Edmund—I mean, this morning?"

"Well, I didn't see him until a short while ago. He came out to heat a kettle of water, I think. But we had sat up late last night, and when he didn't appear first thing I assumed he was still asleep. Though to be perfectly honest I didn't see how he could be."

"Was there any indication last night?"

"He wasn't behaving like a sane man, if that what's you mean. I tried to get him to look at the situation, to understand that Timmons was going to arrest him, but he wouldn't hear it. The harder I tried to reason with him, the more irrational he became. I assured him that we had a good chance for acquittal, but he absolutely refused to consider it, said he couldn't expose his mother and Miss Hattie to a sordid trial. But he said he would not plead guilty either. I'll tell you the truth, gentlemen, I was at my wit's end."

Edmund DeSaussure took a panatella from a coat pocket and cut off the end.

"Was he drinking?" Hugh asked.

"A right good bit last night. He left the house yesterday afternoon. That was another thing. Going out in that driving rain. I tried my best to stop him, but he was bound and determined. He'd been drinking when he came in."

"You don't know where he went?" Hugh asked.

"I think he just wandered off in the woods somewhere. He didn't get back home until way after dark. Soaked to the skin, of course. Do any of y'all want to go in?"

Jim started toward the dog pen.

"Hey," Hugh called. "Where are you going?"

"I'm going to take a walk."

"We're getting ready to go in."

"Go ahead. I'm staying out here."

Jim wanted to see the little Lewallyn setter. *No, darling, you ain't going today. We'll take you another time.* Had Hart still believed as late as yesterday afternoon that he would continue into the future, still assumed as others might that he would have all the time he needed to train that little dog? When had he changed his mind? Alone in Jennie's cabin, dripping rainwater, waiting for her to come? If only Jim had obeyed the impulse of his hand, if only he had offered by that touch the assurance that he cared. He could all but feel in his palm right now the hard, muscled shoulder beneath Hart's shirt. The man had wanted to talk, and he, Jim Creighton, professor of language, had not offered a single word. Jim squeezed his eyes shut against the image of Hart standing wet at Jennie's mantel, looking up with expectation at every little creaking sound.

"Jim!"

Wade and Edmund DeSaussaure were still standing in the yard, looking toward the cottage door where Hugh, his mouth wide open, was calling out, "Come quick! I think he's still alive."

Jim rushed past Wade and the lawyer, who seemed planted to the spot, but as he met Hugh at the door they were coming up the steps behind him.

The window shade was drawn in Hart's room, making it hard to see. Jim wondered why Brother had not raised it. Then he saw. He would have had to step across Hart's body. It lay sprawled face down on the rug and just beyond the outflung hand the dull gleam of a little pistol.

"I heard him groan. I swear to God I did."

Jim knelt beside the body, placed his hand on a shoulder, and lowered his ear to Hart's face.

"Hart," he whispered.

Hart's lips moved.

"Here, Brother, give me a hand."

Jim gently turned Hart onto his back, then caught him under the arms. The left side was warm and wet. He jerked his hand away, wanting to wipe it clean. But Hugh, trying to lift the stockinged feet, had let them slip from his grasp. Jim ignored the blood.

"For God's sake, Brother. Grab him under the thighs. Easy now."

The inert body was almost too heavy for them, but with quick, stumbling, baby steps they lifted Hart onto the bed. The front of his shirt was soaked dark and one side of his face shone darkly in the gloom. He kept moving his lips but no sound came.

Jim's hand was sticky. While he looked around for a towel, Hugh perched on the side of the bed and leaned over the stricken man. "Hart. Do you know who this is?"

Hart whispered "Hugh," barely audible.

"Why did you do this, Hart?"

Jim was bending over Hugh, his hand tingling for attention. He saw the movement of Hart's lips but did not hear his answer.

"What did he say?" Jim whispered.

"'Just so.' He said, 'Just so.'"

Directing himself to Hart, Hugh asked if he had anything to say about Tison.

There was not even a movement of lips.

"Listen to me, Hart. God will not forgive an unconfessed soul."

"For God's sake, Brother," Jim said. "Move."

Jim edged his brother aside and bent his face to Hart's ear. "This is Jimmy, Hart. Do you have anything you want to say?"

"Pray," Hart said, his voice light and husky.

Jim took his hand. "Pray these words along with me, Hart. Will you do that?"

Hart said, "Yes," stronger and clearer than before.

"Father, forgive me."

Hart moved his lips.

"Of all of my sins."

The lips moved.

"And receive my soul."

Hart groaned.

"Into thine eternal life."

Hart said, "Life."

"In Jesus' name, amen," Jim said, then bowed his head.

Hart lay still, staring at the ceiling.

The blood on Jim's hand and wrist was growing tacky. He passed his hand before Hart's face and then he closed the dead man's eyes and once again he said, "Amen."

The two brothers stood, uncertain as to what to do, embarrassed to look at one another. Jim felt like a man who had intruded upon another's utmost privacy. He bent down to pick up the pistol.

Hugh said, "Better not move that," but Jim had already taken it up, the stubby barrel in his fingertips. It was the rickety little owlhead that Hart carried for snakes, but Tison had been shot with a .38. If Hart owned a pistol of the larger caliber, why had he not used it this morning? He placed the weapon on the desk beneath the window and raised the shade. Sunlight filled the room.

"God in heaven," cried Hugh. "Look at this, Jimmy. He shot himself in the head too. How in the world did he manage that?"

Jim did not want to look, did not care to understand. He had just found a letter, its ink hardly dry.

: : :

Out on the porch. Jim noticed for the first time Hart's old setter Dan, lying beside the banister, its head between its paws, a forlorn expression on its whitened face.

Dogs know more than we think they do, Jim thought.

Wade was sitting on the steps, his head in his hands. He did not look up.

Edmund DeSaussure approached, a question on his smooth tan face.

"He's gone," Hugh said.

"But he was still alive when you went in? I could have sworn he was dead when I—"

"Well, he wasn't," Jim said.

"Was he able to say anything?"

"No."

"We better go ahead and call the coroner. But we're going to have to do something about them first." The lawyer indicated with a jerk of his head the big house where Hattie and Pinck and Miss Emma were going about their morning, unaware. "Y'all have any ideas?"

Let Brother answer that one, Jim decided. He was on his way back down to the dog pens.

The pointer and the little setter bitch began to whine and wag their tails when they saw Jim coming. Who would take care of them now? he wondered. Somebody could make a decent dog out of Flint. He had found four coveys for them yesterday morning and busted only one. All it would take was regular work. Jim did not know the setter's name. He had not heard her called anything but "darling."

He walked around to the far side, upwind of the stink of dogshit. The blood on his hand had dried. He wanted to think about the note. "Y'all don't know what's happening, do you?"

The setter whined, stood up against the hogwire, eager for his touch.

Hart had been clean-shaven. Jim was just now realizing that. He must have stood before the mirror this morning, stropped his razor and lathered his face, leaned in close to the glass and scraped with careful strokes, his mind made up. Then he had made up the bed. Then he had sat down at his desk beneath the window and gazed out upon dripping trees.

Jim did not want to look at this: Hart opening the drawer of the desk and removing paper, a bottle of black ink, a fountain pen, that pistol, arranging them before him.

Jim knew the negligible weight of the little pistol. He wished he didn't. Imagined in spite of himself the hard press of the muzzle through the shirt.

He stepped over to the gate of the setter's pen and removed the staple from the hasp. When he opened the gate the pretty black-ticked bitch sprang out and leapt all around him while Flint, aggrieved, barked his resentment.

"You want out too? You hardheaded son of a bitch?"

Jim opened the gate and the dog took off just as he had yesterday morning, and the little setter followed, doing her best to keep up. The dogs went careening through the bare backyard, skidding around corners, scattering hens, flushing guineas into the low branches of a live oak.

And still Hart Bonner pulled the trigger. The shot slammed him hard against the back of the chair, and his reaction pitched him forward, face down on the desk. The pistol hit the pine floor with a small noise.

How long did he lie there, slumped and soaking the front of his shirt, before he realized that it was taking too long to die, before he fumbled at his feet for the dropped pistol?

Jim looked around for something to pick up—a piece of plow point, a broken singletree, a length of rusted chain—it didn't matter as long as he could grip it in his hands. But no such thing presented itself. Brother was calling him. He took out his pocketknife and began to work carefully at a post of the pen. It was a cedar post. The silver shavings curled away from the blade. The exposed wood was red. He put his nose to it.

"What in God's name are you doing down here?"

"Seeing to Hart's dogs."

Hugh shook his head. "We're ready. Come on."

"Have you been up to the big house?"

"Edmund's up there now. We decided to tell them that Hart was cleaning his gun."

"Will they believe that?"

"If they need to bad enough. That crowd don't live in the same world we do. Come on now. We've got to get on back and call Bert Akers."

"I've got to get these dogs up first," Jim said.

"James can do that. We have telephone calls to make."

"I let them out. I need to get them back in."

"What in the hell did you do that for?"

Jim looked at his brother. Hugh was fidgeting, anxious to get on with what had to be done. Jim knew that there was no way to answer his question. "I'm going to take that little Darling back to Spartanburg."

Part *Four*

JENNIE

*J*ennie remembered Jim Creighton kneeling by her chair in the sunlight and then the hot jolt of bourbon that restored her to the hated day, but her terrible cry she had no recollection of. Nor did she recall anything about the rest of Saturday afternoon and night. In her memory those hours would be forever blotted out by Hart's face—the face she never saw, waiting in the paltry light of her cabin for her to open the door. Whether she tried to blind herself to it by staring out the window at the January glare or closed her eyes against it in the darkness, its expression never changed.

: : :

Sunday morning. The sounds of the family moving about the house, the slow steps in the rooms overhead, the faint smells of breakfast. The wallpaper was driving her crazy. Hardly fifteen years since the house was built, and the posies in its pattern had faded to a ghost of color. They may have once been blue. A place by the mirror, on the wall opposite the four-poster, had blistered. She scratched at it with the strong nail of her index finger. The paper was of heavy stock but dry and punky, and it tore easily. Placing her fingers beneath it, she lifted it away from the wall, peeling off a strip that was shaped like a dagger.

When then? he had asked, the last words to her from him who had been her first and truly her only man. They had echoed in her ears a thousand times since yesterday morning, demanding an answer that now she could never give.

Another strip of paper came loose. She dropped it with the others at her feet.

She might at least have said, "tomorrow," or the day after that, or any of the thousands their lifetime might yet have granted them, but she had not.

When then?

Not Friday afternoon in the pouring rain. Jim had advised her against it, but she would have gone anyway had she not been afraid. Not of the sheriffs but of him, of what he had wanted so badly to tell her that he had walked two miles through the rain. By four-thirty she had convinced herself that she knew what it was: that he had killed his brother and had done it for her sake. And she had not been prepared to accept that gift. She would see him another time.

When then?

And so he had waited at the cold fireplace, sopping wet and chilled to the bone, leaning against the mantel, head down but listening through the rain on the tin roof above for the sound of an opening door. And when at last he had known she was not coming, he must have asked, if not now, when? And answered the question for them both.

Jennie could not stop weeping.

She knelt by her cot and tried again to pray. She didn't know if it did any good to pray for the soul of a man already dead— dead by his own hand too—but such was the impulse that seized her. She prayed with closed eyes and moving lips that she might be granted some day to see his face on the other side and to know by his eyes that he forgave her. But the petitions sank like tired balloons at the end of a birthday party and piled up around her where she knelt.

She rose wearily to her feet. There had been a time, and that not long ago, when her prayers, even as they rose groaning from her inmost self and uttered themselves into language, resonated in the chambers of her faith, blessing her with the assurance that they were heard. But not now. The bleak, cracked ceiling dropped a little lower with each creeping hour. God had been on vacation for a week now. If He could not return to her when she needed Him, He might as well stay gone. She saw no reason for living. Yet no sooner had she framed that terrible thought than the prospect of herself alone, abandoned and unassisted, clutched her bones with an icy grip.

: : :

They buried Hart on Monday afternoon, a brief graveside service attended by a small gathering of uncomfortable kinfolk. The preacher had balked at first; he had never presided at the funeral of a suicide, and this was consecrated ground. But Hugh reminded him that he was a Methodist. Besides, old Miss Emma would not understand; she had been told that Hart was cleaning his guns. If the preacher liked his situation, he would think again. The mourners had to take care not to step on the still raw mound of Tison's grave.

: : :

By Monday evening Jennie had exposed a large section of the plaster beneath the paper. The next morning, when Sallie brought her breakfast, she looked at the damage and her eyes swam with tears. "I've been wanting to speak to you for several days now, Jennie. We're concerned about you. All of us are."

Poor Sallie, Jennie thought, trouble in her house, and she can't even bring herself to name it cause then she'd have to talk about it, and she don't know what to say.

Jennie was sitting on the cot, still in her nightgown. Sallie walked over and touched her on the shoulder, then turned toward the door. Then stopped. "You know, Jennie, the Bible says that we will have tribulation, in this world we will. 'But be of good cheer,' it says, 'for I have overcome the world.' I am trying hard to remember that. I hope you will too."

Good cheer was as far beyond Jennie's means as a crackling fire to a cold fireplace, but her soul leapt at the news of its possibility.

⁖ ⁖ ⁖

Jennie had been asleep when Sallie brought her supper, and Sallie had not awakened her. When she did open her eyes, the room was dark. Without a clock she had no idea of the time, but a soft yellow light was shining through the crack beneath the door, reflected off the polished pine boards. People were still up. She rose from the cot and crossed the room to draw the curtains, but through the window something caught her eye—out there near her cabin: torches, spooky tongues of fire flaring in the wind, and by their orange light figures moving about the yard. They moved in random ways, to no purpose that Jennie could understand, and then two of them bent at her cabin window and peered inside. She felt violated, exactly as she would have if she had been sitting out there in her room, and she was terrified. Where was everybody? Had she been left alone, helpless against those torches? Paralyzed by pity for her unprotected little house, she tried to cry out, to scream an alarm, but no sound came. Then, by a surge not of herself, she was plunging through the dark room, banging into furniture, bursting out into the hall.

Jim and Hugh and John Baird were sitting by the fire in the front room, Jim with his stockinged feet propped up on the cherry butler's table, reading a book. All three looked up as she stumbled in, alarmed by the terror in her face.

"There are people," she cried. "Out there."

Jim caught her by the arms. "Easy now," he said. "People out where?"

"Torches." She pointed and tried to hide behind him.

"Okay, Jennie. Calm down now. No one's going to hurt you.

I promise you that. John Baird, get the guns. And the shells. They're on the shelf."

John Baird returned with a gun on each arm, the box of shells in his hand. Jim took the older gun and left the Smith for his brother. They were dropping shells into the chambers when Sallie and Mattie came rushing in from the kitchen, still in their aprons. Jennie flew to Sallie's arms.

"Do be careful, boys," Sallie pled.

The breeches of the shotguns snapped and clicked.

"John Baird," Hugh said, "I want you to stay in here and look after the ladies. I don't want you out there, you hear?"

"He's not going a place in this world," his mother said, "but upstairs with us."

Like a mother hen herding her brood, Sallie guided Jennie and Mattie toward the staircase. John Baird followed. But they all stopped at the foot of the steps. Torches were gathering at the front gate. In the flaring light men in white sheets and peaked hats. Some wore hoods. Jim stepped behind a post on the porch, but Hugh advanced to the steps, the barrels of his gun picking up the orange torchlight.

"You people get on away from here," he yelled, his voice shrill and testy. "You don't have any business here."

A murmur from the crowd. One man not hooded stepped forward as far as the gate. "We just come for the nigger girl. We don't want no trouble with y'all. Just tell us where she's at."

"We've got women and children in here," Hugh said. "I'll not have you good-for-nothing white trash coming up to my front door and scaring them to death. Now get on away from here."

There were jeers from the mob, muffled threats, and the torches flared.

"You better watch your mouth now, Mr. Creighton. It's a sight more of us than it is of y'all."

"Yeah," said Hugh, "but it ain't us that's looking up the barrels of these shotguns, and I'm real nervous. If you don't believe me, just come on through that gate."

"Ain't nobody coming through no gate, Mr. Creighton. You just tell us where that girl's at and we'll leave you be."

Jim stepped from the post where he had been standing and joined his brother, shoulder to shoulder. "Didn't you hear what he said? The ladies are inside the house, and that's where they're going to stay."

It took a second or two for Jim's message to sink in. A muffled voice spoke. "Well I'll be goddamn. If that ain't enough by God to gag a possum. Lording it up and down the big road like y'all was somebody and ain't the first damn one of you fit for decent folks."

Jennie knew that voice. It was Leonard Coe. Jim descended two steps, past Hugh, and brought the gun up, across his chest, as though he were coming up behind a dog on point. "That's enough out of you, Coe," he said. "We've already had to run you off one time. Now get the hell out of here before you get hurt."

The men around him laughed, as much at Coe as at the Creightons, and the torches stirred. A small man stepped through the gate, adjusting his bedsheet so that he might see through the eyeholes. "Come on, boys, they ain't going to do nothing." The voice of Coe again. "They ain't got the balls."

Hugh fired, right past Jim's ear, and all the women jumped. Torches and sheeted figures scattered, shouting threats. "God-almighty, Brother," Jim said, holding his hand to his ear. "Are you crazy?"

"I warned them." Hugh's hands, still holding the gun, were trembling violently. "I just shot up in the air."

"Well, you made an impression."

The torches were wavering in the darkness, farther and farther down the avenue, like despairing little spirits. The family drew together in the doorway, each one warmed by the nearness of the others. When the torches had diminished to small points of fire, Jim and Hugh leaned their guns against the wall.

Jim asked Jennie if she was all right and held out his arm as though to gather her to himself. She nodded and moved closer to him. He patted her on the back.

Halfway down the black tunnel of the avenue, automobile headlights came on, no more than small white discs at that distance, and the people on the porch heard the *chug chug* of engines being cranked. From the pitch and swing of the lights, the night riders were having trouble backing and filling in the narrow lane.

"I should have blown the bastards to kingdom come," Hugh said, and his voice quavered like a child's.

Jennie commenced to tremble. She was cold and about to wet herself. "Oh Jesus," she whimpered and would have fallen had Jim not reached out and caught her.

: : :

Jennie awoke the next morning in the gray light of a room she failed to recognize. There was a pallet on the floor beside her bed. Someone had slept on it. She looked around. This was Buddy's room, where Jim and Mattie were staying. Of course, it was. Jennie had not been up here in a long time. It must have been Mattie who had slept on the floor. Jennie had a fuzzy recollection now. She had wanted someone to stay beside her. Mattie had sat on the foot of her bed. That was the last thing she remembered, Mattie assuring her that Hugh and Jim were keeping watch through the night, Mattie singing softly.

People were stirring around downstairs. She might get up and raise the shades, flood her fears with honest daylight, but her bed was a cozy nest. She lay at the warm center of a stronghold, fortified by the solid wall of family—a lady of the house, Jim Creighton had said. If she could just go on staying there.

When she next awoke, the window shades were back-lighted brightly, yellow squares aglow in the dimness of the room. She could think of no reason to get out of bed, nothing she had to do. If she went down to the kitchen—the only room in the house where she felt entirely comfortable—she would not be able to sit idle while Sallie did the work that she was accustomed to, but neither could she roll up her sleeves without Sallie making a big to-do. Her only choice was to stay where they had put her and let them wait on her.

There was a knock at the door—Sallie bringing coffee. Jennie said, "Come in." But the visitor wasn't Sallie. It was Mattie, pushing the door open with her foot, presenting a steaming breakfast tray and chirping good morning.

Jennie started, pulling the blanket up to her bosom, embarrassed to have been caught by Mattie still in bed at such an hour. She touched her hair, tucked in a strand. "I should have been up a long time ago."

"I'm glad you were able to sleep, the way you thrashed around all night."

"Oh, I must have kept you awake."

"I was not the one who needed the rest. Now. I hope you have an appetite because we've fixed you a good breakfast, and goodness knows you need to eat. You go ahead now, and after you get dressed I'll come back for the tray."

Mattie reminded Jennie of a little bird with her quick, efficient movements. "Thank you, Miss Mattie, but I can take the tray. I ain't an invalid."

"Let me come back for it, Jennie. There's something I want to speak with you about."

: : :

Jennie should have known. She had known. Deep down she had. But she hadn't thought it would be so soon, or that Mattie would be the one they sent to tell her.

She sipped coffee from her saucer but merely picked at her hominy and eggs, rearranging the food on her plate. When the coffee was gone, she got up and raised the shades. Sun poured in, touching the dark mahogany furniture with warm red light, bouncing from the mirror and shimmering on the walls. Jennie stood before the dresser. She let her gown slip from her shoulders and fall down around her hips and settle in a soft pile about her ankles. She stepped out of it. A gaunt figure stood before her, breasts wasted, ribs in bold relief. Jennie was reminded of the skeletons of cows—knobby hips and curved rib cages—bleaching in the piney woods. She didn't care. Whether she put on flesh again or dried up and blew away in the next strong wind made no difference to her. The day outside, streaming gloriously through the window, was to her no more than portal to a gray desolation, a new year that stretched featureless and unremarkable for as far as she could see.

From a bowl of water on the marble-top stand she soaped a cloth and bathed her underarms. At the rag's cold touch and the streaming of water down her sides, goose bumps rose and her dark nipples puckered. She rinsed quickly and washed away the suds, ran the rag between her legs and toweled her body dry. That would have to do until she found a warmer place to bathe.

She was fastening the last button on her bodice when she heard a tap at her door.

Mattie came straight to the point. "Jim and I have discussed it, Jennie, and we would like for you to go back to Spartanburg with us. We have a precious little room off the back of the house that was just made for you, and goodness knows I can use your help. How does that sound?"

"Are they so scared I'll grieve before their face, Miss Mattie?"

"Oh, Jennie. It's not that. It's not that at all. It's just that Jim and I think it might be best for you to get away for a while. Now I can help you pack. We want to get an early start tomorrow."

A precious little room just made for you. That was what Sallie had said to her when she came back from Florida twelve years ago: We have the dearest little cabin, just made for you.

"Slow down a minute, Miss Mattie. I need some time to think. I'll be down before long."

Mattie took the tray and left. Jennie walked over to the window. A precious little room just made for you. Below, the tin roof of her cabin shone brightly in the sun. The dearest little cabin, just made for you. Mr. Johnny had built that cabin himself, soon after she came back from Florida. He had built it a little larger and a little sturdier than the general run of servant houses, and he had put glass lights in the windows, befitting the status of the kind of cook Sallie was looking for. But it was still a nigger house.

From the back of her cabin Hart's path stood out plain, a white ribbon coming up through the brown weedy field from the woods, right past the barn and into the lane that ran behind her house: an announcement to anyone who stopped at that window and took the time to look.

He would not have cared. She could just hear him: To hell with them if they don't want to understand. Had it not been for her he would have invited not just the family but the whole county to line up at this window. How often through the years had she had to remind him that it was only people's voluntary blindness that allowed him to wear that path? How proud of her he would have been for what she had told the sheriff: "I refused to have intercourse with Mr. J. T. Bonner because I was true to Mr. Hart Bonner." And they had put it in the newspaper. Maybe that's what brought those Ku Kluxers last night. She took a deep breath and placed her trembling fingertips upon the dusty windowsill. "After all those times I had to stop you from saying something, and then you went and left me to do your telling for you." She spoke out loud, as though believing that he might hear her.

A framed display of arrowheads hung on the wall—Buddy's collection—eight pretty ones, all of a size but each of different colored stone. She took her little reticule from the table by the bed and from it drew the arrowpoint that Hart had sent to her by Jim, the gift that had caused her to drop the china plate she'd been drying. Of white stone, it was the second he had given her, a reminder of the first one twelve years ago, right after Bonner Creighton's death. He had brought it one night to her cabin—a nearly perfect artifact, salmon pink with streaks of deeper red. Heart's blood, Hart had called those streaks, Cupid's arrow.

Hart's blood. His blood. Shed for her.

To save her from a trial. She saw that clearly now, saw how he must have foreseen the lurid spectacle—herself the killer's nigger whore, dragged in and degraded before the lascivious eyes of white men. No darker prospect than that. Not even death. The only way he could think of. Yet what had it availed?

Her life was still in danger as long as she remained in Cypress Swamp. She had been saved last night not by his but by her Creighton blood. A lady of the house, Jimmy had told those Ku Kluxers. She remembered a hot Sunday afternoon not long after she'd returned and gone to work for Sallie. Mr. Johnny had just bought a new Kodak and Sallie, wanting to use it, had herded the family out onto the porch after dinner. They had all been there that day—Sallie and Mr. Johnny, Hugh and Wade with their new wives, Jimmy and the old folks, Miss Sadie and Marse Bonner. At the last minute, when the old man was grumbling about the heat, Sallie had thought of her and made everybody wait. Jennie had resisted. No one else in the family had ever been so willing to acknowledge, well, who she was, and for her to take her place on the porch with the Creightons, especially with that old man, was more than she could do. But Sallie had insisted, dragging her playfully up the hall. And then Sallie had said a startling thing: "If they don't like it, Jennie, they can just pretend that you're the servant." Jimmy had been the photographer, the only one in that crowd who knew how to take a picture, and Jennie had made him back up. "Come in a little closer, Jennie," he had ordered, but she had stood her ground, off to the right, keeping a space between herself and the Creightons.

What were they pretending now? And what was her position? She was the Creightons' colored sister. That's what she'd always been, and that's what she would go right on being if she moved into Mattie's precious little room. But she did not have to do that. By Hart's death her Creighton blood had lost its power.

For the first time since they had moved her into the big house, Jennie could imagine the possibility of feeling good again. Maybe her prayers had been heard after all. Whatever happened to her now would be not of their will but His.

"I can't go, Miss Mattie," Jennie said when Mattie had come back up. I thank you, tell Mr. Jimmy, but I need to stay right here."

"Oh, Jennie," Mattie said, her eyes swimming with tears. "They won't let you stay. Don't you know that?"

Jennie had smiled. "They ain't got nothing to do with it, Miss Mattie."

"I don't understand."

"Hart set me free, Miss Mattie."

"I just don't understand."

"By what he did. I don't think that's what he meant, but that's the way I have to take it."

: : :

Jennie sat on the bed and unlaced her high-top shoes, then slipped from the bedroom into the dark hall and crept in stocking feet down the long staircase, wincing at each creaking step. Having told Mattie of her decision, she had thought that it was over, that she would be allowed to remain in that upstairs room until they came and told her to pack. But Hart had not let her be. On the table by her bed lay the paper that contained his private words. She read them again, his words and her public ones—what she had told the sheriff, calling Hart by name. But he had not called hers, had not written it in his note nor spoken it to a soul. And now she knew why. He had left her to do his telling for him because he would have exposed her to danger if he had done it himself, would have brought about the very thing that he was dying to prevent. The poor, dear fool. It had almost happened anyway. It mattered little now, but he had counted on her at least to understand. Well, she did.

They would never assist her in what she had to do, nor would they allow her to do it alone. She had to get out of the house without being seen.

The coast clear, she was quickly down the stairs and out the door, headed toward her cabin in the blinding sun, her poor feet freezing as she crossed the dead lawn. Without smoke coming from its chimney, the cabin looked lifeless too, as though the terror of the night before had scared it to death. Since last leaving it—the morning after he had waited wet and dripping by the hearth—she had dreaded having to enter it again. The hurt it contained, like an unaired mugginess, would be too thick to breathe, and she was terrified by the prospect of finding that wet place by the hearth, a permanent reproach refusing to dry.

But now, invigorated by her purpose, she opened the door and walked straight to the corner where her meager wardrobe hung. The cabin was cold, colder even than the air outside, but sun streamed in through the back window, allowing her the light she needed to find the dress she wanted. It was a satin gown with a ruffled bodice and long tight sleeves, an old-fashioned hand-me-down from Clara Creighton, years ago, hardly warm enough for a day like today but the closest thing she owned to the black of widow's garb. She brushed at dust on the ruffles, then laid it on the bed, unbuttoned the dress she was wearing, and stepped out of it.

The gown hung loose in the shoulders and bagged around her hips, testimony to the weight she had lost, but that wouldn't matter where she was going. The cameo brooch that he had given her for Christmas was in a cigar box on her dresser, along with the red arrowhead. She fastened the cameo at her throat. From a shelf she took down a large hatbox, removed the hat, and placed it on the bed. It was an extravagant piece of millinery, fashionable among young ladies at the time Hart had bought it for her, but that was ten years ago. By current tastes, its wide brim seemed outrageous, its spray of crimson roses ostentatious. There were three of them, full-blown. She had told him that she had nowhere to wear it, but he had said no matter, he'd just wanted to see it on her. She had laughed at her reflection in the mirror, and he had got his feelings hurt. The roses stood for something, he had said—what, she could not remember now. Ever since, the hat had sat in its box on the shelf. She wished she had a black veil to drape from the front, but the hat's color matched the dress, close enough. Stooping to the mirror, she placed it on her head, backing away to see it in all its wide-brimmed glory. Satisfied, she stabbed it down with two long pins, one on either side, and pronounced herself ready.

She stuck her head out the back door, looking for Nathaniel in the kitchen yard, but he was nowhere to be seen. Maybe she would find him at the barn, passing the time with John Earl and Willie Tee. She hurried along the privet hedge, out of sight of the big house. The morning seemed remarkably still and quiet. By the time she reached the barn she understood. It was last night. The people on the place had their ways of disappearing. She would have to hitch up the buggy herself. She hoped she knew how.

The buggy was in the carriage shed, next to the surrey. She was grateful to see that a lap robe lay folded on the seat. Anxious that she might be observed from the big house, afraid she'd soon be missed, she backed between the shafts, caught one in each hand, and started toward the barn. The buggy rolled easily on its bright red wheels.

From the January glare Jennie entered the barn, a darkness latticed by slants of dusty sun and reeking of ammonia. Chittering sparrows fluttered away at her approach, and from the back a horse blew softly. Looking about for a place where harness might be kept, she stepped into cold, wet straw and flinched. She had an old pair of shoes in the cabin, but she had chosen not to wear them. Prepared now, she strode forward, indifferent to the floor.

The harness was where she'd hoped it would be—in a room on the left—but opening the door she was baffled by the confusion of hames, collars, bridles, straps, lines, and buckles. She grabbed the first collar she saw, hoping it would fit, and lifted from a peg a set of oiled leather straps. The contraption, hames attached, looked complicated. Figuring it out was going to give the big house that much more time to miss her.

Jennie was no stranger to the buggy horse Molly. She had often driven the placid mare down to Cypress Swamp. But whether the mare would stand still for a woman who didn't know what she was doing remained to be seen. Jennie called her by name as she entered the stall and stroked the smooth crest of her neck. Cooing softly, she pulled the bridle over the long head and ears, worked the bit between the lips, and, catching the horse by the cheek strap, led her out into the hall.

The collar was easy, but the harness gave her trouble. Working carefully but as quickly as she could, she arranged it along Molly's back, buckled the bellyband, pulled the tail over the back band, fitted the hames snug to the collar, and snapped the lines to the bridle rings. It looked right so far. She led Molly to the buggy, traces trailing, and the mare backed readily into the shafts. Jennie hooked the traces to the singletree but saw that straps from the britching hung free. Maybe they buckled to those places on the shafts.

Perched on the seat, she was confident for the first time since leaving the house that she was actually going to make it, escape from the yard undetected. She lifted the lines high in both hands. Despite the chill and her freezing feet, she felt good, in charge. She slapped the lines along Molly's back. "Get up, Moll."

For a short space between the barn and the head of the avenue, a horse and buggy could be seen from the house, should anyone happen to be looking. She prayed that no one was. She turned into the avenue, and the mare's iron hooves rang on the iron-hard sand. She removed the whip from its socket and stung the mare on the rump, right hard, leaning forward in her eagerness. Molly broke into a trot, and a squeaking hub increased in tempo. That danger passed, she was safe, she hoped, until she reached Cypress Swamp. How she would get through the village, she could not guess, but the Lord had seen her this far; He would see her all the way.

She was past Wade's avenue when she remembered that she had meant to say goodbye—not to Wade and Clara, though she bore that sweet man no ill will—but to the little cabin yard out back where she had spent her childhood. And to her memory of the red-faced white man who used to give her oranges for Christmas. Oranges were all he ever gave her. To this day she couldn't stand the taste. He had always spoken gently to her mother—she remembered that—but she had hated the way her mother used to change whenever he came around. Now she could leave him behind, lay his ghost to rest in that same dooryard, and do it without a twinge of regret. But without particular pleasure either, she noticed.

The sun stood straight overhead, but her wide hat brim cast its shadow like a chilly mantle upon her shoulders. She wrapped her cold feet in the lap robe and looked back. The road behind her was empty. She entered a tunnel of live oaks, their moss-draped branches shutting out the sun, and passed the avenue to Miss Emma Bonner's house. Along this stretch of road she had always imagined the little backyard cottage he had told her of, but he didn't live there now. She didn't even look as she rode by.

: : :

Ahead lay Cypress Swamp and the gallery of Thompson's General Merchandise that caught every scrap of trash that blew through Heyward County, as Hart used to say. Once he had threatened to sweep it clean and she had had to stop him from buckling on his pistol. Now that the gallery posed a real danger to her, he was not here to do it.

She knew she was in trouble when she heard the whistle of the train. It was the 12:05 bound for Columbia. She had not thought of that. There would be a crowd at the station—the ne'er-do-wells from Thompson's who seemed to think that the train would not come in unless they were down at the station to greet it. The big event of their day. She considered the chances of her racing through the village, but if the train beat her there, she would have to stop at the crossing, after having attracted the attention of every eye.

She could see smoke from the engine as she entered the wide, dusty street. The crowd was not as large as she had feared—perhaps because of the cold—but large enough to include some of the ruffians who had come last night. She touched Molly with the whip. She had to get across the tracks before the train came in. She saw that she would make it. The engine, bold with brass fittings, was approaching slowly from the right, clanging its bell and blowing steam—an immense black machine, as high as a house, huffing and chuffing toward the crossing, but it seemed now to be slowing to a stop. The mare threw her head and her eye rolled white, but Jennie pushed her up the incline toward the tracks, the steam hissing in her ears, the brass bell ringing.

"Hey, little lady! Hold up here!" A brakeman on her left reached for the horse's head. "What in the world's wrong with you? Don't you see that train?"

Molly tried to avoid the hand, but the brakeman caught the line. And suddenly there were others, overalls and black felt hats, crowding around the horse. "Well I'll just be goddamn if that ain't who I think it is. Y'all looka here."

Faces turned to her, white faces all, whiskers and hungry eyes, grinning like stray dogs.

"Now where are you in such a hurry to get to, gal, all by yourself?"

Not one familiar face in the crowd, no one to appeal to. She gripped the handle of the whip.

Above the clanging of the bell came from behind them the imperious *ooga ooga* of an automobile horn. Heads turned to look. Jennie rose from the seat and slashed the whip across the arm of the brakeman. "Get up!" she yelled, and Molly bolted forward. Jennie sat down hard. The buggy bounced and clattered across the tracks, directly beneath the face of the looming engine's headlamp. She could have reached out and touched it.

: : :

The little white frame church gleamed like a light in the midday glare. Jennie guided the mare among the tall pines and pulled her to a stop before an iron hitching post at the edge of the church-yard. She was fastening the lines when the Creightons drove in behind her, two automobiles, but she was through the wrought-iron gate by the time they climbed out. She paused to close the gate behind her—her only word of caution to anyone who might think to stop her now—and someone called out her name. Sallie's voice. Jennie had thought just the men. But she did not turn around.

The graveyard stretched before her, a wide sunlit field crowded with granite markers and falling away to the wooded stream that gave the place its name. To think that Cypress Swamp could populate a community of this size. So many dead. And these were just white people, and Methodists at that. The Baptist cemetary was just as big. Not to mention the Episcopalian.

But there was only one grave that she cared about—a mound of dirt too new for a stone. She craned her neck and turned her head, looking and looking.

The Creightons had respected the closed gate. She was glad of that. She knew how she must look to them in that dark, old-fashioned gown, that extravagant hat, wandering barefoot among the granite lambs and ornate spires like a woman just released from an insane asylum. Well, let them look; let them think what they would.

Suddenly, she remembered when they buried Mr. Johnny. And where. Down on the edge of the woods it had been. The thawing grass was wet underfoot as she made her way down the gentle slope. And there it was. Or there they were. Two, of course, side by side. She had completely forgotten Tison Bonner.

There was a space between the graves, room for one more, and that's where Jennie stood, looking from one mound to the other. Just like that old man, she thought, to turn up where he ain't welcome. The dirt on the left looked rained on, that on the right recently turned. She decided on the right and knelt at the foot. And there she prayed—not in words but with an image of him, being lifted from shadow by the love that made the world into brighter light than the world had ever known.

Finished, she removed the pins from her hat, set the hat upon the grass, and in full view of those who stood watching at the gate she lay face down upon the mound, her cheek pressed to the sand, her arms outflung. She lay there until the chill of the earth seeped through her bosom, until the doves in the pine trees begged her to rise, until she heard him say what she had been listening for, and then she forgave him too. As she got to her feet, the pain of her abraded soul, of the places rubbed raw and bleeding, began to ease. She brushed sand from her bosom, knowing that the healing had begun. "I would have brought you flowers," she said, "but it's the wrong time of year."

She bent to pick up the hat, its garish roses in full bloom, scarlet against the dark material. Oh, how he'd tried to glorify them roses. She smiled to think of it. Then knelt again and placed the hat upon the mound, about where his chest would be, and fixed it to the soil with the two hat pins. "There," she said. "That's the best I can do for now."

She looked toward the gate and there they were: Sallie with Buddy standing by her, Jimmy and Mattie, Wade too. She didn't even notice that Hugh was missing until she saw a person sitting at the wheel of the Model T.

With her hair tumbling down upon her neck, she walked straight toward them, barefoot across the cold, dead graveyard grass.

EPILOGUE

*T*runks of pine trees, columns rising from a flat pine-needle floor, a dreary sameness in all directions. Jim Creighton was lost in his own backyard. He was also a stranger among his own people. Once he returned to Spartanburg, he would not come back to Cypress Swamp. The Bonners were dead—all but Pinck and Hattie. Hart was dead. Their house was empty. And Jennie banished, sent into exile, driven by Hugh to Orangeburg. Though a visitor, just arrived as Jennie was leaving this morning, might have almost thought from the way she looked in that green velvet suit, that she was a pampered daughter about to depart for the Grand Tour. Oh how she had held herself when she came out of her cabin, attended like a princess by her mother, her head held high, her step sure and certain, and how she had smiled. One would have thought that she was actually looking forward to the trip.

Maybe she had no tears left, but her eyes were dry as she bade farewell to each member of the family. Even Miss Sadie offered her hand. Mattie she hugged for a long time but not him, nor did she have for him a valediction, but she saved him for last, and when she took his hand her eyes were glistening. It was he who assisted her into the automobile, onto the back seat, for Sallie was going with them, and he who closed the door.

Lo and behold, a flash of white among the trees up ahead. That little Darling. She had seen him, and here she came. He knelt and she bathed his face with her tongue. As he rumpled her neck, he caught the gagging odor of decay. She had been rolling in something rotten. He felt it on his hands and got to his feet. A dead cow probably. He wiped his hands in the pine straw. He would have to give her a bath when he got back, whenever that might be. One more thing to do.

"How do we get home, Darling?"

By way of answer, the setter trotted ahead, making sure that he did not fall behind. In a matter of minutes they came upon a woods road so faint he would have missed it had it not been for the dog. She turned into it, and he noticed the shallow ruts. She seemed to know where she was going. He hoped so. She ran ahead, opening the distance between them. He called to her and she stopped. There was a building up ahead, an old, abandoned tenant house, he reckoned. This far back in the woods, it must date from slavery times. Assured that he was coming, the setter took off, racing toward the cabin, barking as she ran. Jim hurried along, calling out to her. The cabin, he saw now, might once have been a church; the skeleton of a squat steeple perched upon the roof beam above the front door.

From behind the building, flushed by the dog, rose a great black cloud of flapping vultures—*whump, whump, whump*—forty or fifty birds, beating the air into spreading waves of stench. They did not go far, alighting heavily on the branches of pines, a few on the roof of the building. Darling kept up her barking. Jim approached with caution. Behind the church lay a graveyard enclosed by a fence of rusted wrought-iron spikes. From one of the spikes hung a deer, head down, impaled through a hind-quarter. Jim was puzzled. The fence was not high. The deer should have cleared it easily. For some reason this one must have miscalculated its leap. He told the setter to hush and circled around to the left, out of the foul stream of carrion. The animal's head and neck lay upon the ground. It was a buck, a young six-point, as far as he could tell. Something must have driven it toward the fence, for there was nothing inside the enclosure that might have enticed it to jump. Feral dogs probably. And the buck in flight may not have seen until too late the rusty spikes against the background of pine straw. The spike had caught the hind leg and snatched the buck right out of its leap. Had not punctured the muscle but only the skin, a narrow strip but strong enough to snag and hold the deer. It must have taken a long time for the poor creature to die, hanging thirsty on the fence, and the buzzards would not have waited. What a desperate cluster they must have made, grasping by their weak feet any purchase they could find. From the back the deer's coat still held its sheen, but Jim did not want to examine the other side.

Sickened, he turned away. He walked around to the front of the church. The door had long since fallen from its hinges. He sat in the doorway. Darling came up and lay at his feet, exhausted now that she had shown him her great discovery. Jim filled the bowl of his pipe and struck a match to it.

And those who had worshiped in this sad sanctuary had also died, as would he too some day, and Mattie, and the children they yet hoped to have, each impaled uncomprehending upon what dread spike? he wondered.

And he saw Jennie's face, as she had come up from Hart's grave yesterday, hatless, her hair a glory in the sun, walking straight toward them, and her stride. That was something.